Classical Arabic Stories

Classical Arabic Stories

AN ANTHOLOGY

Edited and with an introduction
by Salma Khadra Jayyusi

COLUMBIA UNIVERSITY PRESS
NEW YORK

Columbia University Press wishes to express its appreciation for assistance given by The Pushkin Fund toward the cost of publishing this book.

Salma Khadra Jayyusi would like to extend her thanks to Dr. Ahmad al-Uthaim for his kind support toward the preparation of this anthology.

Columbia University Press
Publishers Since 1893
New York   Chichester, West Sussex

Paperback edition, 2012

Library of Congress Cataloging-in-Publication Data
Classical Arabic stories : an anthology / edited by Salma Khadra Jayyusi.
p.   cm.
Includes bibliographical references and index.
Translated from the Arabic.
ISBN 978-0-231-14922-8 (cloth : alk. paper) — ISBN 978-0-231-14923-5 (pbk. : alk. paper) — ISBN 978-0-231-52027-0 (e-book)
1. Arabic literature—Translations into English. I. Jayyusi, Salma Khadra. II. Title.
PJ7694.E1C56   2010
892.7'08—dc22
2009049504

Columbia University Press books are printed on permanent and durable acid-free paper.

This book was printed on paper with recycled content.

Printed in the United States of America

To my father, Subhi al-Khadra, my first mentor and model, who, with keen insight and a deep sense of duty, taught me from childhood how to love and revere a heritage of great value, and how to inhabit two ages simultaneously—our brilliant classical age and our beleaguered modern one—and to serve them both.

To him this book, that embodies his vision, with love and lasting gratitude.

Contents

Preface and Acknowledgments

This anthology is intended to fill a substantial gap in the study of classical Arabic literary prose. My realization of the great injustice to Arabic culture in modern times, even by Arabs themselves, through the neglect of its rich heritage in creative prose genres motivated my decision to bring about this anthology (as well as a book of essays, now in press [at E. J. Brill], *The Classical and Post-Classical Arabic Story: Genres, History and Influences*, by some of the best current scholars, Arabs and Arabists).

Despite their secondary status in the Arab critical tradition, classical narratives in Arabic continued to grow, finding new adventures and exploring as yet untried possibilities in Arabic literary prose. The inventiveness and skillful treatment of style, language, and subject matter should constitute points of interest for all students of world literature. However, as I discuss in my introduction to this volume (and elsewhere), it has been the attachment to poetry, the most-cherished literary form, which Arabs have sustained throughout their literary history, that has kept at bay the discovery and enjoyment of Arabic creative prose and the cultural enhancement it can afford. This anthology, however, limits itself to the story type, itself demonstrating great variety and creativity.

I must here thank first and foremost noted Saudi writer ʿAbdallah al-Nasser, former cultural representative of the Saudi Ministry of Higher Education in London, where I first met him, for the decisive part he played in bringing support to this anthology. His help was prompted by his devotion to Arabic culture and its dissemination in the world, a devotion that has culminated in the accomplishment of several works of discourse and translation as part of the projects of *PROTA* and East-West Nexus. It was he who spoke to the well-known businessman Dr. Ahmad al-ʿUthaim, who graciously donated the subsidy needed for this work, proving once again that the love of literature and the pride Arabs take in their literary heritage are still very much alive. I thank him heartily for his immediate and positive response to this work's needs, and for the gracious courtesy he showed me when, because of circumstances beyond my control, the work on this anthology was a little delayed. It is only through individuals of this outlook that Arabic business can be a major channel for cultural dissemination beyond the Arab world.

And many thanks to the colleagues who helped in assembling the work. My gratitude goes to Leila al-Khalidi al-Husseini, a lifetime friend and intellectual, who helped me with the selections for this volume; to my cousin Sawsan Nuweihid Ajlouni for her suggestions of several religious selections; to the novelist Laila al-Atrash for many cogent suggestions in the selection phase of this anthology, to Ghada Jayyusi-Lehn, professor at the American University in Sharjah, the United Arab Emirates, for her volunteer help in researching certain important matters for this work's references, and to Antoine Raffoul for his kind help volunteered in the last preparation of a publisher's copy of this book.

Heartfelt thanks go to the translators of these stories, ʿAbd al-Wahid Luʾluʾa, Ibrahim Mumayiz, Bassam Abou Ghazaleh, Fayez Suyyagh, Roger Allen, Matthew Sorenson, Lena Jayyusi, and my brother, Faisal al-Khadra. Much effort and expertise went into creating an accurate and viable first translation. The second translation, the final polishing, was done mainly by Christopher Tingley with his usual care and precision and with the great benefit of his proficiency in English medieval literature. I cannot thank the translators enough for their painstaking, expert work. Jaʿfar al-ʿUqaili was a wonderful assistant who did much for this book and for other East-West Nexus and *PROTA* books, and I owe him many thanks.

Salma Khadra Jayyusi
Editor
Director of East-West Nexus/*PROTA*

Classical Arabic Stories

Introduction

Arabic fictional genres have suffered a great injustice throughout their history, mainly through the secondary status they acquired in the rich Arabic critical tradition. Their importance and great variety and originality were overlooked in favor of poetry, the tradition's oldest and most favored art form. The Arabic critical concept of literature in classical times, represented by a long list of critics and literary historians, concentrated disproportionately on poetry and bestowed much less attention on fiction. Poetry was regarded, and, to an extent, still is, even with the rise of a strong fictional tradition in the twentieth century, as the Arabs' primary artistic expression. This well-entrenched attitude caused the many prose genres (both fiction and nonfiction) attempted by classical Arabs over the centuries to retreat into the dusty corners of world literature, unknown to most and unexplored fully in their artistic and semantic value even in the eyes of their own Arab inheritors. Moreover, this widely undervalued contribution, which boasted both charm and finesse in many of its forms, received far less attention than poetry not only from literary critics but also from the royalty and nobility of medieval times, most of whom gave bountifully both status and sustenance to the poets of their times.

Despite this lesser status, prose genres in classical Arabic continued to grow, enjoying great variety and finding cause for constant adventure, reflecting in part their explorations of the unbounded possibilities of Arabic literary prose. To my knowledge, the Arabic fictional prose venture was perhaps unmatched in its scope and aesthetic value among medieval cultures, at least west of India.

This is not to say that there has been no serious scholarship in modern times engaged in studying the various prose genres medieval and premodern Arab authors left us. In answer to a changed outlook on the study of

Arabic literature, discourse on Arabic creative prose by both Arab scholars and Arabists has increased in size and grown in sophistication. In addition, a fair number of Arabic compendiums of creative prose selections have been assembled, particularly by Egyptian scholars. As part of my quest to introduce Arabic culture to non-Arab audiences, I have felt a need to offer the fruits of this recent research on Arabic literary accomplishments in the field of creative prose.[1] Focusing on the classical Arabic story,[2] I have left the very rich genres of other types of creative prose: oratory, epistles, advice literature, legacies, meditative essays, proverbs, and others, for another effort.

I began with a study on the history and development of the classical Arabic story, inviting to the venture some of the best specialists, Arabs and Arabists, to participate. They graciously offered the fruits of their specializations in the various fictional and other story-type genres to help me produce as comprehensive a book as possible revealing the wide vista of what Arabic fictional talent has offered throughout its long history, beginning with pre-Islamic times. This resulted in a volume of studies (forthcoming from E. J. Brill) detailing the genres of the old Arabic story, its development, its ramifications, and its influences east and west both in the past and at the present time.[3] I felt, too, the pressing need to offer selected examples of the Arabic classical story to non-Arab readers, bringing to light the human condition in its many aspects, taking readers on a trip to an intimate knowledge of the other, those living at a different time and in a different culture, thus showing the universality and the pertinence of human experience across cultures and through time. This purpose could be attained only through offering selections from the literature itself, through translation; hence this anthology.

A description of the various genres of the classical Arabic story, their history and influences, will be especially useful to the nonspecialist. The selections in this collection range from pre-Islamic and Islamic stories of love and adventure to anecdotes on various experiences to the more complex narratives of the *maqamat* (assemblies). There is also within these genres variation, from short tales, sometimes very short, as in the *khabar* genre, to longer accounts, arriving at novel writing in the Andalusian philosopher Ibn Tufail's famous philosophical novel *Hayy ibn Yaqzan.* In fact, the study of the development of the old Arabic story is also a study of linguistic and stylistic changes in the history of Arabic literary prose. For we begin with the well-balanced style and sentence construction that we see in early literary prose and move, at the beginning of the empire-building era in the first century A.H. (seventh–eighth centuries C.E.), to the extremely succinct style befitting the exchange of urgent messages between the center in Hijaz and the ongoing armies spreading east and west. This was still, one must remember, a semi-oral age, and transmitted messages had to be short but cogent and memorable. Orality depended on factors that preserved its message: meter and rhyme in poetry, economy of words in prose. The *khabar* became a major vehicle of storytelling for which the succinct, condensed style was the most suitable. Later, two major innovations took hold of creative prose: complexity and fluidity of style. Mention must be made here of ʿAbd al-Hamid al-Katib, who, with the spread of literacy, had greater freedom to write in a more elaborate style. The development of this new freedom in linguistic virtuosity is seen in the *maqamat*, first of al-Hamadhani (356 / 968–398 / 1008); its rhyming and linguistic wealth finding greater elaboration and complexity by al-Maʿarri, in his *Epistle of Forgiveness*; by the other writer of the *maqamat*, al-Hariri; and by numerous other writers in the Arab east and, westward, in Muslim Spain (al-Andalus), Portugal, and Muslim Sicily.

Poetry, on the other hand, did not follow the same history of development, neither in style, diction, nor vision. Indeed, while the adventure of language and style in prose was heading toward complexity and, later on, in the postclassical centuries, often toward repetitiveness, redundancies, and the use of conceits and embellishments, including *sajʿ* (rhymed prose), language and style in poetry were growing more in the direction of simplicity and a greater affiliation with the contemporary language, as evident in such Mamluk and Ottoman poets as Ibn Nubata al-Misri, al-Shabb al-Dharif, Ibn Sanaʾ al-Mulk, and al-Bahaʾ Zuhair. The latter made occasional use of contemporary colloquial words that modern revivalists abstained from using. A comparison of the diverging directions of medieval prose and poetry represents, in my view, a rich field of investigation.

I have arranged the pre-Islamic tales chronologically in a section of their own, while the other stories are grouped thematically. This grouping of the pre-Islamic tales allows interested scholars to look for possible differences with the tales known to have been created during the Islamic period and consider whether they signify any major changes in outlook on the world, where, in pre-Islamic times, a mainly pagan worldview dominated. One must of course keep in mind the later revisions and omissions imposed in Islamic times on some of these texts in cases where they veered too far from a monotheistic outlook on the universe. The pertinent question remains whether the advent of Islam initiated a change in narrative development, causing, as it clearly did in poetry,[4] a rupture in the evolution of this art form.

There has been much debate among historians of Arabic literature about the actuality of fictional narratives before Islam. However, there are no peoples without lore, and pre-Islamic Arabs, both Bedouins and townspeople, certainly had rich experiences to narrate. This is not the place, however, to put this issue to any lengthy argument, and the assumption here is that pre-Islamic tales existed and were transmitted to the later Islamic centuries, perhaps with some modification wrought intentionally (for example, when texts contradicted the monotheistic beliefs of Islam) or unintentionally, as happens always with oral works. Many of the stories in this anthology come from *The Book of Crowns on the Kings of Himyar*, perhaps the richest source of purportedly pre-Islamic tales. Its stories, legends, and mythological adventures would fit an ancient, multicultural selectivity well known in other cultures and assume a scope far beyond normal possibilities—men living hundreds of years, corpses of dead kings that do not decay, fantastic, superhuman feats, soaring imaginations unchecked by the limitations of established religious belief.

The first two centuries of Islam was the period when adherence to truth was becoming a devotional requirement in literature, and when a story form such as that of the *khabar* began its spread in Arabic letters with its often short form and its chain of transmitters to lend authority (or the semblance of authority) to factual claims.

I have attempted to represent the many genres selected from important collections or single works. However, I do not offer samples from the *Arabian Nights* because the *Nights* are represented well in translation.

Observing the development of the old Arabic story, one can see that, although Islam's early insistence on veracity in literature interfered with its natural development, it was able, in a short period, to resume its normal pace, constantly veering toward complexity, reflecting an active and engaging art of storytelling. Perhaps the most important observation in this process is that the art of literary prose opted out of poetry's focus on the higher echelons of society and gazed at the whole of an Islamic public that was growing firmly in urbanity, depicting a people many of whom came from lower social strata: wily beggars, tricksters, party crashers, and others who resorted to tricks and simulations to survive. The antihero appears quite early in Arabic fictional history. A world inhabited by personalities who were neglected, almost unseen for centuries in much of world fiction, is depicted now, as early as the second century after Islam/

ninth century C.E.,[5] as alive with humor and mischief, a virtual presence of an acknowledged rogue in a thriving civilization.

A short description here of pre-Islamic literary genres will be of use. The art of storytelling has universal features and, in many of its genres in any one culture, coincides with its prototypes in other cultures, particularly in the chronological story with a beginning, a middle, and an end. Nonetheless, there are at least three major genres that are specifically Arab in origin: the *khabar*, the short anecdote that usually takes a genealogical list of transmitters (*isnad*) as an introduction to the story; the assemblies, or *maqamat*; and the visit to Heaven, exemplified first and foremost in the story of the Prophet's ascension to stand at the hands of God.

The Myths of Arabia

For myth is at the beginning of literature . . .
—Jorge Luis Borges

The mythic apprehension of experience is the early human gaze at the universe, the outcome of the human encounter with its mysteries, of the desperate desire born in the human heart to fathom its insoluble dilemmas. It was also the answer to man's desire to overcome the hindrances of his life, the evil that can beset it, and the incapacities and human limitations that he discovers in himself. This is where man's deep interest in magic and superhuman solutions took a grip on the mind and heart.

This has been a universal phenomenon in literature. Before Islam, the Arabian Peninsula was teeming with myths and legends,[6] but the advent of Islam as a major doctrine interrupted the progression of this early human conceptualization of the universe, quickly arresting and transcending the mythic stage of the human confrontation with the mysteries of the cosmos as it offered a finalized explanation of human life and of the universe. A humanization of experience was sought, away from the world of fantasy and mythic apprehension of the cosmos. The former outlook on an awesome world full of wondrous visions and superhuman marvels, lodged in the intriguing realm of mystery, was now restrained by the new religion that left almost nothing unaccounted for. Under the wing of Islam, that intriguing world of mystery and uncanny powers was now deciphered, its enigmatic phenomena laid bare by the clear capacity to see in all this the hand of the One Unseen God, who can never be represented or portrayed but who controls everything.

The world of mystery in pre-Islamic times, the world of inexplicable phenomena that had dominion over the human mind, had created a deeply perplexed human being, posing great challenge to his mortal powers and capabilities. This was conducive to a magnificent retaliation, to a great creative invasion of the mysteries surrounding man, to a creation, often wild, of fictive accounts depicting feats of human conquest where "human" was aggrandized and invested with the potency of the gods. All this disappeared in early Islam and would recur only centuries later when the need for popular romance, refreshing memories of conquests and potency after political defeats, became a major force.

The Arab imagination was conquered by the Word, the magnificence and rhetorical sweep of the Quran. All fictive delineations of the unseen God were taboo. Even early Arabic poetry after Islam refrained from actual rapport with the divine. It would be much later that the Sufis, the Islamic mystics, would approach the Holy with all their senses, merging poetry with sensuous faith and familiarizing the never-seen, the never-imagined face of God.

Christianity, which is very much alive in Islam, did not experience the same tightly secured horizons built around intrinsic human limitations; the story of Christ, his short, immaculate life, his suffering and violent death, his glorious resurrection, never failed to bring out a surge of fervent devotion in believers. This gave expression, over and over again, to a magnificent play of visual religious representations that gave scope to the greatest display of inventiveness and creative passion. The Christian religion, moreover, was a miracle-making creed: the crippled made ambulant, the blind given sight again, the dead resurrected. It confirmed the miraculous and the superhuman, reflecting a continuation of some pre-Christian beliefs and imaginings. Islam, and I am speaking here of early Sunni Islam, when it came to superhuman expectations, was austere, alien to a continued age of miracles. Even the jinn in the Quran were humanized. Although the story of the birth of Jesus and of Maryam's virginity and immaculate conception are reiterated in one of the most sublime chapters of the Quran (surat Maryam) and were made part of basic Islamic belief, the crucifixion was rejected: no precedence to killing prophets should be considered possible. The stories of the other Jewish prophets were repeated with awesome reverence, but they, like the story of Jesus, were easily isolated from everyday Islamic devotional preoccupations and did not reside in the Islamic imagination. Islam stood within the boundaries of the rational, and Muhammad performed no miracles. Although there remained a reverence for the wonders of nature, often alluded to in the Quran itself with great literary power, the factual and rational, not the miraculous, were the gateway to the faith. Conviction came through a disposition, ripe and ready, for a more comprehensible order of belief, an answer to the long Arabian search for God; it needed no miracles. Creative minds could not happily improvise on the given Word, contemplate fantastic devotional meanderings, not in this early period. Except for the Prophet's nocturnal trip to the Aqsa mosque in Jerusalem and his ascent to Heaven to stand before God, Sunni Islam would remain rational. There was a kind of sustained completeness about the early Islamic message that allowed few diversions in literature, and hence few fantastic turns. Except for the intriguing verbal images of Paradise, described in the Quran in luminous and picturesque detail, pictorial representation of the holy personages was not allowed. The Muslim was left to embrace abstract concepts, which he could not negotiate at will, add to or question at will, except in short periods of Islamic history, as during the time of the rational movement of al-Muʿtazila in the second to third (eighth to ninth) centuries.

This situation affected the progress of the story, the workings of the creative imagination. The early Muslims were restricted to the dictated word, to the given description of the details of the Islamic call and the life of the Prophet and his companions. Any myths surrounding their lives and those of the people around them were impossible. Many intrusions into the details occurred, but never to the degree approaching mythic exposition and delineation. Sunni Islam retained a rational explanation of the universe. The age itself accommodated, sometimes to the point of fanaticism, a concept of veracity and an insistence on truth. The religious tale one expects to have been nurtured in early Islam did not develop enough to become a genre in itself and was replaced by the Quran's teachings.

Modern Arabs, perhaps heedless of the natural affinity of early cultures with mythic conceptions of the universe, have thought of their history as remarkably devoid of mythologies. The main cause behind this unawareness has perhaps been Islamic pietism, for not only did a prudent adherence to the letter of the creed arrest the development of mythic thinking, but also, in order to secure concepts of life within the strictly defined precincts of monotheistic Islamic devotion and belief, it discouraged a circulation of myths suggesting an alternative interpretation of the world. Pre-Islamic poetry was cleansed of any devotional mention of pagan gods, and, though enough remained for later scholars to collect, myths were not part of the early Islamic imagination and engagement. A return to mythic dramatization was inevitable in time, however, even in some Islamic sects.

Nonetheless, despite the prohibiting atmosphere dominating the early Islamic narrative scene, some transmitters of prose lore, even during the first century, related mythic tales of wonders and marvels resisting religious stricture. However, Arabic stories of superhuman marvels and wonders would return with force in later centuries, as can be seen in some travel books and in the folk romances, among which the fourteenth-century folk romance of Sayf Ben Dhi Yazan[7] is a prime example.

In modern times various efforts to reconnect with the mythologies of the pre-Islamic past were made in the early decades of the twentieth century, first mainly by Arab poets, particularly the expatriate poets in the Americas,[8] followed in midcentury by a number of scholars working to uncover the rich presence of myths in pre-Islamic Arabia, whose work has indeed added greatly to our knowledge in this still only partially mined field of Arab cultural history. Modern Arab writers and intellectuals in general, with no extant Arabian myths about them, only skimmed this area of knowledge, made available to them by modern Arab scholars through painstaking research.[9] They seemed unable to assimilate into their consciousnesses the vivid presence of myths in pre-Islamic Arabia and their significance, their very normalcy, and to realize their activity in all cultures, a testimony to the unity of human creativity, to a cohesive universal vision as all cultures yield to the same basic conditions of life on earth and to the awesomeness of the cosmos and its incomprehensible phenomena.[10]

Legends of Heroism and Chivalry: Ayyam al-ᶜArab

From this encounter with the mysteries of the cosmos, a deep longing was born in man to conquer its dangers and hazards and assert man's potency. Hence the persistent recourse to heroism, conquest, the transcendent capacity to overcome human vulnerability and, by virtue of man's own might and courage, triumph through encounters with its own kind.

Besides stories built around myths and the superhuman hero, the desert Arabs, who had to fight for survival in a region of great scarcity, knew memorable encounters of tribe with tribe, in fights to secure proprietorship, hegemony, or status. It was normal that, around these encounters, intricate war legends celebrating heroism, loyalty, and tribal vendettas arose. The Bedouin Arabs in pre-Islamic Arabia seem to have been fond of their battle legends, all initially committed to memory and passed on generation to generation. Many are still extant. From these early pre-Islamic days, the Arabic predilection for factuality in their accounts is clear. These tales, despite their inevitable dramatic exaggeration, do not, as a rule in this period, touch on the supernatural or mythic. The legends that have come down to us, adorned with poetry expressive of the conflict and chivalry of such encounters, are well-crafted factual accounts. Many told not only of courage and chivalry but also of sometimes heartrending emotional conflict.

An example is the story of ʿAntara, a black poet of note in the pre-Islamic period who was the son of a notable Arab from the southern ʿAbs tribe and an Abyssinian slave mother and who was himself regarded as a slave by his father. The story is dramatic enough in its own right, with ʿAntara's desperate love for ʿAbla, his white cousin, and his feats of courage in defense of the tribe, which procured his emancipation and marriage to his love. The happy conclusion of ʿAntara's story did not necessarily characterize other tales, which can be tragic, as in the Kulaib / Bassous heroic tale. The elaborate story woven around Kulaib, head of the tribe of Taghlib, depicting his arrogance and megalomania, his confiscation of people's rights and property, and finally his punitive death at the hands of his brother-in-law, Jassas, of the tribe of Bakr, sister tribe to Taghlib, is interwoven with the agonized experience of Jalila, Kulaib's wife, also the sister of Jassas. Caught in the clutches of a treacherous fate that made her a pawn between husband and brother, she experienced great suffering, especially felt in the story's tragic end: Jalila was pregnant with Kulaib's child when he was killed. Having been sent back to her tribe after her husband's demise, Kulaib's son is born in the Bakr tribe and grows up unaware that the uncle bringing him up was the killer of his father. According to the old Arabian tribal laws, it was the duty of the son to kill his father's killer, and therefore, when he eventually learns the truth, he has no alternative but to kill the man who has loved and raised him.[11]

Such tales of conflict show a sophistication unexpected at that early age in the life of the Arabic story. Although mirroring a possible experience within the well-established traditions in the culture, the interpretation of the conflict and its introduction into the story reflect a complexity and a sensibility of great significance. Even if one were to argue the possibility of these tales' having been improvised after Islam, the same impression would hold, as it would still belong to a remote time in Arabic literary history.

The Romantic Love Story

The romantic love story took hold of the Arabic popular imagination during the Umayyad period, a period reflecting, in certain parts of the peninsula, particularly in the region of Hijaz, where most of these love stories thrived, many signs of a romantic apprehension of experience. These enduring and charming love accounts formed a genre by themselves and were the purest expression of the ancient Arabian soul, full of nostalgia, loyalty, chivalry, and a catching tenderness toward women that cannot fail to touch one's heart even after many centuries. They were sometimes tragic or semi-tragic accounts, but always anguished stories of unrequited attachments and unreachable dreams; they spoke of a great, idealized love, the love that brings delirium to the heart, that in some cases dements, claiming not only the length of life but also sometimes life itself. Madness is the lot of Qais ibn al-Mulawwah, known as Majnun Laila (Laila's Madman [d. 68 / 688]), whose beloved Laila was married by her father to another man because the poet had announced his love for her in his verse. The story repeats itself again and again. Its pattern had been set by the tragic experience of al-Muraqqash al-Akbar[12] in pre-Islamic times, and the change in fortune in the Umayyad age, in lifestyle, in possibilities did not arrest its relentless perpetuation. At first glance one may think there is no difference between one story and the other. The men were steadfast, anguished, and inconsolable, totally dedicated to the object of their love; the women were mainly passive, loving in silence, their serene suffering, their defenseless acquiescence setting the stage for millions of women in the long Arabian future. Volition in love was denied to both.

The Umayyad period (40 / 660–132 / 750) was a formative time when major changes took place in Arabic literature, in both poetry and prose. It was in this period that the Arabic love story took front stage, particularly in the Hijaz region, its prominent place pointing to the rise of a romantic current in literature in answer to the deep anxiety that had taken hold of the pre-Islamic Arabs with the advent of a new, all-controlling religion, the sudden changes and contradictions that had beset Arabian life and the difficulty of achieving a complete adjustment to a growing new urbanization. Added to this in Hijaz was the region's deprivation of its former status as the center of political life and the anxiety among the thwarted Hijazi aristocracy who remained there. There was political struggle with rising hopes for some and disappointments for others; there was formidable social change accompanying developing urbanization and the influx of multitudes of non-Arabs to the growing cities, old and new,[13] including slave girls and singers. There was a psychological resistance to the new lifestyle, which was threatening the inherited, well-established mores and attitudes that had heretofore shown resilience to change. Also present was the enticing opportunity for migration to more fertile lands away from the beloved but barren desert habitat that had sheltered, for countless centuries, their history and particular character. Despite the great improvements that changed fortunes for and opened far wider horizons to the new Muslims, the abrupt and numerous changes imposed on them brought bewilderment and fear, and a feeling of nostalgia for the lost ways of life, particularly to the Bedouins. Literature itself had a need for change as an art. After this massive transformation, and the influence of Quranic language and style, there arose an imperative necessity for change in the subject matter, language, and style of literature. Literature needed to capture and express the new restiveness of the age.

The new centers of literature during the Umayyad period were, first, Hijaz, the birthplace and early seat of Islam, which had just lost its central power to the Umayyads in Damascus; Iraq, forever a place of strife and unrest; and the seat of power in the Damascene region. These three centers exhibited different literary features. While Damascus encouraged eulogy in particular, the major poets living in Basra and Kufa, in Iraq, foremost of whom were al-Farazdaq (24 / 640–111 / 729) and Jarir (33 / 653–113 / 730), found their outlet in skillful and sometimes hilarious satire. But the rest of Arabia, particularly the region of Hijaz, the area of thwarted dreams, tended to concentrate more on the literature of love; Hijaz was the center of music, the lyric, and the love story. If the heavy satire in Iraq had a streak, too early acquired, of decadent romanticism, a purer, more immediate kind of romanticism illumined the rich love literature, especially that of the chaste lovers of the Umayyad age.

Many literary historians have attributed the phenomenon of love stories mainly to social and political causes. The region of Hijaz, where the greatest spiritual revolution had taken place and from where the most forceful thrust into the world had been effected only a few decades earlier, was now, in the Umayyad period, suffering, as noted above, from political impotency after the citadel of government had moved to Damascus, a move intended to leave the Hijaz area as depoliticized as possible. However, this was a period of great anxiety for all Arabs, whose whole way of life had been altered within the span of a single generation. The radical change in fortune, lifestyle, and expectations, which had so quickly overtaken them, was not immediately internalized, and they found themselves engulfed by political upheavals, civil wars, and sectarian factionalism. A tense and nervous spirit was released, informed by the need for escapism or sensationalism, expressing itself not only in individual rebellions but also, in Hijaz, in romantic eroticism and, in the famous Iraqi souqs of al-Mirbad, in Basra, and al-Kunasa, in Kufa, in satirical poetry. The two genres represented a sort of poetic catharsis. Both the erotic and the satiric proved to be in great popular demand.

The love accounts, in both poetry and prose, assumed the two opposing features of chaste and profane love, establishing a fabulous convention of unforgettable love lore to posterity that has never died down.

It is important to note that these two kinds of love stories were not purely Umayyad; the stage had already been set earlier in pre-Islamic times with such stories as "Midad and Mai," in the *Book of Crowns* (see below). This is one of the stories making up an early pattern of the romantic and tragic chaste love story that became widespread in the Umayyad period. "Midad and Mai" is the story of the unconsummated love between Midad, a young dignitary from Mecca, and his cousin Mai, which ends with the self-inflicted death by thirst of the two lovers, who, broken down with despair and anguish for each other, willfully deny themselves water and, separately, die of thirst (hence the non-Islamic nature of the story).[14]

A similar story, more akin, for its involvement with a poet, to the chaste Umayyad love stories involving more than a few famous Umayyad poets, is the sixth-century tale of al-Muraqqash al-Akbar. The story of his love for his cousin Asmaʾ is one of a desperate attachment to the beloved, who is married off to another man, causing the devoted lover to pine and, in this case, die in the process of looking for her. Only about twelve poems remain from the verse of this poet, but the story is a lovely and complex account not simply of his love for Asmaʾ but also of the greed and treachery of her father, who had promised her to him on condition he would leave in search of money but then, in his absence, married her off to a richer man; of the cruelty and intrigue of the maid and her husband, who accompanied al-Muraqqash on his quest for Asmaʾ but later abandoned him to die alone in a cave; of a brother's loyalty, who discovers the situation and rushes to help him only to arrive too late. It is an intricate story fit for a modern-day film.

On the other hand, the story of al-Muraqqash al-Asghar, also of pre-Islamic times, belongs to the realm of the profane. The protagonist is also a poet, and his illicit relationship with a Yemeni princess, the daughter of the king, and also with her chambermaid is more profane than any of the erotic stories narrated from the Umayyad period. Her father orders the princess kept under constant guard, allowing no man to enter the premises. However, al-Muraqqash is carried to her nightly on the back of her chambermaid, but an observant watchman sees how the footprints of the chambermaid are deep on entering the premises but lighter on going out, and the trick is discovered.

Despite the restrictions imposed on love by a people so zealous about their women throughout the known Arab history, lovers in the early classical period continued to choose their own destiny. They adulated the object of their love, allowing their passions to make apparent their undying yearnings to the beloved, even sometimes to the extent of delirium, as in the case of Qais ibn al-Mulawwah, known as *majnun* Laila (Laila's Madman). For after Laila was married off to a man from another tribe, Qais spent the rest of his life roaming the wilderness, mourning his love in a poetry aesthetically potent and emotionally moving. His love, even with all the torment it produced, was a most desired attachment that he steadfastly coveted. Witness the madman, insatiable, unrelenting, holding on to the curtains of the Kaaba and beseeching God to increase his love for her, affirm and intensify it, and bolster it in his heart. The story of Qais ibn Dharih (d. 68 / 688) and his love for Lubna, his adored but childless wife, whom he is forced, through the intrigues of his parents and their rigid insistence, to divorce, recounts the same kind of anguish and single-minded quest for the beloved. What is amazing in these stories is not only the perpetual freshness of every encounter with the beloved but also the demonstration of an unwavering constancy in the male lover, belying what is regarded as virile masculine qualities: inconsistency and instability in love. A number of these idealized stories survived the centuries because their protagonists were well-known poets.[15] Perhaps the best known among them is Jamil ibn Maᶜmar, known as Jamil Buthaina, whose love for Buthaina lasted all his life, until his death in Egypt in 82 / 701. It is the same story of forced separation and of permanent fidelity. Jamil was a famous figure in the Hijaz, and there is no doubt that the story attached to him is authentic. Some of the most charming and tender verse on love and the beloved was written by Jamil.[16]

These tragic love stories,[17] which reflected extreme situations, also suited the general mood. However, the accumulation of so many love stories showing great similarity to one another points to the rise of a literary fashion that dominated the literary milieu in the Hijaz for a time, then disappeared. A fashion is not a trend; it takes shape, in literature, when an individual work expressing something found to be exciting and suitable to the prevailing tastes is taken up by a number of authors in a certain period, runs its course, then is overtaken by the forces of change, often through aesthetic fatigue, and dies out. A trend, on the other hand, does not disappear completely; it dissipates, giving way slowly to a new, often corrective trend that coexists with it for some time. This internal movement in the creative realm explains why, in some literary ages, we invariably have at once the old and the new, the traditional and the innovative.

The stories were also an implicit rebellion against existing social norms, an indictment of the strict taboos of the culture, which were accentuated by Islam. But this rebellion was never realized. No hard-hearted patriarch was ever defied and brought down, and the chastity of the Arab woman was going to remain forever at the heart of the highest morality, the proof of family honor and a never-violated ethical code. The longing for volition in love, for the attainment of love's greatest ecstasy, was to linger for centuries in the Arab soul, transcending the rich urban centuries of the empire, with their abated, colorful male sexuality, their open negotiations with the erotic, to surface again in various periods and areas of the Arab world, then assert its hard command among modern Arab poets and writers of fiction in the first half of the twentieth century. Umayyad ʿUdhri love, as it came to be called with reference to the ʿUdhra tribe in the Hijaz, which boasted the greatest number of lovers annihilated by love ("a people who, when they love, they die"),[18] was a battle in which the lovers were always defeated, their resistance and constancy only a symbol of a vanquished soul that gallantly persevered.

The perseverance in love was not, would never be permeated with the hope for union and bliss. It often ended in stalemate, sometimes, as in the case of Laila's tormented lover, in madness and death. But the love story that aspires to immortality has perforce to revolve around deprivation and loss and the attempt to transcend them or defy them with an avowal of constancy. The best, the most memorable love literature is not usually created out of the delight of fulfilled passion and permanent union.

It is interesting to observe the contradictory situations during the Umayyad age. While the most powerful *public* drama was taking place in Damascus, where the citadel of government had moved, and on the vast frontiers of the quickly expanding Arab domains, a concentration on the most private of experiences was demonstrated in the Hijaz, where, instead of the brisk public energy with which that region had reverberated only a few decades earlier, the self-absorption in these stories signaled a retreat from public involvement, and, despite the similarities the love tales show, a concentration on individualized, private experience is paramount and the intimate voice of the bereft lover is heard. There is a clearly discernible inwardness of the lover in these stories, an attitude perhaps seen here very early in literary history but regarded today as the earmark of the modern novel.

Not to be overlooked is the other, contrasting vogue that existed side by side in the Umayyad era with that of chaste and unfulfilled love: while those wretched, mostly Bedouin lovers were mourning their fate, there was a group of other lovers, mainly in the cities of Hijaz, now flourishing with a new wealth and great resurgence in the arts of music and song, who knew well how to enjoy life. Led by that blithe-spirited poet ʿUmar ibn Abi Rabiʿa (23 / 643–93 / 711), they had no patience with constancy and sorrow. A number of them were poets, and some of the most charming stories were about them. Both kinds of experiences were the result of the same motivation: the need for escapism.

As mentioned, it was with the establishment of urban life in the many cities that mushroomed in the vast Abbasid empire (which began in 132 / 750) that much of the emotional attachment to the purity of love and its constancy subsided. Except for rare instances, we do not find, in the long Abbasid era, that burning out of the soul for the sake of the beloved, that concentration and permanent devotion, that tenderness and chastity. The profane erotic trend became almost the norm in the Abbasid age, and with the great influx of all kinds of slaves of both genders and of many races, the nature of love changed on the whole and became inured to the pursuit of pleasure, at times targeting a homosexual experience. Love proves capable of undergoing many transformations, of experiencing mutations of mood and intensity; and fiction will have a wide variety of themes, away from the unrequited love stories of the Umayyads. But for the Umayyads, these tragic stories were a great representation of a private tragedy begun very early in Arabic culture.

Whether the love stories were all genuine, concerning real historical figures or not (some, such as the story of ʿUmar ibn Abi Rabiʿa and Jamil ibn Maʿmar, or Jamil Buthaina, are certainly genuine), their existence, often in elaborate construction, in an age of eroticism remains of relevance. They reflected a culture neither repressive nor permissive[19] that shaped their existential experience. Whereas the stories of unfulfilled, chaste love and enduring constancy were more popular, there was profanity even in the first century, however well camouflaged.[20] This other kind of love developed with the centuries, including in part the homosexual experience of lovers in the breadth and length of the Islamic empire, from Cordova to Baghdad.

The Short Anecdote

There are many examples from the *khabar* (pl. *akhbar*) genre in this anthology. The *khabar* is usually a short anecdote, resembling the very short story of modern times.[21] It often has a pretension to truth and revolves around real or the simulation of real protagonists and thus is always one step away from pure fiction. It is found in abundance in the many large and small collections assembled by various anthologists, medieval and modern. *Khabar* anecdotes reflect medieval Arabic social and intellectual life, its beliefs, mores, experiences, and colorful diversity. These anecdotes usually begin with a list of genealogical transmitters forwarding the individual *khabar*, a practice that was the result of the need to proclaim "truth" in narration, which Islam, particularly in its earlier phases, demanded of believers. Through this procedure, accounts that might have been imaginary assumed the appearance of truth.

The issue of veracity in studying the *khabar* genre should be crucial when looking for the social aspects of medieval Arabic life. However, whether a single *khabar* anecdote is based on truth or fiction, it is its aspects as an art form that engage the critic and literary historian, whose primary interest is to observe the development of the art of storytelling in Arabic. The most interesting artistic aspects of this genre are its terseness of expression, its closed structure, and its conciseness, which entails great control of language and expression, as well as its immediacy. Some anecdotes are short stories or episodes, some no more than brief comments, wise or comic, on various aspects of life,[22] and other longer accounts of more complex events or stories. They always develop toward a conclusive ending. The language of these narratives usually lacks the intimacy that would arouse ardor, nostalgia, or deep compassion. That was the provenance of the Umayyad love story and the endearingly subjective love poetry that often accompanied such stories. It must be kept in mind that the age when the *khabar* flourished, the height of Abbasid hegemony, was a realistic age, one that had abandoned the romanticism of the Umayyad age.

The *khabar* is a purely Arabic genre, issuing from both the early Islamic discouragement of purely fictitious narratives but also the old Arabic mastery, since pre-Islamic times, of succinct, cogent expression, with little of the redundancies or flabbiness afflicting Arabic prose much later. It was also a direct contradiction to the endless tales found in the *Book of Crowns*, where one story grows out of another. The interest in the many compendiums containing hundreds of anecdotes[23] stems from other human incentives: the curiosity about Arabic and particularly Abbasid life revealed, pulsating with all kinds of experience and with the smells, sounds, colors, and rhythms of place, and the interest found in the variety of human encounters, some of an amusing, even a mischievous and comic appeal. The history of a place, a people, the very conscience of the Abbasid experience are brought to light in these narratives. Indeed, the whole Arab cultural and social heritage, during one of its richest periods, has a genuine treasure in these many dictionaries and compendiums.

The insistence on veracity began early after Islam. The first Islamic century displayed a close attention, whether spontaneous or imposed, to the demands of the new faith in its urge to spread the message of the new religion to the surrounding world. Islam brought fame, wealth, and conquest to this half-forgotten area of the planet. Arabia had burst out into the world, and from desert harshness and scarcity a landscape of fruits and flowers and running waters was attained. This sudden and decisive movement opened many avenues to the Arabs, who had been hemmed in in the vast and mostly arid desert of Arabia, counteracting, but only to a limited extent, the strong tribal identity of Bedouin Arabs now entering the age of urban life. It also eventually brought a sense of a new Arab / Islamic identity, which thereafter remained vivid in the Arab consciousness.

The *khabar* is linked with the ninth-century scholar, philologist, and anthologist al-Asmaʿi (124 / 741–216 / 831), and such later linguists as Ibn Duraid (223 / 837–321 / 933). By the fourth / tenth century, the form had become widespread. Because of the fear of exaggeration and waywardness and the possible dissemination of narratives estranged from Islamic teachings, fiction in early Islam was suspect. Religious authorities wanted the new Muslims to concentrate on the Quran and on the teachings of the Prophet, which enveloped everything. Much later, the jurist, linguist, and religious savant Ibn al-Jawzi (511 / 1117–597 / 1200) gave six main factors he felt had negatively affected the storytelling art: first, people tended to reject anything that had not existed at the time of the Prophet; second, the stories of the ancients were regarded as rarely accurate, especially those about the Israelites.[24] Third, storytelling tended, it was felt, to distract from the study of religious texts; fourth, there were many narratives in the Quran and among the traditions of the Prophet that rendered these unreliable stories superfluous; fifth, some of the narrators who adopted Islam introduced into their stories alien elements that tended to change the hearts of the public; and sixth, most storytellers, whether from ignorance or a lack of genuine piety, did not pay enough attention to a story's veracity.[25]

The *khabar* established itself strongly and for many centuries as a major method of narration, factual and fictive, and constituted numerous entries in the many large compendiums and dictionaries in which Arabic heritage is so rich. They coexisted with new fictive genres created by the Arabs themselves or imported from the conquered worlds of India and Persia.

The importance in Arabic literature of the broad public is seen even in pre-Islamic times. With the romantic love stories in the Umayyad age, its place was firmly established. And even after the full evolution in the Abbasid period of a royal caliphate, with its pomp and ceremony, a new proud and mighty upper class, a vast bureaucracy and complex infrastructure, a large, powerful merchant class with great economic power, and the introduction of luxury and city refinements into the lives of the upper echelon of society,[26] the interest of both the humbler urban public and the desert Bedouins continued in prose literature. At this point, and I am talking here of the classical Abbasid centuries, poetry and prose took divergent paths. On the one hand, formal poetry preserved, even augmented its elitist status,[27] sustaining the sublime rhetoric and sonorous tones of the eulogy, elegy, and satire and achieving, in some special experiments, an elaborate and intricate grace in a poetry that reflected an art for art's sake approach devoted to painting nature with words. This art form had begun in Arabic in pre-Islamic times with the minute descriptions of both domesticated animals (the camel and the horse) and the desert and its fauna but flourished later, in the early fourth / tenth century and thereafter, with elaborate descriptions of fertile nature (a point to ponder in the context of literary history and comparative literature). On the other hand, the Arabic fictional experience seems to contradict Northrop Frye's categorization of fiction in the West according to neat differentiations and gradations in the status of the hero (which is not exactly accurate for the West either).[28] Right from its earlier experiments we see a rather inclusive attitude toward social levels, and a mixture of protagonists from varied strata of life is presented.

In addition to depicting the lifestyle and full range of daily habits and usages of the urbanized Arabs and Arabized Muslims in the flourishing cities of the empire, *khabar* prose narratives also recorded the changing language of the Abbasids,[29] for while they remained capable of the greatest sublimity and eloquence, they were also able to accommodate the tones and echoes of the marketplace, of the language of rowdy ruffians and uncouth plebeians. Philologists interested in historical linguistics can benefit greatly from the scrutiny of these prose narrations. Indeed, in the

Abbasid period, when the greatest mixture of races and languages took place, it was, as mentioned above, mainly in the prose narratives, not in poetry, that linguistic change was best effected.

Thus the *khabar* enjoyed a splendid freedom from the formal constraints of rhetorical language that poetry could not enjoy. However, Arabic prose later experienced great restraint with the resurgence of an intricate rhetorical style decked with internal rhyme and ornate figures of speech. This can be seen in the restrictive form of the *maqamat* and in the eloquent and complex *Epistle of Forgiveness*, by the major poet al-Maʿarri (363/973–449/1057), and numerous later prose writers of the Mamluk and Ottoman ages, but while this trend pursued its own course a wealth of historical, scientific, social, linguistic, and literary knowledge continued to be gained from the numerous compendiums of *akhbar* on general or specialized topics. Only recently have scholars, Arab and Arabists, started to more fully appreciate the value of the *khabar* genre and study its techniques and characteristics.

Many compendiums and smaller books were written using the form. Al-Asmaʿi's anecdotes, which included original tales (*nawadir*) and amusing stories (*mulah*), appeared in later compendiums of *akhbar*. Their writers lived in the very heart of the bustling Abbasid era, when urban cultural phenomena had been firmly set and Arabian city life had acquired its particular rhythms and conventions, informed by an amalgam of cultures, concepts, and behavior patterns not completely harmonious with the old, pre-Abbasid patterns. Remarkable among them was al-Jahiz (159 / 775–254 / 868), a much earlier writer and anthologist. Although he was also greatly interested in language and style, al-Jahiz was also deeply concerned with lived life, human nature and the nature of all beings. Some of the most famous compendiums on general and specialized subjects were authored by him, recording numerous anecdotes and interesting tales. Of special note is his book *The Misers* (*al-Bukhalaʾ*), from which a number of anecdotes are presented in this anthology. His work in this and in other books reflects not only his humor and dexterity in the use of irony but also his genuine interest in common people, even in the most lowly, as part of his interest in human behavior itself. The book reflects the firm establishment of an urban culture in the Abbasid cities and the rise of both a middle class conscious of money matters and self-interested preservation of wealth and a lower class trying to survive in an environment marked by materialistic acquisition. Many colorful episodes[30] are recorded in *The Misers* depicting marginal social characters: naive people, lighthearted tricksters, beggars, and thieves.[31] The humor reflects the great change that had happened to the Arab author since his Bedouin days, when he was bound to a more serious approach. The desert had produced little humor, but city life was showing its impact on this aspect of the range of human responses, usually linked to urban cultures.[32] This formed a basis for the later appearance of the *maqamat*. Indeed, the work of al-Jahiz was a great cultural achievement that appeared a century and a half before the end of the first millennium.

The *khabar* genre is abundantly represented in the renowned *Book of Songs* (*Kitab al-aghani*), of Abu ʾl-Faraj al-Asbahani (284 / 897–355 / 966),[33] and in many other famous dictionaries and compendiums. But it is in the narratives of Abu ʿAli ʾl-Tanukhi (327–384 / 938–994) where the *khabar* achieves great effect: in his various compendia the *khabar*, often a short, dramatic story, not only entertains the reader but also exhibits great knowledge and breadth of vision. Among al-Tanukhi's several works, *Reprieve After Hardship* (*Al-faraj baʿda ʾl-shidda*) revolves around episodes from the lives of real people, often including advice and examples from religious texts, but it is generally devoid of humor. It reveals the intimate secrets of political life, the tyranny of rulers, and the terror they instilled in the hearts of people from all walks of life. His most remarkable work is the entertaining and enlightening eight-volume book *Nishwar al-muhadara wa akhbar al-mudhakara* (*Snippets of Conversation and Memorable Tales*, or, according to D. S. Margoliouth, *Table Talk of a Mesopotamian Judge*), devoted to general social and cultural themes. His third work, *Al-mustajad min fiʿlat al-ajwad* (*The Admirable Deeds of Munificent Men*), focuses on another specialized theme. It is interesting to see how, in the first two volumes, he uses words from the contemporary colloquial, evoking a feeling of familiarity and immediacy in the stories, while in the third book, on the subject of generosity and hospitality, a revered Arabic ideal inherited from pre-Islamic times, he reverts to a higher language. Another important characteristic of these writings is the interest shown in the common man, an interest, as mentioned, common in the Arabic writings of the time. The individual is also often depicted as an autonomous person with his own feelings, whims, tastes, and choices, a situation dramatically reversed when the author depicts the studied and self-conscious reactions of caliphs and men of power.[34]

As a form, the *khabar* has its limitations, a major one of which is its narrow scope for diversity of technique. Arab writers, however, discovered several other means of diversifying their fictional techniques, and some were strikingly original.

The Visit to the Afterworld: Hell and Heaven

The story of Isra᾽ (night journey) and Miʿraj (ascension) depicts the Prophet's ascension to Heaven at night, starting at the Holy Mosque (al-Kaʿba), in Mecca, arriving at the mosque of al-Aqsa, in Jerusalem, and back to Mecca the same night. The Miʿraj is the tale of the Prophet's ascent to Heaven and appearance before God with the archangel Gabriel as guide. His ascent allowed him to witness the tortures of Hell and the luminous beauty of Paradise. The Isra᾽ and Miʿraj journeys represent the pinnacle of Islamic tales of marvel and were immediately popular, a sign of people's great infatuation with miracles and marvels, and became widespread also outside the Islamic world, pointing to the fascination of people with miracles and the supernatural. The Miʿraj story, which has many versions, features fascinating descriptions of Paradise and Hell, as in the following excerpt in ʿAbd al-Wahid Lu᾽lu᾽a's words:

> In several versions of the Muslim narrative, the Prophet saw hell from his position in the third heaven. It had several floors where the sinners were cast according to the seriousness of their sin . . . hell is deep down under Jerusalem, the centre of the earth . . . [It] had the shape of an overturned cone, a series of concentric circular strata, descending from top to bottom. [It also] has seven gates. The heavens are seven, indicating the special significance of the number seven in Islamic culture . . . The Muslim paradise has four rivers . . . The journey seeks the Divine Throne, where the light is dazzling. The ascension begins in Jerusalem.[35]

Lu᾽lu᾽a continues:

> The equally ethereal beauty of the Muslim paradise, especially in this emphasis on light and sound in both works: light always dazzling, and sound is either that of nature, trees, birds, or sound of *tasbih*, chanting, glorifying the Lord . . . "God is the Light of heavens and earth" is the leitmotif of the Muslim chants, based on the descriptions in the Holy Quran. Lights are full of color . . . angels, as well, appear in fantastic colors.[36]

The ascension to Heaven was later adapted by the famous poet Abu ᾽l-ʿAla᾽ al-Maʿarri in his *Risalat al-Ghufran* (*Epistle of Forgiveness*) and by the Andalusian poet Ibn Shuhayd (383 / 992–426 / 1035) in his *Al-Tawabiʿ wa ᾽l-Zawabiʿ* (*Treatise of Familiar Spirits and Demons*). It was also translated into such languages as Castilian, French, and Latin. Its possible influence on

Dante's *Divina Commedia* has been suggested by many observers. ʿAbd al-Wahid Luʾluʾa has written at length on the many similarities in the Arabic and Dante's versions so as to leave little doubt as to the possibility of Dante's borrowing from this Islamic legend.

Fables

Several types of sophisticated fictional genres had been produced in Arabic by the beginning of the Abbasid age. One of the earliest such works was *Kalila and Dimna*, a collection of fables translated by Ibn al-Muqaffaʿ (102 / 720–139 / 756) from the Persian translation of an Indian collection. An Arabized Persian and a new convert to Islam, Ibn al-Muqaffaʿ used his lucid, succinct style and command of language to produce an immortal text that has enjoyed a considerable amount of critical study and translations, one that has not lost its charm in modern times. Fables have been attractive to writers in many cultures, often employed to express human observations on life and morals. *Kalila and Dimna* is based on the answers allegedly given to Dabshalim, a king of India, by his vizier, a Brahman philosopher called Bidpai, in the form of fables in which animals act and speak and furnish subtle allusions to human life and experience. The intention is to illuminate, in each episode, one or more of life's aspects or furnish solutions to problems that people encounter or give a lesson as to the correct behavior. This is done by comparing a human situation or action to an incident that has happened to one or more animals, or reiterating an idea said by another, or expressing an emotional state experienced by a third, but which are all, in fact, representative of human experience and immediately accessible to the reader as such. Although the intention of fables is didactic, they are usually enjoyable and often charming. To provide profound wisdom from the mouth of animals is, in fact, to make it more easily savored, animals being always capable of arousing more sympathy in people and less antagonism. In a turbulent and dangerous age like that in which Ibn al-Muqaffaʿ lived and in which he prematurely and brutally died at the hands of the Abbasid state, the resort to this kind of obliqueness was a clever way of camouflaging criticism of the state of things. All through the book, King Dabshalim suggests a topic to Bidpai or presents an issue, and Bidpai answers by saying something like, "When the lion saw the bones in his den . . ." before continuing with the fable.

Whether these fables were translated by Ibn al-Muqaffaʿ in their entirety or partly so and partly written by him, as some scholars claim,[37] they were eminently successful. Desert Arabs had lived with animals at close range, and animals had a vital role in their lives. In pre-Islamic literature, animals are described in minute detail, those that are hunted and those that hunt and those that are a source of food or a means of travel, on which survival in the desert depended. The allusions and symbolization contained in the work of Ibn al-Muqaffaᶜ were commensurate with the artistic treatment animals received from major Arab poets. The Bedouin poet's description of them had arrived at archetypal and symbolic dimensions in the hands of Labid, in pre-Islamic times, and especially Dhu ᵓl-Rummah (77 / 696–117 / 735), in the Umayyad period, who took a most sophisticated approach.

The Arabic fables of Ibn al-Muqaffaᶜ were followed by other attempts in much the same fashion later in the Abbasid period. We find them in the *Arabian Nights*, often relayed in a convoluted fashion. Ferial Ghazoul has written a detailed account of the use of fables in that work. She has also written of their adoption by the group of philosophers known as Ikhwan al-Safa, whose treatment of fables reflects the continuation and elevation of this genre in classical Arabic. In the *Arabian Nights* fables reveal behavior patterns in people and offer advice against human weakness. Their incorporation by the Brethren of Purity in their works represents a serious consideration, where philosophy is served by the symbolization and metaphorical power of fables. Defining their intention, Ikhwan al-Safa said: "We made [our intention] evident in the mouths of animals so that it comes out more effectively and clearer in address, more attractive as stories, more delicious to the ears, and furnishes greater benefit, prompting the reader to think deeply."[38] Excerpts of these are represented in this anthology.

As Ghazoul explains, however, the brethren had another purpose, a scientific one. They tried to show that, according to their theory of the origin of species, life-forms were not created all at once but, according to God's wisdom, were created in stages, first the plants, then the animals, then man.[39]

The Assemblies

A striking change in technique, variety, language, and style took place in creative prose after the Umayyad period, one that far outstripped what happened in its contemporaneous poetry. Perhaps the greatest change poetry experienced was its slow alienation from the pre-Islamic conventions, particularly regarding the pre-Islamic description of animals and the deserted campsites.[40] Although other elements of the poem were certainly undergoing change during the Abbasid period, the changes in creative prose were more sudden and radical. The new genres introduced into prose and the changes of language and style point to the wide range open to prose as compared to the strict conventions of poetry and the dictates of its history.

The open inventiveness of prose literature produced, in the fourth / tenth century, the totally urban assemblies, or *maqamat*. These constitute the third genre of narrative literature purely Arabic in origin. The assemblies were mainly picaresque tales offering a comic representation of experience, often depicting the life of wandering rogues and frequently revolving around the personality of a trickster. However, under their comic surface, they contained incisive social criticism.

The father of the art of the *maqamat* was Badiᶜ al-Zaman al-Hamadhani, who took the humor and irony found in such earlier writers as al-Jahiz, particularly in *The Misers*, to a new literary form and thus produced a completely novel fictive genre.

Also of note about them is that they, like a number of other tales in the Abbasid period, depicted the life and manners also of the lower classes, arriving at the delineation of the antihero so many centuries before this kind of protagonist had become central to fiction in Europe. Of course, al-Jahiz, that great genius of the second to third century A.H. (eighth to ninth century C.E.), had already given the type his creative attention. The early entry of this type of protagonist—ruffians, thieves, tricksters, outcasts, vagrants, naive dupes, party crashers, nouveaux riches—into Arabic fiction can only denote a fast-growing urbanism and a sophistication that broke the bonds of the conventionally exclusive concern with those of the upper ranks, relegating those of lower status to little or no narrative importance.

Al-Hamadhani was a writer with a particular originality, one who invented a new fictive form and brought it to great success. His achievement was not only improvising an unprecedented organizational scheme but also devising purely fictional content built around imaginary protagonists. The *khabar*, as we have seen, had pretensions to veracity and concerned real or possibly real protagonists and was thus shy of being pure fiction. However, by his double contribution, al-Hamadhani was able to offer a new and interesting addition to the limited forms of fiction in the literary world anywhere, providing a framework and substance to the great cultural, social, and literary changes that had taken place in various aspects of medieval Arab life.

Writers before him had long been experimenting with the ironic mode, al-Jahiz constituting a brilliant early example. Al-Hamadhani, however, brought the ironic mode in the art of fiction to its fullness, a marked signal of an irreversibly changed sensibility reflecting a striking contrast to poetry's lingering idealizations and elevated forms of address almost throughout the Abbasid ages. The diverse personalities populating the *maqamat*, taken from the social milieu of Abbasid society, were, with rare exceptions,[41] invisible to the eloquent poet, haughtily overlooked by him, comfortably neglected. In mode and intention, the introduction of the *maqamat* was a triumphant departure from the obsessive concentration on social grandeur and the pomp of status; it forged an almost perfect split between formal poetry and prose fiction in the fourth century A.H.

In the fifty-one *maqamat* remaining to posterity (the author claimed he had written four hundred), al-Hamadhani manifests farsightedness, linguistic dexterity, great descriptive capacity, and an ability to write skillfully on many topics. In style and language, al-Hamadhani's *maqamat* are eloquent, marked by high rhetoric (in contrast to their humble subject matter) and rhymed prose (*saj*ʿ), sustaining a rhythmic flow and sometimes incorporating quotes from poetry as illustration or embellishment. In structure, his *maqamat* have two protagonists, the first, the main protagonist, whom al-Hamadhani calls Abu ʾl-Fat-h al-Iskandari, is the one who undergoes the various adventures and describes them in an elevated, eloquent language that is transmitted to his narrator, here called ʿIsa ibn Hisham. And it is the latter who relates them to the reading or listening audience.

Always witty and often hilarious, each *maqama* is a tableau of a single experience, of an isolated adventure complete within itself that concentrates on both action and dialogue, the action usually limited in time and space, dramatic and intense, and the dialogue often intriguing and entertaining. The problematic world of the main protagonist, usually a trickster, often loosens its binding limits so he can override it triumphantly. Indeed, he seems to be the master of his time and fate.

Al-Hamadhani's work was destined to continue and thrive. This schema of his *maqamat* was adopted by later writers, with a change of the names of the two protagonists. The genre he established quickly traveled to North Africa and Muslim Spain, attracting several writers in Andalusia, such as the prominent poet Ibn Shuhayd. Al-Hamadhani's most famous successor, however, was Abu Muhammad al-Qasim al-Hariri (446 / 1054–516 / 1122) in the east, who made the *maqamat* form the medium of a grand exercise in linguistic dexterity, filling his *maqamat* with embellishments and artful improvisations. His *maqamat* concentrate on a continuous experiment in stylistic magnificence and the inclusion of complex figures of speech. They are longer than those of al-Hamadhani and are masterpieces of linguistic virtuosity. Al-Hariri had the greatest influence on Arab writers after him, even up to the nineteenth century with the beginning of the Arabic literary renaissance, when some of the foremost pioneers of the reawakening, such as Nasif al-Yaziji (1800–1883) and Ahmad Faris al-Shidyaq (1801–1887), wrote their share of *maqamat*.[42]

The Epistle of Forgiveness

The intricate and highly rhetorical *Epistle of Forgiveness*, by the famous poet Abu ʾl-ʿAlaʾ al-Maʿarri, was a riposte to a letter sent to him by a writer called ʿAli ibn al-Qarih, whose questions of heresy and faith and reactionary attitude and seeming bias in his critical comments on some major literary figures provoked al-Maʿarri to write his *Epistle*. It is a narrative on an imaginary journey to the afterworld, in which al-Maʿarri sends Ibn al-Qarih to both Paradise and Hell, meeting and holding conversations with poets, men of letters, linguists, musicians, and narrators. Al-Maʿarri, irked and challenged by the pretentiousness of Ibn al-Qarih's letter, improvised this trip to the afterworld to expose Ibn al-Qarih's flagrantly less-commendable qualifications and to show off his own vast knowledge of Arabic culture, his mastery of the Arabic language, grammar, and rhetoric, his proficiency in religious knowledge, his expertise on the *khabar* collections and Arabic poetry of the pre-Islamic and early Islamic periods, and his extensive general erudition. This major work, which was a great experiment in intellectual and linguistic virtuosity, was also a major literary venture in that it succeeded in transforming the epistle genre into a new, distinct literary form.

The work is narrated in the voice of al-Maʿarri. The protagonist, Ibn al-Qarih, moves from Paradise to Hell, then returns to Paradise, and with every move, several fictional episodes, often of genuine interest to the reader, take place. The narrator follows the footsteps of the protagonist, watching every move he makes, and monitors his conversations with the inhabitants of the afterworld. The narrator knows everything that goes on in the minds of all the people concerned.

This was a suitable opportunity for al-Maʿarri to voice many of his observations on the ideas and ideologies widespread in his period. In a sarcastic manner he attacks, among other things, several of the religious creeds as well as the Sufis in the person of al-Hallaj.

A notable characteristic of this work is its inclusion of various episodes in each segment of the journey, each episode preserving its integrity, a great difference to the complex strategy of *Kalila and Dimna* and the *Arabian*

Nights, where a single story often branches out before it ends. The narrative keeps an artistic balance between description and dialogue, and the dialogue unfolds in a way that exposes Ibn al-Qarih's pedantry, pretentiousness, egotism, and attachment to sensuous pleasures but also reveals al-Maʿarri's erudition and ironic bent. Despite the difficulty of the language of these episodes, they preserve their charm and interest even after so many centuries.

Al-Maʿarri's *Epistle* was followed by several more of the same genre by other writers, the most famous of which is the *Risalat al-tawabiʿwa ʾl zawabiʿ* (*Epistle of Familiar Spirits and Demons*) by Ibn Shuhayd in Muslim Spain. Ibn Shuhayd, who was younger than al-Maʿarri and died at a relatively young age, was clearly aware of the experiments in literature of the Arab east and quick to adopt them.

The suggestion has often been made that *The Epistle of Forgiveness* may have formed the basis of Dante's *Divina Commedia*. It is astonishing that most European literary historians in investigating the history of the various nascent literatures that developed in the second millennium around Muslim Spain and the shores of the Mediterranean, particularly Muslim Sicily, show no attempts whatsoever to examine the influences that must have existed in some of the literary works in these languages; the songs of the troubadours and the lyrical poetry in the south of Italy, especially in Sicily, where Arabs ruled for over two hundred years, until the end of the eleventh century, are two examples. It is beyond the scope of this essay to go into the details of these influences, but surely it cannot happen that a civilization should flourish for centuries in a certain place, achieving brilliant heights, and leave no influences.[43] The apparent Arabic influences in Spanish and other languages have been acknowledged and studied, to an extent.[44] The other influences of the culture have largely been overlooked by the old guard of Western literary history.

An Early Novel in Arabic

The philosophical novel *Hayy ibn Yaqzan*, by the Andalusi philosopher Ibn Tufail, is one of the treasures of classical Arabic literature. A mixture of philosophical reflection and storytelling, it has preserved its literary and intellectual excellence throughout the centuries.

"*Hayy ibn Yaqzan* is the tale of a man who grows up on an uninhabited island and attains the highest degree of insight, both philosophical and religious, by dint of his inborn capacities, by his experiences, perceptions and reflections."[45] J. C. Burgel regards this novel as a turning point in Arabic philosophical writings.[46]

The story begins with Hayy's birth by spontaneous generation from the mud on the shore and upbringing by a gazelle, a story already known about the founders of Rome. His gazelle mother dies before he reaches puberty. Having grown up in nature, he imitates the animals but spends his time studying nature.

Absal, the second protagonist in the novel, is from another island. He teaches Hayy human speech, and when he explains his own religion to Hayy, they discover they share the same convictions. Hayy then visits Absal's island, where he finds the people there to be superficial believers attached to physical pleasures. "He tries to open their eyes to the higher realities of their world, but in vain. He and Absal thereupon leave them and decide to retire to the lonely island and spend the rest of their lives in devotions there."[47]

It is a unique novel, authentically Arabic in origin, a story that is at once philosophy, vision, and literature, representing a way of some philosophers to explain their philosophical ideas through stories, tales, and symbolic visions. Through symbols mystics express their passionate feelings and show how a mystic can say what cannot be said in ordinary language and describe what cannot be described. They rely on sensuous and concrete representations from the outside world, often images from mundane love poetry and the pleasures of life on earth, and use them by elevating them to spiritual experience.

This is because love is its own goal. But the Sufi lover is elevated. His love is pregnant with ideas, meanings, and flavor and is directed toward a unique purpose. It is stronger and loftier than all other loves. The Sufis are certainly the masters of love and truth in love, having given the most fantastic examples of the most wonderful spiritual aspirations. Islamic mysticism met a lot of rejection because of these sensuous expressions and images. We can describe the novel as "the story of human life in nature, or the adventure of the human mind in the universe." Ibn Tufail depicts, most skillfully, some of the stages through which human life or the mind passes.

The meeting of Hayy with Absal, who appears on Hayy's island when Hayy has matured in thought, and their eventual harmony symbolize the meeting of the philosophic mind and the canons of law brought forth by the prophets. His failure with the inhabitants of the second island symbolizes the failure of the masses to realize the aims of philosophers and their abstractions.

Ibn Tufail wanted to intimate his understanding of life and resurrection and the nature of recompense and punishment, and express his wish to criticize the society he lived in.

Hayy ibn Yaqzan is a well-written, well-organized novel, but it did not inspire other Arabic writers to write novels. The reason seems obvious. A novel, written by a literary philosopher, as in this case, was not meant for public dissemination but to be read as a philosophical reflection. The eleventh century could not sustain the production of long fictional narratives on a popular level.

The Folk Epic

The incorporation of mythology into the story and of episodes of marvels and wonders side by side with stories of superheroic action or penetrating wisdom was fully revived later, particularly with the rise of folk epics. As a genre, the folk epic was not an early fruit of the Arabic creative imagination, although some features can be found in *Ayyam al-ʿArab* (*Battles of the Arabs*) and in *Kitab al-Tijan* (*Book of Crowns*). However, the Arabic folk epic proper arose mainly during the Mamluk and Ottoman periods, when life was plagued by political instability and non-Arab hegemony.[48]

Arabic folk epics are original and individual, with marked variations in theme and resolutions, although keeping the general epic features common to all. Adventure and love are the main topics, but there are also wars and great feats of courage, physical prowess and moral integrity, often meshed with magic and superhuman events.

These epics have preserved their attraction in the Arabic world to the present time: they are still narrated in the cafés of some old Arabian cities, such as Damascus, and in villages and in the less-modernized habitats of the Arabic world. They are also found in many of the libraries housing Oriental manuscripts. Many printings of them are available in various Arab cities, and there are scholars of Arabic literature specializing in them and teaching them at Arab universities.

The most famous of these folk epics are:[49]

1. *The Epic of ʿAntara ibn Shaddad* (around 4,000 pages)
2. *The Epic of Hamza al-Bahlawan* (around 2,000 pages)
3. The famous Hilali epic, *Sirat Bani Hilal*, which has two major renditions: a prose rendition of about two thousand pages, and a poetry rendition

collected and recorded by the poet ʿAbd al-Rahman al-Abnudi and constituting a quarter of a million poetry quartets
4. *The Epic of Princess Dhat al-Himma, the Loafer and Her Son, Prince ʿAbdul Wahhab* (around 5,000 pages)
5. *The Epic of al-Dhahir Baibars* (around 5,000 pages)
6. *The Epic of ʿAli ʾl-Zeibaq*, which resembles the story of Robin Hood
7. The fourteenth-century epic *The Adventures of Sayf Ben Dhi Yazan*, which reflects the domination of mythological and superstitious thought above reality

An excerpt from the latter is included in this anthology. Sayf Ben Dhi Yazan was a historical figure, a pre-Islamic Yemeni king with quite a few recorded exploits to his name. In the fourteenth century his story was transformed into a folk romance of great fascination, a folk epic offering a full range of stories of wonders and miracles, mythic events, superhuman feats, as well as all-too-human experiences, with all the necessary ingredients of a magical account of heroism, in which this epic surpasses all others. It depicts Sayf's prodigious exploits, mainly for love, and his intricate personal life. In this epic, he is presented as a Muslim.[50]

Notes

1. S. Leder has edited a substantial book of studies on *Story-Telling in the Framework of Non-fictional Arabic Literature* (Wiesbaden: Harrassowitz, 1998). In addition to the present anthology, *PROTA* plans to prepare an anthology of nonfictional prose genres in English translation.
2. I say "story" here rather than "fiction" because some narrations were not perceived as fictive accounts but as factual stories.
3. In addition to the book of studies I have edited on the old Arabic story, tentatively titled *The Classical Arabic Story: Genres, History and Influences*, forthcoming from Brill, I also offer a brief account of the emergence and development of this story in my introduction to *Modern Arabic Fiction: An Anthology* (New York: Columbia University Press, 2005), where I briefly describe the rich and varied vista of the classical Arabic story.
4. The short era from the first Hijri year (1 / 622) to the end of the Orthodox Caliphate in the year 40 / 660 marked a strong rupture in the development of poetry, an art that, during this short period, was stigmatized and discouraged in religious circles. The direct relationship with pre-Islamic poetry, with few exceptions, such as that of Dhu ʾl-Rumma (77/697–117/735), was weakened and sometimes lost, and poets, even great poets such as al-Farazdaq, lost touch in part with some pre-Islamic conventions. On this, see my chapter, "Umayyad Poetry," in *Arabic Literature to the End of the Umayyad Period*, ed. E. F. L. Beeston et al. (Cambridge: Cambridge University

Press, 1983), 390 *et seq.* (on al-Farazdaq, see p. 405); see also the account in that chapter of Dhu ʾl-Rumma's firm relationship with the inherited poetic traditions and his further development of their symbolic significance (430–31).

5. See, for a single example, *The Misers*, by the renowned scholar al-Jahiz (159 / 775–254 / 868).
6. H. T. Norris, "Fables and Legends in Pre-Islamic and Early Islamic Times," in Beeston, *Arabic Literature*, 1:374–86.
7. See the translated excerpt from this tale in this anthology.
8. For a summary of these attempts, see my *Trends and Movements in Modern Arabic Poetry* (Leiden: Brill, 1977), 1:74–78, where the experiments of Shafiq al-Maʿluf are discussed, and 2:720–21 n. These efforts culminated in the fifties and early sixties with the employment of the Phoenician fertility myths of Tammuz, Ishtar, and similar deities, a commendable effort describing the vision of a resurrection after death to coincide with the situation of Arab life after the Palestine debacle of 1948 and hope of its rebirth. However, these myths cannot be included under the symbolic reference of myths alive in people's consciousness, which would trigger a telling experience of the past to symbolize the present. Even educated Arab readers had to study these myths in order to understand the poems that incorporated them.
9. See Mahmoud al-Hoot, *Fi tariq al-mythologia ʿind al-ʿArab: Bahth mushab fi ʾl-muʿtaqadat wa ʾl-asatir al-ʿArabiyya qabla ʾl-Islam (A Detailed Introduction to Arabic Mythology and Beliefs About Islam)* (1953); Shukri ʿAyyad, *Al-batal fi ʾl-adab wa ʾl-asatir (The Hero in Literature and Mythology)* (Cairo: Dar al-Maʿrifa, 1959); ʿAbd al-Muʾid Khan, *Al-asatir al-ʿArabiyya qabl al-Islam (Arabic Myths Before Islam)* (N.p.: Lajnat al-Taʾlif, 1937); Firas Suwwah, *Mughamarat al-ʿAql al-Ula: Dirasa fi ʾl-ustura (Suriya-Ard al-Rafidain) (The Mind's First Adventure: A Study in Myths [Syria–Iraq])* (Damascus: Ittihad al-Kuttab al-ʿArab, 1976); Mustafa al-Jozo, *Min al-asatir al-ʿArabiyya w ʾl-khurafat (Of Arab Myths and Fables)* (Beirut: Dar al-Taliʿa, 1977); and the comprehensive, two-volume work by Muhammad ʿAjina, *Mawsuʿat asatir al-ʿArab ʿan al-jahiliyya wa dalalatuha (Encyclopedia of Arabic Myths of Pre-Islamic Times, and Their Significance)* (Beirut: Dar al-Farabi, 1994).
10. See the discussion by Jamal Barout and Saʿd al-Din Kulaib, "On Fantastic Arabic Narrative," in my forthcoming book of studies, *The Classical Arabic Story: Genres, History, and Influences.*
11. For an analysis of the Ayyam al-ʿArab tales, see Peter Heath, "Ayyam al-ʿArab," ibid.
12. The notion, generally asserted in modern times, that the devotion and purity of Umayyad lovers was due to the influence of Islam is discredited by the fact that such stories, of which the Midad and Mai story and that of al-Muraqqash al-Akbar and Asmaʾ are but two, existed in pre-Islamic times, pointing to other reasons behind the development of this genre.
13. Apart from such pre-Islamic cities as Damascus, Mecca, Medina, and Taʾif, the new Muslims early founded Basra (14 / 636) and Kufa (17 / 139), which became great centers of literary and linguistic exchange during the Umayyad period and later.
14. Suicide is against Islamic strictures.
15. There has been wide speculation regarding the existence of Qais ibn al-Mulawwah and several other such poets who had romantic stories knit around their lives. Nonetheless, the poetry ascribed to Qais ibn al-Mulawwah and Qais ibn Dharih,

two of the most famous ʿUdhri poets of the period, rings most genuine. The anguish in it is too real, the tenderness, the fervor, the yearning too strong to believe it was invented by poetry reciters. This question is in any case outside the scope of this introduction. Whether the protagonists were real people or invented is irrelevant to the fact that the stories existed, and we are interested here in the stuff of fiction, not in the actual identity of its protagonists.

16. Jamil ibn Maʿmar (or Jamil Buthaina, after his beloved) was one of those famous poet lovers. He was denied marriage to her and spent the rest of his life caught in the grip of that early love. In the following verses, they have met in middle age, and, seeing his hair colored with henna to cover the white, she taunts him with having grown old: "You've grown old, Jamil, your youth is spent!" He reminds her of their youth, how he swathed his raven hair with perfume and walked dragging his train behind him, ending in these lines:

    All this was changed by fickle time. But you
    like the Marzuban's* pearl, still in the sap of youth,
    We were neighbors once, shared the same playground
    How is it I grew old
    and you did not?

    *Marzuban is the name of a Persian chief, signifying, in this instance, a very wealthy person.

17. The greater concentration on love and suffering was also in vogue in other ancient fiction. Margaret Doody shows how " 'fate', 'suffering', and 'love' were played out in the ancient Greek, Roman and other novelistic literatures and where the heroes and heroines undergo ordeals" (*The True Story of the Novel* [New Brunswick, N.J.: Rutgers University Press, 1997], 33).
18. See Jaʿfar al-Sarraj, *Masariʿ al-ʿushshaq* (*The Tragic End of Lovers*) (Beirut: Dar Sadir, ca. 1958), 2:186.
19. Islam did not repress love, only illicit relationships. A famous tradition alludes to the Prophet's having said: "He who loves and hides his passion, then dies, dies a martyr." This is repeated in several of the less-famous collections of the Prophet's traditions and is therefore not regarded as a bona fide saying. However, the fact that it found currency and was preserved shows at least the sympathy that Islam had for love and lovers so long as chastity was observed.
20. For more on the Umayyad period, see my "Umayyad Poetry," 1:387–432, and, on love literature, see pp. 419–27; see also the cogent discussion by al-Muncif al-Wahaibi, "Arab Lovers, or the Sons of the Rainbow," in *The Classical Arabic Story* (forthcoming).
21. See Geert Jan van Gelder, "Brevity and Short Stories in Classical Arabic," and Antonella Ghersetti, "Arabic Anecdotes and Medieval *Narratio Brevis*," both in ibid.
22. Such as the following short definition by a Bedouin woman when asked to describe love: "Love is that which excites the dormant and calms down the anxious."
23. Such as in Ibn al-Jawzi's book, *Akhbar al-hamqa wa ʾl-mughaffalin* (*Stories of the Stupid and Dim-Witted*) and many other similar books by him; and al-Muhassin al-

Tanukhi's (d. 384 / 994) collection *Al-faraj baʿda ʾl-shidda* (*Relief After Affliction*), full of wise advice and religious exhortations and descriptions of the repression and violence done to people by rulers and their officials. Another by al-Tanukhi is *Al-mustajad min fiʿlat al-ajwad* (*The Admirable in the Deeds of Generous Men*). A third is by al-Raqqam al-Basri (d. 321 / 933), *Al-ʿafwu wa ʾl-iʿtidhar* (*Forgiveness and Apology*), which deals mainly with various meanings of forgiveness, reprieve, and apology; it speaks of felons and how they were forgiven, giving a clear picture of the Arab personality in those times and of many of the social habits and the relations of rulers with subjects, as well as the habits of people in their quarrels and differences, depicting some of the major historic figures, such as al-Hajjaj, ruler of Basra, and the poet al-Farazdaq; and there is Ibn al-Daya's (d. 330? / 941) charming book *Al-mukafaʾa* (*The Recompense*). With the development of city life, many books were written about sexual and sometimes illicit topics, such as books written by the encyclopedic writer Shihab al-Din al-Tifashi (580 / 1184–651 / 1253), *Nuzhat al-albab fima la yujad fi kitab* (*A Recreation for the Mind by What Is Not to Be Found in Books*), which contains details of sexual practices of his time. Another, also by al-Tifashi, *Rujuʿ al-shaikh ila sibah* (*The Return of the Old Man to His Youth*), and others.

24. For a single example: the story of David's trick on Uriah, when he sent him "out to fight in order that he might be killed and then marry his wife" was categorically rejected by Muslims, who regarded it as impossible to be true, because it gave such a bad example. Prophets, the new Muslims believed, should be above this. See Ibn al-Jawzi, *Kitab al-qussas wa ʾl-mudhakkirin* (*The Book of Storytellers and Preachers*), ed. and trans. Merlin Swartz (Beirut: Dar al-Machriq, 1971), p. 10 for the Arabic, p. 97 for Swartz's translation.
25. Ibid., 10–11.
26. See, in my *Modern Arabic Fiction*, the excerpt from Jurji Zaydan's novel, *Al-Amin wa ʾl-Maʾmun*, 1047–56, especially 1049–50, describing the luxurious procession of al-Amin's mother, Queen Zubaida, the wife of Harun al-Rashid.
27. Folk poetry also began early in both Muslim Spain and Baghdad; however, it was never recognized as genuine poetry by poets and critics but was referred to according to its genre: *muwashshah*, *zajal*, and so on.
28. Northrop Frye, *Anatomy of Criticism: Four Essays* (Princeton, N.J.: Princeton University Press, 1957); see in particular chap. 1.
29. The Arabic language underwent many changes in the Abbasid period, with the appearance of hundreds of newly coined words and expressions and an influx of a large vocabulary introduced from other languages, particularly words pertaining to foods and dress and the new urban and civic usages arriving from the conquered urban centers of the surrounding lands.
30. ʿImad Ismaʿil, Jalal Khayyat, and ʿAli ʿAbbas, eds., *Mukhtarat min athar al-Jahiz* (*Selections from the Books of al-Jahiz*) (Baghdad, 1980).
31. On beggars and thieves he wrote two additional works, *Hiyal al-mukaddin* (*The Trickery of Beggars*) and *Hiyal al-lusus* (*The Trickery of Thieves*), containing many colorful situations.
32. On the rise and evolution of humor at the end of the Umayyad period, see ʿAbd al-Karim al-Yafi, *Dirasat fi ʾl-adab al-ʿArabi* (*Studies in Arabic Literature*) (Damascus,

1963), especially the chap. "Tatawwur al-mujtamaʿ min khilal tatawwur al-fukaha" (The Development of Society [as Seen] from the Development of Humor) 489–624.

33. A study by Hilary Kilpatrick on this topic illuminates the method and intention of these *akhbar*, "Context and the Enhancement of the Meaning of *Akhbar* in the *Kitab al-Aghani*," *Arabica*, tome 38, 1991.
34. A very interesting book is *Al-mukafaʾa* (*The Recompense*), by Ahmad B. Yusuf, known as Ibn al-Daya (d. 340? / 951), who lived in Egypt and was knowledgeable about many disciplines, including letters, medicine, clairvoyance, mathematics, and others. In this book, the author tries to show how people get rewarded in this life according to what they do. The writer speaks of people high and low, avoiding a highly elevated language and including many words from Persian and from the local vernacular of Egypt and other parts of the Arab domains.
35. Excerpt from ʿAbd al-Wahid Luʾluʾa's essay, "Echoes of Israʾ and Miʿraj in the *Divine Comedy*," in my *Classical Arabic Story*.
36. Ibid.
37. Mahmoud Dhuhni presents a long discussion on this point, trying to prove, not without logic, that at least part of the book's sections were completely the creation of Ibn al-Muqaffaʿ; see his long chapter on him in *Al-Qissa fi ʾl-adab al-ʿArabi ʾl-qadim* (*The Story in Old Arabic Literature*) (Cairo: Maktabat al-Anglo ʾl-Misriyya, 1973), 150–201.
38. As quoted by Ferial Ghazoul in her illuminating article on the fables in the *Arabian Nights* and in *The Epistles of the Brethren of Purity* ("Qisas al-hayawan baina mawruthina al-shaʿbi wa turathina ʾl-falsafi" [Fables Between Our Popular and Philosophical Heritage], in *Fusul*, special number on heritage, autumn 1994, 134–52, quotation on p. 136).
39. Ibid., 145.
40. When the great Umayyad poet Dhu ʾl-Rumma read his wonderful *baʾiyya* poem at al-Mirbad, one of his best, he asked al-Farazdaq, who admired the poem, why he was not regarded among the greats (*fuhul*). Al-Farazdaq's answer shows the alienation of town poets like al-Farazdaq from pre-Islamic conventions: "This is because you keep describing the campsites and the camels." These conventions nonetheless persisted among some major poets, such as al-Sharif al-Radi, several centuries later.
41. The minor poet Abu Dulaf al-Khazraji, of the fourth / tenth century, opposed the elevated trend of major poets. His poem "Al-qasida ʿl-Sasaniyya" (The Sassanid Poem) portrays the life of marginal members of society, including beggars, linked, in this poem and elsewhere, with the Banu Sasan, of Persia; see the two-volume work by C. E. Bosworth, *The Medieval Islamic Underworld: The Banu Sasan in Arabic Society and Literature* (Leiden: Brill, 1976). This kind of verse by Abu Dulaf and a few others was not, however, destined to become a tradition in poetry.
42. For more on the *maqamat*, see Abdallah Cheikh-Moussa, "Reality and Fiction in the Maqamat of al-Hamadhani, Abu ʾl-ʿAnbas al-Saymari and Abu l-Fath al-Iskandari," and Devin Stuart, "Classical Arabic Maqamat and the Picaresque Novel," both in *The Classical Arabic Story* (forthcoming).
43. On some of these influences, see, among others, Luce López-Baralt, "The Legacy of Islam in Spanish Literature," in *The Legacy of Muslim Spain*, ed. Salma Khadra

Jayyusi, 505–52 (Leiden: Brill, 1977); and María Rosa Menocal, "Al-Andalus and 1492: The Ways of Remembering," ibid., 483–504; and Roger Boase, "Arab Influences on European Love Poetry," ibid., 457–82, for a cogent discussion of influences and similarities.

44. Federico Corriente, "Linguistic Interference between Arabic and the Romance Languages," ibid., 443–51; and Dieter Messner, "Further Listings and Categorizations of Arabic Words in Ibero-Romance Languages," ibid., 452–556.

45. J. C. Burgel, "Ibn Tufail and His *Hayy ibn Yaqzan*: A Turning Point in Arabic Philosophical Writing," in Jayyusi, *Legacy of Muslim Spain*, 831.

46. Ibid.

47. Ibid. For a compelling discussion of this novel, see ʿAbd al-Fattah Kilito, "The Intruder: Hayy ibn Yaqzan," in my *Classical Arabic Story*.

48. Muhammad Rajab al-Najjar, "Epic Stories in the Arab Heritage: Structure, Significance and Function," ibid.

49. Ibid.

50. Harry Norris, "Introduction," in *The Adventures of Sayf Ben Dhi Yazan: An Arab Folk Epic*, part translation, part retelling by Lena Jayyusi (Bloomington: Indiana University Press, 1996).

I

Pre-Islamic Tales

I

The Sons of Nizar

When Nizar[1] felt himself about to die, he called his sons Mudar, Iyad, Rabiᶜa, and Anmar.

"Sons," he told them, "this red tent" (which was of leather) "is to be Mudar's; and this black horse and black woolen tent are to be Rabiᶜa's; and this gray-haired servant" (she was of middle age) "is to be Iyad's; and this reception room is to be Anmar's, in which he will sit. If you find any difficulty in dividing [the inheritance], then go and consult with the Serpent of Jurhum [the High Priest], who lives in Najran."[2]

When Nizar died, they found themselves quarreling over the inheritance and so went to visit the Serpent of Jurhum. On their way, Mudar, seeing the remains of grass that had been used for pasture, said:

"The camel that ate this grass was one-eyed."

"And it was lame," Rabiᶜa said.

"And it was short-tailed," Iyad said.

"It was certainly a stray camel," Anmar said.

As they walked on, they met a man looking for his camel, and he asked them if they had seen one.

"Was it one-eyed?" Mudar asked him.

"Yes," he said.

"Was it lame?" Rabiᶜa asked.

"Yes," the man said.

---

1. Nizar ibn Rabiᶜa is regarded as the founder of the southern Arabs in what is now called Yemen.
2. Najran was one of the most important ancient cities of Yemen. The title "Serpent of Najran" was given to this priest on account of his celebrated wisdom, the serpent being a symbol of wisdom for the ancient Arabs.

"Was it short-tailed?" Iyad asked.

"Yes," answered the man.

"Was it a stray camel?" Anmar asked finally.

"Yes," the man answered, "that's the very camel! Take me to where it is."

"By God," they said, "we never saw it."

"You're lying!" the man retorted. Then he laid hold of them. "How am I to believe you," he went on, "when you describe my camel down to the last detail?" He stayed close by them till they reached Najran.

When they alighted, the camel owner cried:

"These men have taken my camel. They've just described it to me."

"We never saw it," the brothers said.

They went to the Serpent of Najran, who was a wise man and a judge among the Arabs, and laid their case before him.

"How were you able to describe it," he asked, "when you'd never seen it?"

"I saw," Mudar answered, "how it had grazed on one side of the pasture and left the other. And so I decided it must be one-eyed."

"I saw how one of its feet had left clear tracks," said Rabiʿa, "while the others had left weak ones. And so I decided it must be lame."

"I knew it had a short tail," Iyad said, "because its dung was in a single heap. Had it had a long tail, the dung would have been scattered."

"I knew it was a stray camel," Anmar said finally, "because it had grazed in one lush place, thick with grass, then left it for another with poorer, ranker grass."

The Serpent of Najran told the man:

"These men didn't take your camel. Go and search for it."

"Who are you?" he asked them then. And, when they told him, he welcomed them, and they told him the reason for their visit.

"How can you be in need of me," he asked, "when you are as you are?"

Then he gave them his hospitality, killing a goat for them, and he brought in wine, then sat where he could hear them without their seeing him.

"I should never have eaten more delicious meat," Rabiʿa said, "had the goat not been fed on the milk of a bitch."

"I should never have drunk better wine," Mudar said, "if the vine had not been growing on a grave."

"I should never, to this day," said Iyad, "have seen a man more noble than this one, if only he had come from the father he claimed."

"I have never," Anmar said finally, "heard words more profitable to us than our words today."

All this was uttered in the Serpent's hearing, and he said to himself: "These are devilish men."

With that he called the server and asked him about the wine and where it had come from.

"It came," the man told him, "from a shoot I planted on our father's grave. And what wine was ever more delicious?"

Next he asked the herdsman:

"What was the matter with this goat?"

"It was a small goat," the herdsman answered, "whose mother had died, and there was no female in milk among the goats we had. And so I had to suckle it on a bitch's milk."

Then he approached his mother and asked her who his father was. She had, she told him, been married to a king of great wealth who could not beget children. "I was afraid," she went on, "he would die childless and all his wealth would be lost."

The Serpent returned to the young men and explained these matters to them. They in turn told him of their father's advice.

"Whatever wealth falls under the color red," he told them, "that belongs to Mudar." And Mudar took all the dinars and all the red camels, and was called thereafter Mudar the Red.

"As for him," the Serpent said, "to whom the black horse and the black tent were given, he shall have all that is black." And Rabiʿa inherited all the black horses and was called thereafter Rabiʿa the Horse.

"And all," the Serpent continued, "that resembles the gray-haired maid-servant belongs to Iyad." And Iyad inherited all the white and gray sheep, and was called thereafter Iyad the Gray.

As for Anmar, the Serpent assigned him all the dirhams and whatever else remained of the inheritance, and he was called thereafter Anmar the Remnant.

From *Kitab al-Tijan fi Muluk Himyar* (*The Book of Crowns Concerning the Kings of Himyar*), as narrated by Abu Muhammad ibn Hisham, from Asad ibn Musa, from Abi Idris ibn Sinan, from his grandfather Wahb ibn Munabbih. Edited and published by the Center for Yemeni Studies, Sanaa, Yemen, A.H. 1347.

2

The Priestess of the Banu Saᶜd

ᶜAbd al-Muttalib[1] vowed that, should he have ten sons and find them all men around him, he would sacrifice one of them at the Kaᶜba in honor of the [pagan] god.

When all his sons had grown to the age of ten, he told them:

"Sons, I made a vow of which you know. What do you have to say?"

"The choice is yours," they said. "We are all in your hands."

"Let each of you take his arrow," ᶜAbd al-Muttalib said, "and write his name on it."

They did so and gave him the arrows. Then ᶜAbd al-Muttalib summoned the man responsible for casting the arrows [as divination] and gave him their arrows, telling him: "Shake them slowly."

ᶜAbd Allah was the son dearest to him. The man cast the arrows, and it was ᶜAbd Allah's arrow that came out. ᶜAbd al-Muttalib took a great knife and brought ᶜAbd Allah and had him lie between the two Quraish idols, Isaf and Naʾila.[2] But as he was about to slay him, the boy's brother Abu Talib leaped in and stayed his father's hand.

When the Abu Makhzoum, who were ᶜAbd Allah's maternal uncles, heard of this, they all came furiously to ᶜAbd al-Muttalib.

"We shall not allow you," they said, "to slay our nephew. Go and slay whomever you wish from your other children."

---

1. ᶜAbd al-Muttalib was the grandfather of Prophet Muhammad and brought him up after the Prophet's father, ᶜAbd Allah, died before he was born.
2. At al-Safa and Marwa, near the Kaᶜba, where sacrifices were offered.
3. Abu Talib was ᶜAbd Allah's full brother and the uncle who took over the task of the Prophet's upbringing when the grandfather died. He was also the father of ᶜAli, the Prophet's cousin and son-in-law, who became the fourth Orthodox Caliph, ruling from 35 / 656 to 40 / 661.

"I have made a vow," ʿAbd al-Muttalib said, "and the arrow came on ʿAbd Allah. He must be slain."

"No," they said. "This shall never be, so long as we have breath in us! We are ready to sacrifice for his safety all our wealth, inherited or acquired."

Then the chiefs of the Quraish came to ʿAbd al-Muttalib and counseled him, saying:

"The thing you intend to do is fearful. Should you slay your son, you will never enjoy life after him. Only have patience, and we will go with you to the priestess of Saʿd. Whatever she commands you to do, then do it."

"I consent to this," ʿAbd al-Muttalib said.

He went with a group of the Banu Makhzoum to the priestess in Damascus. When ʿAbd al-Muttalib had told her of his intention to slay his son, the priestess said: "Leave now." And so they left.

Next morning they returned. "How much," she asked, "is the head price of a [slain] man in your [community]?"

"Ten camels," they answered.

"Return to your country," she told them, "and bring forward this boy intended for sacrifice, and bring with him ten camels. Then cast the arrows on him and on the camels. If a camel's arrow comes, then slaughter it; and if it comes on your son, then add ten camels more till your god accepts the price offered."

The group returned to Mecca, telling ʿAbd al-Muttalib:

"You have a good example in Ibrahim, for you know how he had meant to sacrifice his son Ismaʿil. You are the master of Ismaʿil's progeny. Therefore offer your money in place of your son."

In the morning, ʿAbd al-Muttalib brought ʿAbd Allah and ten camels, then called the dealer of the [lots for the] sacrifice and told him: "Cast, but do not be hasty."

The arrow came on ʿAbd Allah. ʿAbd al-Muttalib made them twenty, and again the arrow came on ʿAbd Allah; then he made them thirty—then forty—and, each time the arrow came on ʿAbd Allah. [Still] he increased the camels by ten, till they were a hundred camels. Then he cast the arrows and it came on the camels.

"The god is great!" ʿAbd Allah exclaimed. And the men of Quraish did the same. "Your god is satisfied," they told ʿAbd al-Muttalib, "and your son is safe."

"No," ʿAbd al-Muttalib said. "No, by the god, this shall not be till I have tried this three times."

He cast a second time, and the arrow came on the camels, and then he tried a third time, and again the arrow came on the camels. So ʿAbd al-Muttalib knew he had won his god's acceptance in redeeming his son.

A hundred camels, of the best breed ʿAbd al-Muttalib owned, were brought forward and sacrificed, then left in the place of slaughter for anyone to take. And ʿAbd al-Muttalib returned home, joyful his son was redeemed.

From *Bulough al-Arab fi Maʿrifat Ahwal al-ʿArab* (*Attaining the Goal in Knowing the Life of the Arabs*) by Mahmoud Shukri ʾl-Alusi; in *Qisas al-ʿArab* (*Stories of the Arabs*), vol. 1.

3

Faithfulness and Sense of Honor

Once, it is said, al-Nuʿman ibn al-Mundhir[1] went out hunting on his mare called al-Yahmoum [the black]. The mare took him astray in the open country, and, unable to control it, he was separated from his companions. Then the rains assailed him and he sought out a shelter, finding a house in which there was a man called Hanzala, from the tribe of Tayʾ, along with his wife.

"May I take shelter here?" al-Nuʿman asked.

Hanzala agreed, and came out to him and helped him dismount. Hanzala, who did not know al-Nuʿman, had only one goat.

"This man," he told his wife, "is, I see, of dignified bearing. He may be some noble, important personage. What are we to do?"

"I have some flour," his wife said, "which I have stored. Slaughter the goat, and I shall make bread with the flour."

The woman baked, and the Taʾi man milked the goat, then slaughtered it, made a *madira* broth[2] and gave al-Nuʿman meat to eat and milk to drink. Then he sat conversing with al-Nuʿman for the rest of the evening.

In the morning, al-Nuʿman put on his clothes, mounted his mare, then said:

"O man from Tayʾ! Seek your reward from me, I am King al-Nuʿman."

"I shall do so, God willing," answered the man.

Al-Nuʿman was able to rejoin his group of riders, and they all returned to al-Hira. As for the Taʾi, he remained there for some time, till he became afflicted by disaster and by toil, and fell on evil days.

---

1. Al-Nuʿman was a pre-Islamic king of al-Hira, in the north of the Arabian Peninsula. He died in 616, just a few years before the advent of Islam.
2. *Madira* is a broth made by cooking meat in pure milk until the meat is cooked and the liquid thick.

"Why not go to the king?" his wife said. "He will be generous to you."

When the man came to al-Hira, it chanced to be the day of al-Nuʿman's doom.[3] Al-Nuʿman was standing all armed with his horsemen. When he saw Hanzala, he recognized him and was greatly disquieted.

"Are you not," he asked, "the Taʾi who was my host?"

"Yes," Hanzala answered.

"And could you not," al-Nuʿman said, "have come on some other day?"

"Your Majesty," Hanzala said, "how could I have known of this day?"

"Even if the man were [my son] Qabous himself," came the reply, "there would be no other course but to kill him. So, ask whatever worldly things you wish, for you are doomed."

"Your Majesty," Hanzala answered, "what will I do with worldly things when I am no more?"

"There is no other way," al-Nuʿman said.

"Then," Hanzala said, "I ask you to delay my sentence till I have gone to my family and settled their affairs, arranging for their livelihood. Then I will return to you."

"Find me a guarantor, then," al-Nuʿman said, "so I know you will return."

The Taʾi turned to Sharik ibn ʿAmr, al-Nuʿman's companion, who was standing next to al-Nuʿman, and called on him to be his warranty. Sharik, though, would not do it. But a man from the tribe of Kalb, called Qurad ibn Ajdaʿ, said to al-Nuʿman: "I will be his guarantor, Your Majesty." With that al-Nuʿman ordered that the Taʾi be given five hundred she-camels, and the Taʾi went to his tribe, agreeing to return in one year to the day.

When the year had passed, and just one day remained, al-Nuʿman said to Qurad: "You will surely die tomorrow."

In the morning, al-Nuʿman rode out with his horsemen and foot soldiers, fully armed as usual, till he came to the two tall buildings called al-Ghariyyan, where doomed men were killed. Al-Nuʿman stood between the two buildings, bringing Qurad with him. But his ministers said: "You have no right to kill him before the day is over." So he left him, though his wish was to kill him so that the Taʾi could escape the punishment.

No sooner had the sun begun to set, with Qurad standing on the leather [execution] mat and the executioner standing beside him, than the man's wife came keening to him; and, as they stood in this fashion, a man was seen far off.

---

3. While still a pagan, al-Nuʿman had two kinds of days, one of "bliss" and the other of "doom," on which he would kill the first man he saw.

"You cannot kill him," people said then, "before this man reaches us, and you know who he is."

So he held back the order till the man reached them; and it was indeed the Taʾi.

Al-Nuʿman, distressed that the Taʾi had come, asked him:

"What made you return after you escaped death the first time?"

"Faithfulness to my promise," the Taʾi said.

"And what," al-Nuʿman asked, "inspires you to such faithfulness?"

"My religion," Hanzala replied.

"And what is your religion?" al-Nuʿman asked.

"The Christian religion," Hanzala replied.

"Tell us of this," al-Nuʿman commanded.

The man told him, and al-Nuʿman [thereupon] embraced the Christian religion with all the people of al-Hira, killing no more people from that day on, and commanding, too, that al-Ghariyyan should be torn down. He pardoned the Taʾi, marveling, and saying:

"By God, I do not know who is the more faithful, he who escaped being killed yet returned, or he who stood as his guarantor. By God, I will not be the meanest in spirit of the three of us."

From *Amthal al-Maidani* (*The Maidani Proverbs*) by Abu ʾl-Fadl Ahmad al-Maidani; *al-Mustatraf fi Kulli Fannin Mustazraf* (*The Exquisite in Every Appealing Art*) by Shihab al-Din al-Abshihi; *Kitab al-Aghani* (*Book of Songs*) by Abu ʾl-Faraj al-Asfahani: *Muʿjam al-Buldan* (*Dictionary of Countries*) by Yaqut al-Hamawi; *Al-Mahasin wa ʾl-Addad* (*Merits and Their Opposites*) by al-Jahiz; *Bulough al-Arab fi Maʿrifat Ahwal al-ʿArab* (*Attaining the Goal in Knowing the Life of the Arabs*) by Mahmoud Shukri ʾl-Alusi; *Al-Mahasin wa ʾl-Masawiʾ* (*Merits and Faults*) by Ibrahim ibn Muhammad al-Bayhaqi; in *Qisas al-ʿArab* (*Stories of the Arabs*), vol. 1.

Editor's Note: *Qisas al-ʿArab* is a four-volume anthology of the old Arabic stories prepared by Ahmad Jad al-Mawla, Muhammad ʿAbd al-Fadl Ibrahim, and Muhammad al-Bijjawi, who have collected rich material from major Arab story compendia in classical times. Among the many classical books they have consulted are the list attached to the above translated story. I felt it would be helpful to mention their titles and authors for the benefit of students of Arabic doing further studies on the subject, because they are basic reference books. No page numbers and other details are displayed here because most of them are available in two or more editions that differ in date, place of publication, size, and pagination, having been printed in various Eastern and North African Muslim countries. This anthology will also give further references for the classical Arabic stories.

4

Al-Nuʿman's Outfit

ʿAmr ibn al-ʿAlaaʾ said:

Al-Nuʿman sat one day clothed in an outfit studded with jewels, the like of which had never been seen. He gave audience to the Arabs, among whom was Aws ibn Haritha,[1] and those present gazed long and hard on the clothing.

"Never," each said to his friend, "have I seen an outfit to match this one, nor have I heard that any king was ever able to possess one like it."

Aws ibn Haritha, though, sat with his head bowed, not looking at it.

"I have seen," al-Nuʿman said to him, "how all those who entered admired this outfit and spoke of it to their friends—all except you. I have not seen you admire it or even look at it."

"May God send you happiness," Aws replied, "an outfit is pleasing in the hands of a merchant. But when it is on a king, and his face is radiant through it, then it is on him that my gaze will be." The king found the answer good.

As they left, al-Nuʿman told them:

"Gather here tomorrow, for I am presenting this outfit to the master of the Arabs."

The Arabs left, each supposing he was the one on whom it would be bestowed. Next morning, they donned the best clothes they had, and put on their best swords, and rode their finest horses, and came to al-Nuʿman. Aws, though, was not among them.

"Why," the group asked him, "don't you come with us to the king's assembly? It may be you are the one on whom the outfit will be bestowed."

1. Aws ibn Haritha was one of the most important fathers of the pre-Islamic Arabs. Originally from Yemen, he emigrated to Medina before the advent of Islam.

"If," Aws replied, "I am the master of my own tribe, then I am not, it seems to me, the master of the Arabs. If I go, and do not receive it, I shall leave feeling diminished. And if I were indeed the one meant to be singled out for it, then my rank would be known [in any case]."

Al-Nuᶜman gazed at all the faces, but did not find the face of Aws ibn Haritha. He summoned some of his special aides, telling them: "Go and bring news of Aws."

Al-Nuᶜman's messenger went, made inquiry of some of Aws's friends, and was given news of him that he brought back to al-Nuᶜman. Al-Nuᶜman then sent him a messenger, saying: "Come in peace, free of all fear." So Aws came, dressed in the same clothes he had worn the day before. The other Arabs had been overjoyed at his absence, fearing he would be the one chosen for the outfit.

When he had taken his place in the assembly, al-Nuᶜman said:

"I see you have not changed your clothes today. So here, put on this outfit to make your person more handsome."

With that he took off his clothing and gave it to Aws to wear. The other Arabs, though, were filled with rancor and envy.

"We have no remedy for this," they said, "except to ask one of the poets to satirize him harshly, for only through poetry can his status be diminished."

They gathered together five hundred she-camels and went to the poet al-Hutaiᶜa.

"Take all of these," they told him, "and satirize Aws ibn Haritha for us."

Al-Hutaiᶜa was the most famous Arab poet of his time, and the most skilled in satire. But he said:

"How can I satirize a man of great and undisputed lineage, of boundless generosity, a judge whose opinion is never at fault, so brave that his guest is never ill treated, full of charity? All I see in my house is from his bounty."

Another poet, Bishr ibn Abi Khazim, heard of the matter and coveted the reward. He took the five hundred she-camels and satirized Aws, making reference to his mother, Suᶜda. When Aws heard of this, he pursued him, and Bishr fled, leaving behind his she-camels, which were brought to Aws. Aws took them, then went in strong pursuit of him once more.

As for Bishr, he wandered among the many tribes of the Arabs, seeking someone who would protect him from Aws. Everyone he sought, however, told him:

"I would protect you from any except Aws ibn Haritha. From him I cannot give you refuge."

Aws had sent many scouts in search of him, and at last Bishr was captured and brought to Aws. When the man stood before him, Aws said:

"Woe to you! You satirize my mother, when our age has none to match her?"

"So it was," Bishr said.

"I shall kill you," Aws said, "in such a way as to restore Suʿda's name."

With that Aws went in to see his mother, Suʿda.

"I have," he told her, "brought you the poet who satirized you, and I have decided to kill him in a way that will restore your name."

"But surely, son," she said, "there is a better course?"

"And what is that?" he asked.

"He has," she said, "found no one who will give him refuge from you, and we are a people who see no harm in doing good. Set him free, I entreat you, and return his camels to him. And give him bounty from your wealth and equally from mine, and send him back safe and sound to his tribe; for they have despaired of his return."

Aws went out and asked Bishr:

"What do you suppose I am going to do with you?"

"You are surely going to kill me," Bishr said.

"And is that what you deserve?" Aws asked.

"Yes," came the answer.

"Suʿda," Aws said, "whom you satirized, has advised such and such."

With that he ordered Bishr should be freed from the rope with which he was bound. Then he told him:

"Go now to your people, safe and sound, and take with you what you have been given."

Bishr raised his hand to the sky.

"God," he said, "You are my Witness that I shall never again recite any poetry except in praise of Aws!"

From *Al-Mukhtar min Nawadir al-Akhbar* (*Selections from Rare Anecdotes*) by Muhammad ibn Ahmad al-Maqqari; in *Qisas al-ʿArab* (*Stories of the Arabs*), vol. 1.

5

A Lowly Man Gains a Wife

A man from the Asad tribe recounted a story, as follows:

Some of my camels had lost their way, and I sought them among the Quda^{c}a tribe. When night fell, I found myself close to a house that had a hospitable air. I called, and a woman of shining beauty, like the sun, came out.

"Come down," she said. "You're welcome."

She had me sit by a fire to warm myself and brought me a platter of food, sitting to talk with me as I ate. After this a herd of many camels came toward the house, and a man with them. She went to him, along with a little boy she had been playing with, and he took hold of the boy and began kissing him. So ugly was this man I supposed he must be a slave, till he sat down beside her and asked:

"Where has our guest come from?"

"From Asad," she replied.

I realized then he must be her husband, and I started reflecting on how different they looked.

"You seem," he said, noticing this, "to be wondering about us."

"I am indeed," I replied.

"I'll tell you," he said, "how she came to be my wife."

"Yes," I said. "I'd be most interested to hear."

You should know (he began) that I was the youngest of seven brothers—and to look at me you would have thought I was their slave. They'd send me off to see to their grazing, and one day a camel strayed.

"Go and find it," they told me.

"That's not fair on me," I replied.

"Go and do it, you cursed boy," my father said, "or I'll make this day your last." And with that he threatened to beat me.

So off I went in the most wretched state, cold and hungry. That evening I encountered an old woman who seemed affluent and highborn, and alongside her was this young woman. The young woman began to mock me.

"Why don't you come in," she said, "when we've all finished sleeping? I'd like to talk to you. I've never seen a finer-looking lad!"

"Leave me be," I said.

Her father came with seven brothers, and they all slept close by the tent. Warm and full from the food I'd had, I felt tempted and went into the tent.

She sensed my presence there.

"Who's that?" she called.

"It's me," I replied. "The guest."

"Out with you!" she cried. "May God never greet you!"

I left in a panic. Their dog came up, making to bite me, and I was holding him off with my stick. Then he got his teeth into the woollen cloak I was wearing, and we struggled together till, at last, we fell into a dry hole. The young woman came out to see what had happened.

"I would have liked to make this your grave," she said. "Only I'm afraid of the consequences." And with that she threw me a rope.

"Come on out," she said.

As I reached the top of the hole, it collapsed under her feet and we both fell down in. Next morning the others missed her, and, unable to find her, they came with swords and stones, meaning to kill us. Her father, though, said: "I know my daughter. She's above suspicion."

They got hold of us and pulled us out. Her father came toward me.

"What sort of man are you?" he asked. "Can I marry her to you, and avoid any scandal?"

"How would I do anything else?" I said, sensing my life might be safe now.

He thereupon married her to me, the dowry fifty camels, a bondwoman, and a slave. I went back to my father and told him of all this, and he fetched her. And here she is, witness to what I've just said.

From Dawud al-Antaki, *Tazyin al-Aswaq bi Tafsil Ashwaq al-ʿUshshaq* (*Adorning the Markets with Tales of Lovers' Longing*), vol. 1, ed. Muhammad al-Tunji (Beirut: ʿAlam al-Kutub, 1993).

6

A Charitable Gift

Hammad told the following, which he learned from the chieftains of the Tayy tribe:

So generous and munificent was ʿUnbah bint ʿAfif, mother of Hatim [al-Taʿi], that she could withhold nothing. Her brothers strove to restrain her, but she would not listen to them; and, since she was wealthy, her brothers confined her in a house for a year, providing her with food, in the hope she would learn to hold back. Then, after a year, supposing her to have changed her ways, they released her and gave her a flock of camels [between twenty and fifty in number].

A woman from Hawazin then came to her, begging charity. She gave the woman the flock.

"By God," she said, "I was touched by such hunger, I made a vow to withhold nothing from any who asked."

From Ibn Qutaiba, *ʿUyun al-Akhbar* (*The Book of Useful Knowledge*), vol. 1.

7

A Cunning Message

Abu Hatim, quoting al-Asmaʿi, told me how a certain Bedouin had related as follows:

A man fell in love with a woman and married her, sending her a gift of thirty sheep and a skin of wine. On his way the messenger drank some of the wine and slaughtered a sheep. As he made to leave, she told him:

"Greet your master, and tell him our month is one day short, and that Sahim, the shepherd minding our ewe, brought it to us sucked."

When he reached his master and told him this, his master beat him till he confessed his crime.

From Ibn Qutaiba, *ʿUyun al-Akhbar* (*The Book of Useful Knowledge*), vol. 2.

8

A Noble Wife

[THE FOLLOWING PIECE IS INCLUDED HERE AS AN INDICATION OF THE SOCIAL TENSIONS THAT COULD ARISE IMMEDIATELY FOLLOWING THE ARRIVAL OF ISLAM.]

I spoke of the eloquence of women to Ziyad bin Abih, telling him as follows:

Qais bin ʿAsim converted to Islam while he had a wife from the Hanifa tribe. Her relatives and her father refused to do the same, and they feared she herself would convert. Should she do so, they vowed, they would have nothing more to do with her as long as she lived.

Qais accordingly parted with her, and, when she was borne off to her people and some of them were in attendance, Qais stood up and praised her, saying he had separated from her against his will; that she herself had wished for this following his conversion to Islam.

"The praise you have given," the wife said then, "accords with your noble lineage and your goodness. And, by God, you have been full of affection, have been distinguished far above others, and failed seldom, embracing solitude after the Prophet's message. For me my widowhood in your lifetime is easier than it would have been after your death. Know that I shall remain in the nest of no husband, after you."

From Abu ʾl-Faraj al-Asfahani, *al-Aghani* (*Book of Songs*), from Ahmad ibn Abi Tahir Tayfur, *Balaghat al-Nisaʾ* (*The Eloquence of Women*).

9

The Exile of al-Harith ibn Midad

[ACCORDING TO AN ANCIENT STORY, THE SONS OF ISRAEL HAD ABANDONED THE FAITH OF DAWUD (DAVID) AND SULAIMAN (SOLOMON) AND CHANGED THE WORDS OF AL-ZABUR, THE HOLY BOOK THAT GOD HAD GIVEN TO DAWUD. THE SONS OF ISRAEL, BEARING WITH THEM A COFFER CONTAINING SOME PRECIOUS HOLY SCRIPTS, LAUNCHED A MILITARY CAMPAIGN AGAINST MECCA. WHEN AL-HARITH IBN MIDAD AL-JURHUMI, KING OF MECCA AT THE TIME, DEFEATED THEM, THEY ABANDONED THE COFFER. THE PEOPLE OF THE JURHUM AND ʿIMLAQ TRIBES BURIED IT BENEATH ONE OF THE DUNG HEAPS IN MECCA; BUT AL-HARITH IBN MIDAD, AWARE OF THE PRECIOUS NATURE OF THE CONTENTS, OBJECTED TO THIS, ORDERING THAT THE COFFER SHOULD BE EXHUMED BY NIGHT. THE SONS OF JURHUM AND ʿIMLAQ, HAVING DISHONORED THE HOLY SCRIPTS IN THE COFFER, SUBSEQUENTLY VANISHED, AND AL-HARITH IBN MIDAD, IN HIS DISTRESS, EXILED HIMSELF FOR THREE HUNDRED YEARS. "THE EXILE OF AL-HARITH IBN MIDAD" BECAME PROVERBIAL IN ARABIC.]

It was related on the part of Iyad ibn Nizar ibn Maʿadd that he gave the following account when asked about the sources of his wealth:

When my father, Nizar, died, he left behind him, along with myself, my three younger brothers, Mudar, Rabiʿa, and Anmar. As I was his eldest son, he had entrusted them to me, telling me I should seek the opinion of the wise Qulmus, the Serpent of Najran,[1] if we had disputes over the inheritance. When we went to him, he decided the camels and sheep

1. Najran was one of the most important ancient cities of Yemen. "Serpent of Najran" refers to this priest's celebrated wisdom, the serpent being a symbol of wisdom for the ancient Arabs.

should go to me, the dome to Mudar, the mare to Rabiʿa, and the land to Anmar.

After a time a great disaster struck us, and I lost all my wealth except for ten camels. These I began to hire out to feed my family. One day I hired out my camels, and my brothers did the same, for a journey to Damascus, and from there I returned to Medina. There I could find no one to hire my camels back to Mecca. The caravans were due to leave next morning, and there were ten staging posts between the two cities.

Suddenly, in my distress, I heard a voice crying out:

"Oh people, can anyone give me a mount to the holy city? If so, for the ride of a camel, I will pay him as much as his camel can bear in pearls and rubies and gold."

No one, though, was inclined to accept his offer, for people were busy with their own affairs. "Why," I said to myself, "do I not offer him a camel? If he is speaking the truth, I shall be rich, and if he is lying, I have nothing to lose." I sought out the voice, and came upon an old man as tall as a palm tree, blind, and with a beard reaching to his knees. Perturbed on account of his great size, I approached nonetheless.

"Old man," I said, "I have what you are seeking."

"Come nearer, son," he said.

As I drew closer, he placed his hand on my shoulder, and I felt it like the weight of a mountain.

"Are you Iyad ibn Nizar?" he asked.

"Yes," I said. "How do you know my name?"

"I know from my father and my grandfather," he said, "that Iyad ibn Nizar will bring al-Harith ibn Midad al-Jurhumi back to Mecca after a long exile. How many camels do you have?"

"Ten," I replied.

"That will be enough," he said.

"Do you have others with you?" I asked.

"No," he said. "But I shall ride each camel for a single day, after which it will be crippled."

Resolved to honor my word and help him, I agreed.

"Take me to your home," he said then, "to spend the night."

He spent the night with me there, and next morning, when people set out for Mecca, I joined them, taking just the old man with me. We traveled the whole day, till sunset, and the camel was crippled. Next morning I supplied another camel to carry him, and so we went on, with camel after camel crippled by the end of the day. Finally we reached Mecca and were on Mount al-Matabikh.

"Son," he said, "I feel the camel pulling up. Have you reached Mount al-Matabikh?"

"Yes," I replied.

"Is there anyone close by," he went on, "who can hear what I say?"

"No," I said. "There are some people in front and some behind."

Then he asked:

"Do you know who I am?"

"No," I said.

"I am al-Harith ibn Midad ibn ʿAbd al-Masih ibn Nufayla . . . ibn Jurhum ibn Qahtan," he said . . . "I was king of Mecca and the lands around . . . The king before me was my brother ʿAmr ibn Midad. We were crowned kings, and one day we would wear the crown on our heads, the other day we would hang it at the gate of al-Bayt al-ʿAtiq [in Mecca].[2] It so happened that a merchant from among the sons of Israel came to Mecca to sell pearls and rubies, and my brother, King ʿAmr, bought from him all he had. And the king reshaped the crown, adding more jewels to it so it looked like a shield. The Israeli, though, had hidden his best jewels and offered them to others.

"When the king learned of this, he had the Israeli brought before him.

" 'Is it a fact,' he asked, 'that you hid your best jewels from me and sold me the meanest ones? Did I not ask you for the best?'

" 'Yes, Your Majesty,' the man answered.

" 'Why then did you do this?' asked the king.

" 'The goods are mine, Your Majesty,' the Israeli said, 'and I am free to sell what I wish and hold back what I wish.'

"The king was so angry he commanded that the man's pearls and rubies, few though they were, should be seized. The Israeli, though, lay in wait for the man who hung the crown at the Bayt al-ʿAtiq, killed him, and took the crown, fleeing by night on a strong camel. Next morning, when the matter came to light, people did not know who the culprit was, till at last they had news from Jerusalem. King ʿAmr then sent to the Israelites, whose ruler was Faran ibn Yaʿqub ibn Sibt ibn Yamin, ordering him to return the crown and pay the price for the blood that had been shed; and to admit to the crime and formally proclaim his regret . . . Faran, though, refused.

"King ʿAmr then wrote to him that the crown was always hung at the door of the holy al-Bayt al-ʿAtiq in Mecca, and that nothing in the crown

2. Al-Bayt al-ʿAtiq (The Old House) refers to the Kaʿba, now the central place of the annual Muslim pilgrimage. It was so called because it was thought to be the first house built by Ibrahim (Abraham) as a place of prayer to God.

had ever been taken by force or treachery. To this Faran replied that he wished to hang it in Jerusalem. 'God is rich,' King ʿAmr wrote then. 'How can you rob one holy house for the sake of another, to honor God through trickery?' Faran, though, answered: 'We are faithful people with a holy book, and we know God better than you.' 'He knows God best who obeys Him,' King ʿAmr said. 'I see not one house of God robbed for another house of God, but rather one king robbing another.'

"We launched a campaign against them, with a hundred thousand men from Jurhum and a further hundred thousand from ʿImlaq, and we were supported with fifty thousand by al-Ahwas ibn ʿAmr al-ʿAbdudi of ʿAbdud ibn Kulayb, a branch of the Qudaʿa ibn Himyar tribe. Faran, son of Yaʿqub, sought help from his Byzantine allies, whose head, Shunayf ibn Hiraql, supported him with a hundred thousand men. Faran himself was at the head of a further hundred thousand from the sons of Israel, supported by a hundred thousand from the people of al-Sham [Syria]. Faran ibn Yaʿqub halted with his men at this mountain, Mount al-Matabikh, and we did the same. Do you know how it came to be given this name?"

"No," I said.

"When Faran and Shunayf," he said, "halted on the eastern side of the mountain, they kindled a fire and cooked their food. We, for our part, halted on the western side of the mountain, lit a fire, and cooked our food. So the mountain came to be called Mount al-Matabikh [the Mountain of Cooking] . . . When the two armies were facing each other, my brother, King ʿAmr, came to me and said: 'Harith, you shall be my successor.' Then he went to the opposing army and asked: 'Who is your king? Here am I, ʿAmr ibn Midad.' When Shunayf stood up, ʿAmr said: 'Why should people die for you and me? Let us fight in single combat. If you kill me, my people will give you their obedience; and if I kill you, your people will give me their obedience.' Shunayf consented to this, and the outcome was that ʿAmr killed him . . . When, though, ʿAmr asked Faran to give him what he and Shunayf had agreed, Faran said he would give him from the wealth of the people of Mecca when he conquered it. Thereupon ʿAmr sent him a message saying: 'This breach of honor you have shown is the same as you showed before. Tomorrow I shall fight you.'

"Before the battle, al-Ahwas ibn ʿAmr al-ʿAbdudi made a speech to his people. 'Oh my people,' he said. 'Things may not be, tomorrow, as they are today. I urge you to be thankful to Him Who is the Source of all goodness, to safeguard your sanctuary, to uphold good qualities, to hold back from reminding others of your favors, to maintain chivalry, which is the essence of honor, to reject the humiliation that leads to self-destruction. Do not hasten to war, for this leads to the loss of souls; but, if attacked against your will, face the assault firmly, and do not ever be deceived by uncertainty, for war has uncertainties and desires such as can blind men's eyes. Beware the deception of wars, for it may destroy your authority and deprive you of glory. Remember you are the holders of old kingdoms and the masters of wars, whereas the sons of Israel and the Byzantines are violators of kingdoms and wars. If you lose the war, your ancient kingdom will be destroyed, and, the moment it falls, your people will be wiped out. Endure, then, and God will grant you life.'

"Then King ʿAmr attacked them with his men and they attacked us. We fought long together, and we crushed them with our swords, and won the battle that was called the Day of Shunayf. And King ʿAmr seized Faran ibn Yaʿqub on a hill and killed him, and that hill has since been called the Hill of Faran . . . After that he pursued them to Jerusalem, and at last they gave him their obedience and restored to him the crown of the kingdom.

"One of their women, named Barrah bint Shamʿun, was very beautiful; no other woman of the progeny of Yusuf ibn Yaʿqub [Joseph, son of Jacob] could be compared to her. Dressed in her finery and jewels, she was sent to King ʿAmr, who, when he saw her, was utterly smitten; and he married her. This, though, was a ruse the sons of Israel had hatched against the king. When Barrah was alone with King ʿAmr, she asked him: 'Did I give you satisfaction?' 'Yes,' he answered. 'Then give satisfaction to me,' she said. 'I am in your hands,' he replied. 'What is your wish?' 'Let my people be,' she said, 'and do them no harm. They have asked me to intercede for them.' 'Your wish is granted,' he said. And so he let them be and returned to Mecca, but he took with him as hostages a hundred wellborn men from the sons of Israel, along with their women and children . . . Then ʿAmr's wife, Barrah bint Shamʿun, having made ready strong camels and men to take her back to Jerusalem, placed a piece of sharp, poisoned iron in his bed; and, when ʿAmr lay down in his bed, he was wounded by the iron and died. With that she swiftly fled, along with the hundred men who had been taken as hostages. Knowing they had no option but to pass by the Hill of Faran, I went there with the horsemen of Jurhum and ʿImlaq. When they arrived, I arrested them all and brought them back to Mecca. There I buried King ʿAmr . . . and gave orders for the prisoners to be executed. I was crowned king, and then I launched a campaign against the sons of Israel, the Byzantines, and the non-Arabs of Syria. Leading a hundred thousand men from Jurhum, and a further hundred thousand from ʿImlaq, I fought against them and defeated them all . . . After that I was minded to kill Barrah, but she claimed she had been tricked at the king's court, that it was the chief among the sons of Israel, the first man to be executed, who had come to the king and done what was done, without her knowledge. 'How, indeed, could I have done such a thing,' she said, 'when I am pregnant by him?' I ordered the midwives [to examine her] and they confirmed what she had said. ʿAmr had had just two daughters and no male offspring. When I was sure she was pregnant, I took pity on her and sent her inside the palace, placing her under guard; and finally she gave birth to a boy, whom I named Midad, after his grandfather. When he grew up, he was the handsomest young man there ever was. I thought once more of killing Barrah, but I feared her son might take vengeance on me. I would, I decided, leave the matter to him; let him deal with his mother over the matter of his father . . ."

When we reached Mecca, he asked me to go with him to the olive orchards.

"Son," he said, "when someone renders you a service, you must thank him; and you have rendered me a great service. Let me, then, thank you and give you a piece of advice. I shall tell you, son, what will protect you. You should understand that what brings you knowledge is better than what brings you wealth. Has a boy named Muhammad been born to the sons of the tribe of Mudar?"

"No," I said.

"Then he will be born," he said, "and his time will come and his faith will be exalted. Should you be living at that time, then truly you must believe what he says, and must kiss the mole between his two shoulders, may peace be upon him. And you must say to him: 'You, who are the best born man proclaiming the great worshipped God! . . .' "

Al-Harith ibn Midad then asked me if we had reached the two olive trees, and I told him we had. He asked me to help him dismount and to take him to these trees. Between them was a great, well-chiseled rock, in the form of a cube, and this he went around, touching all its sides. Then he said:

"Son, this place is called the Place of Death."

With that he wept till his face and beard were wet with his tears.

Next morning he asked me to walk on with him till we reached a rock laid over another rock, with a narrow opening between them. Holding my arm, he moved the rock, and I saw a path beneath the earth, with snakes hissing to the left and right. We walked inside till our way was blocked by a further rock overlaid by a rock. He took hold of my shoulder and entered, placed his left hand beneath the rock, and turned it over; and we saw another path. He took a firm grip of my shoulder to stop me from fleeing. On we walked, till we reached a room filled with light, though where this light came from I could not tell.

"Have no fear of what you see," he told me. "You will come out safely, and from your progeny many tribes will walk the earth."

There came out a black dragon with red eyes, turning around the room, like a huge mountain. I entered the room and saw four beds there. On three of them lay three dead men, while the fourth was empty. [The three dead men were his father, grandfather and great-grandfather. The fourth bed was to be his.] In the middle of the room was a sack of pearls, rubies, silver, and gold.

"Take as much as your camel can carry," al-Harith told me, "but no more." He was a Hanifi, who believed in the religion of his forefathers, Ibrahim, Ismail, and Ishaq, may God bless them.

[Iyad said:] I took what my camel could carry in rubies and gold, choosing the finest, and the rest I left. Then I came out.

From *Kitab al-Tijan fi Muluk Himyar* (*The Book of Crowns Concerning the Kings of Himyar*).

10

The Story of the Cave Where Shaddad ibn ʿAad Was

HOW THE ADVENTURERS ENTERED AND WHAT HAPPENED TO THEM THERE

Wahb ibn Munabbeh said: "I was told by Abu Muhammad ʿAbd al-Malek ibn Hisham how he was told by Ziyad ibn ʿAbd al-Malek al-Bukaʾi, who was told by Muhammad ibn Ishaq al-Muttalibi, who was told by ʿUbaid ibn Shirya al-Jurhumi, that a very old man from Yemen, who was well informed about the kings of Himyar and its affairs, related the following story at Sanaa during the year of the renegades."

There was a man in Yemen among the descendants of the ʿAad ibn Qahtan—the junior ʿAad, for the descendants of the senior ʿAad had all died out. God said [in the Quran]: "Do you see any of them still alive?"

This man from the ʿAad was called al-Humaysiʿ ibn Bakr, and he was brave and dauntless, famed for fearing no one. Venturesome men and outlaws would come to him from all parts of the earth. He was a great adventurer in the mountains of Yemen, Oman, and Bahrain.

One day, two venturesome men, one from the ʿAbs tribe, the other from Khuzaʿa, came to him.

"Humaysiʿ," they told him, "command whatever you wish and we will do it."

So al-Humaysiʿ went with them, and they came to a mountain where there was a wild forest full of snakes, where no one would venture. A number of times al-Humaysiʿ had gone to the mountain alone, but always, when he saw the snakes, he had been struck with terror and had held back from entering. Now, with the two venturesome men alongside, he took courage from their company.

"Place your head between two," he told himself, "even if it is covered to the ears."[1]

---

1. An old Arabic saying.

With that he took his sword, his firestone, his torches, and his food, and he went along with the two till he reached the mountain. The snakes fled at the first sight of them, and so it went on till finally they reached the entrance to a great cave—so vast it seemed as though mountains were standing on their shoulders. The men felt utterly desolate, and they could hear a mighty noise from inside the cave. On the entrance were written words in the Himyari language. The other two asked al-Humaysiᶜ to read the words to them, and he uttered these two lines of poetry engraved there:

Only the venturesome, or the vain and ignorant, shall enter this house.
He who determines the lengths of lives shall deal with him who
enters this cave.

Al-Khuzaᶜi was straightaway seized with terror. Al-ᶜAbsi was seized, too, but managed to stand firm. Then al-Khuzaᶜi said: "Oh Humaysiᶜ, how many have lived in this world, and never suffered this!" And with that he ran off.[2]

"Shall we enter this cave?" al-Humaysiᶜ asked.

"Let us do so," said al-ᶜAbsi.

And so they walked some way into the cave. Suddenly they saw snakes hissing from right and left, and there were winds blowing on the two men, from within the cave. And they heard a mighty noise there.

"This is a tight corner you've brought yourself to," al-ᶜAbsi said. "Are you sure of this cave, Humaysiᶜ?

"I am sure," said al-Humaysiᶜ, "of what my eye has seen. And I live in hope."

"My fear is," said al-ᶜAbsi, "that you are rousing the snakes. I would wager my life, Humaysiᶜ, you have sold your soul at the lowest price."

Al-Humaysiᶜ, though, paid him no heed. On he walked, through the cave, till he came to another entrance still greater, still fuller of foreboding than the first. The mighty noise and the murmuring voices grew greater around them, and they saw more writing in the Himyari language. All this heightened their terror. Then al-ᶜAbsi asked al-Humaysiᶜ to read the words engraved there, and al-Humaysiᶜ read the following:

Look to your saddle, let it not be moved, or certain death will befall it.
Oh dwellers of the Shammam mounts, the Covenant may cancel your
violation.
Rise for that person, his entrance will summon the day of separation.

2. This corrects a discrepancy in the original, where it is al-ᶜAbsi who flees.

"May God punish the man from ʿAad for his rashness!" al-ʿAbsi said. And with that he fled in utter terror, not looking back when al-Humaysiʿ called to him. Al-Humaysiʿ, too, felt driven to flee. Yet he resolved to follow the harder course. On he walked till he came to an entrance still greater, still more terrifying than the two first. On this, too, were words in the Himyari language, with the following text:

There was a counselor once, showing you truth to enter your ears.
The ignorance of the ignorant was manifest in his error, that his
heart was no longer watchful.

He went in through the third entrance and heard a still mightier noise, like thunder. Suddenly, as he was in this plight, a red-eyed dragon appeared before him, its mouth agape. When al-Humaysiʿ saw it, he drew swiftly back. The dragon grew silent and the man of ʿAad stood his ground.

"It's seen me," he thought. "Had it been a [true] beast, it would never have let me be. It must be a talisman."

On he went once more, and the dragon appeared again. He walked toward it, then, hearing a mighty noise, ran off. Then he realized from the noise that the dragon was withdrawing. Convinced now that it sprang from magic, he took care not to accost it, treading lightly, step-by-step, till his foot reached a point where the dragon moved and let out a mighty noise. He thereupon took an axe he had with him and began digging, on this spot, till he found some chains on pulleys. At this point night fell, and he hurried from the cave. He collected some wood from the forest round about, lit a fire, and lay down to sleep, close to the entrance of the cave. During the night he heard weeping and moaning from inside the cave, and, apprehensive now, saw a great fire issuing from the cave. He remained where he was even so, till it engulfed him; and, enduring it patiently, he found it gave no pain. Then another fire, greater than the first, engulfed him once more, and again he endured it with patience. When it had gone, he took the torch he had lit and went and struck it against the walls of the cave, right and left. At last he heard a call from within the cave: "Oh al-Humaysiʿ, your presence is not wished for here." And so he remained outside till dawn. Then he went in through the entrance to the cave, and walked on till he reached the entrance where he had seen the dragon; and he dug around the dragon until it fell. Thereupon he snatched its eyes, to find they were made of red ruby of no value. On he walked till he reached a further entrance still greater, still more terrifying than the one before. When he tried to open it, he heard a mighty noise and saw a huge lion. He stepped back and the lion stepped back, too, with a resounding roar. As he had done with the dragon, he dug around the place from which the lion had retreated, till its movement ceased. Then he snatched its eyes, and once more they were of red ruby of no value. He went in through the entrance and found himself in a great hall, with a room in the midst of which was a gold bedstead, and an old man lying there with a gold board above his head. The ceiling of the room was studded with different kinds of jewels. Over his head, on the wall, the gold board was engraved with the following words: "I am Shaddad, son of ʿAad. I lived for five hundred years. I deflowered a thousand virgins, killed a thousand fighters, and rode a thousand pedigree horses." And below this was engraved the following verse:

> Who is this, oh Shaddad of ʿAad, whose hopes have been dashed?
> Let he who sees me learn well; for I ruled so many years,
> Then hastened away like a guest, as though I were some dream.
> Beware time's treacheries, never feel safe amid life's shifts.
> Take no offense at my words, oh dweller of the forests and wild places.

He said: "I turned to his right side then, and saw a gold bedstead on which were lying two young maidens. Above their heads, on the wall, was a gold board on which were engraved the following words: "I am Habba and this is Labba, daughters of Shaddad ibn ʿAad. We lived through times where we spent all our old wealth, earned or inherited, on our slaves. Then [came the day when] we asked for a measure of wheat, for a measure of jewels, but did not find it. Let any who sees us have no trust in time's shifts. Let him know well that time brings bad times along with good."

Then al-Humaysiʿ took the boards, along with any jewels he found in the house, and withdrew.

From *Kitab al-Tijan fi Muluk Himyar* (*The Book of Crowns Concerning the Kings of Himyar*).

11
Luqman

Wahb said:

The ʿAad al-Asghar ben Qahtan were a devious and treacherous tribe. No wayfarer could feel secure with them, no neighbor would trust them; no stranger would ever visit them, no one would venture to make a covenant with them. A branch of this tribe, the Banu Karkar Ben ʿAad ben Qahtan, lived in the far reaches of Yemen and was at war with all the tribes of ʿAad. These last had as allies the Banu Ghanem and the Banu Zalem ben Qahtan, and they were victorious over the Banu Karkar. When the Banu Karkar saw the abject depths to which they had sunk, how they were subject to degradation after honor, and loss and hard toil after prosperity, they complained of their adversity to their master, al-Sumaidiʿ ben Zuhair.

"Banu Karkar," al-Sumaidiʿ told them, "you have been a treacherous and devious people, one no kin or stranger could trust, of whom neither friend nor foe could feel sure. You have given a hostage to fate, and now fate is demanding its due."

"We see now," they answered, "how we have opened the door of death upon ourselves. Guide us to the door of life."

"Here this cannot be," he said. "Go rather to the Himyari chief, Luqman ben ʿAad, for he has wisdom and goodness, prays to God, and is open to the doors of charity. He who never ceases to invoke God's help is kept safe from harm."

"All this is now in your hands," they told him. "Take us to him."

"Banu Karkar," he told them, "this is a mighty task you have placed on me, for God is pleased with none of your deeds." . . .

Al-Sumaidiʿ went with them to Luqman ben ʿAad. Luqman offered them his trust and they embraced it, and he married from among them a beautiful woman called Sawdaʿ bint Umama. Luqman, who was a jealous man, confined her to a vast cave atop a very high rock, to which he alone could gain access on account of his great stature. In this cave, too, he would worship, and it was his custom each year to gather the people there, both men and women, to pray with him; and he invited the Banu Karkar along with the rest.

There, al-Humaisiᶜ ben al-Sumaidiᶜ saw Luqman's wife and desired her.

"Oh people of ᶜAad," he told the Banu Karkar, "if you do not, by God, find me a way to Luqman's wife, I shall kill Luqman, and then Himyar will see the end of you."

He was a most bold and brutal man, and they knew well enough he would carry out his threat unless they helped him. And so they worked with him to contrive a way to bring the two together without Luqman's knowledge.

But a man among them, called ᶜAmer ben Malik, addressed them as follows:

"You are betraying hospitality and trust, and your end will be no better than your past state. There can be no safety after devious deeds, no excuse for treachery, no falling away from a covenant. You have obeyed a beguiling, lecherous man, and your own tempting devils, against the one who welcomed you. The other Arabs struck you all with a single arrow, and here you are now betraying Luqman, who gave you refuge, with his own women."

They, though, would not hear him, still persisting in their wrongful course . . . As for al-Humaisiᶜ ben al-Sumaidiᶜ, he struck the man. "This man seeks your destruction," he told the Banu Karkar. "Kill him." And so they killed him.

Then they came to Luqman.

"We fear," they told him, "a war is liable to break out among us. If, though, you will store our weapons in your cave, we shall be powerless to spill blood, and kill our own kindred, even though we might quarrel."

"Do so," Luqman said.

And so they brought out their weapons and placed al-Humaisiᶜ ben al-Sumaidiᶜ inside the bundle, hidden from view on all sides. Then they gave the bundle to Luqman, who took it up into the cave.

When Luqman had gone, al-Humaisiᶜ spoke to Sawdaᶜ, Luqmanᶜs wife, telling her: "I am al-Humaisiᶜ ben al-Sumaidiᶜ."

She brought him out, and he [made love to her]. Then she offered him food and drink and put him back in the bundle. This went on for a while, until at last he ventured to sleep with her on Luqman's own bed; and he spat up onto the roof of the cave. Later Luqman came, and, feeling very tired, flung himself down on his bed. Then, looking up, he saw the spittle where it had stuck on the cave roof.

"Whose spittle is that?" he asked his wife.

"Mine," she answered.

He told her to spit, but her spittle could not reach the ceiling.

"But," she said, "I was seated when I spat."

Thereupon he told her to be seated and spit. And still she could not reach so high with her spittle.

"I was standing," she told him then.

And so he told her to stand up and spit. She stood, and spat, but still could not reach so far. He saw then what had happened.

"This," he said, "came from the weapons." And with that he opened the bundle of weapons and brought al-Humaisiᶜ out. Then he called together the Banu Himyar.

"What do you have to say of the Banu Karkar?" he asked them.

"Luqman," they said, "the Banu Karkar were driven from the lands of Himyar because they are a faithless and devious people, fit only to sow treachery among us and fill us with rancor."

Luqman ordered the Banu Karkar to leave his protection. Then he went to the cave on the mountain, put his wife, along with al-Humaisiᶜ, in the bundle of weapons, and flung them down from the heights. Then he stoned them, and all the rest of his people stoned them with him, till the two had been killed. As for the Banu Karkar, they were sent away and lost Luqman's protection.

From *Kitab al-Tijan fi Muluk Himyar* (*The Book of Crowns Concerning the Kings of Himyar*).

II

Tales of Rulers and Other Notable Persons

12

ʿAmara the Faqih and ʿAbd al-Malik ibn Marwan

ʿAmara the Faqih said:

I sat often with ʿAbd al-Malik ibn Marwan in the shadow of the Kaʿba. One day he told me:

"ʿAmara, if you live long enough, you will see people craning their necks toward me and people's hopes aspiring to me. If this should happen, do not hesitate to make me the means to fulfill your needs and the target to realize your hopes. By God, if you do this, I shall fill your hands with joy and bestow a bountiful bliss upon you."

Sometime after, ʿAbd al-Malik went to Damascus and became caliph. I went to visit him there, and, requesting entry to his court, was permitted to go in. After I had greeted him in proper fashion, he said: "Welcome to my brother." Then he called one of his servants and told him: "Have a house prepared for this man to stay in, and see he has comfort and every means to enjoy his stay, and honor him above all my other friends."

So it was done, and I stayed twenty days, attending all his lunches and dinners. When I expressed the wish to leave and return to my family, he ordered I should be given twenty thousand dinars and two hundred thousand dirhams, and a hundred camels all with their tenders and garb. Then he asked me:

"Have I filled your hands with joy, ʿAmara?"

"God be praised, Prince of the Faithful," I replied. "You still remember this?"

"Yes," he said. "There is no good in a man who forgets what he promises and remembers only what he threatens. How long has this been, ʿAmara?"

"It seems as though just yesterday," I said. "Yet the time has been long, Prince of the Faithful."

"This," he said, "was not on account of any piece of news we learned, or any tradition we recorded or chronicle we narrated. Rather, I have, since my first youth, acted in certain ways whereby I hoped to raise my status and spread my name."

"And what might those be, Prince of the Faithful?" I asked.

"I never flattered anyone," he answered, "and never quarreled with anyone. And I never revealed anyone's secrets, never committed any unlawful deed forbidden by God, never envied anyone, or oppressed anyone. And I was always the central bead in a necklace [binding everything together] for my people. I would honor anyone sitting with me, even though he were not a good man, and raise the status of the man of letters, and honor those who were steadfast; and I was forbearing with those of evil tongue, and had mercy on the weak. By this means, God has raised my status. Make ready to leave now, ʿAmara, and go on your way filled with honor."

From Burhan al-Din al-Kutubi, *Ghurar al-Khasaʾis* (*The Finest Attributes*); in *Qisas al-ʿArab* (*Stories of the Arabs*), vol. 1.

13

The Justice of ʿAdud al-Dawla

A man came to Baghdad on his way to the pilgrimage. He was wearing a necklace valued at a thousand dinars, which he tried to sell, but to no avail. And so he left it in the care of a perfume seller and went on the pilgrimage. When he returned, he brought the perfume seller a gift.

"Who are you?" the perfume seller asked.

"I'm the owner of the necklace," the man replied. "The one I entrusted to your keeping."

No sooner were the words out of his mouth than the perfume seller kicked him, then flung him out of his shop.

"You dare," he said, "to make a claim like that against me?"

People gathered around the pilgrim.

"Woe to you!" they said. "This is a good man. Couldn't you find anyone else to make your claim against?"

The pilgrim was confounded, yet kept returning to the man, who only went on cursing and beating him. Then someone told him:

"You should go to ʿAdud al-Dawla. He has great skill in seeking out the truth."

The pilgrim wrote down his account and took it to ʿAdud al-Dawla. ʿAdud al-Dawla summoned him and inquired about his problem, and the pilgrim recounted what had happened. ʿAdud al-Dawla told him then:

"Go tomorrow to the perfume seller and sit beside his shop; and, if he should prevent you, then sit beside the shop opposite him. Do this from morning till sunset, but do not speak to him. Repeat this for three days, and on the fourth I shall pass by where you are and stop to greet you. Do not rise for me, only return my greeting and answer exactly what I ask you. Once I have left, demand the necklace once more, then come and tell me what he says. If he should give it to you, then bring it to me."

[Next morning] the man went to the vendor's shop, but was prevented from sitting there, so he sat down beside the shop opposite, for three days. On the fourth, ʿAdud al-Dawla passed with a great retinue, and, when he saw the pilgrim from Khorasan, stopped and said: "Greetings to you."

The pilgrim made no movement.

"And to you," he said.

"Brother," said ʿAdud al-Dawla, "you come here, and do not come to us and tell us of your needs?"

The pilgrim made some answer, while ʿAdud al-Dawla, standing there with his soldiers around him, went on inquiring about the man, with repeated questions, while the perfume seller almost fainted from fear.

When ʿAdud al-Dawla had left, the vendor looked toward him and said:

"Woe to you, when did you leave that necklace in my care? What was it wrapped in? Remind me, and I might remember."

The pilgrim described it to him, and the vendor got up and searched, then shook a pitcher he had and the necklace fell out from it.

"I'd forgotten," he said. "If you hadn't reminded me, I should never have remembered."

The pilgrim took the necklace. "What good is there in informing ʿAdud al-Dawla?" he wondered. Then he said to himself: "It could be he wishes to buy it." So he went to him and told him.

ʿAdud al-Dawla thereupon sent the necklace to the perfume seller's shop, and had it hung around his neck. Then he had him crucified at the door of the shop and had the crier call out: "Such is the punishment of those who withhold that with which they are entrusted." At the end of the day, the guard removed the necklace and gave it to the pilgrim, saying: "Take it and go."

From Ibn al-Jawzi, *Al-Adhkiyaʾ* (*Smart People*); in *Qisas al-ʿArab* (*Stories of the Arabs*), vol. 1.

14

The Piety of ʿUmar ibn ʿAbd al-ʿAziz

After the burial of [Caliph] Sulaiman [ibn ʿAbd al-Malik], ʿUmar ibn ʿAbd al-ʿAziz became caliph, and riding wagons were brought in to him.

"What are these?" he asked.

"These," he was told, "are riding wagons never used by anyone, kept for the caliph to be first to use, when he ascends to the caliphate."

He left them and went out to seek his mule, saying:

"Muzahim, add these [riding wagons] to the treasury."

New canopies and pavilions were pitched for him, which no one before him had ever sat in.

"And what are these?" he asked.

"These," he was told, "are canopies and pavilions never used by anyone. They are for the [new] caliph to sit in, when he ascends to the caliphate."

"Muzahim," he said, "add these to the revenue of the Muslims."

Then he mounted his mule and went to where new carpets and mats had been laid for the new caliph. He went on shifting them with his foot till only the straw mats remained, then said:

"Muzahim, add these to the Muslim treasury."

Caliph Sulaiman's family were quick to begin pouring perfumes and creams from one [newly opened] bottle into another bottle, and to put on clothes that had never been worn, so as to make them look used—for it was the tradition that, when a caliph died, all bottles he had opened and clothes he had worn were inherited by his children, while all that had not been touched went to the next caliph.

"All this," ʿUmar said, "is neither mine, nor Sulaiman's, nor yours. Muzahim, add these to the treasury of the Muslims."

The ministers began to plot together.

"As for riding wagons," they said, "and canopies and pavilions, and clothes and carpets, these are already beyond our reach. But one thing still remains, and that is the slave girls. Let us show them to him, hoping something may be gained from them. Otherwise, there is no hope of gaining anything."

The slave girls were brought in, their appearance that of dolls. When he saw them, he began to inquire of each where she had come from and to whom she had been sold. The slave girl would tell him where she had come from, and who now owned her, and he would order that she be returned to her country and people. So he did with all of them. When his men saw this, they were in despair, knowing he would impose justice.

After this he spent three days quite alone, with no one permitted to enter. And all the while the Umayyad dignitaries and the noblest of the Arabs, and the army, and the leaders, all waited at his door, to see what would come from him. After three days, he sat before the people, imposed the law by justice and right, remedying all wrongs done and reviving the law of the Book [the Quran] and traditions, and behaved with [scrupulous] justice, rejecting the world and concerned only to obey God's ordinances. And so he went on till the day he died.

From Muhammad ibn ʿAbd al-Hakam, *Sirat ʿUmar ibn ʿAbd al-ʿAziz* (*The Life of ʿUmar ibn ʿAbd al-ʿAziz*) (Cairo: Maktabat Wahba, 1983); in *Qisas al-ʿArab* (*Stories of the Arabs*), vol. 3.

15

A Furthur Story of ʿUmar ibn ʿAbd al-ʿAziz

Before ascending to the caliphate, ʿUmar ibn ʿAbd al-ʿAziz had a village in Yemen known as al-Sahla, which produced an abundant revenue from which he and his family lived.

When he became caliph, he told his freed slave, Muzahim:

"I have decided to return al-Sahla to the Muslim treasury."

"But," Muzahim said, "do you not know how many your children are? They are such and such a number."

ʿUmar ibn ʿAbd al-ʿAziz wept, wiping away his tears with his middle finger, and said:

"I trust in God concerning them. I trust in God concerning them."

Muzahim went to ʿUmar's son, ʿAbd al-Malik.

"Do you know," he said, "what your father means to do? He means to return al-Sahla [to the Muslim treasury]."

"And what did you say to him?" ʿAbd al-Malik asked.

"I reminded him of his children," Muzahim answered, "and he wept and wiped away his tears with his middle finger, saying: 'I trust in God concerning them.'"

"And you," ʿAbd al-Malik said, "call yourself a promoter of religion?"

With that he hurried to his father, telling the chamberlain to request permission to enter.

"He's just begun his sleep," the chamberlain said.

"Go," ʿAbd al-Malik said, "and request permission for me to enter."

"Do you have no pity on him?" the chamberlain asked. "Through the whole night and day, he has just this one hour at noon to rest."

But ʿAbd al-Malik insisted.

"Go and request permission," he said.

ʿUmar, hearing their exchange, said: "Let ʿAbd al-Malik enter." And so he went in.

"What have you decided?" he asked.

"To return al-Sahla [to the Muslim treasury]," ʿUmar replied.

"Don't delay then," ʿAbd al-Malik replied. "Rise now and do this thing."

ʿUmar raised his hands [in supplication].

"God be praised," he said, "for sending me progeny able to aid me in my religion. Yes, son, I shall pray the noon prayer, then mount the pulpit and announce its return openly, before the people."

"And how do you know," ʿAbd al-Malik asked, "that you'll live till noon? Or, if you live till noon, that you'll remain steadfast in your intention?"

At that ʿUmar rose, mounted the pulpit, and announced the return of al-Sahla to the treasury.

From Ibn Abi ʾl-Hadeed, *Sharh Nahj al-Balagha* (*Explicating the Method of Literary Eloquence*), 4; in *Qisas al-ʿArab* (*Stories of the Arabs*), vol. 3.

16

The Chief of Police and Caliph al-Hadi

ʿA*bd Allah ibn Malik said:*

I was once chief of police to [Caliph] al-Mahdi. He would order me to go to the companions of his son al-Hadi and have them beaten and imprisoned, so as to protect al-Hadi from them. Al-Hadi would send asking me to treat them with mildness, but I never heeded his requests and would proceed as al-Mahdi had instructed me.

When al-Hadi ascended to the caliphate, I was sure things would go badly with me. One day he sent for me, and I entered his presence sensing death before me. I found him sitting in his seat with the sword and the leather execution mat before him. I greeted him.

"May God never greet you," he replied. "Do you remember how I sent to you, asking you not to beat al-Harrani as the Prince of the Faithful had ordered you, and also that other time?" He named his companions.

"Yes, Prince of the Faithful," I said. "Will you permit me to speak?"

"Very well," he said.

"By God," I said, "would it please you if you were to appoint me to the post to which your father appointed me, and you gave me a command, and then, if your children sent me an order contrary to yours, I disobeyed your order and followed theirs?"

"No," he said.

"I should be with you," I said, "just as I was with your father."

He told me to approach, and I kissed his hand. Then he ordered that I be given precious gifts, and I returned home reflecting on what had happened.

"It may be," I said to myself, "that he'll speak to his [former] companions about this. And now they're not simply his drinking comrades but his ministers and secretaries. Who knows, they may lead him to change his mind about me and urge him to something I dread to think of."

Now, as I was sitting eating with my children, warming pieces of bread and putting paste on them, I heard a great commotion outside, from the hoofs of horses, as though an earthquake had broken out. "Ha!" I said. "The hour has come!" The door opened, and the servants entered with al-Hadi in their midst.

I sprang up and kissed his hand and foot.

"ʿAbd Allah," he said, "after you left, I reflected on your case. You might (I felt) think that, if I sat among your old enemies that you treated so sternly, they might lead me to reconsider my good opinion of you. This might cause you great anxiety and rob you of your peace. And so I've come to your house, to set your mind at rest and let you know that all grudges are at an end. Here, give me something from what you were eating. By that you will know all fears and misgivings are over, protected as you are by what I've eaten from you, and by my visit to your house."

I offered him the plate with the paste and bread, and he ate. Then he said [to his men]:

"Here, fetch in what you've brought for ʿAbd Allah from my court."

Many mules were brought in [to the yard], laden with money and foodstuffs.

"All this," he said, "is for you to help support you, the mules along with the rest. And now I appoint you to the same post to which my father appointed you."

With that he left, and I became one of his men.

From Ibn ʿAbd Rabbihi, *Al-ʿIqd al-Farid li ʾl-Malik al-Saʿid* (*The Unique Necklace*); also Ahmad Farid al-Rifaʿi, *ʿAsr al-Maʾmun* (*The Age of al-Maʾmun*) (Cairo: Dar al-Kutub al-Misriyya, 1927), 1.107; in *Qisas al-ʿArab* (*Stories of the Arabs*), vol. 3.

17

At Khosrow's Court

Abu Sufyan traveled out [from Mecca] with the aim of making trading arrangements in Iraq. He was accompanied by a group from the Quraish. After three days, Abu Sufyan gathered them together and said:

"We're faced with danger on our journey, for we're coming to [the realm of] an invincible king, who hasn't given us leave to enter his territory. His land is no trading place for us. But let one among you go in with the camels. If he should be harmed, we'll say we're innocent of his blood; and if he's successful, he shall have half the profits."

"Let me go then," Ghailan ibn Salama said. "I'm ready to try."

When he reached the land of Khosrow, he perfumed himself, put on two yellow robes, made himself known, then sat at Khosrow's door till the king granted him leave to enter his court. A translator was brought, who said to him:

"The king asks you: 'Why did you venture to enter my country without my leave?' "

"Tell him," he said to the translator, "that I belong to none of his enemies, nor have I come as a spy for one of his adversaries. I have rather come on a mission of trade, whose goods he may enjoy. If he wishes them for himself, they shall be his; if not, and if he will agree for me to sell them to his subjects, then I will sell them thus."

He went on speaking, and, if ever he heard Khosrow's voice, he knelt.

"The king asks you," the translator said, " 'Why did you kneel?' "

"I heard a loud voice," he replied, "where no voice should rise, out of deference to the king, and I knew no one would dare speak so loud except the king himself. And so I knelt to show my deep respect for him."

Khosrow was pleased by these words, and ordered that a pillow should be placed under Ghailan. But, when they brought it, Ghailan saw the king's picture on it, and placed it on his head. Khosrow, supposing him to be a foolish, uncultivated man, told the translator:

"We sent for this pillow so he could be seated on it."

"I know that," Ghailan said, "but when I saw the king's picture on it, I thought a person such as I had no right to be seated on it, for it ought to be revered. And so I placed it on my head, which is the noblest part of my body."

Khosrow, pleased by this, asked him:

"Do you have any progeny?"

"I do," Ghailan said.

"And which of your children," Khosrow asked, "do you love above the others?"

Ghailan answered:

"The smallest till he has grown, the sick till he is cured, the absent till he returns."

"*Zeh!*" Khosrow said. "It is your good fortune that brought you in to me and showed you how to speak and behave. These are the actions and words of a wise man. Yet you are from a rough people, without wisdom. What do you eat?"

"Wheat bread," Ghailan replied.

"Such a mind," Khosrow said, "does indeed come from eating wheat bread, not from milk and dates [the major Arab Bedouin food]."

Then Khosrow bought his goods for many times their proper price, presented him with a new suit of clothes, and sent along with him a number of Persian builders, who built him a palace in al-Ta'if [in Hijaz], the first to be built there.

From *Bulough al-Arab* (*Attaining the Goal*), 1; also *Al-ʿIqd al-Farid* (*The Unique Necklace*), 1; in *Qisas al-ʿArab* (*Stories of the Arabs*), vol. 1.

18

An Arab at Khosrow's Court

A man of Arabia, Hajib ibn Zirara, requested an audience with Khosrow. The chamberlain asked who he was, and he said: "A man of the Arabs." He was permitted to enter.

When he was standing before Khosrow, the king asked: "Who are you?"

"I am the chief of the Arabs," Hajib said.

"But did you not say before," Khosrow asked, "that you were a man of the Arabs?"

"Yes," Hajib answered, "but then I was standing at the king's door. When I entered his court, I became the chief of the Arabs."

Khosrow, liking the answer, said: "*Zeh!*" Then he ordered that Hajib's mouth be filled with gems.

From Ibn al-Jawzi, *Akhbar al-Zurraf wa ʾl-Mutamajinin* (*Anecdotes of Humorists and Jesters*), Damascus (from the copy in the Taimuriyya Library), A.H. 1347.

19

I Take Refuge in Your Justice, Prince of the Faithful

It has been told how, one hot day, Muʿawiya ibn Abi Sufyan held his court along one of the streets of Damascus, which was open on all sides to the breezes. While he was installed on his official seat, surrounded by citizens of his kingdom, he saw a barefoot man walking hurriedly toward him. Muʿawiya pondered about him, and—the day being so hot—said to his assembly: "God never created any man I have need of on a day like this." Then he said to one of his attendants:

"Go to him and see what his trouble is, and what his circumstances are. By God, if he is poor, I shall make him prosperous; and if he has a complaint, I shall give him justice; and if he has been oppressed, I shall be his champion; and if he is rich, I shall make him poor."

The messenger went to meet the man, and, having greeted him, asked: "Where are you from?"

"Sir," the man answered, "I am a Bedouin from the ʿUdhra tribe, and I have come to see the Prince of the Faithful to complain of an injustice done to me by one of his viceroys."

"Very well," said the messenger. And with that he conducted him to Muʿawiya. The Bedouin greeted him in a manner fitting for caliphs, then recited some lines of poetry:

Muʿawiya, of knowledge, clemency, virtue,
Of generosity and liberal gifts,
I came to you when all paths were blocked,
So do not cut off my hopes of justice
And give me my rights from an oppressor
Who has tortured me where killing would have been lighter.
He snatched Suʿda from me, assailed me, and oppressed me.
I went to him in hope, but he cast me in prison

And put me to torture in chains.
He almost killed me, but death stayed its hand,
My life was not yet due to end.
Help me, I beg you, God's paradise be your reward.
My mind is gone from my grief for Su'da.

When he had finished his recital, Mu'awiya said:

"I see, Bedouin, that you speak of one of our viceroys but have not named him."

"It is your cousin," replied the Bedouin. "Marwan ibn al-Hakam, the viceroy of Medina."

"And what is your story?" Mu'awiya asked.

"May God guide the Prince," the Bedouin said, "I had a cousin whose hand I asked from her father, and he gave her to me in marriage. I loved her devotedly, on account of her perfect beauty and character, her sensible mind, and her kinship to me. For a time, Prince of the Faithful, we lived together in the greatest possible happiness, and my mind was perfectly at peace. During that time I had a herd of camels, and a flock of sheep, from which I was able to keep her and myself. But God's decree and the shifts of time changed all that: the beasts were struck by disease, and I was left with nothing. I was brought low and filled with anxiety. My situation grew ever worse, till I was ready to lose my mind; I felt myself a burden on the face of the earth. When news of this reached her father, he came between us and stopped my seeing her, denied me my rights, cast me out, and hid her away from me. I felt helpless, with no one to stand for me. And so I went to Marwan ibn al-Hakam to complain of my uncle. He sent for my uncle, and, when he was standing there in front of him, asked:

" 'Man, why did you come between your nephew and his wife?'

" 'May God guide the Prince,' my uncle answered, 'he has no wife from me. I never married my daughter to him.'

" 'May God guide the Prince,' I said, 'I have every trust in the maiden. Let the Prince send for her and ask her.'

"He sent for her, and she came promptly. When she was standing there in front of him, and he saw her beauty, he coveted her; and, Prince of the Faithful, becoming suddenly hostile to me, he rebuked me and ordered me to be imprisoned. I felt as though I had tumbled from the sky into the deepest pit. Then he said to her father:

" 'If you will marry her to me, I will give you a thousand dinars, and add ten thousand dirhams for you to spend. In the meantime, I shall vouch for her divorce.'

" 'If you will do this,' he replied, 'then I will give her to you in marriage.'

"Next morning, Marwan sent for me. When I was standing there in front of him, he looked at me like a raging lion. Then he said:

" 'Bedouin, divorce Suᶜda.'

" 'I will not,' I said.

"He ordered me to be flogged, then sent me back to prison. Next morning, he sent for me once more.

" 'Divorce Suᶜda,' he said again.

" 'I will not,' I answered.

"He then set his slaves on me, and they beat me quite savagely. Then he sent me back to prison. The third day he sent for me yet again, and, when I came, ordered the sword and the leather mat to be brought, and called in the executioner.

"Bedouin,' he said, 'by the majesty of my God and the dignity of my father, if you will not divorce Suᶜda, I shall part your head from your body.'

"Fearing for my life, I divorced her, but once only. Again he sent me back to prison, till her time of waiting was over.[1] Then he married her, and released me. And I have come to you, Prince of the Faithful, seeking justice. I beg you to have mercy on me. Lack of sleep has worn me out, worries have wasted my body, and I am losing my mind for love of her."

With that he burst into tears, having first recited a short poem to describe the state of his mind:

Fire in my heart, harboring destruction,
My body so sick it confounds the physician,
My eyes shedding tears like rain.
A heavy weight I bear that frets my patience.
My night is not night, nor my day day.
Have mercy on me then, a downcast man whose heart is in flight.
Return my Suᶜda to me, and the mighty God will reward you.

With that he fainted, there in the caliph's presence, ready to die as it seemed. Muᶜawiya had been reclining till this moment, but now he sat up.

"Marwan ibn al-Hakam," he said, "was overbearing and harmful, according to the law of the Muslims." Then, gazing at the Bedouin, he went on: "By God, Bedouin, you have come to me with a story like no other I have heard."

---

1. When a Muslim woman divorces or is widowed, she cannot remarry before waiting four months and ten days to show she is not pregnant by her former husband.

He called for paper and ink and wrote to Marwan as follows:

"I hear that you have acted overbearingly against certain of your people, contrary to the rules of religion, and have abused the sanctity of a Muslim. One governing over a city or a province should curb his passions and restrain his pleasures. An administrator is like a shepherd to his flock. Should he treat them with care, then they will stay with him; and if he becomes a wolf to them, then no one will contain them after him."

Sealing the letter, he called for two of his messengers and instructed them to hand the letter to Marwan in person; and this they did. Marwan read the letter many times over, then went in to Suʿda in tears.

"Sir," she said, "why are you weeping?"

"A letter," he answered, "has come to me from the Prince of the Faithful, ordering me to divorce you and send you on to him. If only he had left me with you for two years more, then killed me. That would have been far happier for me."

Thereupon he divorced her and sent her on to Muʿawiya, sending him, also, the following poem denying his guilt:

Forgive what I've done, for, should you see her,
You'd weep floods of tears.
What I send you now is a sun
No man or jinn could match.
Were it not for the caliph himself,
I'd never divorce her till I am in my shroud.

When Muʿawiya read the poem, he said: "He did well in the poem, but ill as to himself." Then, calling for the maiden, he was struck in turn by the beauty of a white-skinned, soft, exquisite girl whose loveliness and perfection were such as to rob any who saw her of their mind. Muʿawiya, filled with awe and admiration, gazed at his assembly, and said:

"This girl is perfect in her physical beauty. Were she eloquent, too, then she would be blessed and fully endowed."

With that he had her speak, only to find her the most eloquent of Arab women. He called out:

"Bring the Bedouin here to me."

When the Bedouin stood there in his presence, Muʿawiya said to him:

"If you will forget her, I will compensate you with three virgins, each with a thousand dirhams and ten suits of clothes of various silks and linen, then order, for you and for them, a regular allowance and gifts."

When Muʿawiya had finished, the Bedouin swallowed hard, then fainted away as though dead. When he came to himself, Muʿawiya asked:

"What is troubling you, Bedouin?"

"The worst of all troubles," he replied. "That I took refuge in your justice, asking God to ward Marwan's oppression off from me."

He recited a short poem describing his state. Then he said:

"By God, Prince of the Faithful, were you to give me all that the caliphate holds, I should never accept it in exchange for Suʿda. Laila's Madman[2] spoke truly when he said:

The heart rejects all but Laila's love.
All other women, though pure, are hateful to me.
When I glimpse her suddenly, I am struck with awe.
And stand dumbfounded.

When he had finished, Muʿawiya said:

"Bedouin, you acknowledged before that you divorced her. The truth is, she has been divorced by you and by Marwan. Still, we shall ask her to choose between us."

"Do so, Prince of the Faithful," the Bedouin said.

With that Muʿawiya turned to her.

"Suʿda," he said, "which do you choose, the Prince of the Faithful with his pomp and honor and palaces, or Marwan with his tyranny and violation, or this Bedouin with his hunger and rags?"

The girl pointed to her cousin, saying:

This one with his hunger and rags
Is dearer to me than kinfolk and neighbors,
And the man with the crown or his viceroy Marwan,
And every rich man in the world.

"Prince of the Faithful," she went on, "I would not desert him on account of time's shifts. My life with him was beautiful before, and I shall uphold him in riches and poverty, in ease and hardship, in sickness and in health, and according to the fate God has decreed for me with him."

Muʿawiya and his council were struck with admiration at her mind, and at her perfection and loyalty; and he ordered ten thousand dirhams

2. On Laila's Madman, see the discussion on love in the introduction.

to be given her, and had her registered in the charitable allowance of the Muslims.

From al-Nuwairi, *Nihayat al-Arab* (*The Highest Aspiration*), II; in *Qisas al-ʿArab* (*Stories of the Arabs*), vol. 4.

20

Tricked She Was

A*l-Haytham ibn ʿAdi, reporting to Ibn ʿAbbas, said:*

ʿAtika, daughter of Yazid ibn Muʿawiya, was married to [Caliph] ʿAbd al-Malik ibn Marwan, who loved her deeply. One day she became angry with him and would not be reconciled for all his efforts. He was much concerned by this and complained of the matter to his close entourage.

"What will you give me," asked ʿUmar ibn al-Asadi, "if I am able to appease her?"

"Whatever you wish," Marwan replied.

ʿUmar went and sat at the entrance to her chambers, weeping.

"What is troubling you, Abu Hafs?" her chambermaid asked.

"I have come to my cousin [ʿAtika]," he said, "on a very grave matter. Please, ask her to grant me an audience. It may be she can resolve my problem."

"What is it you wish to tell me?" ʿAtika asked.

"You know my situation," he replied, "with the Prince of the Faithful. I had just two sons, and one attacked the other and killed him. I told the Prince of the Faithful: 'I am the one legally responsible; and I forgive him.' But the Prince of the Faithful would not hear of it. 'I will not,' he said, 'let this become a practice among my people.' He is to have my son killed tomorrow. I beg you, for the grace of God, to speak to him of this, to ask him to leave me this one son. In so doing you will save two lives in one; for, if he should be killed, I shall kill myself."

"I will not speak to him!" ʿAtika said.

"Surely," he said, "you could gain nothing better than the saving of two lives." And with that he began to weep and went on weeping, bitterly.

Her attendants, entourage and servants alike, urged her insistently to help him. At last she cried: "Bring me my garments."

She dressed and had the door between herself and the caliph (which she had ordered to be blocked up) freed once more. Then she entered [the court].

One of the caliph's attendants promptly went to him.

"Prince of the Faithful," he said. "ʿAtika is here."

"What are you saying?" the caliph asked. "Have you seen her?"

"I have, Prince of the Faithful," he replied.

At this moment ʿAtika appeared there where ʿAbd al-Malik was seated on his throne. She greeted him, but he said nothing.

"By God," she said, "were it not for the sake of ʿUmar ibn Bilal, I would never have come to you. If one of his sons attacked the other and killed him, and he is responsible, and yet he forgives him, is it for you to decree he should be killed?"

"Indeed," said the caliph, "I shall do this, whatever he says."

"I entreat you," she said, "in the name of God, not to do it."

With that she approached him and took his hand; then, as he still looked away, kissed his foot. At this he leant over her and held her to his breast, raised her up on to his throne, and said: "I have forgiven him." So they were reconciled.

Later, as ʿAbd al-Malik was sitting with his close entourage, ʿUmar ibn Bilal came to him.

"Abu Hafs," the caliph said, "you have shown yourself most resourceful. How may I reward you?"

"Prince of the Faithful," said ʿUmar, "a thousand dinars, and a plantation with all the necessary slaves and tools."

"It is yours," the caliph said.

"And places of rest," ʿUmar continued, "for my sons and family."

"Those, too, are yours," said the caliph.

"Woe to the pimp!" ʿAtika cried, on learning of this. "He tricked me!"

From Ibn Qayyim al-Jawziyya, *Akhbar al-Nisaaʾ* (*Tales of Women*) (Beirut: Dar al-Kutub al-ʿIlmiyya, 1990).

21

Um Asya the Midwife and the Palace of Khumarawayh

I was with Um Asya, the midwife of Khumarawayh ibn Tulun's wife (a pious woman who conducted herself most excellently and enjoyed a favored status with Khumarawayh), and we were discussing how God's grace intervened in the livelihood of His worshippers, and how He warded evil away from them. She told me the following story.

Two brothers (she said) married me and my sister. My sister's husband grew rich, but my own became very poor and at last died in great penury, leaving me with several daughters. My sister's husband died, too, but left her and her children a rich inheritance: houses, orchards, and other possessions.

I'd toil (she went on) to feed my children; and, if I had nothing left, I'd go to my sister and ask her to lend me this or that, ashamed to ask her to give it. Ramadan came around, and, when we'd reached the middle of the fasting month, my children told me how they longed for some sweets for the feast.

I went to my sister.

"Please," I said, "lend me a dinar to make some sweets for the children, for the feast."

"Sister," she said, "it's getting on my nerves, the way you keep saying 'lend me.' If I did lend you something, how would you pay it back? From your orchards, maybe, or from the rent from your houses? I wish you'd simply say 'give me.'"

"I'll repay you," I told her, "from what I'm sent by God, Whose ways none can foretell."

She laughed.

"That, by God," she said, "is just a wishful dream. Only fools have dreams like that."

I left her and plodded off home.

Now, in our quarter there lived a black servant of Bint al-Yatim's, Khumarawayh's wife. When I'd reached there, he intercepted me.

"A neighbor of ours is in labor," he said, "and she's having a difficult time. Could you go in and help her? She doesn't have a midwife."

I tell you (Um Asya went on), I'd never even seen a woman in labor! Still, I went in to her, passed my hand over her stomach, and set her on the labor chair, the way the midwife had done with me when I had my own children. Within an hour she'd given birth. When she stopped screaming, the servant came to ask how she was, and I told him she'd actually given birth already. He was amazed how fast it had happened and supposed it was all on account of my own skill. And he went to his mistress, who was pregnant herself with Khumarawayh's first child and whose confinement was imminent. She'd interviewed a number of midwives and found none of them pleasing.

"In our quarter," the slave told her now, "there's a midwife we took to a woman in labor. She passed her hand over the woman's stomach, and the woman gave birth straightaway." And he went on to describe me in terms God himself might have used.

"Tomorrow," she told the servant, "bring her here."

He came and summoned me to his mistress, and I responded with a cheerful manner and faith in God. She took a liking to me.

"You," she said, "will be with me in my labor."

At that moment she felt a pain in her stomach, of the kind women feel when they're about to go into labor. I put out my hand and rubbed her stomach, secretly praying to God for success. I was murmuring a prayer to God to help me, but everyone around thought what I was murmuring was some kind of talisman to help her. Her pain subsided, and she sensed I'd brought her blessed relief.

At this point Khumarawayh came in.

"What was the matter?" he asked.

"I felt a violent stomach pain," she told him, "and a midwife I'd chosen passed her hand over my stomach, and all the pain went away." And with that she told me to come out and meet him.

"I pray to God," he said, "that He'll save her through the relief you bring."

We'd now (Um Asya continued) reached the last ten days of Ramadan, and I prayed to God with more fervor than even those hermits and ascetics could have done who wander the mountains and leave worldly things. And all was for fear of seeing my sister gloat. Within three days, Khumarawayh's wife went into labor. I put her on the labor chair, and there she sat for two hours before giving birth, very easily, to a baby boy. Khumarawayh, meanwhile, was pacing to and fro outside. She'd expected a dreadful time giving birth, but, when the baby emerged, she said:

"Is this what labor is?"

"Yes," I replied.

At that she kissed my eyes with joy, while Khumarawayh cried out to me:

"Tell me how she is, you blessed one!"

"By the Prince's life," I answered, "all's well with her. She's given birth to a son, perfectly formed."

He sent me a thousand dinars and insisted on seeing her, such was the care and tenderness he felt toward her. I, though, kept him outside till I'd moved away everything connected with the labor. Then I told her:

"Mistress, please, when you see him, smile at him."

When he came in, she smiled at him, and he distributed plentiful alms in honor of her and the infant.

On the seventh day (Um Asya said), which also happened to be the day of the Ramadan feast, she ordered I should be given five hundred dinars; and I received a further thousand from her entourage. So, I now had two thousand five hundred dinars. She also presented me with more than thirty suits of clothes, and I received, from what had been prepared for the feast at their palace, enough food to make up three sumptuous meals. I went home and sent my sister the food for one of these, and she came to see me, congratulating me and filled with shame.

"You criticized me," I told her, "for saying 'lend me.' And all the time I was going to pay you back from this. Never belittle those God favors, those who have trust in Him and in His recompense."

Thereafter, Um Asya gained a good deal of money from Khumarawayh and rendered many great services to the dignitaries of the city.

From Abu Jaʿfar Ahmad ibn Yusuf, *Al-Mukafaʾa* (*The Recompense*), ed. Ahmad Amin and ʿAli ʾl-Jarim (Cairo, 1941).

22

Yazid and Habbaba

Habbaba was owned at first by the famous Umayyad poet al-Ahwas. Yazid ibn ʿAbd al-Malik, the brother of the caliph then ruling, heard her singing and bought her for four thousand dinars. His brother the caliph, though, when he heard of this, decided to indict him.

Yazid was already married to Suʿda bint ʿAbd Allah ibn ʿUthman and to Rabiha bint ʿAbd Allah ibn Jaʿfar. He had grown deeply attached to Habbaba, but, fearing the indictment, he suppressed his regrets and sold her to a man from Ifriqiya. In due course, when he himself became caliph, Suʿda sent a freedman of hers in search of Habbaba.

The freedman was told she was in Medina, and he looked for her there, only to learn she had moved on to Egypt; and, when he looked for her in Egypt, he was told she had moved on to Ifriqiya. In Ifriqiya he spoke to her master and strove to coax him into selling her. The man refused at first, but—when the envoy told him the caliph would otherwise seize her by force—eventually agreed to sell her for a hundred thousand dirhams.

As the envoy was passing with her through Mecca, around two hundred men came out to see her off, and they asked her to sing for them. She sang two verses to them, then wrote down their names; and later, when she showed the list to Yazid, he sent each of the men a thousand dirhams.

When she arrived in Damascus, Suʿda dressed her in fine clothes and endowed her lavishly with jewels and perfumes. She then approached the caliph.

"God," she said, knowing what was in his heart, "has granted you the caliphate. Is there anything else you desire?"

"No," he replied.

"I have a notion even so," she went on. "Tell me, and perhaps I can help you to your wish."

"Habbaba," he said.

"And would you," she asked him, "recognize her if you saw her?"

"Yes," he answered.

With that she took him by the hand and conducted him to Habbaba. He was filled with joy, and Suʿda's standing rose greatly in his eyes. Habbaba had pledged that, whatever Suʿda wished for from the caliph, she herself would ensure she acquired it, and that Suʿda's son should be appointed successor to the caliphate. This Habbaba fulfilled.

Rabiha, for her part, had bought the singer Sallama, who had been with another man from Medina. Yazid had seen her and had felt a deep love for her, too. When the two singers had come into his keeping, he said:

Now the search is over, there is no more parting;
As if a man settled happy after long absence.

His regard for Habbaba grew when he entered one day and heard her singing behind a curtain:

Your love, Yazid, almost brought death to me;
Before we met once more, would have destroyed me.

He lifted the curtain and, finding her seated with her face to the wall, realized she had not seen him. He flung himself upon her, and she became very precious to him.

Habbaba was the most beautiful woman of her time; and she combined gentleness and knowledge, together with adroitness in literature, in the use of musical instruments, and in singing, having learned all the singing from such famous singers as Maʿbad, Jamila, Um ʿAwf, and others. Before becoming caliph, Yazid would visit Um ʿAwf and suggest particular verses to her. Now he asked Habbaba to sing them. Habbaba, not wishing to malign Um ʿAwf directly, combated Yazid's devotion for Um ʿAwf by singing as follows:

The heart would have only Um ʿAwf and her love,
An old woman. Whoever loves old women is brought down.

Yazid laughed at this.

"Who," he asked, "made these verses?"

"Malik," she told him.

One day he asked her and Sallama to sing to him what each thought he desired to hear; and, if one of them guessed correctly, she could ask for whatever she wished. Sallama sang first, but was not successful. Then Habbaba sang as follows:

A troop from the Kinana tribe around me
In Palestine, swiftly mounting their steeds.

These were in fact the verses he had in mind, and he told her to ask for whatever she wished.

"I wish you," she said, "to give me Sallama and all her possessions."

"Ask for some other thing," Yazid said. She, though, insisted.

"Very well," Yazid said at last. "You have gained Sallama and whatever she owns."

Sallama was much cast down by this, since she had been such a fine student when studying music with Maᶜbad, who had instructed her in turn to train Habbaba. She reminded Habbaba of this.

"You will see nothing but good," Habbaba told her.

Yazid then asked Habbaba to sell Sallama to him. She freed her accordingly and asked Yazid to betroth himself to her, and he married her. One day the two singers disagreed over a tune improvised by Maᶜbad on two verses of the poet Jarir. Yazid called upon Maᶜbad himself to act as arbiter, telling him he favored Habbaba's argument. And Maᶜbad came down on Habbaba's side.

"You only decided like that," Sallama said, "because of her standing." Then, gazing at the caliph, she said: "Permit me, Prince of the Faithful, to offer him gifts, on account of the debt of gratitude I owe him."

He did so, and Maᶜbad found, in due course, that Sallama's gifts had arrived before Habbaba's. And she went on sending gifts to him till he left.

[The caliph] lavished his time on Habbaba, and on merriment, singing, and drinking. He would, it is said, have a fountain filled with wine; and, whenever he became enraptured with music and singing, he would throw himself into it and rip an outfit costing a thousand dinars.

It is said, too, that when later [in the Abbasid period] the name of his brother, [Caliph] Sulaiman [ibn ᶜAbd al-Malik], came up before [Caliph Haroun] al-Rashid, al-Asmaᶜi said:

"He [Sulaiman] had a ravenous appetite. When the table was laid, he would not wait till the food had cooled but would take the meat with his sleeve."

"And as for his brother Yazid," al-Rashid told al-Asmaᶜi in turn, "he would tumble into wine fully dressed. How much you know of people! By God, I have their clothes here. Sulaiman's sleeves are full of grease, and there are traces of wine in Yazid's clothing."

So Yazid went on. He had assumed the caliphate in succession to ʿUmar ibn ʿAbd al-ʿAziz [see above], may God bless him, when people had become accustomed to justice and reform. Now, as things ceased to run smoothly, people began to find his behavior intolerable, and there was loud protest. His brother Maslama went to him to rebuke and advise him, reminding him of ʿUmar's righteousness. "By God," he is supposed to have replied, " ʿUmar does not need God more than I do."

For some days, accordingly, he turned aside from his concubines and his drinking, sitting there in state for the people.

"I trust," he told Maslama, "you will cease to blame me now."

All this went down badly with Habbaba. She sent for the poet al-Ahwas, who wrote some verses, then summoned Maʿbad, who set them to music. Then she contrived to have the caliph hear the verses sung. According to one version, she crossed his path as he was going out to pray. According to another, she bribed one of the caliph's favored servants to let her stand where the caliph would hear her as she sang al-Ahwas's verses.

The caliph was quite enraptured.

"Tell Maslama," he said (another version has it that he stipulated the chief of police), "to lead the people in prayer." And he cursed anyone who condemned him for this. Then he returned to his former self-indulgent ways.

The verses Habbaba sang spoke of love and of the glory of the caliph. The following is an example:

If you do not love, have not known passion,
Then be a stone cut from the heaviest rock.
Life is simply what you desire, enjoy,
Even when those who hate life blame you . . .
A noble man of the Quraysh,
His sway acknowledged in youth and manhood,
He gave money for praise; and he is
An imam of guidance, does what he's accustomed to.
He inherited glory from his father and grandfather,
Who inherited a well-built citadel of glory . . .

"Who wrote this?" Yazid asked Habbaba when he heard the poem sung.

"Al-Ahwas," she replied.

So he summoned al-Ahwas and presented him with gifts.

When Habbaba sang him this song, his passion would well up.

"Well done, my love," he would say. "Make me soar aloft!"

"And to whom," Habbaba would say, "will you bequeath the nation?"

"To you!" would come the answer.

One day his passion for her grew so great that he said: "I appoint you caliph, and I appoint such and such to be your deputy."

"I dismiss him forthwith," she said.

"I appoint him," he said, "and you dismiss him?"

He stormed off, but she took it lightly enough.

As the day wore on, he summoned one of her servants and asked him what Habbaba was doing.

"She is playing with her trinkets," the servant answered.

"If you will have her pass by me here," the caliph said, "I will give you whatever you wish."

The servant went and sported with her for a while, then he snatched one of her trinkets and ran off. She pursued him and, in due course, passed by where the caliph was. He leaped up and embraced her.

"I have appointed him," he said.

"And I dismiss him!" she replied.

They made up and were happy again together. Then, one day, he said:

"I have been told no one can know pure happiness for a whole day. I wish to test this out."

Summoning his guards, he instructed them to admit no one. Then he vanished, with Habbaba, into an orchard near al-Ghuta. There he stayed with her in perfect happiness until midday. Then, sporting with her, he threw a pomegranate seed at her, or a grape. She, so it is said, tried to swallow it, but she choked and died. So intense was Yazid's grief that he held her there in his arms for three days, embracing and kissing her, till her state began to change. Severely condemned for this, he gave orders for her to be made ready for burial. He, though, could not stand to pray, and it is said he was borne on people's shoulders. According to another version, Maslama told Yazid he would go in his place, but never did so. Yazid summoned a woman who had been one of Habbaba's servants and took consolation from her closeness. "Here we used to sit," he would tell her, and other such things.

After fifteen days, he was once more gripped by panic and gave orders she should be exhumed. This, though, his brother prevented. "People would suppose," he told Yazid, "that your mind has become unhinged, and they would depose you." Yazid thereupon withdrew the order. According to another version, he did in fact exhume her and was told she had changed.

"I see her today," he is supposed to have said, "better than she was before." Then he died. Still another version has it that he lived on after her for forty days, then died and was buried alongside her. He is the only caliph known to have died for love.

As for Sallama, she survived them, living on into the days of the Abbasid caliph al-Mansour.[1]

From Dawud al-Antaki, *Tazyin al-Aswaq bi Tafsil Ashwaq al-ʿUshshaq* (*Adorning the Markets with Tales of Lovers' Longing*), vol. 1, ed. Muhammad al-Tunji (Beirut: ʿAlam al-Kutub, 1993).

1. Al-Mansour was the second Abbasid caliph and ruled from 136 / 754 to 158 / 775.

23

A Ruse of Muʿawiya

Yazid ibn Muʿawiya heard of the beauty of Zainab bint Ishaq, the wife of ʿAbd Allah ibn Salam the Qurashi. She was indeed one of the most beautiful women of her time, and also one of the most learned and one of the wealthiest. He became enchanted by her. When at last he could bear the situation no longer, he mentioned the matter to one of his father's entourage, a man named Rafiq, who in turn divulged it to Muʿawiya.

"Yazid," he told Muʿawiya, "has come to feel the deepest longing for her."

Muʿawiya sent for Yazid and asked him about this, and Yazid told his father of his agonized passion.

"Have patience, Yazid," Muʿawiya said.

"How can you instruct me to patience," Yazid asked, "when there is no hope?"

"Where then," Muʿawiya asked, "is your chivalry, your serenity, your piety?"

"If anyone," Yazid rejoined, "could have profited from piety in his passion, or from wisdom in thrusting away what was afflicting him, then would David [the King of Israel] not have done it?"

"Hide your suffering, son," Muʿawiya said. "You will gain no profit from making your state known. God will do with you as He wills. What will be will be."

Muʿawiya began, even so, to scheme how Yazid might attain his desire, writing to Zainab's husband, ʿAbd Allah ibn Salam, who was his viceroy in Iraq.

"When my letter reaches you," he told him, "come [to Damascus] for a reason that, God willing, will bring you great profit. Do not linger."

ʿAbd Allah quickly came, and Muʿawiya lodged him in a house he had had specially prepared for him.

Now at this time Muʿawiya had two dignitaries as his guests, Abu Huraira and Abu ʾl-Dardaʾ.

"God," he told them, "has divided this world among His worshippers and has granted them many blessings, for which they should be thankful and that they should preserve. On me He has bestowed the highest honors and the most illustrious name. He has granted me wealth and made me the guardian of His people, His trusty ruler in His lands, and the judge of His worshippers, to try me and see if I should prove thankful or blasphemous. The first thing needful is to inquire into the state of those under him.

"I have a daughter who has come of age, and I wish to give her in marriage. I must therefore seek a suitable husband for her, so that the one who rules after me will do the same; for it might be he would allow the devil to dictate his course—that he would keep the girls of the family unmarried, thinking no one suitable for them. In the case of my daughter, it would please me if—on account of his piety, his honor, his good deeds, his chivalry, and his learning—she were to marry Ibn Salam the Qurashi."

"You," they answered, "are the one most able to safeguard God's gifts, to give Him thanks for them and seek His blessings."

"Then," Muʿawiya said, "make this known to him on my part. I also mean to give her the right to choose for herself. I hope, though, she will not make a choice different from my own."

They left him, went to ʿAbd Allah ibn Salam, and told him what had taken place. As for Muʿawiya, he went to his daughter.

"If," he told her, "Abu ʾl-Dardaʾ and Abu Huraira should come and speak to you of ʿAbd Allah ibn Salam, urging you to heed my wish forthwith, tell them this: 'He is a worthy nobleman and a near relative, but he is married to Zainab bint Ishaq. I fear I shall fall prey to jealousy like other women, then do what will anger Almighty God and so receive His punishment. No, I will not marry him till he divorces her.' "

When Abu ʾl-Dardaʾ and Abu Huraira met with ʿAbd Allah and told him what Muʿawiya had said, he told them to return to Muʿawiya and ask for his daughter's hand. This they did.

"You are well aware," Muʿawiya said, "how acceptable he is to me, how eager I am to have him marry my daughter. But, as I told you, I leave the choice to her. Go to her now and let her know what I intend for her."

They went to her and told her, and she answered as her father had instructed her. They then went back to ʿAbd Allah and informed him how matters stood.

When it struck him that nothing stood between him and marriage to her except divorcing Zainab, he made them witnesses to the divorce, then sent them back to Muʿawiya's daughter. They went to Muʿawiya, too, and told him how ʿAbd Allah had divorced his wife so as to marry Muʿawiya's daughter. He made a show of displeasure.

"His divorce of his wife," he told them, "displeases me. I do not find it good. Still, go in peace, then come back to receive [my daughter's] consent."

They left, then returned to him. And he commanded them to go in to his daughter and receive her consent.

"It is not for me," he told them, "to force her. I have left the choice in her hands."

They went in and told her how ʿAbd Allah had divorced his wife in order to please her; and they mentioned his good qualities and his noble lineage.

"He holds a lofty position among the Quraysh," she said. "I will make inquiry about him till I know his innermost qualities, then inform you how God has inspired me. There is no power save in God."

"May God," they answered, "guide your steps in the right path and make the choice for you."

With that they left her and told ʿAbd Allah what she had said.

People began to gossip about ʿAbd Allah's divorce of Zainab and his approach to marry Muʿawiya's daughter. He was, they said, to blame for divorcing his wife so hastily, before making sure the engagement would actually take place.

ʿAbd Allah now urged Abu ʾl-Dardaʾ and Abu Huraira to obtain an answer from Muʿawiya's daughter. They went to her.

"Do as you intend," they said, "and seek guidance from God. He will guide whoever asks."

"I trust," she said, "that God has indeed chosen for me. I have inquired most closely about ʿAbd Allah and find he does not suit me, does not meet my requirements. Those I consulted differed in their opinion. Some advised me against marrying him, while others urged me to proceed. It was their disagreement I found displeasing."

When they told ʿAbd Allah what she had said, he realized he had been deceived.

"God's will," he said, "is sovereign, and what is destined cannot be averted. Even when a man has grown wise, when his mind has found serenity and his judgment been nourished and proved, no opinion or wile of his can thrust away his fate. Perhaps, though, their present happiness will not last. Perhaps the consequences will haunt them."

Word of what had been done to him spread everywhere, becoming common knowledge among the people. "Muʿawiya," they said, "tricked him into divorcing his wife, when all he wanted was to have her for his son." There was no question they found his deed hateful.

The ruse had indeed worked to perfection, but fate took a contrary hand. When Zainab's period of waiting was over,[1] Muʿawiya sent Abu ʾl-Dardaʾ to Iraq to ask for her hand for his son Yazid. Abu ʾl-Dardaʾ journeyed as far as Kufa, where al-Husayn ibn ʿAli was then living, and turned aside to visit al-Husayn. When he was there with him, al-Husayn asked him why he had come [to Iraq].

"Muʿawiya," Abu ʾl-Dardaʾ told him, "has sent me to ask for the hand of Zainab bint Ishaq, for his son Yazid."

"I myself," al-Husayn told him, "wished to marry her, and I had planned, when her time of waiting was over, to send to ask for her hand. What held me back was the need to find someone like you as my envoy, and now God has sent you. Do, I ask you, request her hand on his behalf and mine, and let her decide which one of us God wishes her to take. May God be merciful to you. This trust will weigh upon you till you fulfill it. I will give as large a dowry as Muʿawiya will do for his son."

Abu ʾl-Dardaʾ agreed to this.

"Madam," he told Zainab, when he had entered her presence, "God has created all things with His power and formed them with His might; has fashioned the fate of all things and accorded every fate a reason. None can evade God's destined will or elude His decision. It may be that what happened to you, the fate that befell you in being divorced from ʿAbd Allah ibn Salam, will bring you no harm but rather great profit. For the prince of this nation, the son of its king and his successor to the throne, Yazid ibn Muʿawiya, has sent me to ask for your hand. And so, too, has al-Husayn, son of the daughter of the Prophet, peace be upon him, and master of the young men of Paradise. You know the greatness of these two lofty persons, their luster and their goodness. I have come to ask for your hand. Choose which of them you wish to take."

She was silent for a long time.

"Abu ʾl-Dardaʾ," she said at last, "had this thing come upon me in your absence, I would have sent messengers to you to ask your opinion and would have made no decision without you. Now that you yourself are the messenger, I shall place the matter in your hands and pass on the decision, after God, to you. Choose for me now, whichever is more pleasing to you, and, as God is our witness, discharge this after all due reflection, letting

---

1. See note on page 88.

no personal feeling hold you back from a just judgment. You are not ignorant of their qualities, nor are you insensible to the task with which I am entrusting you."

"Madam," he answered, "my mission is only to let you know of these things. The choice is for you to make."

"God forgive you," she said, "I am the daughter of your friend and brother and cannot act without your help. Do not hold back, for fear of anyone, from speaking the truth on this matter. It is your duty now to fulfill the trust I have placed in you. It is God we should truly fear and please. He knows us all and is merciful to us all."

When he saw no course but to give his own opinion, he said:

"Daughter, the son of the daughter of the Prophet, peace be upon him, is nearer to my heart and more suitable in my eyes. Only God, even so, knows which of the two is better for you."

"He is the one I choose," she said, "the one I wish for and accept."

Al-Husayn married her accordingly, bestowing a large dowry on her. When Muʿawiya heard of this, he was enraged and blamed Abu ʾl-Dardaʾ in scathing terms.

"If a man sends a blind simpleton," he said, "he will end up with the opposite of what he wanted!"

Muʿawiya then dismissed ʿAbd Allah ibn Salam and cut off all his income, because ʿAbd Allah had maligned him and accused him of trickery. And he went on treating him with relentless harshness till ʿAbd Allah, his wealth much reduced, could endure no more and returned to Iraq.

Before ʿAbd Allah divorced Zainab, he had entrusted her with a large amount of money and a great quantity of gems. Now, though, he suspected she might deny this, given that he had treated her so badly, divorcing her for no fault of her own.

He met with al-Husayn and greeted him.

"You know," he told him, "of what has taken place between me and Zainab. But I left some money in her care and did not take it back."

He went on to speak highly of her, then said:

"I would ask you to remind her of this and urge her to return my money."

When al-Husayn went to her, he told her:

"ʿAbd Allah ibn Salam came to me, and he was profuse in his praise of you, making clear what a good companion you had been and how honestly you had always behaved. This pleased me and made me happy. He mentioned, too, that he had entrusted some money to you. I ask you to justify his trust and return his money to him. He has done no more than speak the truth and ask for his right."

"What he said is true," she replied. "He entrusted me with some money, I do not know how much. I will return it to him sealed as he gave it."

Al-Husayn commended her for this.

"It would be best, I think," he went on, "for me to have him come in to you, so you can show him the sum entire, just as he gave it to you."

He then met with ʿAbd Allah.

"She did not deny possession of your money," he said, "and told me it is still sealed as you gave it. Go in to her and take your money back in person."

"Will you not," ʿAbd Allah asked, "charge some other person to bring my money to me?"

"No," al-Husayn said, "you must receive it from her as you gave it."

Al-Husayn went in to her chamber.

"Here is ʿAbd Allah," he said. "He has come to redeem the trust he placed in you."

She produced the bag of money and placed it in ʿAbd Allah's hands.

"Here," she said, "is your money."

ʿAbd Allah thanked her and praised her. When al-Husayn left at this point, ʿAbd Allah broke the seal on his bag and tried to give her some of the money it contained.

"Take this," he said, "as a small gift from myself to you."

The two burst into tears at the disaster that had befallen them, till at last their voices could be heard outside. At this al-Husayn, filled with compassion and tenderness, went in to them.

"As God is my witness," he said, "I divorce her. God, You know I married her neither for her money nor for her beauty, but only to give her the chance to return to her husband."

ʿAbd Allah thereupon asked her to give al-Husayn back the dowry he had paid. She agreed to this, but al-Husayn would not take it.

"All I wish for," he said, "is God's recompense. That is better for me."

When her period of waiting was over, ʿAbd Allah remarried her. As for Yazid ibn Muʿawiya, God had forestalled his marriage to her.

From al-Nuwairi, *Nihayat al-Arab* (*The Highest Aspiration*); in *Qisas al-ʿArab* (*Stories of the Arabs*), vol. 4.

24

Caliph ʿUmar and the Soldier's Wife

ʿAbd al-Razzaq said, following Ibn Juraij:

[Caliph] ʿUmar [ibn al-Khattab], may God be pleased with him, was making one of his rounds of Mecca by night [to assure himself all was well with his subjects]. He heard a woman say:

The night is long and dark,
And no beloved with whom to divert myself.
But for the fear of God beyond compare,
The sides of this bed would be squeaking.

"What is troubling you?" ʿUmar asked her.

"Months back," she told him, "you sent away my beloved husband. Now I long for him."

"Have you done any wrong?" ʿUmar asked her.

"God forbid!" she replied.

"Restrain yourself," ʿUmar told her. "It will be for a short time only, till a message reaches him."

He sent for the man. Then he entered the room of his daughter Hafsa, may God be pleased with her.

"I have come," he said, "to consult you on a matter that has troubled me greatly. I wish you to resolve it for me. How long can a woman stay without feeling the need of her husband?"

Hafsa, bowing her head in modesty, made no answer.

"God," ʿUmar told her then, "does not hold back from the truth."

Hafsa made a sign with her hands, to show that the time would be three or four months. ʿUmar thereupon decreed that the armies should be kept from home for no longer than four months.[1]

From *The Life of the Prophet's Companions* (*Hayat al-Sahaba*), vol. 1, ed. Muhammad Yusuf al-Kandahlawi (Beirut: Dar al-Maʿrifa, 1986).

1. This early acknowledgment of women's sexual rights raises the question whether this was perhaps the earliest *official* acknowledgment of such rights, at least among adherents to monotheistic religions.

25

Al-Akhtal Imprisoned in a Church

Ishaq ibn ʿAbd Allah said:[1]

As a young man I went with my father to Damascus, and there I wandered among its churches and mosques. As I entered one of the churches, I found al-Akhtal imprisoned there and couldn't take my eyes off him. He asked about me and was told of my lineage. Then he addressed me.

"Young man," he said, "you're of noble birth. I wish to ask a favor of you."

"Your request is granted," I answered.

"The priest," he said, "has imprisoned me here. Would you ask him to set me free?"

I went to the priest and told him who I was. He welcomed and honored me. Then I said:

"I have a request to make of you."

"And what is that?" he asked.

"To free al-Akhtal," I replied.

"God save you from such as he," the priest said. "A young man like you shouldn't speak on his behalf. He's a vagabond, speaks ill of people's honor, and makes mock of them."

Still I insisted, and, reluctantly, he went with me, leaning on his cane. He stopped in front of al-Akhtal, then raised the cane.

"Enemy of God!" he said. "Will you return to vilifying people and casting slurs on honorable women?"

Al-Akhtal promised repeatedly, his manner humble and downcast:

"No, I will leave my ways."

---

1. Al-Akhtal (Abu Malik, Ghiyath ibn Ghauth of the tribe of Taghlib, 19–90/640–708) was one of the major poets of the Umayyad period.

"Abu Malik," I told him then, "people stand in awe of you and the caliph honors you. Your status is a lofty one among the people. Yet you humble yourself before this man and obey him?"

"It's religion," he answered. "It's religion!"

From al-Asbahani, *Kitab al-Aghani* (*Books of Songs*), 8; in *Qisas al-ʿArab* (*Stories of the Arabs*), vol. 1.

26

A Miserly Governor

Ziyad ibn ʿAbd Allah al-Harithi, a man of the most miserly and harsh ways, was governor of Medina. One day, one of the secretaries sent him several baskets of food, elegantly covered, which arrived after he had eaten.

"What are these?" he asked.

"Baskets of food," he was told, "sent by the secretary such and such."

"People always send things when it's too late!" he said, highly vexed. "Khaitham ibn Malik [his chief of police], go and invite the people of the *suffa*[1] here to eat this."

Khaitham sent the guards to bring them. Then the messenger who had brought the baskets said to the governor:

"If it pleases you, have the baskets opened and see what there is inside them."

The governor ordered they be opened. There revealed was splendid food—chicken, kids, fish, and *khabisa*,[2] along with sweetmeats.

"Take these baskets away," he said then.

When the people of the *suffa* arrived, he told his chief of police:

"Khaitham, give each of them ten lashes, for I have heard they recite the Prophet's traditional teachings in his holy Mosque."

From al-Nuwairi, *Nihayat al-Arab* (*The Highest Aspiration*), 3; in *Qisas al-ʿArab* (*Stories of the Arabs*), vol. 4.

---

1. *Suffa*: originally a place at the back of the Prophet's mosque where poor and homeless followers took shelter.
2. *Khabisa* is a confection made with semolina and pomegranate.

27

All Lies

Al-Jahiz said:

Muhammad ibn Yasir told me the following of a governor in Persia: While [this governor] was busy with his accounts and affairs, having removed himself as far as he could, a poet came to him and recited poetry in his praise and to his glory. When he had finished, the governor told him, "Very good" and ordered his secretary to give the man ten thousand dirhams. The poet was transported with delight.

When the governor saw this, he told him: "I see this instruction has moved you greatly." He then ordered his secretary to give him twenty thousand dirhams, and the poet became almost crazed with glee. When the governor saw his happiness was doubled, he said: "I see your joy doubles as I double my gift." Then he indicated to his secretary to give the man forty thousand.

The poet's heart almost stopped from happiness. When he had recovered himself, he told the governor:

"You are a most generous man, and I know, as long as you see my happiness ever rising, you will raise the reward. But this I cannot accept, for it would be base ingratitude."

With that he asked God to reward the governor and left.

It is said the governor's secretary approached him, saying:

"God be praised, this man would have been happy to have forty dirhams from you, and yet you instruct me to give him forty thousand?"

"Woe to you," the governor answered. "Do you mean to give him anything?"

"Is there some way, then," the man asked, "not to carry out your instruction?"

"Fool!" the governor rejoined. "This man made us happy with some words, and we made him happy with some words. He claimed I was more handsome than the moon, stronger than the lion; that my tongue was sharper than the sword, my judgments more piercing than the spearhead. Is anything he placed in my hand of lasting use? Don't we know he was lying? But he brought us happiness when he lied to us; and we brought him happiness when we ordered rewards for him, even though a mere lie was intended. When all is said and done, lies [were exchanged] for lies and words for words. But to compensate lies with truth, and words with actions, that would be a loss unheard of before."

From al-Jahiz, *The Misers* (*Al-Bukhala'*), Dar al-Kutub, 1; in *Qisas al-ʿArab* (*Stories of the Arabs*), vol. 4.

28

Two Great Musicians

Ziryab learned music at the hands of Ishaq al-Mawsili[1] in Baghdad. Often he took Ishaq's songs by stealth and was guided to a serious understanding of the art, as well as possessing a fine voice, and he came to excel Ishaq without Ishaq's realizing this—until Ishaq suggested to [Haroun] al-Rashid that he would send him an unknown musician, who knew the art of music well but had not yet gained fame. Ishaq told him of this student:

"He is one of your freed slaves, and I have heard he has good manners and a gentle heart. He renders tunes all of his own invention. He will, I believe, come to be an important musician."

"This is what I seek," al-Rashid said. "Bring him, it may be he has what I require."

So Ishaq brought him. When al-Rashid spoke to him, Ziryab always answered in the most composed terms, with the most succinct phrases. Al-Rashid asked him if he was skilled in music.

"Yes," Ziryab replied, "I know well all that others know well, and most of what I know well, they do not. This skill should be kept for your court, reserved for you alone. If you will give me leave, I can sing for you what no ear has heard before."

Al-Rashid ordered Ishaq's lute to be brought in, but Ziryab would not take it.

"I have," he said, "a lute I made myself, fashioned as I saw fit, and can use no other. It is at the door, and, if the Prince of the Faithful will give me leave, I shall ask for it to be brought in."

---

1. Ishaq al-Mawsili was a great Abbasid musician (150 / 767–235 / 850) who sang at the court of the renowned Abbasid caliph Haroun al-Rashid (170 / 786–193 / 809).

Al-Rashid gazed at Ziryab's lute (which was very like the one brought in to him).

"And what held you back," he asked, "from using the lute of your mentor?"

"If," Ziryab answered, "my lord would like to hear my mentor's singing, that I will do on his lute; but if he wishes to hear my singing, then it must be accompanied by my own lute."

"To me," al-Rashid said, "the two seem exactly the same."

"Sire," Ziryab answered, "their appearance would suggest so. But my lute, though fashioned to the same proportions and using the same wood, weighs only one third of his lute."

Thereupon he described his own lute in a way that aroused al-Rashid's admiration. He ordered Ziryab to sing, and he sang:

Oh King, oh blessed King,
People come seeking you.

When he had sung for al-Rashid, the latter was quite delighted and told Ishaq:

"By God, had I not known you to be truthful, and heard you say you had never heard this before, I should have punished you for leaving this man unknown to me. Take him and care for him till I have time [to attend to the matter]. I have good intentions for him."

Ishaq was nonplussed by this and stirred up by an envy too strong for him to control. When alone with Ziryab, he told him:

"Now, ʿAli, envy is the oldest of human ills, and life on earth is bewitching, and competition in art arouses an enmity none can quell. You deceived me about your fine music, how skilled it was, and all the while I was seeking your profit. Now I have eased myself out from my secure place, and very soon my status will fall while yours will rise—a state of affairs to which I cannot reconcile myself, even though you are like a son to me. Were it not for my loyalty as your mentor, I should end your life without further ado, come what may.

"So, choose one of two things, with no other course permitted. Either you go away from me into the wide world, so that I hear no more of you—you must promise me that with the most sacred oaths, and I will help you with anything you may need, money and other things—or you stay in spite of me and against my wishes, leaving yourself an open target. Take care, for I shall not let you be and shall not hold back from having you killed, paying for it with my wealth and my body. So, make your decision."

Ziryab chose to flee and left at once, knowing Ishaq was well capable of carrying out his threat. Ishaq helped him to this end, giving him enough to support him. Ziryab left, his destination the far western regions of the Muslim world [i.e., Muslim Spain]. Then, at last, Ishaq's mind could be at rest.

When al-Rashid had finished with a matter needing all his attention, he told Ishaq to bring in Ziryab.

"But where am I to find him, Prince of the Faithful?" Ishaq answered. "He is a crazed young man, who claims that the jinn speak to him and nourish him with what he needs to excel in his singing, so that he sees no one in this world equal to him. When the Prince of the Faithful's reward did not arrive swiftly, he supposed this was meant to belittle him and make light of his art, and he left in anger, wandering the world, I have no knowledge where. Almighty God has aided the Prince of the Faithful, for this man is afflicted with a madness that threatens to break all bounds, striking terror in all who see him."

Al-Rashid trusted what Ishaq had said.

"Whatever he is," he said, "we had great pleasure from him."

Ziryab went on to Spain. [Emir] ʿAbd al-Rahman ibn al-Hakam knew of him and wrote to those governing under him that they should treat the man well and have him come to Cordova, instructing, too, that he should be met with mules and good equipment. Arriving at night with his family, Ziryab was given one of the best houses, equipped with all he needed, and presented with gifts from the emir, who also assigned a salary for him and gave him houses and possessions in Cordova and its orchards to the value of forty thousand dinars. When the emir had given him all he wished for and felt he had pleased him and assured his acquiescence, he summoned him. And when he heard his singing, he left all other singing and loved him dearly, promoting him above all other singers.

From Lisan al-Din ibn al-Khatib, *Nafh al-Tib fi Ghusn al-Andalus al-Ratib (Emitted Fragrance from the Moist Branches of al-Andalus)*, vol. 2; in *Qisas al-ʿArab* (*Stories of the Arabs*), vol. 4.

29

An Attendant of al-Hallaj Fasts for Fifteen Days

I was informed by Abu ʾl-Hasan Ahmad ibn Yusuf al-Azraq as follows:[1]

I had heard how [the Sufi leader] Husain ibn Mansur al-Hallaj would eat nothing for a month or more, and he was being closely watched, too. I was amazed at this; and, since there was a friendship between me and Abu ʾl-Faraj ibn Rauhan the Sufi, a pious and devout traditionalist whose sister was married to Qasri, Hallaj's attendant, I asked him about this.

"How Hallaj managed it," he replied, "I have no idea. But my brother-in-law Qasri, his attendant, practiced abstinence from food for years and, by degrees, came to be able to fast for fifteen days, more or less. This he achieved by a means I'd never discovered but that he revealed when he was imprisoned with the other followers of Hallaj.

"'If,' he told me, 'a man's watched closely over a period of time, and no trickery's discovered, then the scrutiny becomes less strict, and, as still no fraud is found, it slackens still further till it becomes neglected altogether, and the person under watch can do as he wishes. These people were watching me for fifteen days and saw me eat nothing in that time. That's the utmost time I can endure hunger; were I to fast one day more, I should perish. Now, take a *ratl*[2] of Khorasani raisins, and another of almonds, pound them to the consistency of oil dregs and make them into thin leaf. Then, when you come to me tomorrow, place it between two leaves of a notebook, which you should carry openly in your hand but rolled up so that what's inside should neither break nor be seen. When you're alone with me, and see there's no one watching, put it under the tails of my coat and leave

1. Al-Hallaj (ca. 244 / 858–309 / 922) was a prominent figure in the early period of Sufi mysticism. During this time Sufism faced mounting hostility from mainstream Islam, and al-Hallaj himself was eventually arrested and executed.
2. A weight measurement.

me. Then I shall secretly eat the cake and drink the water I use to rinse my mouth for ablution, and that will last me a further fifteen days, after which you'll bring me a second supply in the same way. If those people watch me during the third fortnight, they'll find I really do eat nothing before you pay your regular visit with supplies, and then I shall elude their watch once more, and so remain alive.' "

He followed these instructions (the narrator went on) all the time the man was in prison.

••••• •••••

From Abu ʿAli ʾl-Muhassin al-Tanukhi, *Nishwar al-Muhadara wa Akhbar al-Mudhakara* (*Snippets of Conversation and Memorable Tales*).

30

A Vizier Removes a Dessert Stain with Ink

I was told this story by Abu Ishaq ibn Abu ʾl-Dahhak, who was known as al-Dinari because his mother came from Dar Dinar in Baghdad. Abu ʾl-Qasim ʿAli ibn Muqla[1] *told me the same anecdote, in much the same words:*

The vizier Abu ʿAli ibn Muqla, who was also a fine calligrapher, was having a meal one day. The dining table was cleared. As he was washing his hands, he saw on his garment a yellow stain from the sweet dessert he had just been eating. He opened the inkpot, dipped his finger in it, and let a drop of ink fall on the spot, till the spot had been wiped out, replaced by the ink mark.

"That first," he said, "was a shameful stain, because it was a mark of gluttony. But this one is a sign of craftsmanship."

Then he recited the following lines of verse:

Saffron is fragrance for young women,
But ink is the perfume for men.

From Abu ʿAli ʾl-Muhassin al-Tanukhi, *Nishwar al-Muhadara wa Akhbar al-Mudhakara* (*Snippets of Conversation and Memorable Tales*), vol. 3.

---

1. Ibn Muqla (273 / 886–328 / 940) is the reputed inventor of the first cursive style of Arabic script (known as *nashki*). An apparently inveterate political intriguer, he was appointed vizier, and dismissed, three times, ending his life in prison.

31

How a Baghdadi Chief of Police Questioned Suspects

I was told this story by Abu ʾl-Qassem Bahloul ibn ʿAli Abu Talib al-Qadi Muhammad ibn Ahmad ibn Ishaq ibn Bahloul al-Tanukhi, who heard it from the administrator of the Bab al-Sham quarter in the west of Baghdad:

When I worked as a police officer with Abu ʾl-Hassan al-Abzaʿji, the chief of police in Baghdad, he once brought out twenty thieves from prison and sought the caliph's permission to have them crucified near the bridge. Permission was granted, and al-Abzaʿji gave orders for them to be crucified in the early evening, instructing my unit to keep watch over them.

"Stay by these criminals through the evening and night," he said. "Tomorrow I'll have their heads cut off."

We spent the night asleep, and so did our unit commander. One of the thieves thereupon seized his chance, cut his bonds, and came down from the cross. We heard his footsteps, but he was already on the run. The commander and I ran after him, but we couldn't catch him. Then, fearing the other thieves might see what had happened and do the same, we hurried back and sat down, anxious and downcast.

"Al-Abzaʿji," our commander said, "isn't one to accept excuses or overlook mistakes. He'll think one of the thieves bribed me so he could get free and escape. He'll have me beaten till I confess, and if I don't, he'll go on and flog me to death. What am I going to do now?"

"Run off," I said.

"And how and where," he said, "am I going to live then?"

"Listen to me," I told him. "It's midnight now, and no one realizes what's happened. Let's go around. We might come across some unlucky man fated to die. We'll tie him up, crucify him, then tell the chief he can have the twenty convicts he left with us."

"That sounds good to me," he said.

And so we started wandering around. We took the road to the bridge over the Tigris River, and there we spotted a man relieving himself under the bridge. We went down and arrested him.

"What's up with you people?" the man shouted. "What have I done wrong? I'm just a boatman. This is my skiff, look here!"

We started beating him, telling him he was the thief who'd run away from the place of execution. We led him off to where the other convicts were and put him up alongside the rest, in place of the runaway thief.

All night he went on crying and wailing. We felt sorry for him. It was just his bad luck, we thought, but what could we do?

Next morning, Al-Abzaʿji rode off to the prison and came close by the crosses, ready to have the criminals executed.

"Hey," the boatman shouted, "you, the top man! You'll be answerable to Almighty God! Get me down and listen to me. I'm not one of the thieves you want to put to death. I've been trapped into this, it's totally unjust."

The police chief had him brought down.

"What do you have to say to me?" he asked.

The boatman told him exactly what had happened. The chief summoned us.

"Who is this man?" he asked.

"We've no idea what he's talking about," we said. "You left twenty men with us, and here they are."

"You took money from one of the wrongdoers," he said, "and let him go. Then you came across this innocent stranger and arrested him."

"We didn't! This is one of the thieves you handed over to us."

The chief issued orders for the nineteen criminals to be executed, but kept the boatman to one side. Then he instructed all the prison guards to be brought in front of him.

"Is this man one of the twenty wrongdoers we arrested?" he asked.

They took a close look at the man, then said, all together, that he wasn't.

Al-Abzaʿji pondered for a time. Then he gave orders for the boatman to be set free. The man went off, but was then brought straight back to the chief, who asked him to tell his story again. The man repeated what he'd said before.

"And what were you doing just there, at midnight?" the chief asked.

"I was fast asleep in my boat," the man said, "when nature called. So I went up on to the bank and relieved myself."

Once more the police chief pondered for a time. Then he said to the boatman:

"Tell me the truth, and nothing but the truth, and I'll set you free right away. What were you doing there?"

The man repeated his account.

It was al-Abzaʿji's habit, when he wanted to force a confession from someone, to place him between two men holding canes behind their backs. If the accused man scratched his head, he'd get a mighty blow on the back. Then the police chief would yell at the one with the cane: "God cut your hand and leg, you scoundrel! Who told you to do that to this man here? Why did you hit him? Come over here. You, poor fellow, I've spared your life this time." If the offender admitted his guilt, the chief would settle the case in one way or another. But if the man should hesitate, or scratch his head, once, twice, three times more, he'd be thrashed harder and harder, while the chief stepped in every so often with threats and promises.

That was exactly how the boatman was handled, till at last he collapsed and spoke pleadingly to the chief.

"Do you," he asked, "promise me safety and security, in soul and body, if I tell you the truth?"

"Yes," said al-Abzaʿji, "I do."

"I'm a boatman," the man said, "well known among my neighbors for good manners and good conduct. Yesterday, after dark, I was steering my boat alongside the Tuesday market to enjoy the moonlight scene. A servant came out from a house I'm not familiar with, and, as I came closer to the bank, he showed me a pretty, well-dressed woman and two little girls. He gave me a few dirhams and told me to take them to Bab al-Shamasiyya.

"We moved smoothly on for a while, toward the place. When the woman took off her veil, I was enchanted by her lovely face and felt a desire for her. I raised the oars and fixed them to the sides of the boat, and the waves drove us to the middle of the river. I touched the woman and tried to make love to her, but she fended me off and started shouting. So I warned her, if she didn't stop shouting and resisting, I'd drown her in the river. She stopped shouting at that, but, in spite of all my attempts to force myself on her, she kept fighting back.

" 'Who are these girls?' I asked.

" 'My daughters,' she said.

" 'Which one do you love more?' I asked, holding one of the little girls up. 'Let me do what I want, or I'll drop her in the water.'

" 'Whatever you do,' she said, 'I won't give in.'

"I flung the girl in the water, and the woman started wailing. I slapped my hand over her mouth, and, to confuse anyone who might have heard her screaming in the darkness, I shrieked out: 'Over my dead body. I'm not divorcing you!'

"She fell silent again and started weeping. I let her go on for a while, then came back to her.

" 'Let me have what I want,' I said, 'or I'll throw the other girl in.'

" 'I won't let you, by God,' she said.

"I took hold of the second girl and flung her in the water. Then I turned to the woman.

" 'You've nothing left now,' I said. 'Either you let me do it, or you get killed right now.' And I seized hold of her hand and lifted her up to hurl her down in the water.

"She gave in at last. I laid her down in the boat, forced myself on her, then started steering the boat toward the place where I was supposed to go. After a while, though, I realized that once she arrived there, or back at her house, she'd tell people what had happened, and then I'd be chased and caught and killed. So I grasped her hands and legs and flung her into the river.

"After I'd drowned her, I plunged into deep thought, realizing the enormity of my misdeed, the gravity of my crime. I felt like a drunken man who's just come to, filled with repentance and guilt. The only thing I could do now, I thought, was to go down to Basra and hide among the rivers there. So I moved on, then, as I approached the bridge, I felt a call of nature. I'd get out and relieve myself, I thought, then go back to my boat. And while I was doing it, these guards attacked me and put me under arrest."

Al-Abzaʿji gazed casually at the boatman, with a satisfied air.

"Under the circumstances, man," he said, "you're no affair of ours and we're no affair of yours. You can go off now."

Supposing, naively, that the case was closed, the man turned to leave. The chief yelled after him:

"Where are you going, young man? Come back here! You can't leave till you've given us your oath you'll never do anything like this again."

The man came back.

"Now take him," the chief said, "and cut off his hand."

"But, sir," the man pleaded, "you guaranteed my safety and security."

"Safety and security," al-Abzaʿji said, "for a mad dog like you? After you've killed three living human beings, committed adultery, and disturbed the public peace?"

The man's hands were severed, his head cut off, and his body burned there and then.

From Abu ʿAli ʾl-Muhassin al-Tanukhi, *Nishwar al-Muhadara wa Akhbar al-Mudhakara* (*Snippets of Conversation and Memorable Tales*), vol. 3.

32

God Alone Be Thanked

Al-Hajjaj[1] had some wrongdoers brought before him and ordered that they be beheaded. When the time came for the early evening prayer, just one of them remained. He told Qutaiba ibn Muslim: "Take him away with you and bring him back tomorrow."

Later Qutaiba said:

"I went out with the man. As we were going on our way, he asked me:

" 'Do you feel inclined to a charitable deed?'

" 'And what might that be?' I asked.

" 'By God,' he replied, 'I've made no rebellion against the Muslims, nor wished to fight with them. You've seen what I became drawn into. But I have money and other things entrusted to me. If you'd agree to set me free, and let me go to my family and return everything to its owner, then make my will, I promise to return and place my hand in yours.'

"Astonished at his request, I laughed and continued on our way. But he repeated the request, adding:

" 'I vow before God to return to you.'

"I couldn't but grant his request, and told him: 'Go!'

"As he vanished from sight, fear took hold of me. How had I let myself do this? When I reached my family, I was in great distress. They asked me what was making me so anxious, and I told them.

" 'You've been bold with al-Hajjaj,' they said.

"We spent the longest of nights, but, as the dawn call to prayer sounded, there was a knock at the door. I went out, and there was the man.

" 'You've come back!' I exclaimed.

---

1. Al-Hajjaj (d. 95 / 714) was a key provincial governor under the Umayyad dynasty. A man of probity, he was also noted for the severity of his methods.

" 'God be praised,' he answered. 'I gave you my word, taking God as my witness. Would I betray you and not return?'

" 'By God,' I answered, 'I shall strive to help you.' I took him, had him sit at al-Hajjaj's door, and entered.

"When al-Hajjaj saw me, he asked:

" 'Qutaiba, where's your prisoner?'

" 'God be with you, Prince,' I said, 'he's here at the door. But the strangest thing has happened between us.'

" 'And what was that?' he asked.

"I told him the whole story. Then al-Hajjaj asked for the man to be brought in.

" 'Qutaiba,' he said, 'would you like me to give him to you?'

" 'Yes,' I replied.

" 'He's yours,' he said. 'Take him with you.'

"When we'd gone out, I told the man:

" 'Take whichever road you choose.'

"He raised his eyes to the sky, and said: 'God be praised!' But he didn't say a single word to me.

" 'This,' I said to myself, 'must be a madman, by God.'

"Three days later, though, he came to me.

" 'May God,' he said, 'reward you from His bounty. I wasn't mindless of what you did for me, but I couldn't bear to have any of the human race share my praise of God!' "

From al-Kutubi, *Ghurar al-Khasa'is* (*The Finest Attributes*); in *Qisas al-ʿArab* (*Stories of the Arabs*), vol. 3.

33

Al-Hajjaj Orders the Torture of Azadmard

*In a note written by the judge Abu Ja*ʿ*far ibn Bahloul, I found this story that was reported to him by Muhammad ibn Ahmad al-Hashimi:*

The ruler of Iraq, al-Hajjaj ibn Yousuf al-Thaqafi, instructed his assistant, Muhammad ibn al-Muntashir, as follows: "Take Azadmard ibn al-Firand the Zoroastrian[1] and beat his hand and leg till he settles his debts to us."

In a week of courteous discussion (Muhammad said), I managed to recover three thousand dirhams from Azadmard. Al-Hajjaj, though, wasn't satisfied. He brought the man back and handed him over to Maʿad, who was in charge of torture for the government. Maʿad crushed Azadmard's hand and leg but failed to get any more money back from him.

When I was in the market, Azadmard passed me on a mule, his injured limbs wrapped and bandaged up.

"Come closer, Muhammad," he said. I did so.

"When you were charged with this duty before," he said, "you treated me with respect. I paid what I considered reasonable, in good faith and of my own free will. By God, I shall never give out so much as a dirham against my will. That man there owes me three thousand dirhams. If you could kindly recover this money from him, on my behalf, it's yours for the noble work you've done."

"I swear by God," I said, "I'll never take anything from you, seeing the condition you're in."

"Do you know," he asked, "what the people of your religion told me of your Prophet?"

---

1. Being among the "People of the Book," Zoroastrians were permitted to practice their religion openly under Muslim rule.

"No," I replied, "I don't."

"According to them," he went on, "your Prophet said: 'If God wishes people good, He will choose the best of them to be their rulers; and if He wishes harm to them, He will govern them through the worst, and send them untimely rain.'"

And with that Azadmard told the muleteer to move on.

I was still in my place in the market when one of al-Hajjaj's messengers came to say the ruler wished to see me at once. I went to him and found him fuming with rage, his sword unsheathed and set on his lap.

"Come here," he commanded me.

"By God," I answered, "I shall never approach you while you have that sword there ready to use."

Thanks be to God, he gave one of his rare laughs. He sheathed the sword, then asked me:

"What did that heretic say to you?"

"I swear by God," I said, "that I've never cheated you since the time you gave me your trust, or told you any lies since you first placed your confidence in me." And with that I told him the story.

I started to bring up the question of the three thousand dirhams, but he waved it away.

"Say no more about it," he said. "This unbeliever is well informed about the sayings of our Prophet, peace be upon him."

From Abu ʿAli ʾl-Muhassin al-Tanukhi, *Nishwar al-Muhadara wa Akhbar al-Mudhakara* (*Snippets of Conversation and Memorable Tales*), vol. 1.

34

Iyas as Judge

A man gave another some money to keep for him, but the other man denied he had ever been entrusted with it. The first man then took him to Iyas's court, telling Iyas:1

"I gave him some money to keep for me in such and such a place."

"What was in this place?" Iyas asked.

"A tree," the man answered.

Iyas thereupon told the plaintiff:

"Go to the place in question and look at the tree. It may be God will make things clear to you. Or it may be you buried the money beneath the tree, then forgot about it. When you see the tree again, you may remember."

The man went off.

"Sit here," Iyas told the defendant, "till your accuser returns."

Iyas went on with his judicial work, glancing at the man from time to time. Then he asked him:

"Do you think your accuser's reached the place with the tree?"

"No," the defendant answered.

"Enemy of God!" Iyas said. "It's you who are the treacherous one."

The defendant confessed, and Iyas kept him there till his opponent returned. Then he told the other man:

"Take your rightful money from him. He's confessed."

From Muhammad al-Bayhaqi, *Al-Mahasin wa ʾl-Masawiʾ* (*Virtues and Blemishes*) (Beirut: Dar al-Kutub al-ʿIlmiyya, 1999); in *Qisas al-ʿArab* (*Stories of the Arabs*), vol. 1.

1. The judge in question was Iyas ibn Muʿawiya, from the Mazina tribe. Appointed by Caliph ʿUmar ibn ʿAbd al-ʿAziz as judge for the Basra region, he was known for the fairness and mildness of his legal decisions

35

The Wisdom of Judge Iyas

A man placed some money with Iyas's treasurer and went to the Hijaz. When he returned, he claimed it back, but the treasurer denied all knowledge. The man thereupon went to Judge Iyas and told him what had happened.

"Does he know you've come to me?" Iyas asked.

"No," the man said.

"Have you claimed it in the presence of anyone else?" Iyas went on.

"No," the man said.

"Leave then," Iyas said, "and say nothing of this to anyone. Then come back to me in two days."

The man left, and Iyas summoned his treasurer.

"We've received a large sum of money," he said, "and I wish to leave it in your keeping. Is your house secure?"

"Yes," the man said.

"Then arrange for a place to keep the money," Iyas told him, "and for people to fetch it."

The [first] man returned to Iyas, who told him:

"Go to the man. If he gives you the money, then well and good. If he withholds it, tell him: 'I shall inform the judge.' "

The man went to the treasurer.

"Will you give me the money I entrusted to you?" he asked. "If not, I shall make a complaint to the judge."

The treasurer gave him the money, and the man went to Iyas and told him. The treasurer then went to Iyas, who rebuked him, ordering him not to come near him again.

"You traitor!" he concluded.

..... ❦ .....

From Ibn Hujja ʾl-Hamawi, *Thamarat al-Awraq* (*Fruits of Writing*); in *Qisas al-ʿArab* (*Stories of the Arabs*), vol. 1.

36

Why a Judge Pardoned a Fraudster

I was told this story by Abu Ahmad ibn Abu ʾl-Wadr, a sheikh and son of a judge, who heard it from his father. I met him in [A.H.] *349* [971 C.E.]. *He said his father was a close adviser to the judge Abu ʿUmar al-Qadi:*

A man once forged a letter in the name of judge Abu ʿUmar to the governor Abu ʾl-Qassem al-Hiwari, asking for his help and assistance. There was much trust and respect between Abu ʿUmar and al-Hiwari. The man took the forged document to al-Hiwari's office and, having submitted the letter, was asked to wait outside for an answer.

It so happened that judge Abu ʿUmar and I were, on that particular day, paying a courtesy visit to al-Hiwari. The judge, seeing the letter signed with his name, at once realized someone had imposed on him. I saw a brief flash of anger in his face, but I knew from experience that such a prudent and venerable person would not show his true feelings.

"I've just received your letter, Judge," al-Hiwari said, holding it out. "Rest assured the man will be given every possible assistance."

Abu ʿUmar thanked the governor, giving the impression he would indeed never have recommended help had it not been necessary. Shrewd and insightful as he was, he kept his comment general and vague, being unsure of the details of the fraudster's request.

"If the man's still waiting outside," he went on, "have him come in."

The man was brought in, and his face twisted in fear.

"Are you the person," al-Hiwari asked, "who brought this message from our most esteemed judge?"

"Yes, sir," the terrified man replied.

"The governor," said Abu ʿUmar, "may God give him strength, has promised you generous help. Wait outside, will you?"

We spent an hour or so with the governor, in casual chat and small talk. Finally Abu ʿUmar rose and took his leave, then, on his way out, whispered in my ear: "Bring him over."

I hung back, took the man aside, and spoke to him softly and pleasantly. Then I went with him to Abu ʿUmar, who was waiting for us.

"Curse you!" the judge said. "You've forged my handwriting and my signature. You know that whatever I ask for, I get. I protect people's money, reputation, and blood. Suppose Abu ʾl-Qassem were to discover your trick? Wouldn't he cut you in pieces?"

The man began weeping and sobbing.

"I swear by God, your honor," he said, "that what prompted me to this wrongdoing was poverty, hardship, and need. I did it because I had faith in your generosity, and because my misconduct wouldn't affect any verdict or testimony. What I did wouldn't, I thought, do you any harm. I'd benefit myself and be protecting you too."

"My God!" exclaimed Abu ʿUmar. "So it was poverty that drove you to this?"

"I swear by God it was," the man replied.

Abu ʿUmar wept, then called one of his servants and whispered a few words in his ear. The servant left and, after a time, came back carrying a wallet with a hundred dinars and a bag filled with clothes, and handed them to the man.

"This will help you for the present," Abu ʿUmar told the man. "Take it and use these clothes. Go back to al-Hiwari's office, and I'll confirm the earlier recommendation. But give me your pledge you'll never use me fraudulently again."

The man took an oath before Abu ʿUmar, then left. Some months later, he returned on a fine horse and in lavish attire to greet Abu ʿUmar. He began uttering respects and thanks and praying for the judge's health and success. Abu ʿUmar didn't recognize the man till I reminded him of the earlier incident.

"Why are you thanking me?" the judge asked.

"I'm the one," the man said, "who presented the letter to the governor, Abu ʾl-Qassem al-Hiwari, and he provided me with money and rewards. He's given me generous help all this time, till finally I've become what I am now. And since that time I've been invoking God's favor on the honorable judge."

"I can only thank Almighty God," judge Abu ʿUmar said, "that I've served people with such success."

From Abu ʿAli ʾl-Muhassin al-Tanukhi, *Nishwar al-Muhadara wa Akhbar al-Mudhakara* (*Snippets of Conversation and Memorable Tales*), vol. 1.

III

Tales of Danger and Warfare

37

Maʿn ibn Zaʾida and the Black Man

Maʿn ibn Zaʾida said:

When I fled from al-Mansour,[1] it was from the battlefield. I'd spent days in the [burning] sun and thinned my beard and sideburns, and I was wearing a coarse woolen cloak. I mounted a camel and went out toward the desert, but I was pursued by a black man carrying a sword. No sooner had I slipped the guards than this black man caught hold of the camel's nose rope, brought it to its knees, and took me in charge.

"What is it you want?" I asked.

"You are sought," he answered, "by the Prince of the Faithful."

"And who am I," I asked, "that the Prince of the Faithful should seek me?"

"You are Maʿn ibn Zaʾida," he said.

"Fear God, man," I rejoined. "What have I to do with Maʿn?"

"Leave this pretense," he said. "By God, I know you well enough."

"And supposing," I said, "that what you say is true. Here are some jewels I have with me, worth more, many times over, than the prize offered to the man who bears me off to al-Mansour. Take these and don't shed my blood."

"Let me see them," he said.

I let him see them, and he examined them for a time. Then he said: "You're right about their value. But I shan't accept them before asking you something. If you tell me the truth, then I'll release you."

I told him to ask his question.

---

1. Maʿn ibn Zaʾida was one of the most valiant and generous men of his age. He lived during the end of the Umayyad period and the beginning of the Abbasid (which began in 132 / 750). Initially he remained loyal to the Umayyads, and, when Caliph al-Mansour fought the Umayyad loyalist Yazid ibn ʿAmr ibn Hubaira, to whom Maʿn was affiliated, Maʿn fought gallantly at Yazid's side until the latter was killed. Maʿn then fled and was sought by al-Mansour, who eventually pardoned him.

"People," he said, "have spoken of your great generosity. Now tell me, did you ever give away all your wealth?"

"No," I answered.

"Half of it?"

"No."

"A third of it?"

"No."

So he went on till he'd reached a tenth.

"It may be," I said, embarrassed, "that I gave away that amount."

"That's not so much," he said. "I'm a humble man who goes on foot. And I'm taking only twenty dirhams from al-Mansour, while these jewels are worth a thousand dinars. Yet I'm returning them all to you, and sparing your life, too, on account of your famous generosity. You'll know, now, that there are people in this world more generous than you are, and you won't think too highly of yourself. From this time on, think slightly of anything you might do, and don't ever hesitate to perform some noble, generous deed."

With that he threw the bag back to me, released the camel, and made to take his leave.

"Man," I said, "you've put me to shame. The shedding of my blood would have been lighter to me than this thing you've done. I entreat you, take what I gave you. I have no need of it myself."

He laughed at that.

"Did you think," he said, "I was trying to trick you? By God, I won't take it. I'll never take any prize for an act of generosity." And with that he left.

By God, when I was pardoned [by al-Mansour] and felt myself safe, I sought that man, asking anyone who might bring him to me to name his price, but I never heard of him again. It was as though the earth had gaped and swallowed him.

From al-Nuwairi, *Nihayat al-Arab* (*The Highest Aspiration*), 3; in *Qisas al-ʿArab* (*Stories of the Arabs*), vol. 1.

38

Al-Mansour's Pride

When al-Mansour went on pilgrimage, he was shown some jewels of priceless value. Recognizing them, he said:

"These belonged to [Caliph] Hisham ibn ʿAbd al-Malik[1] and were passed on to his son, Muhammad ibn Hisham, the only man left from the Umayyad dynasty. I must seize him."

With that he looked toward his bodyguard al-Rabiʿ.

"When," he said, "I have finished leading prayers tomorrow in the Kaʿba, and when everyone has gathered, close all the doors of the mosque and have them guarded by men you trust. Leave just one door open and stand guard there yourself. Let no one pass unless you know him; and when Muhammad ibn Hisham tries to leave, arrest him and bring him here to me."

Next day, al-Rabiʿ did as al-Mansour had commanded him. Muhammad ibn Hisham was in the mosque and, realizing he was the one sought, was sure he was about to be taken and killed.[2] Confounded, and in clear distress, he was seen by Muhammad ibn Zaid ibn ʿAli ibn al-Husain, who did not know who he was. This Muhammad approached.

"What's troubling you so?" he asked.

"Nothing," came the answer.

"Tell me," Muhammad insisted. "I promise to see you safe."

"Who are you?" ibn Hisham asked.

---

1. Umayyad caliph who reigned from 106 / 724 to 125 / 743.
2. The Abbasids had killed virtually every man of the Umayyad dynasty. The only ones who had escaped were this man and Hisham's grandson, ʿAbd al-Rahman al-Dakhil, who fled to Spain and founded the Umayyad dynasty there.

Muhammad told him his name, and this made ibn Hisham more fearful still. He became mad with fear almost, certain he was about to be killed.[3]

"Have no fear," Muhammad told him. "You have killed neither my father nor my grandfather. I have no vengeance to take against you. I shall strive to save you, God willing. But forgive me, please, for any insult and ill-treatment I might seem to cause you."

"Do whatever you wish," ibn Hisham answered.

With that Muhammad flung ibn Hisham's cloak over his face and pulled him toward the door, till he was close to where al-Rabiᶜ, al-Mansour's bodyguard, was standing. The moment al-Rabiᶜ's eyes fell on them, Muhammad began striking ibn Hisham about the head. Bringing him to al-Rabiᶜ, he said:

"This man's a camel driver from Kufa. He agreed to hire me some camels, then, the moment I'd paid him the due amount, he ran off and hired the camels to some people from Khorasan. I have witnesses against him, and I ask you to send guards to conduct us to the judge, and to hold his camels back from being sent to Khorasan."

Al-Rabiᶜ gave him two guards.

"Stay close by these men," he told them, "till he's with the judge."

Meanwhile, Muhammad kept hold of ibn Hisham's cloak, which hid his face. And so they all left the mosque.

When they had left al-Rabiᶜ far behind, Muhammad said: "Go wherever you wish."

Ibn Hisham kissed his hand and head.

"God alone," he said, "knows where He sends His message." Then he took out some jewels of priceless value, saying: "By God, honor me, son of the Prophet's daughter, by accepting these from my hand."

"Go with your possessions," Muhammad told him. "We are from the Prophet's family and accept no reward for any good deed we might do. Only guard yourself from that man. He is resolved to seek you out."

From Muhammad ibn Ahmad al-Maqqari, *Al-Mukhtar min Nawadir Al-Akhbar* (*Selections from Rare Anecdotes*); in *Qisas al-ᶜArab* (*Stories of the Arabs*), vol. 1.

---

3. Muhammad was the great-grandson of al-Husain ibn ᶜAli who fell in battle with the Umayyads in 62 / 680.

39

With the Byzantines

When [Haroun] al-Rashid began capturing the various [Byzantine] cities and fortresses and destroying them, he came to Heraclea, which was the strongest and best fortified of their strongholds. The people were well entrenched. The gate overlooked a valley and had a ditch all around it. As he was bombarding it ceaselessly with his engines of war, the gate was opened, and one of its men came out in full battle array, calling out:

"Your fighting has been long! Let two of your men come out to meet me."

Still he raised the number, till he had reached twenty men. But no one answered him. He went back inside and closed the gate of the fortress.

Al-Rashid had been asleep and was told of the matter only after the man had gone back inside. He was most angry and regretful at missing [the challenge], blaming his guards for allowing this.

"Because no one took up his challenge," someone said to him then, "he will become more headstrong and overbearing. He will surely come out tomorrow and offer the same challenge."

Al-Rashid's night was long, and the morning found him waiting. The gate opened, and the man came out into a day of burning heat, asking that twenty of the men should face him.

"Who is willing to go out and meet him?" al-Rashid asked.

Most of his leaders answered his call, men of the stamp of al-Hirthama, Yazid ibn Mazyad, ʿAbd Allah ibn Malik, and others, and he decided to send some of them out to face the man. But others, volunteers for jihad, protested, till he heard their protests from afar and allowed twenty of them to approach him. They asked permission to counsel him, and this he granted.

"Prince of the Faithful," their spokesman said, "your leaders are most famous and are celebrated for strength and courage and knowledge in the skills of war. Should one of them go out to meet that unbeliever there, and kill him, that would be nothing great. But if the unbeliever should kill him, it would be a bitter humiliation for the army, a wound never to be healed. It would be best if the Prince of the Faithful permitted us to choose a man to fight the unbeliever. If he should be victorious, those inside the fortress will know that the Prince of the Faithful had their strongest fighter killed at the hands of an unknown common man; and if he should be killed, then it is the martyrdom of a man whose death will not affect the army or cause disquiet to the soldiers; and another like him will go out to meet the Byzantine, and then another, till it is finished."

"I find your counsel good," al-Rashid said.

They chose from among themselves a man called Ibn al-Jazari, known in the vanguard of battle for his fortitude and chivalry.

"Will you go out to meet him?" al-Rashid asked.

"I will," al-Jazari said, "and I shall invoke God's help."

"Give him a horse," al-Rashid said, "a spear, a sword, and a shield."

"I have greater faith," al-Jazari said, "in my own horse, and my spear is more steadfast in my hands. But I accept the sword and the shield."

He donned his battle gear. Al-Rashid called him and bade him farewell, invoking God's blessings on him. Then the man went out to meet the Byzantine with twenty other men from those prepared for jihad.

When they came to the valley, the Byzantine counted their number, then told them:

"I said twenty men, and you have increased the number by one. But it is no matter."

They called to him:

"Only one man will go out to meet you."

When Ibn al-Jazari went out, the Byzantine gazed at him, while most of the other Byzantines stood watching the scene from the fortress, till it seemed [to the Muslims] that all those within the fortress had come to see the fray. Then the two opponents began fighting with their spears. On and on the combat went, with neither so much as scratching the other. Then they laid down their spears and drew the swords from their sheaths, and fought with swords while the heat grew ever more fierce and the two horses began to weaken. Ibn al-Jazari would strike a blow certain, he thought, to win the victory, only to see the Byzantine parry it. His shield was of iron, and made a fearful sound when it was struck.

When each despaired of overcoming the other, Ibn al-Jazari fled, and the Muslims were quite downcast, more than they had ever known, while the Byzantines clamored with joy and pride. Yet it was merely a ruse by the Muslim fighter. The Byzantine followed him, and Ibn al-Jazari contrived to cast a rope that looped perfectly around his neck. Then, galloping, he threw him from his horse, turned toward him, and the Byzantine was slain, his head severed before even he struck the ground. The Muslims' cries of "God is Great!" rose high, and the Byzantines, defeated, withdrew and closed the gate. The news reached al-Rashid, who exclaimed to his leaders:

"Discharge fire from the catapults, on all sides! They are without defense!"

The Muslims did so, placing linen cloth on stones, soaking them with oil, setting them on fire, then hurling them against the walls. The fire would take hold on the walls, which began to weaken and fall. When fire surrounded the whole enclave, they were able to force the gate without fear.

From al-Asbahani, *Al-Aghani* (*Book of Songs*), 17.46; in *Qisas al-ʿArab* (*Stories of the Arabs*), vol. 3.

40

Muslims at the Court of China

Qutaiba ibn Muslim[1] struck deep with his eastern conquests, till he came close to China. The king of China wrote to him, saying:

"Send us one of your noblest men, to tell us of you and answer us concerning your religion."

Qutaiba chose twelve from among his army, all handsome, tall, with strong hair, eloquent, and courageous. He spoke with them and found them wise and able to inspire respect. He ordered they should be equipped with good weapons, good clothes, some of them embroidered, and with soft shoes and perfume, and he sent them off with thoroughbred horses and had them provided with good riding animals.

Among these men was Hubaira ibn al-Mushamraj al-Kilabi, a most eloquent man.

"Hubaira," Qutaiba asked, "what do you intend to do?"

"May God bless the Prince," Hubaira answered, "tell me your wish, and I shall heed it."

"Go with God's blessings," Qutaiba said, "and may success attend you. Do not remove your turbans till you reach that country. When you have an audience with him, let him know I have sworn not to leave till I have trodden their country and taken taxes from them."

They left, with Hubaira at their head, and when they arrived, the king of China sent for them. They entered the bath and left it wearing white clothes over thin garments, putting on perfume and [soft] shoes and cloaks. Then they entered his court, where the greatest of his land were assembled.

---

1. Qutaiba ibn Muslim was a conqueror prince who ruled Khorasan, in Persia, for thirteen years during the reign of al-Walid ibn ʿAbd al-Malik. He attacked the border regions of China and imposed *jizya* taxes on them. He was killed in 96 / 715.

They sat, but no one spoke to them, neither the king nor his entourage. [At last] they rose [and left].

The king asked those present at his court:

"What do you say to these men?"

"We have seen," they replied, "a people no better than women. Their fragrance was apparent to all."

The next day the king sent for them [once more]. They put on embroidered clothes and turbans and went to his court. When they entered, the king ordered them to return, then asked his courtiers:

"What do you say to these men?"

"Now," came the reply, "they seem nearer to men."

On the third day, he sent for them [yet once more]. They wore their weapons, and their helmets and shields, left their canes, and rode their horses. The king of China gazed at them and saw men like walking mountains. When they arrived, they struck the ground with their spears, then came forward, ready to fight. So fearful was their aspect, they were told to return even before they had entered.

They left, carrying their spears and riding their horses, galloping off as if racing their mounts. The king asked his courtiers:

"What do you say to these men?"

They answered:

"We have never seen their like before!"

The king sent to them, telling them to send their leader, the best man among them; and they sent Hubaira to him. As he entered, the king said to him:

"You have all seen the greatness of my empire, and how no one will permit you the upper hand while you are in my country. You are, indeed, like an egg in my palm. But I wish to ask you two questions; and if you do not tell me the truth, I shall kill you."

"Ask then," he said.

"Why did you act as you did, assuming such a different appearance over the three days."

"Our style [of dress] on the first day," Hubaira replied, "was the one we assume within our families, along with the perfumes. Our dress on the second day was the one we assume when we visit our princes. As for the third day, it was the kind we assume for an enemy. When we feel ourselves threatened, we dress in this manner."

"How well you arrange your lives!" the king said. "Return to your leader and tell him to withdraw, for I have come to know how he cherishes his life and how small his army is. If not, I shall send on to you a horde that will lead you and him to perdition."

"How can you say," Hubaira answered, "that his army is small, when the vanguard of his army is in your country and its rearguard in the olive groves [of our homeland]? And how can you claim he cherishes his life, when he has left the opulent life he had and come to invade your country? As for your threat to kill us, we regard our lives as forfeit, and to be slain is the most honorable way to die. We neither hate nor fear such a death."

"What would be pleasing to your leader?" the king asked.

"He has vowed," Hubaira answered, "not to depart till he has trodden the earth of your land and been paid the *jizya*."[2]

"We shall," the king said, "fulfill his vow for him by sending him earth from our country to tread and *jizya* to please him."

Then the king ordered that gold trays should be filled with earth, and he sent them along with silk and gold. He presented, too, gifts of great value to the group, and they left bearing these gifts to Qutaiba. Qutaiba accepted the *jizya* and trod the earth.

From Ibn Jarir al-Tabari, *Tarikh al-Tabari* or *Tarikh al-Umam wa 'l-Muluk* (*History of Nations and Kings*), 8; in *Qisas al-ʿArab* (*Stories of the Arabs*), vol. 3.

2. The *jizya* was a tax levied on non-Muslims, in lieu of military service.

41

Greed and Treason

When Caliph al-Walid ibn Yazid heard that Yazid ibn al-Walid had stirred the hearts of men against him, incited the people of Yemen, and challenged his rule, he withdrew from his companions and summoned one of his servants.[1]

"Go out in disguise," he told him, "and stand by one of the roads, watching those who pass. If you should see an old man in tattered clothes, walking slowly by with his head bent, greet him and whisper in his ear that the Prince of the Faithful wishes to see him. If he answers you at once, then bring him here to me; but if he seems hesitant, then leave him and seek another, till you find a man of the kind I spoke of."

The servant went and brought to him an old man who met the caliph's conditions.

When the man entered al-Walid's presence, he greeted him as custom demanded. Al-Walid ordered him to approach, then gave him time to calm himself. Then, fixing his gaze on him, he asked:

"Are you well qualified to converse with caliphs?"

"Yes, Prince of the Faithful," the man said.

"If you can," al-Walid said, "tell us what this entails."

"Sire," the man answered, "converse means recounting to one who listens, listening to one who recounts, and discussing what is profitable and proper."

"That is well answered," al-Walid said. "I shall test you no further but rather listen to what you have to say."

---

1. Al-Walid ibn Yazid was an Umayyad caliph for around a year following the death of his uncle, Hisham ibn ʿAbd al-Malik, in 125 / 743. He was killed in the rebellions against him and was succeeded (even more briefly) by the Yazid ibn al-Walid mentioned here.

"Indeed, Prince of the Faithful," the old man said. "Yet converse is of two kinds: one kind is to inform about what has been said, and the other is to say what it is the host needs to hear. I have not been told, in the presence of the Prince of the Faithful, which of the two ways I should choose."

"You are right," al-Walid said. "I shall propose to you, then, the path I wish you to follow.

"It has come to our hearing that a subject of ours has sought to harm our reign, and that this has influenced others. This is a painful matter for us. Have you heard of this?"

"Yes, Prince of the Faithful," the old man answered.

"Speak now," al-Walid told him, "according to what you have heard, and tell me how the matter may be remedied."

"I heard once," said the old man, "of something that happened to the Prince of the Faithful ʿAbd al-Malik ibn Marwan.[2] When he chose people to go out with him to fight Ibn al-Zubair in Mecca—may God preserve it—he had ʿAmr ibn Saʿid ibn al-ʿAas accompany him along with the others. But ʿAmr had a wicked intent and evil intentions, and was greedy to usurp the caliphate. Caliph ʿAbd al-Malik had come to know of this but had nonetheless accorded him respect.

"When the Prince of the Faithful was far from [his capital of] Damascus, ʿAmr feigned sickness and asked leave to return to the city. When he entered Damascus, he mounted the pulpit and made a speech to the people, attacking the caliph, and then did the same throughout Damascus, calling on the people to dethrone ʿAbd al-Malik. They did so, giving him their pledge of allegiance. ʿAmr then fortified the walls of the city and defended its territory.

"The news reached ʿAbd al-Malik as he was on his way to fight Ibn al-Zubair. He heard, too, that the ruler of Hims had rebelled against him, and that the people of the border and the coastal towns were now ready to revolt. He summoned his ministers and told them of what he had heard.

" 'ʿAmr,' he said 'has control of Damascus, ʿAbd Allah ibn al-Zubair now rules the Hijaz, Iraq, Yemen, Egypt, and Khorasan, and al-Nuʿman ibn al-Bashir, prince of Hims, and Zufar ibn al-Harith, prince of Palestine, have reneged and sworn allegiance to Ibn al-Zubair.'

---

2. The Umayyad caliph ʿAbd al-Malik ibn Marwan reigned from 65 / 685 to 86 / 705. His campaign against the anticaliph Ibn al-Zubair, a militant opponent of the Umayyad dynasty, resulted in the latter's death in 73 / 692. In contrast to al-Walid ibn Yazid, ʿAbd al-Malik enjoyed a long and notably successful reign.

"When his ministers heard all this, they were utterly confounded. 'Have you nothing to say?' ʿAbd al-Malik asked them. 'I stand in need of your counsel.'

" 'If only,' their leader said, 'I were a bird on a bough in Tihama till these revolts were at an end!'

"When ʿAbd al-Malik heard this, he rose and, ordering them to stay where they were, rode off alone, instructing a band of his bold warriors to follow him at a distance. This they did.

" ʿAbd al-Malik went on and came across a poor, frail old man collecting sumac.[3] He greeted him courteously, putting him at his ease, then said: 'Old man, do you know anything of this army's march?'

" 'Why do you ask?' the old man said.

" 'I am thinking of joining this army.'

" 'I see in you,' the old man said, 'the mark of authority. You should quite forget this idea, for the prince you think to join has had his reign brought to ruin, and the caliphate is like a sea in turmoil!'

" 'It is my heart's desire,' ʿAbd al-Malik said, 'to accompany this prince. Will you guide me with your counsel?'

" 'This disaster fallen on the prince,' the old man said, 'is beyond all bound. I should be loath to see you cast down.'

" 'May God reward you,' ʿAbd al-Malik told him.

" 'If you go to this prince,' the old man said, 'and join his army, mark what he does. If you find him bent on seeking ʿAbd Allah ibn al-Zubair, then shun him. But if you see he has returned whence he came, abandoning the goal he had before, then wish him victory and safety.'

" 'But surely his return to Damascus,' ʿAbd al-Malik said, 'is not more pressing than his campaign against Ibn al-Zubair?'

" 'That appears true enough, I grant,' the old man said. 'But let me solve the puzzle for you. If ʿAbd al-Malik goes to fight Ibn al-Zubair, he takes the form of an oppressor, for Ibn al-Zubair has not leaped to take his throne. But if he should go to ʿAmr ibn Saʿid, he goes in the form of one oppressed, since ibn Saʿid broke the covenant and betrayed his trust, seizing a rule that had never been his or his father's before him, but rather belonged to ʿAbd al-Malik and his father before him. Here ʿAmr is the aggressor.

" 'There is a saying that the fat of the usurper leads to leanness, and the treacherous is dismissed. But let me recount to you a fable that will persuade you and solve the puzzle.

3. The acidic red seeds of the sumac are dried and ground for use as a condiment.

" 'Once, it is said, a fox called Zalim [meaning "oppressor"] had a burrow in which he lived, and that pleased him. One day he went out in search of food and returned to find that a snake had taken the burrow as a hole for itself. He waited for it to come out, but it did not do so, and he realized it had taken the burrow as its home. Since he could not live with the snake, he went in search of a refuge for himself and found, at last, a good-looking burrow in a well-fortified spot with dense trees and flowing water. He liked this burrow, and he was told, on inquiry, that it belonged to another fox called Mufawwad, who had inherited it from his father. Zalim called to him, and the other came out to meet him, welcoming him and inviting him to enter his burrow. When asked about his affairs, Zalim told him of the snake, and Mufawwad felt a deep compassion for him. "Death," he said, "is better than living in shame. I propose you take me to your old home, which was usurped from you, and let me see it. Then we will find some way of regaining it for you."

" 'They went together to the old burrow, and Mufawwad, having gazed at it, told Zalim:

" ' "Come back with me and spend the night at my home, and let me devise some means of resolving this."

" 'They did so, and Mufawwad spent the night in thought, while Zalim, for his part, was admiring Mufawwad's home, noting its qualities, its fortification, and its airiness, till at last he began to covet it. He set himself to devising a ruse to usurp it from Mufawwad and send him into exile.

" 'In the morning, Mufawwad told Zalim:

" ' "I saw that your old burrow is far from water and trees. Why not abandon it and let me help you dig out another burrow in this desirable place?"

" ' "That could never be," Zalim said. "My soul would perish from longing for my old home."

" 'When Mufawwad heard this, of the love he claimed to feel for his old home, he said:

" ' "Let us go, today, and fetch some wood and make it into two bundles. Then, when night falls, let us go to some of those tents and take some fire, then carry the wood and the firebrand to your old home; then let us put the two bundles in the doorway and light them. If the snake comes out, it will be burned; and if it stays inside, it will choke to death."

" ' "A fine idea," Zalim said.

" 'They went and fetched some wood, made it into two bundles, and then, when night fell, Mufawwad went to the edge of the tents and took a brand. [Meanwhile] Zalim took one of the two bundles and hid it, then dragged the other to the entrance of Mufawwad's house and blocked it [with himself inside]—thinking that, when Mufawwad came to his burrow, he would not be able to enter and would have to find another home for himself.

"'Zalim had seen some food in Mufawwad's burrow, which Mufawwad had stored for himself. If, Zalim thought, Mufawwad should come with the firebrand and lay siege to him in the burrow, he could live on this store of food. His greed had quite blinded him to the flaw in his scheme.

"'When Mufawwad came with the firebrand and did not find Zalim, he thought the other must have picked up one of the bundles, to be of assistance, and gone on ahead to his old burrow, where the snake was now living. He himself should, he decided, hurry to catch up with him and help carry the wood.

"'He placed the firebrand next to the [other bundle of] wood, not realizing, in the pitch-darkness, that it was there, totally blocking the entrance. No sooner had he begun to walk from the burrow than the fire caught the wood, making a very thick smoke. Seeing the wood ablaze, he realized Zalim's ruse and knew Zalim was being burned inside the burrow. "This," he said to himself, "comes to him who seeks his own death through crooked ways."

"'When the fire had died down, Mufawwad entered his burrow, brought out Zalim's body, and flung it away, then returned to living in his burrow.

"'This fable I have related to you because it is like what ʿAmr ibn Saʿid has done, in his oppression and treason, to ʿAbd al-Malik. It matches the fox's trick, in taking his kingdom and fortifying it against him.'

"When ʿAbd al-Malik heard the old man's wise words, he said:

"'May God reward you. I should like to see you again at a time we arrange. Tell me where you live, so I can meet with you again.'

"'And what is it,' the old man asked, 'that you want from this?'

"'This,' ʿAbd al-Malik said, 'is so I can reward you for your advice.'

"'I have made a covenant with God,' the old man said, 'never to accept any gift from a miserly man.'

"'And how do you know I am miserly?' ʿAbd al-Malik asked.

"'Because you have held back my reward when you could have given it at once. Why do you not reward me [at once] with what you have?'

"'I swear to you,' ʿAbd al-Malik said, 'it was mere thoughtlessness.' With that he took off his sword, telling the man: 'Accept this from me and take good care of it. Its value is twenty thousand dirhams.'

"'I will not,' the old man said 'accept any reward from a thoughtless man. Leave me to my God, Who is never miserly and never thoughtless. He will suffice for me.'

"These words of the old man aroused great respect in ʿAbd al-Malik, and he recognized his deep piety. 'I am ʿAbd al-Malik,' he told him. 'Let me know, I entreat you, of anything you need.'

" 'I, too, am ʿAbd al-Malik.[4] Let us raise our petitions together, to Him Whose servants we are.'

" ʿAbd al-Malik went on and did as the old man had advised him. Success attended him, and he won the victory over his enemies."

When al-Walid heard what the old man told him, the advice pleased him, and he asked where he had learned it. He was ignorant of the old man's lineage, and, feeling ashamed, he said:

"He who lacks people like you among his subjects is lost indeed."

"Prince of the Faithful," the old man answered, "kings know only those who seek them and stick close to their doors."

"You are right," al-Walid answered. Then he ordered an immediate reward to be given him, and told him to come to him often, so that he could profit from his knowledge and wisdom.

From Ibn Hujja ʾl-Hamawi, *Thamarat al-Awraq* (*Fruits of Writing*), 174; in *Qisas al-ʿArab* (*Stories of the Arabs*), vol. 4.

4. "ʿAbd al-Malik" means "servant of the king." The old man uses *king* to mean God, the King of all mankind.

42

Consequences of Oppression

I was told this story by Muhammad ibn ʿAbdullah al-Ahwazi, who heard it from Abu ʾl-Fadl al-Balkhi, who said it had been reported to him by the qadi of Balkh, al-Khalil ibn Ahmad al-Sijistani:

A battalion commander was sent to our region of Sijistan, with a huge army of soldiers, by Nasr ibn Ahmad, ruler of Khorasan. He took control of Sijistan, and his aides and Khorasani troops began plundering the country. They even molested women in the streets.

People appealed to me and to the legal faqih, putting their grievances to us. We went with them to the army commander—the faqih and I, along with a group of notables—and were given an audience. The faqih, who spoke first, counseled the commander and made it clear to him what was happening.

"My dear sheikh," the commander said, "how can you be so naive? I have with me here thirty thousand soldiers who've left their women behind in Bukhara. What are they supposed to do when lust and desire swell them up? Do you expect them to post their stiff members home to their wives? Aren't they better off putting them in the women here when they feel like it? I'm not going to inflame my men, and set them against me, by denying them this kind of thing. That's all. You can go."

We left accordingly. The crowds, who were waiting for us eagerly, asked: "What did the prince say?"

The faqih repeated what the commander had said, word for word, to the fury of the crowds.

"Those arguments of his are depraved!" they yelled. "He seems to be telling the soldiers to be more debauched than ever. This is a breach of Almighty God's commandments. Do we have the right to oppose him for those words of his?"

"Yes," the faqih replied. "You are justified in opposing him for what he said."

"Will you give us permission to do it?" they asked.

"You have permission," the faqih answered.

The crowds were inspired and full of spirit; and, by the time we had said our early evening prayers, all the Khorasanis had vanished from our town. A great throng of people had gathered, then thrown themselves on the Khorasanis, slaughtering them in vast numbers. The crowd attacked the commander's house, too, and looted it. They wanted his head, but he mounted his horse and fled in panic with those of his troops who were able to escape.

That was the last time we had Khorasani soldiers in our region.

From Abu ʿAli ʾl-Muhassin al-Tanukhi, *Nishwar al-Muhadara wa Akhbar al-Mudhakara* (*Snippets of Conversation and Memorable Tales*), vol. 3.

43

Avoiding a Conflict

ʿAmr ibn Maʿdi Kareb said:

I rode out one day and saw, in one of the quarters, a tethered mare and a spear wedged nearby; and I saw its rider in a hollow [i.e., relieving himself].

"Beware," I told him. "I intend to kill you."

"And who are you?" he asked.

"I'm the son of Maʿdi Kareb," I told him.

"Abu Thaur," he told me, "you're not playing fair. You're mounted on your horse and I'm here in a hollow. Give me your pledge you'll make no attempt to kill me till I'm mounted on my horse and can take measures to defend myself."

I gave him my pledge not to kill him till he was mounted on his horse and could defend himself. He came out from the hollow where he was, put on his sword, then sat down.

"What's this?" I asked him.

"I have no intention," he said, "of mounting my horse and fighting with you. You know best if you should betray your pledge."

I left him and went off. And this was the most skilful trick I ever heard of.

From Ibn al-Jawzi, *Akhbar al-Zurraf wa ʾl-Mutamajinin* (*Anecdotes of Humorists and Jesters*), Damascus, A.H. 1347.

44

The Byzantine Rulers and the Muslim Prisoners

I was told this story by Abu Bakr Muhammad ibn ʿAbd al-Rahman, who heard it from Mukarram ibn Bakran, who said it had been reported to him by Abu Yahya, son of the judge Ibn Mukarram:

I was one of the counselors to the vizier Abu ʾl-Hassan ʿAli ibn ʿIsa, who would often seek my advice. One day I entered his office to find him looking quite distressed, and I suspected he must have received some reprimand from Caliph al-Muqtadir.[1] Hinting along those lines, I asked him what the matter was.

"That isn't the cause of my anxiety," he said. "What concerns me is something far more serious."

"Would you tell me about it?" I asked. "I might perhaps have something to advise."

"Very well," he said. "Our agent on the frontiers has sent me a report about Muslim prisoners in the Byzantine lands. Until very recently they were well and humanely treated. Then, a short while back, two young boys assumed power and embarked on a policy of repression, starvation, deprivation, and rigor against our Muslim brothers, even attempting to convert them to Christianity by force. Our brothers now find themselves in a wretched, intolerable state, and we can do very little to help them. We have no power over those lands. I've been striving, vainly, to persuade the caliph to release funds and prepare our armies to conquer Constantinople."

"Grand vizier," I said, "I suggest a different means of seeing this problem resolved."

"And what's that, may God bless your soul?"

---

1. An Abbasid caliph who ruled from 295 / 908 to 320 / 932.

"The Christians," I said, "have a senior leader in Antioch, whom they call the Patriarch, and another in Bait al-Maqdis [Jerusalem], called the Bishop. Both of them have influence over the Byzantine ruler. They can even install a ruler or dethrone him. No monarch may be enthroned without their blessing, and that only after he has pledged loyalty, submission, and respect to them. The Byzantines believe anyone defying either of these two heads should be declared a blasphemous offender. The two cities are in our dominion, and the two religious leaders among our subjects. Will the vizier then write to the rulers of these two provinces, asking them to send these powerful heads, so we can tell them how things stand with our prisoners of war? It is not, they will be told, the proper way of good kings to treat prisoners in this manner. We must make it clear to them that they will be held responsible for the misconduct of the Byzantine rulers. Then, let us see how they handle the matter."

The vizier summoned his scribe and dictated two letters to this effect, instructing him to see them dispatched at once.

"You've greatly relieved my mind," he said. And with that I took my leave of him.

Two months and a few days later, when this conversation had slipped from my mind, a messenger arrived with instructions to go to the vizier. I rode to him on my horse, anxious and unaware of the reason for the summons. When I entered his office, he received me warmly.

"Welcome to my dear counselor!" he said. "May God reward you well for all you did on behalf of your religion, yourself, and myself."

"What is this?" I asked, surprised. "Please tell me."

"Your advice about our prisoners was providential! There's the messenger of our ruler, bearing the good news." He indicated a man among his audience. "Tell us what happened," he said.

"Our ruler," the man said, "sent me to Constantinople, with a messenger carrying letters from the Patriarch and the Bishop to the young Byzantine rulers. And here is what they said in the two letters:

" 'You have contravened the teachings of Christ by your misdeeds and your mishandling of the prisoners. This you should not do, since it is forbidden and unlawful. It stands against the way Christ has commanded us to act.' " (Here the letter cited a number of Christian directives.) " 'You must refrain from such action, begin treating them with humanity and kindness, and cease your attempts to force them to Christianity. Otherwise we shall denounce you, depose you from your seats of authority, and excommunicate you.'

"I moved on with the messenger till we reached Constantinople. I was not permitted to see the two young rulers, who had long discussions with the messenger in private. Then, after a few days, they summoned me. I greeted them, and their interpreter advised me of their response. The young rulers, he said, wished to inform the ruler of the Arabs that what he had heard about the prisoners was the merest lie and utter fabrication. 'They will,' the man continued, 'shortly allow you entry to the courtyards, to see for yourself that the conditions of your prisoners are not as they were portrayed to you. Contrary to what you have been told, you will hear them expressing gratitude for our treatment of them.'

"I was taken to the courtyard, where I saw the prisoners. Their faces were very pale, as though they had just been brought out from their graves. Written on those faces was the story of the agony and anguish they had been enduring before our arrival. They seemed in a far better state now, their appearance evidently marked by a sudden recent comfort. Inspecting their clothes, I saw they were all brand-new. I realized then that I had been kept away from the prisoners until their clothes had been changed and their condition improved.

" 'We are thankful,' the prisoners said, 'to the two rulers, may God bestow His blessings on them.' Then they turned to me, and went on: 'Our state was as bad as it was reported to you but has been alleviated and eased since you arrived in this country. How did you know about us? Who told you of the state we were in? Who sent you to see to our welfare?'

" 'The office of the grand vizier,' I said, 'has recently fallen upon ʿAli ibn ʿIsa, and he quickly came to know of your state. Accordingly, he made immediate contact with the religious heads of Antioch and Bait al-Maqdis, and they, in turn, sent their emissaries to Baghdad. And I joined these last on their way to Constantinople.'

"The prisoners began applauding the vizier and heaping praises on him, asking Almighty God to bestow His blessings and grace upon him.

"Then I heard a passionate cry from one of the women prisoners:

" 'ʿAli ibn ʿIsa, Almighty God will confer good fortune and blessings on you for all your favors to us!'

"I returned to Baghdad, and, when ʿAli ibn ʿIsa heard of all this from me, he was so moved he began to weep. He knelt and prayed, praising Almighty God. Then he rewarded the emissary of the Patriarch and the Bishop, and sent him back."

"Grand vizier," I said, "you have often complained to me of the burden of your duties at the ministry, and expressed the wish to leave the office for fear of any grave mistakes you might make while carrying out your functions. Suppose you were now living quietly at home? Could you have earned all these heavenly rewards, even if you had spent most of your fortune? So, don't think any longer of stepping down, and don't carp at your responsibilities. May God give you the power to do more such noble deeds. So you will please Him and enjoy His blessing in the life to come, just as He has honored you with this prime ministry."

From Abu ʿAli ʾl-Muhassin al-Tanukhi, *Nishwar al-Muhadara wa Akhbar al-Mudhakara* (*Snippets of Conversation and Memorable Tales*), vol. 1.

45

From *The Lion and the Diver*

The diver talks to the lion in a ploy to win a quest:

"It has been told[1] how [the king of Persia] Khosrow Abrawiz dispatched [his general] Shahrabraz to fight the Byzantines. Shahrabraz tightened his grip on their king in Constantinople till he was almost ready to surrender and pay the *jizya* imposed on the conquered.[2] Still, the Byzantine king gathered on board ships all the weaponry and engines of war and ammunition he could, prepared to cross the Bay of Constantinople and face Shahrabraz with his assembled strength. When all was ready and at sea, a storm blew up and tossed the ships, driving them to the camp of Shahrabraz, who captured them all. He thereupon sent all the spoils to Abrawiz, who rejoiced at this, the merit of Shahrabraz enhanced in his eyes. He expressed his pleasure with Shahrabraz constantly at his court, where all the dignitaries of the kingdom were in attendance.

"As these took their leave, a prominent courtier who envied Shahrabraz came to the king.

"'For all your knowledge and wisdom, Your Majesty,' he said, 'a point has escaped you. Shahrabraz sent you all these things only after keeping back a far greater share of the spoils for himself. If Your Majesty wishes to learn the truth of this, you need only summon him back. He will have to bring all the spoils with him, for he cannot leave them behind. Then you will know for certain.'

---

1. The following anecdotes are narrated by a jackal in the animal kingdom. The jackal is known for his capacity for reflection and is accordingly nicknamed the "diver" because he delves, or dives, into meanings and brings out the essence of things. Here he is advising the king (the lion) to resort to ploys in the face of his powerful enemy—an enormous ox that has been devastating the neighborhood of the lion's kingdom.
2. The *jizya* was a tax levied on non-Muslims, in lieu of military service.

"Abrawiz assented to this, writing to order that Shahrabraz should return home and leave his brother in his place, so that he, Abrawiz, could confer with him on matters that could not be resolved by letter. This he sent with a messenger, giving the man two letters: one of them urging Shahrabraz to return quickly, the other saying that, having considered the matter, he found it better for Shahrabraz to remain to confront the full strength of the enemy. 'If,' he told the messenger, 'you find he has announced his intention to return and begun preparations, then give him the letter in which I urge him to return. And if you find he has made no arrangements for this and has made no announcement on that score, then give him the other letter.'

"Shahrabraz, though, came to hear of this, and he sent words of conciliation to the Byzantine king, suggesting they should join forces to fight Abrawiz.

"'No,' the Byzantine king answered. 'You stay in my country and I will go to fight Abrawiz.'

"He marched to fight Abrawiz with an army four hundred thousand strong, surprising Abrawiz, who was without a full army. Fearing the worst now, Abrawiz summoned one of his Christian subjects who had benefited from the court's favor.

"'You know how beholden you are to me,' he told the man, 'for my munificent treatment of you. I wish you to take this cane and deliver it personally to Shahrabraz. Be careful on no account to hand it over to another.'

"The Persian king had made a hole in the cane, inserting in it a letter supposedly sent to Shahrabraz. 'When my letter reaches you,' it told him, 'I wish you to burn the seat of the Byzantine kingdom, to kill their fighters, and take their children hostage. Know that I shall be attacking the Byzantine king on the day here specified. This should be the date for your own attack.' Abrawiz then ordered money to be given to the Christian messenger, cautioning him once more to give the cane to none but Shahrabraz.

"The Christian went off, passing close by where the Byzantines were encamped. There he heard twenty thousand church bells ringing, and on hearing them, his heart was filled with tenderness. 'Oh soul,' he said to himself, 'cursed you are if you become a cause of destruction to the religion of the Christians!'

"He went accordingly and stood at the door of the Byzantine king, asked leave to see him, and gave him an account of the matter. The king opened the cane, brought out the letter, and read it. 'Shahrabraz has deceived me!' he snorted. 'By God, if I come upon him, I shall kill him without further ado!' And so saying, he retreated at once with his army.

"When the news reached Abrawiz, he laughed.

"'A single word that defeats four thousand soldiers,' he said, 'is of priceless value and splendid consequence.'"

Having heard this story, the lion answered majestically: "I will not consent, with all the strength and courage I possess, to resort to ploys. Such things are done only by feeble beasts." The diver countered with wise arguments, then narrated the following anecdotes:

"It has been told how a man, defeated in battle, was speeding away on a horse he cherished greatly, and another fugitive asked him to take him up on his horse, too. The man let him ride behind, but, a short while later, looked back and saw his enemies galloping along behind, about to catch up with him.

"'Get down,' he requested the man. 'If not we shall both be killed.'

"'By God,' the man said, 'I will not agree to dismount, but rather hold on to what I have gained. If we are to be saved, then let us be saved together. If not, let us perish together.'

"'If there is no help for it but to be killed,' the horseman told him, 'then it is better I should die facing the enemy boldly than flee in disgrace.' And with that he turned toward the enemies as if intending to confront them.

"When the other man saw the horseman was indeed about to fling himself into the midst of the enemy, he leaped from the horse, and the horseman, turning back once more, galloped safely away."

From *Al-Asad wa ʾl-Ghawwas* (*The Lion and the Diver*), an Arab fable from the fifth / eleventh century, ed. Ridwan al-Sayyid, 2nd ed. (Beirut, 1992).

IV

Tales of Religion

46

The Tale of Kaᶜb ibn Malek

OF HIS REPENTANCE AND THAT OF HIS TWO FRIENDS

I was told by Abu ʾl-Taher, Ahmad ibn ʿAmr ibn ʿAbd Allah ibn ʿAmr ibn Surayj, a slave of the Bani Umayyah, that he was told by Ibn Wahb, who was told by Ibn Yunes, who was told by Ibn Shihab, who said that the Prophet Muhammad undertook the Tabouk Conquest against the Byzantines and the Arab Christians of Syria.

Ibn Shihab said: I was told by ʿAbd al-Rahman ibn ʿAbd Allah ibn Kaᶜb ibn Malek that ʿAbd Allah ibn Kaᶜb was the leader of the Kaᶜb when he became blind. He said: I heard Kaᶜb ibn Malek tell of how he did not join the Messenger of God [the Prophet Muhammad][1] *at the Tabouk raid:*

Kaᶜb ibn Malek said:

I never held back from joining the Prophet in any conquest he undertook except for that of Tabouk. I did indeed take no part in the battle of Badr, but he blamed no one for failing to join him then, for he had left the city with the Muslims to capture the herds of the Quraysh,[2] and it was by chance, not contrivance, that God brought them face-to-face with their enemy. I had joined the Prophet on the Night of al-Aqaba,[3] when we

1. "Messenger of God" is the common expression used here and elsewhere for the Prophet Muhammad. For literary conciseness, the translation "the Prophet" will be used throughout.
2. The Quraysh was the majority tribe in Mecca, to which the Prophet belonged and which rejected his proclamation of Islam and took up arms against him. Muhammad and his followers thereupon took refuge in the town of Yathrib, to the north of Mecca, later called Medina. Some there had already been converted to Islam, and they invited Muhammad to take refuge with them. They were therefore called al-Ansar (the supporters), while the refugees from Mecca were called al-Muhajirun (the emigrants).
3. The Night of al-ʿAqaba was when the supporters proclaimed their faith in Islam before the Prophet and gave him their word to provide him with asylum and support.

faithfully adopted Islam, and I would not give up this for [the privilege of] fighting at the battle of Badr, even though Badr is more famous.

When I held back from joining the Prophet at Tabouk, I had never been so strong or affluent. Never before, by God, had I owned two riding camels together; only in preparation for that conquest. The Prophet made his assault on a very hot day, having traveled a long distance through a great wilderness and in the face of great numbers of the enemy. Making the Muslims ready for the assault, he clearly explained the plight they were in and the goal they were to accomplish. Though the Muslims alongside the Prophet were many, no register was kept. Yet hardly a man wished to leave thinking he would be unnoticed. The Prophet achieved that conquest when the fruits were ripe and the shadows were broad, and I was most inclined to play my part.

The Prophet was prepared, along with the Muslims, and I began to make myself ready, too, striving vainly to do what was necessary, telling myself I could do it if I had the will. But I remained, unable to prepare my equipment, till finally the Prophet and the Muslims had gone into battle and I had accomplished nothing. I strove once more to make ready so as to join up with them—if only I could!—but such was not my destiny.

After the Prophet had set out, I was filled with grief whenever I met with others, for I was, I found, the only [competent] one to have stayed behind. The others who had stayed were, here, a man well known for hypocrisy, or, there, a man feeble enough to be excused. The Prophet called me to mind only when he had reached Tabouk. Then, sitting there with his people, he asked:

"What has become of Kaᶜb ibn Malek?"

"Oh Prophet," said a man from the Bani Salimah, "he held back, gazing at his cloak and his figure."[4]

Muᶜadh ibn Jabal, though, rejoined:

"That is a poor answer indeed! Oh Prophet, I swear by God, we know him to be a good man."

The Prophet said nothing . . .

[Kaᶜb ibn Malek continued:] When I learned that the Prophet had set out on his return from Tabouk, I was filled with grief and began to seek some way to justify myself. How, I wondered, could I avert his anger the next day? I sought counsel too from all the wise men among my people. I learned the Prophet was approaching [the city], and I was convinced now I could find no way of excusing myself. So, I decided to tell him the truth.

4. An old Arab expression meaning that he was an admirer of himself.

Next morning the Prophet arrived. It was his custom, when returning from an expedition, to go first to the mosque to pray for a short while; and so he did this time. Then he sat to receive the people, and those who had declined to take part in the expedition came to express their regret and to swear allegiance to him once more. They were around eighty men. The Prophet accepted their excuses, gave them his assurance, and asked God to forgive them, leaving it to Almighty God alone to judge the secrets of their hearts. I came in and greeted him. He smiled in an angry fashion. Then he said:

"Come closer!"

I approached and sat before him.

"What held you back?" he asked. "Had you not bought a mount?"

"Oh Prophet," I said, "if I were, by God, to excuse myself to any other man in all this world, I should seek to avert his anger (being well spoken as I am) with some plausible reason. Yet I know, should I utter some pleasing lie, God will swiftly rouse your anger against me. If, though, I tell the truth, this may indeed make you angry, but God will, I hope, be good to me. By God, I have no excuse. I was never as strong, never as affluent, as at the time I failed to join you."

"This man has told the truth," the Prophet said then. [He looked at me and said:] "Rise and go, and await what judgment God may pass upon you."

So I rose, and some men from the Bani Salimah rose, too, and followed me.

"By God," they said to me, "we never knew you commit a guilty act before. Could you not have given the Prophet some excuse, the way those others did who stayed behind? Then your guilt would have been absolved by the forgiveness the Prophet asked for you."

[Kaᶜb continued:] By God, still they reproached me, till I was on the point of returning to the Prophet to tell my own lie. Then I said to them:

"Has any other here embraced the course I did?"

"Yes," they said. "Two others told the truth as you did, and they were given the same answer."

"And who were they?" I asked.

"Murarah ibn Rabiᶜa al-ᶜAamiri,"[5] came the answer, "and Hilal ibn Umayyah al-Waqifi."

These were two good men, who had taken part at Badr and were an example to others. When I heard their names, I went on my way.

[He said:] Then the Prophet ordered the Muslims that all those who had not held back [from the expedition] should no longer speak to the three of us.

5. The name is disputed, other scholars calling him al-Amri.

[He said:] And so people avoided us. Their manner toward us was changed, so much so that I felt a stranger in the world; it was no longer the world I had known. So things went on for fifty days. My two friends submitted to this and stayed weeping at home, but I was stronger and more patient. I would go out to attend prayers and wander about the marketplace. But no one would talk to me. I would sit with the Prophet, too, and greet him at his assembly after prayers, asking myself, did he really move his lips in response to my greeting? I would pray alongside him, sending secret glances in his direction. When I moved forward to pray, he would look at me; but when I looked at him, he would take no notice of me.

The Muslims continued to ignore me for a long time. At last I walked and climbed the house wall of Abu Qutada, my most-beloved cousin. When I greeted him, I swear he did not respond. Then I said to him:

"Abu Qutada, for the sake of God, do you not know I love God and His Prophet?"

Still he said nothing. Again I besought him in the name of God. He remained silent. Then, still once more, I besought him in the name of God. Then he said: "God and His Prophet know best." I turned back, my eyes filled with tears, then leaped over the house wall and went on my way.

As I was walking in the market of Medina, I heard a Nabataean from Syria, a seller of food in the marketplace, asking: "Who can guide me to Kaᶜb ibn Malek?" People pointed me out to him, and thereupon he came and handed me a letter from the king of Ghassan.[6] The letter read as follows:

"After due salutation, it has come to our notice that your friends have shunned you. But God forbid you should remain in a place of disgrace, where your right is lost. Come to us, and we will take our portion of your grievances."

When I read this, I said to myself: "Here is one evil more." And I took it to the furnace and burned it. When forty nights of the fifty had passed, and God's revelation was slow, a messenger from the Prophet came to me and said:

"The Prophet commands you to keep apart from your wife."

"Am I to divorce her then?" I asked.

"No," he said. "Only keep apart from her and do not approach her." And he sent the same message to my two friends.

---

6. The Ghassanids were a Christian Arab tribe and were allies of the Byzantines, acting as a buffer between the Byzantine Empire and the desert Arabs to the south. They were eventually conquered by the Muslim armies.

"Go to your parents," I told my wife, "and stay there with them, until God passes His judgment."

Then Hilal ibn Umayyah's wife went to the Prophet and said:

"Oh Messenger of God, Hilal ibn Umayyah is an old man with no servant. May I go and serve him?"

"Yes," he said, "but he may not approach you."

"By God," she said, "he can do nothing at all, and, by God, he has been weeping ever since this business began."

[Kaᶜb said:] Some of my people said to me:

"Why not make the same request of the Prophet concerning your own wife? He has allowed Hilal ibn Umayyah's wife to serve him."

"No," I said, "I shall not ask the Prophet's permission in this. How, in any case, can I know what he might say, knowing as he does that I am a young man?"

The matter went on for ten nights more, making fifty nights in all from the time he had forbidden people to talk to us. On the morning of the fiftieth night, I said my dawn prayers on the roof of one of our houses. While I was still afflicted in this state Almighty God had willed for us, stricken with dejection and sensing the earth heavy on my soul, I heard someone on Mount Salᶜ cry out at the top of his voice: "Oh Kaᶜb ibn Malek, rejoice!" When I heard this, I fell on my knees, for I knew relief had come.

[Kaᶜb said:] The Prophet, at dawn prayers, had advised people that God had forgiven us. So it was that people came to us with the good news; and bearers of the news went to my two friends also. One man came to me on his horse, but another, from Aslam, sent me the news from the mountaintop, and the voice was faster than the horse. When this latter man came to me in person with the news, I gave him my full attire in recompense. And, by God, it was the only attire I then had. I borrowed another, put it on, and hurried to the Prophet. People in the street received me in groups, with congratulation for the forgiveness granted.

"May God's forgiveness bring you happiness!" they said.

In due course I entered the mosque, where the Prophet was sitting with people around him. When Talha ibn Ubayd Allah saw me, he rose and came swiftly toward me, shaking my hands and congratulating me. By God, no other emigrant[7] did this except him.

[The narrator said:] Kaᶜb would never forget what Talha did.

[Kaᶜb said:] When I greeted the Prophet, his face lit up with pleasure.

---

7. See n. 2.

"Rejoice!" he said. "This is the best day you have known since the time your mother gave birth to you."

"Is it from you, Prophet?" I asked. "Or is it from God?"

"No," he said. "It is from God."

When the Prophet was pleased, his face would brighten as though it were part of the moon. We all knew this.

Sitting there at his disposal, I told him:

"Oh Prophet, part of my repentance will be to give away my wealth for the sake of God and His Messenger."

He, though, told me:

"Keep some of your wealth. That is better for you."

"I shall, then," I said, "keep my share from the Khaybar battle."

Then I added:

"Oh Prophet, God has indeed saved me by virtue of my truthfulness, and part of my repentance will be to speak the truth so long as I live."

And, by God, from the moment I told the Prophet this, I have known of no Muslim with whom God was so generous for his truthfulness as He has been with me. To this day, by God, I have never tried to tell a lie, and I pray God He will keep me so for the rest of my life.

From *Sahih Muslim* (*Famous Authentic Compilation of the Prophet's Traditions*), "Kitab al-Tawba" (Book of Repentance), ed. Muhammad Fuʾad ʿAbd al-Baqi, vol. 4 (Beirut: Dar al-Fikr, 1368/1978).

47

The Tale of Jurayj the Worshipper

SHOWING HOW ATTENDING TO PARENTS HAS PRIORITY OVER PRAYER

*We have been told by Shayban ibn Farroukh, who was told by Sulaiman ibn al-Mughirah, who was told by Humayd ibn Hilal, who was told by Abu Rafi*ᶜ*, who was told by Abu Huraira, that Prophet Muhammad had said:*

Jurayj was worshipping at a hermitage when his mother came to him.

[Humayd said:] "Abu Rafiᶜ described to us how Abu Huraira had repeated the Prophet's account of the way Jurayj's mother had called him.

"She placed her hand over her brows, raised her head, and called out: 'Jurayj, here I am, your mother. Will you speak with me?' Then she realized he was praying.

"Hearing his mother call him, Jurayj said: 'Oh God! My mother or my prayers?' And he chose his prayers.

"She withdrew accordingly but returned later and called: 'Jurayj, here I am, your mother. Will you speak with me?'

"He said: 'Oh God! My mother or my prayers?' And he chose his prayers.

" 'Oh, my God,' she said. 'Here is Jurayj, my son. I call him and he refuses to speak with me. I ask you, God, let him know whores before you send him to his death.'

"Then [the Prophet] said: 'Had she asked God to let him be bewitched by them, He would have done so.' He also said: 'A shepherd was accustomed to come to this hermitage, and a woman from the village met with him. The shepherd had relations with her, and she became pregnant, giving birth to a baby boy. "How did this come about?" someone asked her. "It was the man at that hermitage," came her reply.'

"So, the people came to Jurayj, with their axes and other iron tools. When they called to him, he was praying and would not speak with them; and they began tearing down his hermitage. When he saw what they were doing, he came down to them.

" 'Ask this woman why,' they said.

"He smiled and passed his hand over the baby's head.

" 'Who is your father?' he asked.

" 'The shepherd is my father,' the baby rejoined.

"When they heard the baby's answer, they said:

" 'We shall rebuild, with gold and silver, all of your hermitage we have torn down.'

" 'No,' he said. 'Only restore it to the way it was.'

"Then he stood over it."

•••••

[Another version was related by Zuhayr ibn Harb, as related to him by Yazid ibn Haroun, as related by Jarir ibn Hazem, as related by Muhammad ibn Sirin, as related by Ibn Huraira, as he heard the Prophet Muhammad say:]

Only three people have talked when they were infants: [among them] ʿIsa [Jesus], son of Mary, and a person linked to Jurayj. Jurayj was a faithful man who was praying at his hermitage when his mother came and called to him.

"Oh God," he said, "my mother or my prayers?" And he chose his prayers.

His mother went away and came the next morning, calling to him while he was praying. Again he said: "Oh God, my mother or my prayers?" And he chose his prayers.

So his mother said: "Oh God, let him not die before you show him the faces of whores."

As the sons of Israel were speaking of Jurayj and his worship, a whore all too famous for her beauty told them: "I can seduce him for you, if that is your wish."

She came to where he was, but he did not look at her. Then she went to a shepherd who was there at his hermitage, seduced him, and became pregnant by him; and when she gave birth to her baby, she said it was by Jurayj. Thereupon people came to him, beat him, and tore down his hermitage.

When he asked them for a reason, they said: "You committed adultery with this whore, and she had a baby by you."

"Where is this baby?" he asked.

---

1. "Fulan" is a name given in Arabic to an unknown man (the feminine form is Fulana). A rough English equivalent would be so-and-so.

When they brought the baby, he said: "Let me first pray to God." When he had finished his prayers, he came to the baby and poked it gently in the stomach.

"Boy," he said, "who is your father?"

"Fulan the shepherd,"[1] the baby said.

The people then went to Jurayj, kissing him and tendering their apologies.

"We shall build a golden hermitage for you," they said.

"No," he said. "Simply return it to the way it was, of clay."

And so they did.

From *Sahih Muslim* (*Famous Authentic Compilation of the Prophet's Traditions*), "Kitab birr al-walidayn" (Book of Munificence to Parents), ed. Muhammad Fuʾad ʿAbd al-Baqi, vol. 4 (Beirut: Dar al-Fikr, 1368/1978).

48

The Tale of the Crevice People, and of the Magician, the Monk, and the Young Man

We were told by Haddab ibn Khaled that he had been told by Hammad ibn Salamah that he had been told by Thabet that he had been told by ʿAbd al-Rahman ibn Layla that he had been told by Suhayb that:

The Prophet Muhammad said:

There was once a king who had a magician working for him. When the magician grew old, he said to the king:

"I have grown old, my lord. I beg you to let me have a young man to whom I can teach the art of magic."

The king accordingly sent a young man for him to teach. On the way where this young man [habitually] passed, there was a monk with whom he would sit, listening to what the man said. So impressed was he by the man's words that, whenever he went to visit the magician, he would pass by the monk and sit with him; whereupon the magician would beat him for being late. When he complained of this to the monk, the monk told him:

"If you fear the magician, tell him you have been held back by your parents. And if you fear your parents, tell them you have been held back by the magician."

One day the young man encountered a great monster that prevented people's passing that way.

"Today," he said then, "I shall learn who is better, the magician or the monk."

With that he picked up a stone, saying:

"Oh God, if you value the monk's matter over the magician's, then kill this beast, so people may be made free."

Then he flung the stone at the beast and killed it, and the people were made free. He went to the monk and told him what had happened.

"Son," the monk told him, "today you have shown yourself superior to me. I see what you have achieved, and you will be put to the test. When you are put to the test, tell no one about me."

The young man was able to heal the blind, and those with leprosy, and to treat people with sickness of every kind. One of the king's men, who had become blind, heard of this and went to him, bearing many gifts.

"These will be too little for you," he said, "if you can heal me."

"I heal no one," came the answer. "God it is who heals. If you believe in God, then I shall ask Him to heal you, and He will do it."

God healed the man, and the man went to the king and sat with him as usual. When the king saw him, he asked:

"Who restored your sight?"

"It was my lord," the man replied.

"So," the king said, "you have another lord beside me?"

"God," the man said, "is my Lord and yours."

The king had him taken off and put to torture, and finally he confessed about the young man, who was ordered to be brought in.

"Son," the king said, "we have heard of your magic: how you heal the blind and the leper, of the many things you do."

"I heal no one," said the young man. "God it is who does so."

So the king had him taken off and put to torture, and finally he confessed about the monk. The monk was brought in and commanded to renounce his faith, but he refused. The king then called for a saw, which was set on the man's head, and the head was cut into two halves. Next the king's companion was brought in and commanded to renounce his faith. But he refused. And so the saw was set on his head, which was cut into two halves. Then the young man was brought in and commanded to renounce his faith. But he, too, refused. Thereupon the king handed him over to a number of men from among his followers, saying:

"Take him to the mountain, climb it till you reach the peak, then, if he does not renounce his faith, fling him down from there."

So they took him to the mountain and climbed it.

"Oh God," the young man said then, "protect me whichever way You will."

With that the mountain shook so violently that the other men fell from the heights. The young man walked back to the king.

"What has become of the men?" the king asked.

"God has protected me," the young man answered.

The king thereupon handed him over to a number of men from among his followers, telling them:

"Take him in a boat to the middle of the sea. Then, if he does not renounce his faith, fling him in."

So they took him to the sea.

"Oh God," the young man said then, "protect me whichever way You will."

With that the boat capsized and the king's men were drowned. Once more the young man walked back to the king.

"What has become of the men?" the king asked.

"God has protected me," the young man answered.

Then he said to the king:

"You may not kill me till you have done as I tell you."

"And what is that?" asked the king.

"Gather all the people at a high place," he said, "and crucify me on the trunk of a tree. Then take an arrow, set it in a bow, and say: 'In the name of God, the young man's Lord.' Then shoot me with the arrow. If you do this, you will surely kill me."

So the king gathered all the people at a high place and crucified the young man on the trunk of a tree. Next he took an arrow, set it in a bow, and said: "In the name of God, the young man's Lord." Then he shot the young man with the arrow, and the arrow struck the temple of the young man, who put his hand where the arrow had pierced, then died.

At that the people watching said:

"We believe now in the young man's God. We believe now in the young man's God."

Then the king was told:

"Do you see what it was you feared? By God, what you feared has come to pass. People have become believers."

Thereupon the king ordered crevices to be dug and fire to be lit inside the crevices. Then the king said:

"Whoever does not renounce his faith shall be flung into the crevices."

A woman carrying a small boy came and was unwilling to be thrown into the fire. But her small boy said to her:

"Mother, be patient, for you are in the right."

From *Sahih Muslim* (*Famous Authentic Compilation of the Prophet's Traditions*), ed. Muhammad Fuʾad ʿAbd al-Baqi, vol. 4 (Beirut: Dar al-Fikr, 1368/1978).

49

The Tale of the Leper, the Bald Man, and the Blind Man

We were told by Shayban ibn Farroukh that he was told by Hammam, who was told by Ishaq ibn ʿAbd Allah ibn Abi Talhah, who was told by ʿAbd al-Rahman ibn Abi ʿAmra, that Abu Huraira told him that he had heard the Prophet [Muhammad] *say:*

There were once three men among the sons of Israel, one a leper, the second bald, and the third blind. Wishing to test them, God sent an angel to them.

The angel went to the leper and asked him:

"What is it you wish for most?"

"A good complexion," the leper said, "a good skin, and to be rid of what drives people from me."

So the angel passed his hand over the man, and his defect vanished. He was given a good complexion and a good skin. Then the angel asked him:

"What kind of wealth do you wish for most?"

"Camels," the leper said.[1]

So he was given a female camel about to give birth. "May God bless you with it," the angel told him.

Next the angel went to the bald man and asked him:

"What is it you wish for most?"

"Good hair," the bald man said, "and to be rid of what drives people from me."

So the angel passed his hand over the man, and he became like others, being given a good head of hair. Then the angel asked him:

"What kind of wealth do you wish for most?"

---

1. Ishaq is not sure whether in fact he said cattle. However, of the leper and the bald man, one asked for camels and the other for cattle.

"Cattle," he said.

So he was given a pregnant cow. "May God bless you with it," the angel told him.

Then the angel went to the blind man and asked him:

"What is it you wish for most?"

"To have back my sight," the blind man answered, "and to be able to see people."

So the angel passed his hand over him, and his sight was restored. Then the angel asked him:

"What kind of wealth do you wish for most?"

"Sheep," he said. So he was given a ewe with its lamb.

In time the three men had a valley of camels, a valley of cattle, and a valley of sheep, one valley for each.

Then the angel came to the leper in the guise of an old man, and told him:

"I am a poor man, cut off from my people by my journey. I have no hope but in God and in you. I ask you, for the sake of Him who granted you your good complexion, your good skin and your wealth, to give me one camel for use on my journey."

"Requests are many," came the response.

So the angel said to him:

"I know you, I think. Were you not a leper and loathsome to people? Were you not poor and God made you rich?"

"No," said the man. "I inherited this wealth from my fathers and forefathers."

"If you are lying," the angel told him, "may God bring you back to what you were before."

The angel then went to the bald man in his new guise and told him what he had told the first. And the bald man responded in the same way.

"If you are lying," the angel told him, "may God bring you back to what you were before."

The angel then went to the blind man in his new guise, and told him:

"I am a poor man, cut off from my people by my journey. I have no hope but in God and in you. I ask you, for the sake of Him who restored your sight, to give me one ewe for use on my journey."

"I was blind," the blind man said, "and God restored my sight. Take whatever you wish and leave whatever you wish. By God, I shall not hold you back from taking anything you wish, for the sake of God."

Then the angel said to him:

"Keep your wealth. The three of you have been tested, and God is pleased with you and displeased with your two friends."

..... ❦ .....

From *Sahih Muslim* (*Famous Authentic Compilation of the Prophet's Traditions*), "Kitab al-zuhd" (Book of Asceticism), ed. Muhammad Fuʾad ʿAbd al-Baqi, vol. 4 (Beirut: Dar al-Fikr, 1368/1978).

50

Virtue and Divine Reward

It has been related, in the two compilations of authenticated Prophetic traditions, how the Prophet said as follows:

Three men who lived before were walking when it began to rain. They took refuge in a cave, and a fall of rock blocked the mouth. "By God," they said to one another, "nothing will save you now but the truth. Let each relate such [good deeds] as he knows to be true."

"God!" one of them said. "You know I had a hired hand who worked for me measuring rice. When he went away, he left his measure behind. I planted the rice left in his measure, and it flourished, so that I was able, from the proceeds, to buy cattle and a herdsman. Later he came to ask for his wages, and I told him to take all the cattle. 'But,' the man said, 'I left only a measuring tool with you.' 'The cattle,' I told him, 'came from the measuring tool.' And he took them. God! If You know I did this out of awe for You, then grant us release!"

The rock shifted a little.

"God!" said the second man. "You know I had two parents to whom, each evening, I brought milk from my sheep to drink. One evening I was late and found them asleep, while my family had now become hungry. I had never given them milk to drink before my parents had drunk, and now I could not bear to wake my parents—and so I waited till dawn. If You know I did this out of awe for You, then grant us release!"

The rock shifted further, and now they could see the sky.

"God!" said the third man. "You know I had a cousin I loved dearly. I tried to seduce her, and she refused unless I gave her a hundred dinars. I sought to acquire this money, and succeeded, and I took it to her; and she then agreed to let me possess her. As I lay beside her, and was about to fulfill my desire, she said: 'Fear God, and do not deflower what remains sealed except by God's law.' I got up, leaving the hundred dinars. God! If You know I did this out of awe for You, then grant us release!"

And God shifted the rock completely away.

••••• ❦ •••••

From Dawud al-Antaki, *Tazyin al-Aswaq bi Tafsil Ashwaq al-ʿUshshaq* (*Adorning the Markets with Accounts of Lovers' Longing*), vol. 2, ed. Muhammad al-Tunji (Beirut: ʿAlam al-Kutub, 1993).

51

A Vision of the Next World

Your servant wishes to free his hand and pen and set down his impressions, having before been burdened with weariness and exhaustion at the things he has seen, like a small donkey carrying loads only mules are able to bear.[1] I had read nothing of the strange, outlandish happenings in the country, and now I was made furious at what I saw in Damascus and Iraq. I saw squalor in the alleyways, changes of rulers and kings, and pillage by foreigners.

One day, when overcome by sleep, I saw the Day of Judgment. The Summoner of Hell began calling people to give an account of themselves to God. I rose from my grave and headed toward the land of doomsday, weary, fearful, and covered in sweat. "This," I told myself, "is the grimmest, most dreadful day of all." Feeble as I was, so dispirited and frail, I longed for the all-powerful God to provide me here with some refreshing meal—a loaf of hot bread, an omelet of eggs, onion, meat, and cheese, and a flask of Lebanese wine. In this way I might lose my senses, become absent from this world, freed from all these misfortunes.

No sooner had I made my wish than my companion said: "I've just seen some girls with children, who claim you fathered their offspring. Some say you sold them to other owners while they were pregnant."

I could hardly believe my ears.

"Don't, please," I said, "compare me to Hafiz al-Ulaimi, who'd go for young boys, then sell them when their beards started sprouting and get new ones in their place. Don't you see Malik there, the custodian of Hell, coming out of the fire, his eyes wide, a rod in his right hand and a chain

---

1. The author of this piece, Rukn al-Din al-Wahrani (d. 575 / 1179), was a little-known writer born in Wahran (Oran), in what is now Algeria. He traveled to Cairo, Damascus, and Baghdad and wrote down, in the form of a series of dreams and letters, his impressions of the corrupt practices he witnessed there.

in the other, pursuing sodomizers and pimps of the nation of Muhammad, peace be upon him? Stop this talk, won't you? Let's have no more of it."

While we were talking, though, Malik, the custodian of Hell, assailed us. He seized our hands, bound the chain around our necks, and pulled us into the fire. I made my appeal to him.

"Please, sir," I said, "please, Mal, let me for God's sake say a few words."

"Why should I listen to you," he asked, "when you address me and leave out half my name?"

"I was trying to be friendly," I said, "giving you a pet name."

"Very well then," he replied. "Say what you have to say."

"Sir," I said, "I'm one of the people of the Quran, come all the way from the Maghreb. I, too, memorize and repeat the sayings of Muhammad, peace be upon him."

"You reprobate!" he said. "You devise subtle new ways in the art of sodomy. You wrote down the names of Muslim boys, in a great list, in alphabetical order. You, you pig, have led soft-skinned boys to ruin, forcing them to share your bed. But why go on and on listing your vices?"

I was livid with rage.

"I won't," I said, "take that sort of accusation. You'll be sorry for what you've said."

"What are you going to do to me then?" Malik replied. "Pour scorn on me in one of those famous poems or stories of yours?"

When we heard this, my companion and I, we bit back our words and made our tone more conciliatory. And so he left us, and we joined a crowd of people going up to the mount of Aʿraf, the region overlooking the gardens of Paradise. We would, I supposed, have our spirits restored and enjoy a time of ease there. My companion, though, put in a warning word.

"Don't think like that," he said. "We've lost all hope of entering Paradise now. If we were to see the trees and rivers, knowing we'd never reach them, we'd be filled with a sense of loss and sorrow. Our fancies would be a torment to us. My hope, rather, is for an eye that doesn't see and a heart that doesn't suffer."

Turning to one side, I saw Rudwan, the custodian of Paradise; he was holding a scroll and reading aloud. "This," he read, "concerns a man who calls himself a writer but is in truth a mere painter, adorning and embellishing his writings with nothing of substance or value behind them. I shan't permit him to enter Paradise. His empty, embroidered words are good only for concubines, and for women who love other women. Should he venture near Heaven's gate, he'll be struck by ten thousand shoes. If he wrote such words on the thigh of a fat sheep even, the very dogs would shun it."

While all this was being said, we heard a loud report from a corner of the place of doomsday, and saw cheering crowds moving that way, clapping their hands and shrieking with joy. They surrounded four men who were buckling under the whips of the crowd, and yet, at the same time, smiling hopefully. Wondering, I asked Rudwan what all this meant, why these four persons had such a cheerful air.

"Those men," he said, "were once criminals of our nation:[2] ʿAbd al-Rahman bin Murjim al-Muradi, who killed ʿAli bin Abi Talib, God bless his soul; Shummar bin Dhi al-Jawshan al-Dubabi, who had a part in the murder of al-Husain bin ʿAli, the grandson of our Prophet Muhammad, peace be upon him; Hajjaj bin Yousuf al-Thaqafi, the Umayyad ruler of Iraq, who drove out the followers of ʿAli; and Sheikh Abu Murra—Satan himself. They're smiling in the vain hope of God's mercy, buoyed up by the thought that God forgives those who repent and regret their wrongdoing."

We came across ʿUzraʾil,[3] too, praising, ceaselessly and at length, the physicians of the day. Thanks to their shortcomings, he said, he'd been feasted through the sweeping away of so many lost souls. One man's defect may be another man's boon.

At this point the commotion grew louder. A grand convoy approached us, of people like suns and moons in their brightness. They were riding on lustrous horses toward a crystalline spring. We asked who they were. "This," came the answer, "is the master of prophets and messengers, Muhammad bin ʿAbd Allah, peace be upon him, with his companions and the members of his household."

We made our way toward him, straining to reach him, but were held back by the vast throng. We climbed a hilly part of the Aʿraf mount and watched him pass by. Caliph Abu Bakr was on his right, on his left Caliph ʿUmar. Around him were his children, along with al-Hasan and al-Husain, together with ʿUthman, Hamza, al-ʿAbbas, Jaʿfar, and ʿAqil. Other companions, and also the emigrants and supporters,[4] took part in the procession. Now he would

2. The author's attitude to various characters seen in the vision is colored by his Shiʿite loyalties.

3. ʿUzraʾil, the angel of death.

4. The Quraysh was the majority tribe in Mecca, to which the Prophet belonged and which rejected his proclamation of Islam and took up arms against him. Muhammad and his followers thereupon took refuge in the town of Yathrib, to the north of Mecca, later called Medina. Some there had already been converted to Islam, and they invited Muhammad to take refuge with them. They were therefore called al-Ansar (the supporters), while the refugees from Mecca were called al-Muhajirun (the emigrants).

turn to speak with ʿAli, now with ʿUthman. The crowd hailed and wailed in supplication, waving their arms and beseeching him from all sides.

When he came close to the spring, he paused. The Sufis approached him from all sides, carrying their combs and toothpicks, which they then presented to him. The Prophet (peace be upon him) asked:

"Who are these?"

"They are people of your nation," someone said, "who turned into useless, idle hermits. No longer prepared to work for a living, they withdrew into mosques, and there they did nothing but eat and sleep."

"What benefit have they brought to others?" he asked. "What help have they been to them?"

"None at all, peace be upon you. They live like useless castor plants in the garden, wasting water and taking up space."

He turned away from them and moved on toward the spring.

The Ayyubi rulers Najm al-Din and Asad al-Din approached, riding two fine horses like falcons, each carrying with him two garments, one for pilgrimage, the other for holy war. They were joined by Saladin, whom they led to the Prophet (peace be upon him), ordering him to kneel and kiss the Prophet's feet, and this he did. The Prophet asked for God's mercy on him, stroked his head, and prayed for his success and victory, asking him to show kindness to the beleaguered, the ill-treated, and the oppressed. They all stayed some time by the great water source, then returned the way they'd come.

My companion and I sat down to rest and drink. What I needed now, I said, after this long trip, was a piece of soap and some water to wash my beard, covered in dust and sweat. If I didn't clean myself thoroughly, my companion said, I wouldn't be admitted to Paradise; rather, I'd be moved to the gates of Hell, where the custodians would twirl my beard into a wick and burn it.

As we were there, enjoying the leisure of comfort and peace, we heard a mighty tumult coming close, with piercing shrieks and screams, one after the other. Our companions and friends began scattering in all directions.

"What's the matter with these people?" we asked.

This, we were told, was ʿAli ibn Abi Talib (may God bless his soul), coming with horsemen led by his son Muhammad ibn al-Hanafiyya, roaring like a ferocious lion. When he reached us, he cried out and brandished his spear to impale me. And this jerked me from the depths of my slumber, hurling me from my bed to the floor. There I was, wide awake now, with the sweetness of that water still in my mouth, that cry still ringing in my ears, the terror of my fall in my heart, as long as I lived.

Now, sir, what do you have to say of my long ordeal, my feverish vision, stirred up by anger and vengeance?

(And may Almighty God bestow peace upon our Prophet and Master Muhammad, and upon his family and companions.)

From Shaikh Rukn al-Din Muhammad bin Muhammad bin Muhriz al-Wahrani [d. 575 / 1179], *Manamat al-Wahrani* (*The Wahrani Dreams*), ed. Ibrahim Shaʿlan and Muhammad Naghsh (Cairo: Dar al-Kitab al-ʿArabi li-ʾl-Tibaʿa wa ʾl-Nashr, 1968).

V

Comic Tales: Tales of Juha

[JUHA IS A TRADITIONAL CHARACTER AROUND WHOM COUNTLESS COMIC ANECDOTES WERE SPUN, HIS PORTRAYAL VARYING WIDELY FROM THAT OF SAGE TO SIMPLETON. THE HUMOR ITSELF RANGES FROM THE ASTRINGENT TO THE STRAIGHTFORWARDLY HILARIOUS. IT HAS BEEN THOUGHT PREFERABLE TO GIVE THE JUHA STORIES THEIR OWN SECTION SO AS TO HIGHLIGHT THE RANGE OF POPULAR HUMOR THEY EMBODY. THE SELECTIONS WERE MADE FROM VARIOUS EDITIONS OF THE JUHA COMPILATIONS.]

52

Juha as a Vehicle for Satire

[Juha's role here permits not simply general social satire but attack on specific historical individuals of high rank.]

One day Tamerlane[1] summoned the city's governor to confiscate his possessions, on the pretext that he'd stolen large quantities of funds. The truth was, the crops and fruit had been damaged that year by Heaven-sent natural disasters. The previous year's harvest had indeed been plentiful, but this year the earth had produced barely enough for the people to stay alive. The governor had in fact done the best he could, using all his powers of firmness to extract everything possible from what the people had built up.

The man produced his account books, written on the paper of the day—only to see Tamerlane tear them up, then have the soldiers, on Tamerlane's orders, first flog him then force him to eat the torn pages. Tamerlane thereupon confiscated the governor's possessions, leaving him totally destitute.

He then summoned Juha, who had a reputation for honesty, and charged him with supervision of the realm's treasury. The old man tried to wriggle out of the post, citing his failing health, but no excuse was accepted.

At the end of the month, Tamerlane called for the account books, which Juha had prepared on thin layers of bread. Tamerlane asked him just what it was he'd brought.

"Sire," Juha said, "it will end, I know, in your ordering me to swallow these. I'm an old man, not a man of fame and prowess like my predecessor. Indeed, my stomach will scarcely be able to digest even this bread!"

---

1. This is one of a number of stories in which Juha figures alongside the despotic ruler Tamerlane (1336–1405).

One day the governor[2] was walking around, inspecting the city streets, when he sniffed the mouthwatering smell of a grill coming from a bakery nearby. He summoned the baker and a puerile argument ensued, which ended with the governor's ordering the baker to send the grilled goose to his house, and to tell the real owner that it had flown off after being cooked.

"If the owner isn't satisfied," the governor concluded, "then come straight to me and I'll judge between the two of you. I'll deal with him, don't worry."

The baker gave in to the governor and sent the goose to his house. When the owner of the goose arrived to claim it, and the baker told him it had flown off, he was furious. The two of them started quarreling, and the people round about sided with the customer, saying the baker was a thief. They kept on at him till, in the end, he became desperate, panicked, and ran off like a madman, having first given the nearest man such a vicious punch that it knocked out one of his teeth.

The mob's mood grew uglier, but the desperate baker managed to leap into a nearby alley, where he found his path blocked by a pregnant woman returning home with her husband; and he gave her such a kick that she lost the child. The mob, angrier still, kept following him, but off he shot like an arrow from a bow, entered a nearby mosque, and climbed to the top of the minaret. The mob still followed in hot pursuit, and so he jumped from the top of the minaret and landed on one of his pursuers. The man died but the baker survived. As the mob's anger grew fiercer still, the baker fled into a butcher's shop, where he seized hold of a knife, pretending to be crazy.

Now, Juha's donkey was nearby, and, as the baker slashed downward with the knife, he cut off the donkey's tail. Then he ran off to the residence of the governor, Kameesh, the mob still pursuing. Finally they all fetched up in the governor's presence.

Kameesh, for his part, feigned surprise and pretended to have no knowledge of the baker. Then, having heard the full story, he told everyone he believed the baker's claim: that the goose had flown off after being grilled, so demonstrating the power of the Creator, praise be to Him. The goose's owner grew furious at this, whereupon Kameesh, in his capacity as judge, accused him of heresy and lack of faith in the Creator's power, fining him ten dinars accordingly.

---

2. The governor in question, Kameesh, was the living embodiment of the corruption of justice and the judiciary in his time. Clever though he was, and full of mental agility, he was driven by greed and avarice. He had no compunction about cutting corners and no shame about fabricating feeble justifications only the stupidest or most naive person would ever dream of. This is demonstrated in the present anecdote.

The governor then addressed the case of the second plaintiff, who was instructed to strike the baker a single blow that would knock out exactly the same tooth as the one he'd lost—and woe betide him if it was otherwise! The man, realizing how biased the judge was, and despairing of justice, relinquished his case. The governor thereupon fined him ten dinars.

Next it was the turn of the third opponent. "The fault," the judge told him, "lies with your late brother. Why did he have to choose that precise moment to walk under the minaret? Still, let right prevail and justice take its course. You must climb the selfsame minaret and jump down on top of the baker, killing him as he did, indeed, kill your brother." The claimant, realizing the judge's perversity and despairing of justice at his hands, relinquished his right, and the judge ruled he should be fined ten dinars for failing to carry out the decision of the court.

Now it was the turn of the woman who'd lost her child. The judge admonished her for choosing to pass, at that very moment, along a street she knew to be narrow—though in fact (he went on) the real fault lay with her husband, who'd arranged for her to live in such a street. But, be that as it may, justice must take its course. He decreed, accordingly, that the one who'd caused the abortion in her womb must make it pregnant again in lieu. The woman and her husband were stunned, and she relinquished her right. The judge imposed a fine of ten dinars on her for wasting the court's time.

Juha, having witnessed the awesome judgments of this crazed tyrant, fled with his donkey, looking only to make good his escape. The governor, though, forestalled him; whereupon Juha cried out that God had created his donkey without either tail or brains. This the governor, egged on by the baker, refused to accept, and Juha saw it was useless to argue with him. He gazed at the governor.

"My lord governor," Juha said, "so it is. God created my donkey without either tail or brains. Are you denying the might of the Creator? Do you doubt and contend His power?"

The governor, hearing his own reasoning thrown back at him, was dumbstruck and found no reply.

53

The Comic Wit of Juha

[The following anecdotes demonstrate the wit, and also the ingenuity and resource, typical of Juha in many of the traditional stories.]

A merchant went into a restaurant and ordered a chicken and two eggs. He would, he said, pay the restaurant owner in three months' time, when he came back from a business trip. On his return he went to the restaurant and asked to settle the bill in full.

"The account's a high one," the restaurant owner said, "but I'll settle for two hundred dirhams."

"In Heaven's name," the merchant cried, "how could you ask two hundred dirhams, even for two chickens and four eggs?"

"Well," explained the restaurant owner, "if the chicken you ate three months ago had still been alive, and laid one egg a day to be put under a hen, we would have had so many chickens and so many eggs. We could have sold them for hundreds of dirhams."

After a heated argument, they ended up at the court of a judge who was in collusion with the restaurant owner. The judge asked the merchant if he'd agreed upon the price with the restaurant owner three months before, and the merchant said he hadn't. And, pursued the judge, might the chicken and the two eggs not have produced hundreds of eggs and chickens in the meantime?

"Of course they might," said the merchant, "if the chicken had still been alive. But it had been killed and roasted, and the two eggs had been fried."

The judge seemed inclined, even so, to rule against the merchant. And so the merchant asked for a postponement till the next day, when he'd have further evidence to submit. The judge agreed to this.

Next morning the merchant arrived and stated that Juha would be submitting the proof of his case. They waited, but Juha was very late. At last he turned up.

"Why have you been so long?" the judge shouted furiously. "Keeping us waiting like this?"

"Don't be angry, sir," Juha replied meekly. "I was just about to come when my partner, in some land we're going to plant with wheat, came and asked for the seed. So I waited till I'd boiled around two big sackfuls of wheat, then I gave them to him to sow. That's why I'm late."

"An odd sort of excuse that is!" the judge said sarcastically. "Whoever heard of wheat being boiled before it's sown?"

"And," said Juha at once, "whoever heard of a roast chicken and fried eggs reproducing and multiplying so much that they're worth the two hundred dirhams this restaurant owner's claiming?"

The judge, taken aback, ruled in favor of the merchant.

•••••

One night, while Juha and his wife were in bed, he heard footsteps up on the roof. He woke his wife and whispered in her ear to pretend to wake him, then ask him how he'd amassed all his wealth. This she did.

"When I was young," he told her, "I used to rob houses. And whenever I climbed up onto the roof of a house, I'd wait till the moon rose and its beams were shining down on the skylight. Then I'd grab the rays, say "Salaam, salaam" seven times, and slide down on the beams into the house. I didn't need a rope. Once I was finished, I'd climb back up the same way. No one in the house had any idea I was there."

The thief, hearing this, decided he'd picked up a tip that night that was even more precious than anything he might be able to steal. He waited for the moon to rise. Then, when the beams were going down into the skylight, he said "Salaam, salaam" seven times and grabbed at the beams to let himself down through. He fell to the floor and broke his ribs, whereupon Juha rushed over to him, telling his wife to light the lamp before he could escape. But the thief told him:

"Don't have any fears, brother. As long as you're so greatly, wondrously wise, and I'm so stupid, I won't escape you so easily."

••••

Juha bought three pounds of meat and asked his wife to cook it. This she did, but she ate the meat with some of her relatives. Then, when Juha came and asked for the cooked meat, she told him the cat had eaten it while she was busy preparing other things. Juha took hold of the cat and weighed it; it was, he found, exactly three pounds.

"You cunning woman!" he said to his wife. "If this is the cat, then where's the meat? And if this is the meat, then where's the cat?"

•••••

A farmer presented a small rabbit to Juha, who was generous to him in return. The farmer thanked him and went off. Next day, two villagers came and awaited Juha's hospitality. He asked them who they were, and they told him they were the neighbors of the man who'd given the rabbit. So, Juha treated them generously, and they left full of gratitude. On the third day, a group of villagers came to him, and he asked them what they wanted. They were, they said, the neighbors of the neighbors of the man who'd given the rabbit. Juha went into the house, came back with a pot of hot water, and presented it to them.

"Oh neighbors of the neighbors of the man who gave the rabbit," he said, "this is the sauce of the sauce of the rabbit. You can have it to keep."

•••••

Someone hired Juha, then working as a porter, to carry a container with three big bottles in it. On the way, he said, he'd teach Juha three pieces of wisdom that would stand him in good stead.

Juha started carrying the container and, when they'd gone a third of the way, asked the man to teach him the first piece of wisdom.

"If anyone tells you," the man answered, "that it's better to be hungry than to be full, don't believe him."

Juha agreed this was true. Then, when they'd gone two-thirds of the way, he asked the man to teach him the second piece of wisdom.

"If anyone tells you," the man said, "that walking's better than riding, don't believe him."

Again Juha agreed this was true. When they reached the door of the man's house, Juha asked for the third piece of wisdom.

"If anyone tells you," the man said, "you'll be paid a fee for carrying these bottles, don't believe him."

Juha flung the container down on the ground.

"If anyone tells you," he said, "that there's a single bottle in there that isn't broken, don't believe him!"

•••••

Juha attended a banquet given by a wealthy person, and a grilled kid was set in front of him. He started eating with gusto.

"From the way you're tearing into that," remarked the host, who had a malicious streak, "I wonder if the poor creature's mother ever gored you."

"From the sympathy you're showing for it," Juha retorted, "people might think its mother had nursed you at her breast."

•••••

Juha had two wives. One evening, when he was sitting with them and enjoying their company, they decided to trap him by asking which one of them he loved the best.

"I love you both the same," he told them.

"Oh, no," they said, "you can't just slither out of it like that. You're in trouble this time! Now, there's a pool over there. Just choose which of us you'd rather drown in it. Which one of us are you going to toss in the water?"

Juha hesitated, pondering his dilemma. Finally he turned to his first wife.

"I've just remembered, my dear," he said. "You learned to swim some years back, didn't you?"

•••••

A man hit Juha from behind in the middle of the street, looking to make fun of him. Juha grabbed the man by the collar and dragged him in front of the judge. The man claimed he'd mistaken Juha for a friend of his, someone he often joked with in this heavy-handed way. Juha, though, refused to accept his apology.

The judge knew the offender personally and wanted to spare him any punishment. The best thing to do, he declared, was for Juha to hit the man in the same way, or else agree to take ten dirhams from him by way of compensation. Juha couldn't resist the lure of the money, and the judge asked the man if he had it with him.

The offender saw what the judge was driving at. He didn't, he said, have the money with him, but he'd go home and bring it back right away. The judge gave him permission to leave, and he didn't return. After a long wait, Juha got wise to the judge's ruse. He came up close to the judge, as if to whisper in his ear, then gave him a mighty slap. As he left, he said:

"If by any chance the man comes back with the money, then I hereby waive it in your favor."

•••••

An irritating man asked Juha to lend him his donkey to carry out some tasks. Juha's donkey was very dear to him, and he knew, if the donkey struggled under its load or stumbled along the way, that this fat man would probably heap curses and damnation on donkey and owner alike.

So, Juha told him, with apologies, that another friend had borrowed the donkey earlier, to help with his own tasks. The man had no option but to accept the excuse. Then, just as he was leaving, the donkey started braying in the courtyard of the house.

The man was furious.

"Are you telling me, Juha," he inquired sarcastically, "that the donkey isn't here, and yet there it is, braying inside?"

Juha decided to cap the man's cheek with something even cheekier.

"Take it easy, friend," he said. "I've had my say and the donkey's had his. Aren't you ashamed of yourself, accepting the donkey's say-so and calling an old gray-bearded man a liar?"

•••••

When Juha's wife passed away, he married a widow, who regularly brought up the merits of her late husband. And, to spite her, he in his turn would recount the numerous merits of his late wife.

Finally he grew tired of all this. One night, when they were sleeping, he kicked her out of bed and she fell onto the floor. Furious, she went to complain to her father.

"I hope you won't judge me too harshly," Juha told him. "There are four of us sleeping in the same bed: my late wife and myself, and your daughter and her late husband. There isn't room in the bed for four, so your daughter rolled out on the floor. Surely you can't blame me for that?"

•••••

Juha was critically ill.

"Go and put on your smartest clothes and most attractive makeup," he told his wife. "Then come back here to me."

"How can I leave your side," she asked, "when you're here on your deathbed? Do you think I'm ungrateful or weak-willed?"

"No, my dear," Juha said. "You missed my meaning. I can see the angel of death hovering over me. Perhaps if he saw you in your splendid clothes, and looking so attractive, he might leave me and take you instead!"

•••••

Juha visited the city's governor and told him he'd composed a poem in his praise; if the governor so wished, he'd recite it. The governor agreed, but, when he'd heard it, decided he didn't like it. He accordingly presented Juha with a donkey's saddle, which Juha placed on his own back, then left.

As he was leaving the palace, the governor's wife happened to meet him and asked what it was he was carrying on his shoulder.

"My lady," Juha answered, "I recited, to our lord the governor, my most splendid poem in his praise. And he presented me with his most splendid piece of clothing."

•••••

The prince of the country (encouraged by the flattery poured out on him by countless people) always claimed he was a poet; indeed the foremost poet in the region. One day, after he'd recited one of his poems, his entourage started heaping praise, striving to point out the wondrous points of rhetoric and the mastery embodied in the poem—all except Juha, who said nothing.

"Didn't you like it?" the prince asked him. "It's a literary masterpiece surely!"

"I don't see any mastery there," Juha answered.

The prince, furious, ordered Juha to be shut up in the stable, and there he stayed for a whole month.

On a later occasion the prince composed another poem and recited it when Juha was present. Juha quickly rose and made to leave, but the prince stopped him.

"Where are you going?" he asked.

"To the stable, my lord prince!" Juha answered.

54

Juha the Fool

[Sometimes, in sharp contrast to the anecdotes of the previous section, Juha emerges rather as the fool, or as the butt of humorous situations.]

Juha sent his son to buy him some grapes, but the son was away so long that Juha lost patience. When the boy finally came back, with the grapes, Juha asked him about the figs.

"But," the son said, "you didn't ask me to get any figs."

"When I send you to do one thing for me," Juha instructed him, "you ought to do two!"

Sometime after this, Juha fell ill and told his son to fetch a doctor. So the son brought a doctor and another man along with him.

"Who's this second fellow?" Juha asked.

"Didn't you tell me," the son answered, "that, whenever you ask me to do one thing, I ought to do two? So, I brought you the doctor, and, if he cures you, that's fine. If he doesn't, I brought the gravedigger, too."

•••••

One morning Juha went to the marketplace and bought a donkey. Then he started back home, leading the donkey behind him on a rope. Two thieves followed him, and one of them untied the rope from the donkey's neck and put it around his own, while the other one took off with the donkey. Juha, meanwhile, was quite unaware of what was happening.

After a while Juha happened to look behind him and saw a man there in place of the donkey.

"Where's the donkey?" he asked, astonished.

"I'm the donkey," the thief answered.

"How's that?" demanded Juha.

The thief explained.

"I was ungrateful to my mother," he said, "and so she put a curse on me—she prayed the Almighty would turn me into a donkey. Next morning I woke up to find I really had been turned into one. And she took me off to the marketplace and sold me to the man you just bought me from. It seems, God be praised, that I'm now back in my mother's favor and blessing. I've been turned into a human being again."

"All power is in the Almighty," Juha observed. "How could I have used you, when you were human all the time? Off you go now."

With that, Juha untied the rope from around the thief's neck. "Now," he warned the man, "don't upset your mother again! God will compensate me for my loss."

A week later he went to the marketplace to buy a donkey, and there was the same one he'd bought the week before. He went up to it.

"You ill-omened donkey!" he whispered in its ear. "You've been ungrateful to your mother again, after I warned you not to be. You deserve everything that's happened to you!"

•••••

Two imbeciles were walking along a road. "Let's each make a wish," one of them said.

The first man said he wished he had a thousand sheep, and the second said he wished he had a thousand wolves.

"Why's that?" asked the first man.

"So my wolves can eat your sheep," answered the second.

The first man, furious, began heaping abuse on the second, who gave as good as he got in return, till finally they came to blows.

At this point Juha happened to pass by, with two jars of honey on the back of his donkey, and he asked what the matter was. When they told him, he unloaded the two jars of honey and spilled their contents out on the ground.

"May God," he said, "shed my blood as I've spilled this honey, if you aren't a pair of imbeciles!"

•••••

Juha married a woman who was very fat, and he was afraid she'd be too strong for him and do him harm. One day, when she was chasing after him with a cane in her hand, he hid under the bed, where she was too fat to follow him.

"Come here after me," he yelled, feeling safe at last. "If you're man enough!"

•••••

"I heard the most extraordinary yelling and din in your house," a neighbor told him. "It sounded like a quarrel, and then as if something went clattering down the stairs."

"Well," Juha said, "there was a bit of a quarrel between me and my wife. She hit my cloak, and it fell on the floor, then clattered down the stairs. That's what made all the noise."

But how, his neighbor inquired, could a cloak make such a noise?

"Brother," Juha answered, "don't be so fussy over every little detail. I was inside the cloak!"

•••••

Juha was trying vainly to sell a cow he had. A broker in the marketplace saw him and offered to sell it for the usual fee. Juha agreed, and the merchant promptly started crying out details of the cow, noting all its various uses and good qualities, including the fact that it was six months pregnant. The cow was swiftly sold.

Sometime after, matchmakers came to Juha's house to ask for his daughter's hand in marriage to a particular suitor. As they were expanding on his daughter's good qualities, he remembered the one that had led his cow to be sold so quickly.

"She's everything you see, and more," he told the matchmakers. "On top of everything else, she's six months pregnant!"

55

The Logic of Juha

[Special category of anecdotes featuring "Juha the fool" involves the use, by Juha, of an extraordinary, twisted logic. The following anecdotes, some of them not unlike certain kinds of modern surreal humor, illustrate this "logical" process.]

One day Juha rode to the marketplace on his donkey. He bought some vegetables, put them in the saddlebag, then, flinging the saddlebag over his shoulders, he mounted the donkey and rode off.

"Why," a friend asked him, "don't you put the saddlebag on the donkey's back? That way you won't have the work of carrying it yourself."

"Have a fear of God, man!" Juha retorted. "Isn't it enough that I'm riding this poor donkey? Do you want me to tire it out carrying the saddlebag, too?"

•••••

Juha was digging in the ground outside the city of Kufa, and an acquaintance of his passed by.

"What's the matter, Juha?" the man asked. "Why are you digging?"

"I buried some money here in the desert," Juha said, "but I can't find the spot."

"Well," said the other man, "you should have marked it."

"I did," replied Juha. "It was right in the shade of a cloud up there in the sky. And now the shade's completely gone."

•••••

Juha was searching for his lost donkey, muttering the whole time: "Praise be to God!"

"Why do you keep saying that?" people asked him.

"I'm praising God I wasn't riding my donkey," he said. "If I had been, I would have been lost, too."

•••••

"Which is more useful," someone asked Juha, "the sun or the moon?"

He didn't hesitate for a moment.

"The moon," he answered firmly. "No question about it."

"Why's that?" they asked.

"Because," he answered, "the sun rises during the day, when you don't need it. But the moon comes out in the dark. And that's when you need it."

•••••

He was taking along ten donkeys and riding one of them. It occurred to him to count them, and he found there were only nine. So, he got down and started looking for the tenth donkey. Then, before he remounted, he counted them again and found there were ten.

"I'd do better," he said to himself, "to walk and gain a donkey than ride and lose one."

•••••

He was walking down the street, and a thorn stuck painfully in his foot. When he got home, he took it out, then said: "The Lord be praised!"

"What makes you praise God?" his wife asked.

"I'm praising Him," Juha replied, "because I wasn't wearing my new shoes. The thorn would have made a hole in one of them."

56

Juha the Judge

Once, when Juha had been appointed a judge, a cook complained to him how a poor man had found a dry morsel of bread, then passed it over the steam of the food he was cooking, and eaten it. The cook demanded the price of the steam.

Juha took out a bag of coins and counted them, making them jingle as he did it.

"You can take the jingling of the coins," he told the cook, "as the price for the flavorsome steam of your cooking."

•••••

A thief went into a butcher's shop and ordered some meat. Then, while the butcher was busy cutting the meat, he opened the money drawer and stole some silver coins. But the butcher noticed this, grabbed him by the throat, and hauled him off in front of Judge Juha.

When he'd heard each side's story, Juha found himself perplexed as to his judgment. So, he ordered a bowl of hot water to be brought and put the coins in it. Before too long a film of fat appeared on the surface of the water, and by this Juha knew the coins were the butcher's. He returned to the man his coins and ordered the thief to be taken to prison.

•••••

A man was sleeping in an orchard with his cloak over him as a cover. A thief came by and took the cloak, but the man woke, seized hold of the thief, and led him in front of Judge Juha.

There before him, each man claimed the cloak was his own, and Juha was perplexed as to where the truth lay. So he made each man hold one end of the cloak and left them like this for quite some time, while he attended to some papers. Then, suddenly, he yelled out:

"You, the thief, give the cloak back to its owner!"

Taken by surprise, one of the two let go at once. Juha knew then that this man was the thief and ordered him to be imprisoned, while returning the cloak to its owner.

The Juha selections were taken from the numerous collections available to scholars and readers.

V

Other Comic Tales

57

Abu ʾl-Qasim's Slippers

There was, in Baghdad, a man called Abu ʾl-Qasim al-Tunbouri, who had a pair of slippers he wore for seven years. Whenever a tear appeared in them, he would have it patched, till at last they grew very heavy, so much so that they became a byword.

It happened, one day, that he went into the glass market.

"Abu ʾl-Qasim," a broker told him, "today a merchant from Aleppo has come here with a load of gilded glass he couldn't sell. Why don't you buy it from him? I'll sell it for you in no time. You'll double your money with this."

Abu ʾl-Qasim went and bought the glass for sixty dinars. Then he went into the perfume market, and another broker came up to him.

"Abu ʾl-Qasim," the man said, "today a merchant came to us from Nasibin with rose water, but he was so eager to be gone that I was able to buy it from him cheaply. I'll sell it to you, and you'll double your money in no time."

So Abu ʾl-Qasim bought the rose water for another sixty dinars. Then he filled the gilded glass bottles with the rose water and put them on the main shelf of his home.

After that he went to the public bath to wash.

"Abu ʾl-Qasim," one of his friends there said, "I wish you'd change those slippers of yours. They're as ugly as they could be, and, God be thanked, you're a prosperous man."

"You're right," Abu ʾl-Qasim said. "I'll do as you say."

Coming out from the bath, he put on his clothes, then saw a new pair of slippers next to his old ones. His friend, he thought, must have generously bought them for him. He put them on and went home.

But that new pair of slippers belonged to a judge who'd come to the bath. When he went out, he didn't find his slippers.

"Has someone," he asked, "put on my slippers and left his own in their place?"

They searched but found only Abu ʾl-Qasim's old slippers, which they recognized at once. The judge sent his servants to search Abu ʾl-Qasim's house, and they found the judge's slippers there. The judge summoned him, had him beaten, then imprisoned him for a time and fined him some money, before finally releasing him.

Abu ʾl-Qasim left prison and took his slippers, feeling a furious anger against them. He went straight to the Tigris and flung them in. The slippers sank down into the river.

Then a fisherman came and cast his net, and the slippers came up in it. Seeing them, he recognized them and thought they must have fallen from Abu ʾl-Qasim into the Tigris. He took them to Abu ʾl-Qasim's house but didn't find him there. Then, looking around and seeing the window of the main room, he flung the slippers through it, and they hit the shelf where Abu ʾl-Qasim had put the gilded bottles with the rose water. The shelf gave way, the glass bottles fell and broke, and all the rose water spilled out.

When Abu ʾl-Qasim came back home, he realized what had happened. Beating his face, he burst into tears.

"Oh, my money," he cried. "My money! This cursed pair of slippers has made me poor!"

With that he rose and dug a hole to bury the slippers once and for all. But the neighbors, hearing the sound of the digging, thought someone was trying to dig a way into their homes. They appealed to the governor, who summoned Abu ʾl-Qasim.

"How dare you," he said, "dig tunnels into your neighbors' homes!"

He imprisoned him and only released him after fining him some money. Once released, Abu ʾl-Qasim's fury rose once more against his old slippers, and he took them to the latrine at the inn. But the shoes blocked the latrine's pipe so that it overflowed, sending out a fearful stench. The neighbors, finding this intolerable, sought out the cause and found it was a pair of slippers, and, on examining them, realized they were Abu ʾl-Qasim's slippers. They took them to the governor and told him what had happened.

The governor summoned Abu ʾl-Qasim, reprimanded and imprisoned him, and ordered him to repair the latrine. This cost him a good deal of money, and he was fined the same amount again by the governor before he was released.

Abu ʾl-Qasim came out of prison carrying his old slippers.

"By God," he yelled, "I shall never part with these slippers again!"

He gave them a thorough wash, then put them on the roof of his house to dry. A dog saw them and, thinking they were a dead body, took them off to another roof. But the dog dropped them and they landed on the head of a passerby, wounding it badly. People examined the shoes and realized they belonged to Abu ʾl-Qasim.

They complained to the governor, who made Abu ʾl-Qasim pay the wounded man compensation and cover all his medical expenses. This exhausted the last of Abu ʾl-Qasim's money, leaving him with nothing at all.

With that Abu ʾl-Qasim took the slippers, went to the judge, and told him their entire history.

"I ask," he said, "that His Excellency the Judge should set down, on paper, that there is no connection between me and those slippers, and that, whatever they do, I am not to be made liable."

The judge, laughing, gave him some money, and Abu ʾl-Qasim left.

From Luis Sheikho, *Majani ʾl-Adab* (*The Harvest of Literature*), 1889, vol. 3, in *Qisas al-ʿArab* (*Stories of the Arabs*), vol. 4, originally known to have been written by Taqiyy al-Din Ibn Hujja ʾl-Hamawi in the ninth century A.H./fifteenth century C.E.

58

The Party Crashers

[Baghdad apparently contained many professional gate-crashers, who gained a livelihood by attending gatherings uninvited and consuming the food there. The following episode provides an example of this.]

Darraj said:

As I was coming from Baghdad, I happened to pass by a house where a big lunch party was evidently in progress. I saw the host inviting any man he didn't recognize to climb a ladder to a furnished [upper] room. [Having added myself to their number,] I found myself among thirteen people. The host then pulled down the ladder.

The tables below were set for the feast, leaving my companions at a loss, not knowing what to do.

"We've never," I heard them say, "known anything like this happen before!"

"Gallants," I asked them, "what's your line of work?"

"We crash parties," they answered.

"And just what," I asked, "do you intend to do now?"

"We can't see any way out," they said.

"Suppose," I said, "I were to hatch a trick, and have you eat and be released, would you admit I was your master in party crashing?"

"And who are you, by God?" they asked.

"I'm Ibn Darraj," I answered.

"We'll admit it," they said then, "even before you hatch your trick for us."

With that I peered down on the host, as his guests were eating, and yelled out:

"You, the owner of the house!"

"What do you want?" he said.

"Which would you rather have?" I asked. "Will you bring us a big tray filled with food, and we'll eat and go straight afterward? Or shall I throw myself down from this upper room? That way you'll have a dead man leaving the house, and your wedding will be turned straight into a wake."

As I spoke, I made as if to throw myself down.

"Wait!" he shouted. "Woe to you, don't throw yourself down!" And with that he rushed off [to do as I'd said]. "He must be a madman!" I heard him say.

And so they sent up a big tray of food. We ate, and then we left.

From al-Khatib al-Baghdadi, *Kitab al-Tatfeel wa Hikayat al-Tufayliyyin wa Nawadirihim wa Akhbarihim* (*Book on Party Crashing and the Stories of Party Crashers and Their Anecdotes*); in *Qisas al-ʿArab* (*Stories of the Arabs*), vol. 4.

59

Me Too?

Abu ʾl-Hasan said:

There was a man in our town who sank so deep into debt that he had to stay inside his house to keep his creditors at bay. One of the creditors, though, who was owed a small sum of money, managed to get in to him.

"Suppose," this man said, "I find a way for you to appear in public again, safe from your creditors? What will you give me?"

"I'll pay you what I owe you," the man answered, "and as much as you like on top."

The creditor had to make pledges to reassure the man. Then he said:

"Tomorrow, before the time for prayer, tell your servant to sweep in front of your door and courtyard, lay mats on the floor of your shop, and put a recliner there for you to lean on. Then sit down and, whenever anyone passes and greets you, bark in his face. Don't ever do anything more than bark, no matter who the person is. Even if your family and servants speak to you, or anyone else, your creditors included, just keep doing the same till you're taken to the judge. When he talks to you, bark in his face as well, just barking, nothing else at all. When the judge sees how serious the matter is, he'll be sure you're touched in the head, and he'll set you free."

The debtor did as the man had advised him. His neighbor passed, and he barked in his face. Then another neighbor passed, and he did the same, just barking, nothing else at all. Others passed him, too; and then people seized him and took him to the judge. He did the same with the judge, who ordered him to be put in prison and had him watched. But he kept it up, barking and making not a sound otherwise.

When the judge saw this, he ordered his release and had him watched at his home. But still all he'd do was bark. Thereupon the judge, convinced of his state at last, ordered his creditors to stop harassing him.

"This man's sick in the head," he said.

The man stayed like this for a long time. Eventually the creditor who'd shown him the ruse came to ask for the money due to him. When, though, he spoke to the man, all he got back was barking.

"Woe to you, man!" he said. "Me too? When I was the one who showed you the trick?"

Still the man would say nothing, but just went on barking, till his creditor gave up and went off in despair.

From al-Jahiz, *Al-Hayawan* (*Book of Animals*), 2; in *Qisas al-ʿArab* (*Stories of the Arabs*), vol. 4.

60

A Quick-Witted Prisoner

Bakkar ibn Rabah said:

There was a man in Mecca who made arrangements for men and women to meet and provided them with drinks. He was duly reported to the ruler of Mecca, who banished him to Mount Arafat.

There he built himself a house, then sent for his old customers.

"What's stopping you," he asked them, "from going on just as before?"

"But how," they answered, "when you're living on Arafat?"

"Pay out two dirhams for a donkey," he said. "There'll be a safe haven, and a wonderful time, just waiting for you."

So they started riding out to him, and he corrupted the morals of the people of Mecca. Once more he was reported to the ruler, who sent for him.

"Enemy of God!" he said. "I expelled you from God's holy place. And now, with your corruption, you infect the most solemn place of ritual!"

"These people are lying," the man replied.

"To prove what we've said," the informants rejoined, "have all the donkeys in Mecca brought together, then send them off to Arafat with people you trust. If they don't go straight to his house, out of all the houses there, then we're in the wrong."

"This will be a witness and a proof," the ruler said.

The donkeys of Mecca were brought together and sent out. And they all headed straight for the man's house.

"What more is needed?" the ruler asked. "Strip him."

So they stripped him. When he saw the whips, he cried out: "Must I be flogged?"

"You must," the ruler replied.

"By God," the man replied, "the worst of all this is the way the people in Iraq are going to laugh at us. The people in Mecca, they'll say, deal out punishment on the evidence of donkeys!"

And the ruler laughed.

From Ibn al-Jawzi, *Akhbar al-Zurraf wa ʾl-Mutamajinin* (*Anecdotes of Humorists and Jesters*), Damascus (from the copy in the Taimuriyya Library), A.H. 1347.

61

Al-Hajjaj and al-Muttalib

A*bu Ishaq al-Juhaimi said:*

Al-Hajjaj went out in disguise and, passing by al-Muttalib, Abu Lahab's son, asked him:

"What can you tell me about al-Hajjaj?"

"May God's curses descend on him!" al-Muttalib said.

"And when," al-Hajjaj asked, "does he come out [among the people]?"

"May God cause his soul to come out from his breast!" al-Muttalib replied.

"Do you know me?" al-Hajjaj asked then.

"No," said al-Muttalib.

"I am al-Hajjaj," al-Hajjaj said.

"And do you know me?" al-Muttalib asked at once.

"No," al-Hajjaj answered.

Al-Muttalib said:

"I am al-Muttalib, Abu Lahab's son, known to be afflicted by madness three days in the month, and today is the first."

Al-Hajjaj promptly left him.

From Ibn al-Jawzi, *Akhbar al-Zurraf wa' l-Mutamajinin* (*Anecdotes of Humorists and Jesters*), Damascus (from the copy in the Taimuriyya Library), A.H. 1347.

62

A Cunning Marriage Broker

A marriage broker came to a man and said:

"I have a woman who's like a spray of narcissus."

The man married her forthwith, only to find she was old and ugly.

"You deceived me," he told the marriage broker.

"No, by God," she answered. "I didn't. I said she was like a spray of narcissus, because her hair's white, her face is yellow, and her feet are green."

From Ibn al-Jawzi, *Akhbar al-Zurraf wa 'l-Mutamajinin* (*Anecdotes of Humorists and Jesters*), Damascus (from the copy in the Taimuriyya Library), A.H. 1347.

63

Forgery on a Shaky Boat

I was told this story by Abu ʾl-Husain, son of the judge Ibn ʿAyyash:

One windy day in Baghdad, I saw a friend of mine sitting in a boat beneath the bridge over the river Dijla. He was writing there.

"What a fool you are," I said, "writing while you're being tossed about on a stormy day like this."

"I'm about," he said, "to forge a document, in the name of a quivering, tremulous man. I can't use a steady hand to do it. And so I've chosen this place where the waves will shake the boat in the wind. They'll whirl my handwriting around and make it as jagged as his!"

From Abu ʿAli ʾl-Muhassin al-Tanukhi, *Nishwar al-Muhadara wa Akhbar al-Mudhakara* (*Snippets of Conversation and Memorable Tales*), vol. 1.

64

A Tempting Wager

It has been told how a king offered a great sum of money as the price of a mare from the Arabian desert, belonging to a Bedouin. But the Bedouin would not sell. A basket weaver came to the king and told him: "Give a good sum of money to a man, to be handed over to me if I bring the mare. Then I will bring it."

When this had been done, the basket weaver went off to see how the mare was being kept, and he found its owner had appointed a slave whose sole task was to take care of it. The mare was grazing close to him but was securely tethered. The basket weaver went and bought some tasty food, then, sitting down near a stream where the slave could see him, invited the man to come and share the food with him. The slave came and ate with him, and they began to talk together. After they had eaten, the basket weaver said:

"Will you make a wager with me about leaping this stream? Will you wager so many dirhams you can do what I can?"

The slave agreed to this. Thereupon the basket weaver leaped over the stream, and the slave leaped over and was paid the wager. Then the basket weaver told him: "I can do more—I can tie my feet together and leap. If you can do the same, then I will pay you twice as much as I paid you just now."

The slave, greedy and eager to win the money, agreed. "Tie me up," the basket weaver told him. The slave untied the mare, using the straps to bind the other man; whereupon the basket weaver drew his legs together and leaped over the stream.

"I can do the same," said the slave. He untied the basket weaver's feet, used the straps to bind his own, then leaped over the stream. And at the very same moment the basket weaver leaped onto the mare and galloped off.

From *Al-Asad wa ʾl-Ghawwas* (*The Lion and the Diver*), an Arab fable from the fifth/eleventh century, ed. Ridwan al-Sayyid, 2nd ed. (Beirut, 1992).

VI

Tales of the Strange or Supernatural

65

The Strangest Story

When the Abbasids assumed the caliphate, all those Umayyads that were left went into hiding. Among them was Ibrahim ibn Sulaiman. Some of his friends interceded on his behalf with the Abbasid caliph al-Saffah,[1] who granted him safe conduct, then received him at his court and honored him.

One day, al-Saffah said to him:

"Ibrahim, tell me the strangest thing to befall you during the time you were in hiding."

Thereupon Ibrahim recounted the following story:

"I was hiding in al-Hira, in a house looking out on the desert. One day, as I was sitting on the roof of this house, I saw black banners[2] coming from Kufa to al-Hira. I was in great fear, for I supposed the men were searching for me.

"I went off, disguised, till I came to Kufa, not knowing in whose house I could hide. I stayed for a time, pondering what I should do; then I saw a large gate and entered through it. In the courtyard of the house I found a handsome, kindly looking man in clean attire. He asked me who I was and what I wanted.

"'I am,' I said, 'a man in terror for his life. I have come to ask you for shelter and safety.'

"He led me into his house and hid me in a room near his harem, where I stayed enjoying every hospitality of food, drink, and clothing. The man never asked me anything of my circumstances. He would, I noted, ride out each morning at dawn and return a little before noon.

---

1. Caliph al-Saffah, ʿAbd Allah ibn Muhammad, was the first of the Abbasid rulers (r. 132/750–136/754).
2. Abbasid banners were black.

" 'Why is it,' I asked him one day, 'that you always ride out?'

" 'Ibrahim ibn Sulaiman ibn ʿAbd al-Malik killed my father,' he told me, 'and I have been told he's hiding in al-Hira. I go out each day to seek my revenge on him.'[3]

"When I heard this, Prince of the Faithful, my fear grew, and I felt the world narrow before my eyes. I had, I saw, drawn myself to my own death.

"I asked the man his name, and his father's name, and he told me. Then I knew his words were true.

" 'Sir,' I said, 'it is my duty to be truthful with you. In recompense for your generous treatment of me, I shall guide you to your goal.'

" 'Where is he, then?' he asked.

" 'I am the man you have been seeking,' I said. 'Take your vengeance now.'

" 'Has hiding,' he asked, smiling, 'become so wearisome for you, away from your home and family, that you've begun to seek death?'

" 'No, by God,' I said. 'I was speaking the truth. I killed your father, on such and such a day, for such and such a reason.'

"When he heard my words, and realized what I was saying was true, his color changed and his eyes grew red. Then he pondered at length before looking toward me once more.

" 'As for you,' he said, 'you will meet my father in the presence of a Just Judge, and He will take His revenge on you. I shall not betray the pledge of safety I gave you. I ask, even so, that you leave now, for I cannot guarantee your safety if you stay here in my presence.'

"With that he proffered me a thousand dinars, which I declined to accept, and left.

"This was the strangest thing that ever befell me. And this man was the most generous I ever saw or heard of, after you, Prince of the Faithful."

From *Qisas al-ʿArab* (*Stories of the Arabs*), vol. 1.

---

3. It was the duty of a son or brother, as a matter of honor, to avenge the murder of his father or brother, or other close kinsman, by killing the murderer or one of the murderer's kin. This code appears to have been inherited from pre-Islamic times.

66

I Shall Never Eat Elephant Flesh

I was told this story by Ja'far al-Khalidi, who heard it from the prominent Sufi sheikh al-Khawwas:

I took to the sea with a group of other Sufis, and, as we sailed on, our ship was wrecked. We floated on pieces of timber, and some of us were saved, being set ashore, finally, in a place unknown to us. There we stayed for a number of days with nothing to eat. We were starving and close to death.

We came together, and some of us said:

"Let us make a vow to Almighty God: that, should He save us from this place, we will do certain things, or hold back from doing certain things, for His sake."

"I shall fast for the rest of my life," one said.

"We shall pray so many times each day," others pledged.

Yet another person said:

"I shall never tell a lie."

After each had taken his oath, they turned to me and asked:

"What do you have to say?"

"I shall never eat elephant flesh," I replied.

"This," they said, "is no place for joking!"

"By God," I said, "I'm not trying to make fun. But ever since you started on your vows, I've been wondering what promise I could give to Almighty God. I was at a loss. Then it came to me as I've just said. I spoke as my faith directed me."

"It must be something in the air here," they said.

A little later, we began wandering and exploring the land in search of something to eat. At last we came across a plump baby elephant. My companions seized hold of it and tussled with it, till finally they managed to kill it. Then they roasted it.

"Come here and eat," they said.

"A short while back," I said, "I made a vow to Almighty God that I wouldn't do such a thing. Now perhaps I see the reason why. I've eaten nothing for days, and I've no prospect of finding anything else to feed on. But to break my oath to Him by sharing this with you might well be the death of me. Go ahead and eat yourselves." I refused even to go near them.

When they'd eaten their fill, they grew more cheerful. Night fell, and they went off to their sleeping places. I held back, lying down to sleep by the trunk of a tree I'd chosen earlier.

After about an hour, an elephant appeared and began approaching the spot where the baby elephant had been caught. It was trumpeting and rumbling, filling the wilderness with heavy, thunderous roars. It was clearly pursuing us.

"This is the end of us," some of our group said. "There's no escape." And with that they flung themselves flat, their faces to the ground.

The elephant came closer, then went up to them, one after the other, going about and sniffing the body of each man from head to toe. Once it had finished sniffing every part, it raised one of its forelegs, then planted it on the man, crushing his bones. Then, once sure the man had perished, the elephant raised its foreleg, moved to another man, and did just as it had done to the one before, till they were all crushed to death.

Then my turn came. I was sitting upright, taking in what was happening, praying and begging Almighty God for pardon and forgiveness. I didn't lie face down, nor did I flee. The elephant moved toward me, and, when I was within its reach, I lay down on my back. It began sniffing me, every part and limb almost, as it had done with my companions. Then it sniffed me, as it had not done with my comrades, for a second and a third time. Then, stretching out its trunk, it hoisted me into the air. It's going to kill me, I thought, only it's devising some new way of doing it. The trunk held me in its grip, then turned me around and set me on the elephant's back. I sat bolt upright, holding my nerve and thanking Almighty God for keeping me alive up till now. My thoughts went this way and that, wandering between puzzlement and a premonition of death. The elephant was galloping now, running on furiously, till dawn came. Then it stopped and raised its trunk toward me. Now my hour's come, I thought. The elephant wrapped me in its trunk, lowered me gently onto the ground, then went off. I stood there in disbelief, watching it turn and go back where it had come from.

I watched the elephant move further off, till at last it disappeared. Then I thanked Almighty God and said my prayers. I looked at the spot where I was, and round about me, and found I was on a broad, long road. I walked about two leagues, until I reached the borders of a splendid neighborhood. And, traveling on in, I found myself in one of the great cities of India.

The people of the city (al-Khawwas the Sufi went on) were astonished to see me and asked me about myself. I told them what had happened to me, whereupon they said the path taken by the elephant, in that one night, took days to cover usually.

After a while, I excused myself and left these people. Then I wandered from one land to the next, till at last I returned safe to my own country.

From Abu ʿAli ʾl-Muhassin al-Tanukhi, *Nishwar al-Muhadara wa Akhbar al-Mudhakara* (*Snippets of Conversation and Memorable Tales*), vol. 3.

67

A Dream Come True

I was told this story by the state secretary Abu Ahmad ibn Muhammad ibn Suleiman, known as al-Dalji:

One night, Abu Ahmad al-Dalji said:

I had a dream. I was wandering, lost in the wilderness; then, at last, I saw a steep mountain. I climbed it and reached its summit. I was, I felt, very close to the moon, and the moon so close to me I could put out my hand and touch it. I was holding a piece of wood, and I plunged it into the moon and kept on piercing the sphere, till it was riddled with holes. With the same piece of lumber I collected up some of the nearby clouds and pasted them all over the moon. Then I heard a friend of mine asking me: "What are you doing?"

"I've killed the moon," I said, "and I'm covering it with these clouds."

I woke then. But, feeling apprehensive about the dream, I went to visit the scrivener Abu ʾl-Hassan Ahmad ibn ʿUmar al-Talqani. The moment he saw me, he said:

"I had a very strange dream last night. I was just about to call on you and interpret it to you."

"I, too," I said, "had a dream last night that's haunting me. And now, here I am to talk to you about it."

"What did you see?" he asked.

I described my dream to him.

"Don't trouble yourself about it," he said. "You're going to succeed Sahl ibn Bishr, the ruler of Ahwaz. Soon you'll enjoy his position and his wealth."

"Where did you get such a notion?" I asked. "And what did you see in your own dream?"

"In my dream last night," he said, "I met with a good and virtuous man. He must, I thought, be one of the Prophet's companions. I asked him to pray to Almighty God to bestow His blessing on me.

"The man asked me:

" 'Are you a friend of al-Dalji's?'

" 'Yes,' I answered.

" 'Then,' he went on, 'go and tell him this. Ahwaz will be his; but be should be obedient to God, and not offend his wife.'

"Clearly" (Abu ʾl-Hassan concluded) "my dream interprets yours."

I asked him to say nothing of our dreams to anyone. Then I left him and went home.

I wasn't aware I'd offended my wife in any way, except by having concubines. For a year or so, I'd had a maidservant who'd almost taken my wife's place. I sold her straight off, for some thousands of dirhams, and gave the money to my wife.

About a year later, the vizier Ibn Baqiyya came to Ahwaz with ʿIzz al-Din. They captured the army commander, Bakhtukin Azadthruweih, and the ruler, Sahl ibn Bishr, along with the Turks. The commander was later released and appointed chief of protocol, his privileges restored to him. I was given Sahl ibn Bishr's position as ruler of Ahwaz.

Ibn Bishr was imprisoned for a while before being sent to the capital, Baghdad. Then, during the rule of the prince ʿAdud al-Dawla, he was set free and later given the army command and government in Makram, Tastir, and Jundisabour. He seized the chance to settle old scores with me, keeping me confined and demanding money. Then, as he was about to receive the sum, he entered Ahwaz in the name of ʿAdud al-Dawla. For a year and a month he remained in Arjan, then began to incite and stir up the people of Dailam, who became restive, saying they wouldn't accept me as Ibn Bishr's replacement: unless I was dismissed, they said, and Ibn Bishr reinstated as vizier, they wouldn't support the new prince, ʿIzz al-Dawla. Ibn Bishr further lined up the officers and soldiers of the Ahwaz army, who pledged allegiance and loyalty to him. And in [A.H.] 365 [about 975 C.E.], he swore he'd march to Baghdad with his troops to see his demands met.

Prince ʿIzz al-Dawla was enraged. He dispatched his senior counselor, Ibrahim ibn Ismaʿil, with a letter to the people of Dailam, who swiftly thought better of what they'd done, expressing penitence and pledging obedience. Sahl ibn Bishr was arrested and sent to Prince ʿIzz al-Dawla in Baghdad.

As I'd been told in my dream (Abu Ahmad al-Dalji concluded), the Ahwaz province became my domain. I was the only suitable person, and, at a time of need, I was the sole person to be called on.

From Abu ʿAli ʾl-Muhassin al-Tanukhi, *Nishwar al-Muhadara wa Akhbar al-Mudhakara* (*Snippets of Conversation and Memorable Tales*), vol. 3.

68

The Body Snatcher

We were told this story by the poet Abu ʾl-Mughira Muhammad ibn Yaʿqoub al-Asadi of Baghdad, who had heard it from Abu Moussa ʿIsa ibn ʿUbaid Allah al-Baghdadi, who had himself received it from a friend:

I made my way to Ramlah [in Palestine], arriving there at night when the townspeople were sound asleep. So I made my way to the cemetery and went into one of the many vaults built above the graves. I placed my leather shield on the ground to use as a rest and, having slung my sword on the wall above me, lay down. I tried to get some sleep, so as to be ready to go into the town next morning, but I was restless and apprehensive, all alone there. I lay awake all night.

As the night wore on, I heard movements. There must be thieves passing by, I thought. If I confront them, I may not come out safe. And I can't face them anyway if there's a band of them. So I kept still, not moving a muscle. Nervous and frightened, I peered out through one of the holes in the vault and saw, as I thought, a beast, like a bear, moving about. I hid myself but saw how it came close to another vault alongside me, moving around it, exploring for a while, then stepping into one of its openings.

I watched in amazement and disbelief. What, I wondered, was the creature up to? It entered the vault, came out, then went quickly in and out, many times. Then, at last, I saw it go in and strike on one of the graves. The intruder must, I decided, be a body snatcher.

I watched him digging, with both hands, and realized he was using sharp iron instruments. I held back till he'd burrowed down quite deep, and I felt more confident and assured. Then I took hold of my sword and shield, walked forward on tiptoe, and entered the vault. He felt my presence and, as anyone would have done, stood up straight and lunged to slap at me with his hand—whereupon I chopped at his hand with my sword, severing it and seeing it fly off.

"Aaahhh!" he screamed. "You've killed me, God curse you!"

He rushed out, and I stayed on his heels. It was a bright, moonlit night. He kept on running, and I was chasing him, vainly trying to catch up with him, till he got into the town. He passed through endless streets and alleyways, and I was keeping track of the inroads to be sure I wouldn't lose my way. Then he reached a particular house, pushed open the door, went in, and locked the door behind him.

I marked the door, then turned back, following the same route I'd used during my pursuit, till I got back to the vault where I'd met the digger. There I searched for the severed hand and finally found it. I took it out into the moonlight and, after some time and a good deal of effort, managed to pull the hand from the iron instrument, which was like a glove with five channels for fingers. The hand itself was decorated with henna and had two gold rings on it.

I realized then, to my great consternation, that the digger had been a woman. The hand seemed to me, as I looked at it, the most beautiful hand in the world, so delicate, so graceful, so tender, so fresh and elegant. I rubbed the blood from it and fell asleep inside the vault.

Next morning, I went into the town and followed the signs of the roads till I reached the door.

"Whose house is this?" I asked.

"This is the house of the town's judge," came the answer.

A crowd of people had gathered near the door, and in due course a dignified and venerable old man came out to lead the people in their morning prayers, then sat back in the prayer niche [of the mosque]. Utterly astonished, I asked some of the people who the judge was, and they gave me his name. I went on questioning them and found, at last, that the judge had a young daughter and a wife. I was sure now that the digger had been his daughter. I approached him and said:

"God bless you, judge. May I speak to you in private?"

He led me to one of the inner corners of the mosque.

"So," he said, "what is it you have to say?"

I took out the hand.

"Do you recognize this?" I asked him.

"The hand I'm not familiar with," he said. "But these two rings are my young daughter's. What's this all about?"

I told him the whole story.

"Come with me," he said then, and he led me into his house and closed the door. Then he gave instructions for food to be served and called for his wife to come. The servant returned to tell him the woman wouldn't appear with a stranger present.

"Tell her," the judge said, "my guest is a man of honor, and she must come and eat with us."

The woman, though, refused to budge, and the judge began to swear oaths, threatening her with divorce if she refused to obey. So at last his wife came out, weeping, and sat down with us.

"Now tell your daughter to come out and join us," the judge said.

"Are you out of your mind?" the woman said. "What's the matter with you? You've already disgraced me, but at least I'm a mature woman. How dare you give offense to our young daughter?"

The man began once more to swear oaths and threaten to divorce her if she didn't bring the girl in. So the girl was brought in.

Before me was one of the most beautiful young women I'd seen in my life. My eyes were captivated by her charms. She looked, though, very pale and sick, and I knew this was because of what had happened to her hand.

"Eat with us now," the judge said.

She began eating with her right hand, hiding the other inside her clothing.

"Take out your left hand," he told her.

"It has a great abscess on it," the girl said. "It's bandaged up tight."

He insisted, swearing the girl must show her hand. The woman began pleading with her husband.

"Look to yourself, man," she said, "and preserve the honor of your daughter! I swear by God I never saw anything shameful from this girl before yesterday. She came and woke me after midnight, saying: 'Mother, save me, or I'll die!'

" 'What's the matter then?' I asked.

" 'I've had my hand cut off,' she answered. 'I'm losing blood fast. I'll soon be dead. Do something to help me, quickly!'

"With that she showed me her severed hand. I began wailing and beating her face.

" 'Mother!' she said. 'Don't cause me a scandal with your weeping in front of my father and the neighbors. Do something to help me.'

" 'I don't know how to treat you,' I said.

" 'Boil some oil,' she begged, 'and dip my hand in it.'

"I did this and bandaged her hand. Then I said:

" 'Now, tell me, what happened?'

"She refused, but I swore by God, warning her I'd take matters up with her father. At last she gave in.

" 'Two years ago,' she said, 'I became utterly seized by the idea of digging up graves. I told our maidservant to buy me an unshaved goatskin and two iron gloves. When everyone went to bed, I'd tell her to sleep in the hallway and leave the door unlocked. I'd put on the skin and the gloves and leave the house, walking on all fours, so people who saw me from the roofs of their houses would think I was a dog. I'd go to the graveyard, having found out what dignitaries had died that day and where they were buried. Then I'd move to a particular grave, dig it up, and take the shroud, stuffing it inside my skin. After that I'd walk out and come back home, where I'd open the unfastened door, come in, and lock it. I'd take off my goatskin and the iron gloves and give them to the maid, along with the grave clothes I'd snatched. The maid must have over three hundred shrouds stored for me now, in a special room in the house. I don't know what to do with them. But going out to fetch those shrouds, then keeping them as my own, gave me such delight, till this dreadful thing happened to me. Last night a man saw what I was going to do. From his actions, he seemed to be the watchman or guard at the cemetery. When I started digging, he attacked me. And when I tried to cuff his face with my iron hand and drive him off so I could run away and save myself, he struck my left arm with his sword and chopped off my hand.'

" 'Listen,' I said to the girl, 'I'll tell you what to do. First, you have to pretend you've fallen sick with a big abscess on your hand and stay in bed for some time. Your pale face will give support to the story. After a few days, we'll [supposedly] tell your father your hand must be cut off, otherwise your whole body will be poisoned and waste away, and you'll die. He'll give his permission for us to do that, and we'll let it be known we've amputated your hand to save your life. In fact, it's your reputation we'll be saving.'

"And that's exactly what we did—after the young woman had expressed repentance and begged forgiveness, vowing in the name of God never to do such things again.

"I'd intended," the mother told her husband, "to sell the maidservant, have my daughter by my side, and keep a closer eye on her. But now you've shamed me and brought humiliation on yourself!"

"By God," the girl said, "my mother's right. You know I'm sorry now and I'll never do it again."

The judge pointed toward me.

"This," he said, "is your friend who chopped off your hand."

The girl nearly fainted with fear. But the judge turned to me and asked: "Where are you from, young man?"

"I'm from Iraq," I said.

"And why have you come here?"

"To seek an honest living."

"You've found it," came the answer. "It's here for you to enjoy. By God, I had no notion of this malady of my daughter's. Almighty God has blessed us with wealth, and you and I are entrusted with a secret that must not be disclosed. Will you become one of us, and live here in our house? Will you marry my daughter, and let me provide for you from my riches and free you from dependence on other people?"

"I will," I said.

The judge ordered the food to be taken away, then took me out to the mosque, where people were waiting for him. He had, he told them, agreed to my proposal of marriage, and he married me to his daughter. Then he took me back to the house.

I was infatuated with the girl and made love to her. She lived with me for some months, but she clearly disliked me. I did all I could to appease her and make her happy. I wept at the loss of her hand, making the most profuse apology, and she apparently agreed to forgive me. I supposed she was simply grief-stricken at the loss of her hand.

One night, when I was sound asleep, I turned onto my back for a moment and felt, suddenly, a heavy weight on my chest. There she was over me, her legs holding down my arms, boldly raising a knife in her hand, ready to cut my throat. I tried to save myself by thrusting her off, but in vain. Afraid she might plunge down on me if I moved, I stayed still.

"Just tell me," I said, "then act however you want. Why are you doing this?"

"Why am I doing this?" she said. "You cut off my hand, and violated me, and married me, and you really think you're going to get away with it? I swear, by God, you won't!"

"You've missed your chance to kill me now," I said. "You can wound me, of course, but I'll escape death, and then I'll come back and cut your throat. Or maybe I'll just run off and make a scandal for you—hand you over to the sultan, who'll uncover your first crime and your second one. You'll be disowned by your family, then executed."

"Do whatever you want," she said. "You're going to be killed anyway. After all, we're mortal enemies now."

Looking at her, I realized I was in serious danger, that I might get a fatal wound. I'd have, I thought, to resort to trickery.

"I have a solution," I said.

"And what's that?" she asked.

"I'll divorce you on the spot," I said, "and then you can set me free. I'll leave the town, and you won't see me again. Your secret will never be known and you'll never be disgraced. You can marry anyone you like. The townspeople think your hand was amputated because of a poisoned abscess. You'll keep your good name."

"Do you swear," she said, "never to show your face in this town and bring me to disgrace?"

I gave her my most solemn oath. With that she got off my chest, and I lay there as though paralyzed. She ran off abruptly, for fear I might take hold of her. Then she flung away her knife and came back to me. She approached boldly but playfully. She'd only been teasing me, she said.

"Keep away from me!" I yelled. "I've pledged myself not to touch you. Tomorrow morning I'll leave this town and won't come back ever again."

"I see now," she said, "how honest and truthful you are. I swear, if you'd acted any other way, you wouldn't have lived to tell the tale."

She went away briefly, then came back with a bag.

"Here are a hundred dinars," she said. "Take them for your expenses. Write out my divorce paper. And don't ruin my reputation. Now go away!"

I started out from the town after midnight, having written a note to her father, telling him I'd divorced his daughter and left because I was ashamed to face him. I haven't seen them since.

From Abu ʿAli ʾl-Muhassin al-Tanukhi, *Nishwar al-Muhadara wa Akhbar al-Mudhakara* (*Snippets of Conversation and Memorable Tales*), vol. 3.

69

The Old Tailor and His Untimely Call to Prayer

I was told this anecdote by the judge Abu ʾl-Hasan Muhammad ibn Qadi ʿAbd al-Wahid al-Hashimi:

A large sum was owed to a leading tradesman by one of the generals, who constantly put off payment.

"I'd resolved," the tradesman said, "to appeal to al-Muʿtadid,[1] because, whenever I went to try to see the general, he ordered his door to be shut against me and had his slaves insult me. If, on the other hand, I tried gentle means and asked others to mediate, there was no result.

"Then one of my friends said to me: 'I'll recover your money for you, and then you needn't appeal to the caliph. Come with me, now.'

"So I got up, and he took me to a tailor in Tuesday Street, an old man who was seated there sewing and reading the Quran. He told the man what was happening to me and asked him to call on the general and see me righted. The general's residence was near the tailor's, and the tailor started off with us. As we walked along, I lagged behind and said to my friend:

" 'You're exposing this aged man, and yourself, and me, to serious annoyance. When he goes to my debtor's door, he'll be cuffed, and so will you and me with him. The general paid no attention to the urging of so-and-so and such and such, took no notice of the vizier even. Is it likely he'll pay any attention to our friend here?'

"My friend laughed.

" 'Never mind,' he said. 'Let's just walk on and see what happens.'

"We reached the general's door, and, when his slaves saw the tailor, they treated him with reverence, rushing to kiss his hand, which he wouldn't permit. Then they said:

---

1. An Abbasid caliph who reigned from 279 / 892 to 289 / 902.

" 'What brings you here, sir? The master's out riding, but if there's anything we can do, we'll do it at once. If not, then come in and take a seat till he's back.'

"This reassured me, and we went inside and sat down. Presently the man came, and, when he saw the tailor, became most respectful.

" 'You must give me your instructions,' he said, 'before I even go to change my clothes.'

"The tailor then spoke to him of my matter. He assured the tailor he had no more than five thousand dirhams in the house, but begged him to take those and to take his silver and gold harness as pledges for the rest, which he would pay within a month. I readily agreed to this, and he produced the dirhams, along with harness to the value of the remainder; and this latter I took possession of, having the tailor and my friend attest an agreement whereby it should remain with me for a month—after which I would be free to sell it and recoup what I was owed from the proceeds. Having had their attestations, I left with them, and, when we reached the tailor's place, I flung the money down in front of him.

" 'Sir,' I said, 'through you God has restored my property. I should be happy if you'd accept a quarter, a third, a half of it. I make the offer gladly.'

" 'Friend,' he replied, 'you're in haste indeed to return evil for good. Take yourself off with your property, with God's blessing.'

"I had, I told him, one further request. He said I should make it, and I asked him to tell me the reason why the general had yielded to him, when he had treated the greatest men in the empire with contempt.

" 'Sir,' he replied, 'you have what you came for. Leave me, please, to carry on the trade by which I earn my living.'

"I insisted even so, and he related as follows:

" 'For forty years I've been leading the prayers and teaching the Quran in this mosque here, and earning my living by tailoring, which is the only trade I know. Long ago, when I'd said the sunset prayer and was going home, I passed by a Turk who lived in this house. Suddenly a woman with the loveliest of faces passed, and the Turk, who was drunk, seized hold of her and tried to drag her into the house. She resisted and cried out for help, but she found none, for, despite her cries, nobody came forward to save her from the Turk. She was saying, among other things, that her husband had sworn to divorce her if ever she spent a night away from his house. If the Turk forced her to disobey in this, she said, he'd bring her home to ruin, over and above the crime he'd be committing and the disgrace he'd bring on her.

" 'I went up to the Turk and tried to stop him, telling him to let the woman go, but he struck me on the head with a club he was carrying, giving me a painful wound, then forced the woman into the house. I went home, washed off the blood, bound up the wound, then, when the pain had eased, went out to say the evening prayer. When this was over, I said to the congregation:

" ' "Come with me to this godless Turk, to take the matter up with him. Let's not leave till we've forced him to let the woman go."

" 'They rose up at that, and we went and made a great clamor at his door. Soon he came out at the head of a number of his slaves, raining blows on us, and he himself singled me out, striking me a blow that came close to killing me. My neighbors carried me, close to death it seemed, to where I lived. My family treated my wounds, and I slept, but very little on account of the pain, and at midnight I woke, no longer able to sleep for thinking about the matter.

" 'Then I said to myself: The fellow must have been drinking all night, and he won't know what time it is. If I sound the call to prayer, he'll suppose dawn's arrived, and he'll let the woman go so she can reach her house before dawn. That way she'll escape one of the two disasters; her home won't be brought to ruin on top of what's happened to her already. So, I went out to the mosque, walking as best I could, mounted the minaret, and sounded the call. Then I sat and looked out on the street, waiting to see the woman come out. If she didn't come, I thought, then I'd start prayer, so as to leave no doubt in the Turk's mind that it was morning and make him release her.

" 'After a short time had gone by, and the woman was still with him, the street was suddenly filled with horse and foot, and with torches, and men crying: "Who's the one who's been calling to prayer? Where is he?" At first I was too terrified to speak. But then I thought I'd speak to them and maybe find help for the woman. So I called out from the minaret:

" ' "I was the one."

" ' "Come down," they told me, "and answer to the Prince of the Faithful."

" 'Thinking to myself that deliverance was near, I went down and, going with them, found them to be a company of guards with Badr [at their head], who brought me before al-Muʿtadid. I trembled and quaked when I saw him, but he reassured me, then asked what had caused me to alarm Muslims by sounding the call to prayer at the wrong time, so that those who had business would go about it too early, and those who had intended to fast would hold back at a time when they were permitted to eat and drink.

" ' "If," I said, "the Commander of the Faithful will guarantee my safety, I will reveal the truth of the matter."

" 'He told me my life was safe, upon which I told him the story of the Turk, and showed him the marks on me. He immediately commanded Badr to bring the soldier and the woman.

" 'I was led to one side, and, after a short time, the soldier and the woman were brought before them. Al-Muʿtadid proceeded to question the woman about the matter, and her account confirmed mine. He thereupon commanded Badr to send her at once to her husband, with a trustworthy escort who'd take her into her house and explain matters to the husband. They were also to deliver a request to him, from the caliph, not to send the woman away but to treat her kindly. Then he summoned me and, in my hearing, began to question the [Turkish] soldier.

" ' "How much, fellow," he asked, "is your allowance?"

" 'The man told him the amount.

" ' "Your pay?"

" 'So much, he was told.

" ' "Your perquisites?"

" 'So much, he was told.

" 'Then al-Muʿtadid began to list the gratuities the man received, and these the Turk acknowledged, to an enormous sum. Then he asked the man how many slave girls he possessed. He was given the number.

" ' "Were not these," the caliph asked him, "and the ample fortune you enjoyed, sufficient for you, but you must needs violate the commandments of God and injure the majesty of the sultan; and not only commit this offense but, in addition, assault the person who tried to make you do right?"

" 'The soldier, stricken by guilt, could make no reply. The caliph thereupon ordered his men to fetch a sack, some cement makers' pestles, bonds, and fetters. The man was bound, fettered, and placed in the sack, and the attendants were then commanded to pound him with the pestles.

" 'All this was done in my sight. The man screamed for a while, then the voice stopped and he was dead. The caliph ordered the body to be flung into the Tigris, and he told Badr to seize the contents of his house. Then he said to me:

" ' "Sir, whenever you see any kind of wrong committed, great or small—anything of the sort, I say, great or small—then make your protest and order it to be righted, even if this" (he indicated Badr) "should be the one involved. And, if anything should befall you, and you are not listened to, then the signal between us is that you will sound the call to prayer around this time. And I, hearing your voice, will summon you and will do as I have done here to anyone who refuses to listen to you, or who injures you."

" 'I invoked a blessing on him and left. Word of the matter spread among the Dailami and the Turks, and, if ever I've asked any man to see right, or to desist from wrongdoing, he's satisfied my demands for fear of al-Muʿtadid. And so I've never, to this day, needed to sound the call.' "

From Abu ʿAli ʾl-Muhassin al-Tanukhi, *Nishwar al-Muhadara wa Akhbar al-Mudhakara* (*Snippets of Conversation and Memorable Tales*), vol. 1.

70

Crime and Punishment

I was told this story by ʿUbaid Allah ibn Muhammad al-Khaffaf, who heard it from his father, who said it had been reported to him by a friend in the army:

One day, when I happened to find myself in the Karkh quarter of Baghdad, I noticed one of the loveliest women I've seen in my life, and I stopped for a moment to gaze at her. She, though, turned her back and abruptly went off. Then an old woman, who'd been with her, came back and invited me to be the beautiful woman's guest.

"I'm not in the habit of being anyone's guest," I said. "Let the woman come and be my guest."

"Out of the question," the old woman said.

Unable to resist the temptation, or quell my overwhelming desire, I followed her to a place on the outskirts of Baghdad. She went up to a house and knocked on the door.

"Who is it?" a voice asked.

"It's Saʿida," the old woman said.

Suddenly my heart gave a leap, and I turned back, but she called out to me.

"Where are you going, young man?" she asked. "Don't you trust us?"

I changed my mind and went into the house. It was a spacious place, barely furnished. A black maid came with a pot of hot water and a basin, and I washed my face and feet and rested for a while. They served some grubby food, which, being very hungry, I had no option but to eat.

The beautiful young woman appeared once more. They brought wine, and, with her by my side, I drank. I took off my outer garment and turned to her, and she let me embrace her. When, though, I tried to go further, she said:

"I can't do what's forbidden. Wait till someone comes to celebrate our marriage."

Sunset was approaching; it was the time between the two evening prayers. Suddenly there was a knock on the door.

"Oh, heavens," she cried. "My God!"

"What's the matter?" I asked.

"It must be my brother and his attendant," she said. "If he sees you here, I can't answer for your safety. I'll take you somewhere where you can hide till they're asleep. Then I'll join you."

She took me into a small chamber and locked the door behind me. I realized now that I'd been trapped. I was going to be killed for my money, or for something else I had on me. I asked God's pardon and forgiveness for any wrongdoing and vowed to Him never to do anything of the sort again, if He'd only spare me in my plight.

I went up to the door and looked through the peephole, to see and hear what was going on in the room beyond. I saw a monstrous, ugly black lad kissing the woman, who was amorously returning his lust. They lay down, endlessly eating, drinking, and coupling. Between times, he asked her what had happened that day, and she picked up my garment and handed it to him.

"All we've had," she said, "is a worthless ruffian coming here with an empty pocket."

The ugly brute fell into a fury and started cursing and beating the woman.

"What do you call this?" he said. "We need someone with a big bag."

"That's the way it went today," she said. She started begging him, then kissing his feet, weeping and showing how sorry she was, till at last he was satisfied and appeased.

I was sure now that this was the end of me, and I went on praying, still keeping my eye on them. They started their drinking again, with the love-making in between. They must have made love ten times before the man finally collapsed, totally exhausted and drunk.

"Wine seems to have got the better of you, sir," she said. "Why don't you go now and get rid of that ruffian?" I started saying my final prayers.

The door opened and the black man came in, holding a naked sword. Then he slapped me sideways, all over my body, till I stopped shouting and fell, flat and cold. Sure I must be dead, the black man dragged me off and dropped my body into a [shallow] well just by. I could feel the heads of three other people there by my side. The brute then went out of the room, leaving the door wide open.

"What have you done?" I heard the woman ask.

"I've finished him off," came the answer.

He fell asleep by her side, and the old woman came in and covered them. There seemed to be no one else in the house.

Around midnight, I felt life and vigor coming back into my body and decided to save myself. I stood up and, finding the well came only halfway up my height, clambered out and moved, cautiously and on tiptoe, through the room. I could hear nothing but their snoring. I reached the door, opened it, and left unnoticed, arriving home just before dawn.

When my family asked what had happened, I told them how I'd spent the night with a friend of mine, and how, on my way back, a thief had chased after me, grabbed my clothes from behind, and grappled with me, but how I'd slipped away, leaving my outer garment with him.

It took several months of treatment before I was recovered. Then I set myself to finding this woman, in the streets and markets. I changed my looks, dressed differently, and let my beard grow.

One day, passing through the Karkh quarter, I saw her. I didn't speak to her. I went home, changed my clothes, then went back to the spot, walking the way the Khorasanis do, with my hand held behind my back. I saw her again, still in the same place, but she didn't recognize me, and nor did the old woman, who came up to me again with her proposition. Assured she hadn't seen who I was, I spoke to her in Persian.

I followed her to the same house and, as I'd done the first time, stayed with the woman till she said her brother and his attendant had arrived. She took me off to the room and locked the door, where I watched them through the keyhole, with a sharp, slender sword hidden in my clothes.

Having made love to the woman fifteen times, the black man asked:

"What do you have for us today?"

"A plump duck," she said. "A rich man from Khorasan with a heavy bag of money."

"Where is this bag?" he asked.

"Under his belt," she answered.

"Wonderful!" he said.

I pulled out my sword and waited for him behind the door. He ate, drank, and became drunk. When he stepped into the room, I was ready for him. He got past me, to the middle of the chamber, but I went after him and struck him on the leg, and down he went. I followed the first strike with another, at his other leg, and he crumbled like a helpless paralyzed giant. I kept stabbing him till he'd breathed his last, cut his head from his body to be quite sure he'd never testify against me, then stood there without moving.

The woman, growing anxious and impatient at the man's delay, prompted her old attendant, Saʿida, to go and see what had happened. The old woman came close to the door.

"Where are you, sir?" she called. "Why haven't you come out?"

I stayed silent till she stepped in. Then I struck at her leg, crippling her, pulled her other leg inside, then said, with a Persian accent:

"Hello there, Saʿida! You've been a hunter long enough. Now you're the prey."

I killed the old witch, left the chamber, and went into the main room. This time I talked to the young woman in flawless Arabic. She was terrified, well aware she was close to death.

"I'm the man you planned to rob and murder," I said.

"Where's my black lover?" she asked.

"I've killed him," I replied. "And here's his head."

She started wailing bitterly.

"By God," she said, "I beg you, kill me next. I can't live without him!"

"You don't have to ask," I said. "I mean to do just that. But first, where's the money? If you don't show me where the money is, I won't kill you, I'll torture you, then take you off to the sultan. He can decide on the punishment you deserve."

She grew more terrified still.

"No!" she said. "Please, open this closet, and that cabinet—and this locked cupboard, and that storeroom."

As I opened them one after the other, vast wealth poured out into my hands. I turned to her and started pricking and piercing her skin with my sword.

"Show me the goods you've stolen and buried," I said.

The more she resisted or hesitated, the more torment she suffered, till at last she'd uncovered all her hidden treasures. Then, finally, I stabbed her to death.

I picked out the most precious and valuable things I could carry; my bounty came to thousands upon thousands of dinars. After that I never went near the place again. Nor did I ever learn what happened to the house, or the remains of the former victims, or the bodies of the man and the two women.

From Abu ʿAli ʾl-Muhassin al-Tanukhi, *Nishwar al-Muhadara wa Akhbar al-Mudhakara* (*Snippets of Conversation and Memorable Tales*), vol. 5.

71

An Unlucky Encounter

A certain person related as follows:

I once knew a merchant in Basra who was solidly prosperous. He was a friend of mine, but he went to live in Baghdad, and for several years all news of him ceased. Then I met him once more and found him in a very bad way, with almost no money, but I shied away from asking about his evident hardship. Then I noticed that, if ever he saw a woman, his face would change color, and he'd sigh and look away; then, his eyes still averted, he'd grow dejected and go on cursing her till she was out of sight.

I asked him the reason for this.

"I was," he said, "on the point of telling you about the penury I'm in now, and about my long absence, but I couldn't bring myself to do it. Now, though, that you've asked, I'll tell you all about it.

"As you know, I went off to Baghdad. I'd heard of the charm and grace of the women there, and I decided, when I reached the city, that I might well devote half the profit I made on the trip to amusing myself there. So I rented a house and bought some furniture for it, sold my goods, then, with the money I'd gained, went out to look for some female company. As fate would have it, I stumbled at once on a woman of flawless body, plump and delightfully pretty. I beckoned to her, and she came toward me. Then I walked in front of her and entered my house; and she came in after me. No sooner had she come right in than she eased down her drawers, took hold of a peg on the wall, and began writhing around.

"'Just what do you think you're doing?' I asked her.

"'I'm pregnant,' she answered. 'I went to the public bath to make my delivery easier, then, on the way home, the labor pains overtook me, and God, in His mercy, threw you in my way. Now I can give birth in your house.'

"Everything went black before my eyes.

" 'Get out of my house, woman!' I told her. 'Go and give birth in your own house!'

" 'There's no time for me to get home,' she replied. 'And I have my position to keep up. God's blessed me plentifully, and I have a family and a husband, all well off. You won't lose by it, I assure you. I promise that, if you'll help me here now, I'll never leave you all the time you're in Baghdad. I won't take any money except what comes to you as gifts from me and my family.'

"I believed everything she told me. What inclined me to believe her was that her appearance, and the kind of woman she seemed to be, fitted with what she'd said.

" 'Very well,' I told her, 'with God's grace.'

" 'There's just one more thing,' she went on.

" 'And what's that?' I asked.

" 'I need you to call a midwife,' she replied, 'to help me. Women always need one at a time like this.'

" 'But I'm a stranger in Baghdad,' I told her. 'I don't know anyone here.'

" 'I'll tell you where to find her,' she said.

"She described a well-known place and gave me a woman's name. By now, I could see her condition had grown more critical.

" 'Help me, please,' she said, 'before I die right here in your house! I'll do everything I told you, I promise.'

"I went out, feeling like a drunken man, till I reached the place she'd described. There I found the midwife and summoned her, and she came back with me, together with two slave girls she brought along to carry her tools for delivery.

"As we entered the house, we heard the crying of a newborn baby. I rushed forward, in front of the midwife, and found a baby flung down on the floor but no trace of the woman. I was stunned. I felt utterly helpless, not knowing what to say or do, unable to find any explanation.

" 'Perhaps,' I said to the midwife, 'some neighbor took her in because we were so long coming. Maybe they're looking after her and they've left the baby here.'

"The midwife put kohl on the baby's eyes, wrapped him up, then asked for her fee. I paid her what I could, impatient for her to be gone. When she'd left, I started to wonder what I was to do with the infant. I was at a total loss. I thought of killing him, then stopped myself. 'What has he done wrong,' I said to myself, 'for me to take it out on him like that?'

"In the end I decided to put him out in the street, where he could take his chance like any other bastard. His mother, I realized now, was an adulteress of some status. She'd hidden her pregnancy, then, when she felt the labor pains coming, she'd gone out in search of a place to give birth—and, as ill luck would have it, I was the person she'd found.

"When night fell and he'd fallen asleep, I took him out in a wicker basket to a place a long way from the house and set him down close to a wall. Just as I was doing this, he started crying. A woman looked out of her window. Then, when she saw me going off and leaving the crying baby there, she started yelling at me. At that, other women looked out through their windows, and they started yelling, too.

"All this attracted the street guards, and they came and seized me. The first woman told them how she'd seen me putting the wicker basket by the wall, and they hauled me off to the judge, with the basket hung around my neck. The judge asked me what it was all about, and I told him everything.

"He refused to believe a word.

"'Hardly plausible, is it?' he said. 'The truth of the matter is, you killed this child's mother. Now, tell us who she was.'

"When I stuck to my story, I was stripped and beaten to make me confess, but I simply went on repeating what I'd told them. The governor was in no doubt the baby's mother had been killed, or else that the baby was my bastard child by her. I was put in prison, and, while I was there, all my money was seized or stolen. The governor took some, and the judges took some, and the rest was used to buy a slave girl to nurse the infant and to pay her wages. This went on for some time. Then, when the infant was weaned, the slave girl was sold and I had the money from this for a while. The baby died in its third year, but I was kept in prison for four years, because the judge who knew about my case had been dismissed, and there was no one to speak for me. For the rest of the time I lived on the charity of other prisoners, and so things went on till the old caliph died and al-Muqtadir assumed the caliphate. He gave instructions for all prisoners to be freed, and I left prison with nothing to my name. I vowed there and then I'd never look at a woman again till the day I died, and that, if I should catch sight of one, I'd turn my eyes away till she was out of sight."

From Shihab al-Din Ahmad al-Tifashi, *Nuzhat al-Albab Fima la Yujadu fi Kitab* (*Diverting Tales Not Found in Books*), ed. Jamal Jumʿa (London: Riyad al-Rayyis, 1995).

72

The Man and the Lark

A man hunted a lark. When he had her in his hand, the lark asked him: "What are you going to do with me?"

"I'm going to kill you and eat you," the man replied.

"But," she answered, "I'll never satisfy your desire for meat. I'll never fill you up. I could, though, give you three pieces of advice. Wouldn't that bring you a lot more than eating me? The first I'll let you have while I'm still here in your clutch. The second I'll give you when I'm up in the tree, the third when I'm up on the mountain."

"Very well," he said. "Let me have them."

"Never lament for what's past," she said. "And never believe what can't be."

He let her go. When she'd reached the tree, she said:

"You wretched man! If you'd killed me, you would have found two jewels in my craw, weighing 20 mithqals each."[1]

The man bit his lips and heaved a sigh of regret.

"Give me your second piece of advice," he said.

"You've forgotten the first," she said, "so why should I give you three. Didn't I tell you never to lament for what's past, and never to believe what can't be? I don't weigh twenty grains, flesh, blood, feathers and all. So how could there be, in my craw, two jewels weighing twenty mithqals each?" And with that she flew off.

From Ibn Abi ʾl-Hadid, *Sharh Nahj al-Balagha* (*Explicating* The Way to Literary Eloquence); in *Qisas al-ʿArab* (*Stories of the Arabs*), vol. 4.

---

1. A mithqal is around five grams.

73

Two Surrealist Stories from the Desert

Abu ʾl-ʿAmaythal[1] *recounted the following:*

Two Bedouins started to tell each other tall stories. The first said: "Once I set out on a horse of mine and suddenly I noticed a patch of darkness—pitch-black it was. I made for it, and when I got up to it, I saw it was a piece of night that had not noticed that dawn had come. So I kept charging at it on my horse until it dispelled."

The other rejoined: "I shot an arrow at a gazelle one day. The gazelle veered to the right, and the arrow followed it. Then the gazelle swerved to the left, and the arrow swerved after it. The gazelle ran on to high ground, and the arrow flew up behind it. So the gazelle came down again. And then the arrow swooped down on it and struck it."

From Al-Mubarrad, *Al-Kamil fi ʾl-Adab wa ʾl-Lugha*, ed. Muhammad Abu ʾl-Fadl Ibrahim and al-Sayyid Shihata (Cairo: Dar Nahdat Misr, n.d.), vol. 2: 300.

1. Abu ʾl-ʿAmaythal was a minor poet and philologist in Baghdad in the third century A.H. and early ninth century C.E.

74

The Story of Tamim al-Dari

Praise be to God, source of all gifts, and may God bless and bring peace upon our master of the gorgeous face, Muhammad. This is the story of Tamim al-Dari and what happened to him with the jinn and others:

ʿAbdullah bin ʿAbbas told us that when sitting with Amir al Muʾminin [Prince of the Faithful], ʿUmar ibn al Khattab, may God bless him, an Ansari woman came in and said: "My husband has been away for the past seven years, without any news from him. Will you allow me to get married?" "Complete the *ʿudda*[1] for the deceased for four months and ten days," was the amir's answer. She then went away until the end of the *ʿudda* period, after which time she came back and advised the amir of what she had done. ʿUmar looked around at those in his majlis [court] and said: "Muslims, who of you is willing to marry this woman, while I bear her dowry, for an amount of one hundred dirhams from the Muslims' treasury?" A man stood up and said: "I will marry her." ʿUmar then married them and paid her dowry. She then took the man to her house to do what women usually do. She waited for him until he came to her after the evening prayer. She welcomed him and had intimate relations with him for an hour's time, after which she went out to the washroom for a necessity, with the intention of coming back to him. At that moment a man, as tall as a great palm tree, interrupted her progress and said: "Peace be upon thee, So-and-so." "Peace be upon thee," she answered, "and may God protect me from you—who are you?" "How is it you ask God's protection, while I am your cousin and husband?" the man asked in astonishment. "The man you are speaking of," she said,

1. *ʿUdda* is the four months and ten days between a woman's widowhood or divorce and her next marriage. This period of waiting is stipulated in Islamic law to ascertain that a woman is not pregnant by her former husband.

"has been away for the last seven years, and I have no news from him." The argument between the two was long and full, as Ibn ʿAbbas has narrated. Having heard all the argument, the Ansari man went out to them and said to his bride: "To whom are you talking?" Here Tamim answered him, "But, who are you, and what has brought you to my house?" "This is my wife," the Ansari man said. "I was married to her by Amir al Muʾminin, ʿUmar ibn al Khattab, may God bless him." "No, this is my wife," Tamim immediately replied. "I was married to her by the Prophet of God, may God bless him." As the argument between them continued, the woman said: "Let us all be separated until tomorrow morning. Then we will go to the majlis and see what will be decided for us. Both men agreed that what she said was right.

The storyteller said:

When the next morning dawned and spread its light, they came to Amir al Muʾminin, ʿUmar ibn al Khattab, and stood in front of him.

"What is the news?" the amir asked.

Tamim al-Dari answered him in protest, "How is it you marry off my wife while I am still alive?"

ʿUmar, may God bless him, said, "Have you ever seen a man who absents himself from his wife without sending her daily expenses?"

"I was not above the earth," Tamim answered, "I was below the earth, with the jinn, and I am telling you the truth."

While they were talking, Imam ʿAli Ibn Abi Taleb, may God bless him, came in and Amir al Muʾminin, ʿUmar ibn al Khattab, stood up and seated Imam ʿAli beside him. When Imam ʿAli saw Tamim, he recognized him and stood up to welcome him. Imam ʿAli said to Tamim, "My cousin and beloved Muhammad, may God bless him, told us that you would see amazing things no one else had ever seen. Please tell us in full about what you have seen."

"Your wish is my command, Imam," Tamim said. "I confide to you that one of those nights I was with my wife, doing together what men and women usually do. I said to her, 'Fetch me some water to wash up before I go to sleep, for I have heard God's Messenger, may God bless him, saying, "No one may sleep in his bed before washing after sex." ' She went off and fetched the water. As it was completely dark, I said to her, 'Do remain with me and keep me company.' 'You are afraid of darkness,' she said, 'but not afraid of heroes in battles?' Then she said, laughing: 'Take him!'

"At that moment I felt a man, as tall as a high palm tree, carrying me and flying in the air; then he put me down on the fifth earth. There I saw that all its inhabitants were Magians, worshipping fire instead of the Great Lord. I stayed with them for two years, during which time I heard no one attesting that God Almighty is the only one God.

"One day I heard a great turmoil; it was the son of the king of the jinn invading the whole island. He killed a huge number of them, God only knows how many, and took seventy thousand as prisoners, including me. As they brought me to him, I said, 'No God but He.' When the king heard me say this, he asked me, 'Who are you, to which nation do you belong, and who brought you to this island?' I stood up and told him my story. He then took me with him, and I started teaching his children the Holy Quran. He took care of me himself and never left me for a moment. One day I remembered my folks and wept. 'What makes you weep?' he asked. 'I have remembered my folks,' was my answer. 'Between you and your folks,' he said, 'there are mountains, sands, and wilderness inhabited by no human being.' When I heard this I wept even more. So he said, 'I have someone who can take you to your folks.' Then he took me to a cave, where we saw a very ugly afreet, whose eyes were slit. The king looked at him and said, 'What about someone who can rid you of your chains if you take him to his folks?' 'Your wish is my command,' he responded. The king looked at me and said, 'I know that if you ride him, you must say, "You who are wise, just, and generous, O lord of the great throne, keep me safe from all bad incidents, you who are capable of everything." Then the king looked at the afreet and rid him of his chains. He immediately carried me and flew in the air, so I recited what the king had told me. At that moment I heard an angel reading verses from the Quranic chapter "Al-Saffat" [chap. 37]. A comet then burned the afreet and I fell into a green sea. Then a bird jumped on me, gave me water from its beak, saying, 'May God bless you.' I went up to an island, where I spent forty days. While contemplating my condition I saw an animal grazing in the middle of the island. It asked me to come near, so I did and rode it. It went to a monastery, where there was a monk. He came out to meet me and said, 'What is your need and to which nation do you belong?' 'To the nation of Muhammad, may God bless him,' I said, and narrated my story to him. 'Good people they are,' he said. So I talked to him and asked, 'How long have you been in this place?' 'Five hundred years,' he said. 'I am one of the disciples of Jesus, may God bless him.' 'But where do you get your food and clothes from?' I asked. 'I eat from the valley's fruit,' he answered, 'and every year an Indian ship, full of merchandise, anchors at the island. The merchant comes up carrying a woolen cloak and a headdress made of hair that he gives me as fulfillment of a vow, and goes away.' While we were talking, a ship came near and anchored at the island, and the merchant came up carrying what has been mentioned. When he saw the monk, he knelt and kissed his hand and gave him what was with him and made to go back to the ship. The monk asked, 'Would you please carry this man to the city of Muhammad, may God bless him, so you may be blessed?' 'Your wish is my command,' he answered. The merchant then took me with him to the ship and we spent the night at the island. When the morning spread its light all around, the sails were unfolded and we set out on our voyage, having good wind for three days, until the afternoon of the fourth day, when a strong wind blew and destroyed the ship. Everybody was drowned except me. After two days I landed on an island with fruit and rivers, where I stayed for some days. There was a kind of plant that looked like moons, with a protrusion that looked like the mouth of a sheep. I wandered and walked for two days, until I came to a town that was full of buildings and had no wall or gate, no king or vizier. There I spent one night, then walked for two more days, until I saw a cave. As I went in, I found that its floor was spread with pearls and coral. So I collected a lot of it, saying to myself, 'The ship was destroyed for my good fortune.' At this moment a voice said, 'Drop what you have, or you will die.' When I turned, I saw a young man sitting on a carpet, and I asked him, 'Who are you?' He said, 'Beyond you'll find he who will tell you about me and about others.' So I left him and walked for two days, until I came to a great palace, with its gate open. I went in and I saw an afreet sitting on an iron chair. He asked me, 'Are you hungry?' 'Yes,' I said. So he offered me a great table of food, and I ate until I was full. The afreet then turned to me and said, 'If you satisfy my need, I shall take you to your folks.' 'What is your need?' I asked. He then took out four nuts of lead, gave me two, and said, 'Stand up and take me out of this palace.' We came to another palace, where there was a great lion. I approached him with the afreet, who threw one nut at him. The lion ran away from the afreet, who threw the other at the door [which broke open]. So we went in, where we saw a cot of ivory and ebony, with a bed of colored silk, on which a young man was sleeping and on whose finger was a ring of red rubies, from whose light the moon was lit. Above his head was a black snake, and beneath his feet a red snake. I marveled at what I saw, then the afreet turned to me and said, 'Citizen of al-Madinah, if I fall dead, knock me with one nut, and I shall immediately get up alive.' 'Your wish is my command,' I said. The afreet went forward to take the ring. The snake beside the young man's head jumped and struck him, and he fell dead. So I knocked him with one of the nuts I had, and he immediately stood up and went forward to take the ring. The snake beside the young man's feet jumped and struck him, and he fell dead. I knocked him with the second nut, and he immediately stood up alive and said, 'Citizen of al-Madinah, that is why I made you my friend.' Then he walked with caution and went to take the ring. He was immediately turned into a heap of ashes.

I was scared and ran away and went back to the first palace. There I saw a human female slave, who said, 'What has God done with the afreet?' 'He was turned into a heap of ashes,' I said. 'May God not pardon him nor have mercy on him,' she said. Then I asked her, 'Who are you, who brought you here, and who put you in this palace?' 'I am the daughter of the king of al-Andalus,' she said. 'That cursed one kidnapped me from the roof of my palace while my mother was combing my hair, and he brought me to this place, where I have no way back to my folks. I gave birth to two children by him; one died, and the other is still alive.' When I heard this, I cried. 'What makes you cry?' she asked. 'I remembered my folks,' I said. 'Between you and your folks,' she said, 'there are sands and wilderness that you have no power to pass through.' Hearing that, I cried even more. 'Don't cry,' she said. 'I have someone who can take you to your folks.' Then she called, emitting a very high scream. Immediately, a very ugly afreet appeared. 'What is your need?' he asked her. 'I beg you, please,' she said, 'do take this man to his folks and country tonight.' 'Your wish is my command,' he answered. Immediately I found myself carried on his shoulders and taken up into the air. When I saw the sea where I was drowned, the afreet threw me on an island, where I saw a left-eyed old man with a trunk like that of an elephant. He called me, but I did not respond and ran away and walked for two days. Then I saw a huge-looking old man, chained under a tree, with both eyes gouged out. As I looked at him, he said to me, 'To which nation do you belong?' 'To the nation of Muhammad, may God bless him.' I retorted. 'Has Muhammad's time come?' he asked. 'Yes,' I said. 'Come near,' he said. So I did. Then he asked, 'Are the people of Muhammad doing their duties?' 'Yes,' I said. 'Is the Zamzam Spring still there?' he asked. 'Yes,' I said. 'They are about to go astray, until not a drop of water will remain.' Then he asked, 'Have any forbidden acts and great sins been committed?' 'Some have,' I said. He then became very happy and said, 'Now my time has come.' Then he screamed once and someone in the garb of a king came and hit him with a rod of iron. He fell heaped like an island. Then I walked for two days, until I came across a high-rising palace whose blocks were alternately of silver and of gold, with an inscription that read: 'Whoever wishes to come in must say, "No God but He, and Muhammad is His messenger."' When I said this phrase, the door opened. As I entered, I saw curtains of silk, which I lifted, and saw a river, on the bank of which was a table full of food, and I saw people leaning against their swords with blood on them, and they smelled like musk. I also saw two knights [handsome] like moons on white horses, with their heads under the seventh sky and their feet below the lowest earth. I went forward and ate and drank. So they said to me, 'Drink, for God has protected your body from the inferno. When you reach the man with the green turban, say to him that peace be upon him.' I walked for two days, until I saw a mosque, where an old man was sitting dressed in green from head to toe. He addressed me, saying, 'You, who are lost from his people!' I said, 'Yes.' He said, 'You will find in front of you someone who will guide you to what is good for you.' Then I left him and walked on and saw another mosque, where a young man was sitting with a turban on his head. I saluted him, and he responded with a salute. Then I saw a spring and a pomegranate tree, whose fruit was as big as watermelons. He said, 'You are welcome. For years I have been waiting for you.' Then he gave me a pomegranate, which I ate, and I drank some water, performed my ablutions, and prayed. He then said to me, 'Look at that mountain. Behind it there are wonders no one except you has ever seen. Go to it, and tell me of whatever you see.' 'Your wish is my command,' I said, and I went there and saw a land as white as shredded cotton. Curious, I proceeded and saw a bitch as big as a mule carrying her pups, which were barking in her belly. I left her and continued on and saw a woman laden with makeup. I saluted her, but she did not respond. Then I went on and saw an old man pulling water from a well and pouring it into a punctured basin from which the water went back to the well. I said to him, 'It is better if you mend your punctured basin.' 'Mind your own business,' he replied, 'for he who does not mind his own business will hear what he dislikes.' Therefore I left him and walked for two days, until I saw an old man who carried on his shoulder a palm tree trunk swaying right and left. I said to him, 'Put down your load and have an hour's rest.' His answer was, 'Go back to the man with the green turban and ask him about all that you have seen in the mountain and on your way. He will tell you everything.' Hearing this, I went back to the man with the green turban and told him my story and what I had seen in the mountain and on my way. Then I said, 'For the sake of God, sir, do tell me about all I have seen.'

So he said, 'As for the afreet who kidnapped you from your house, his name is Maymoon, the land developer. The place where he brought you is the island of the Magians, who worship fire instead of the Great Lord. As for the one who took you from him, his name is Dahnash ibn Murqan, who disobeyed Suleiman [the Hebrew King Solomon], peace be upon him. The bird who gave you water is called Is-haq, a bird from Paradise. As for the animal on the island, that is the one that comes upon the surface of the earth at the end of time. As for the monk, he is one of the companions of Jesus, may God bless him and give him peace. The ship you embarked on belonged to the king of India, who forbade *zakat*, so his ship was destroyed.

As for the island, it belongs to the nymphs of the sea. Had you not been of the nation of Muhammad, they would have killed you. As for the city full of buildings, it belongs to the people of Yunus [Jonah], may God bless him. The young man in the cave, sitting on the carpet, he is al-Mahdi, who will appear at the end of time. When he comes out, he will not leave a single infidel on the surface of the earth. As for the afreet who took you out of his palace, he is ʿAflaq, the king of afreets. It is he who had kidnapped from the roof of her palace the daughter of the king of al-Andalus, who gave birth to two of his children, one of whom died and the other is still alive. As for he who carried you from where she was, his name is Sahab. The young man who was sleeping on the cot, with a ring on his finger, is Sulaiman, son of Dawood [the Hebrew King David], may God bless both of them. Had ʿAflaq taken the ring, he would have ruled with it over the king of the jinn. As for the one-eyed man with the trunk, that is the cursed Iblis [Satan], and he stays with his soldiers at the island of Bani Raht. As for the blind man chained under the tree, he is the Wicked Man, who comes out at the end of time, carrying Paradise and a fire. His fire is Paradise and his Paradise is fire. Jesus, may God bless him, will kill him in the land of Syria. As for the palace that you have entered, it is one of the palaces of Paradise. As for those leaning on their swords, with blood on them, they are the conquerors in the course of God. The two knights are Jibril [Gabriel] and Mikhaʾil [Michael], peace be upon them. The young man in the mosque, dressed in green from head to toe, that is al-Khidr, and the young man sitting with a green turban is Ilias, peace be upon him. He is one of the good people and one of God's messengers. As for the white land, that is God Almighty's platform, where He judges His creation on doomsday. As for the bitch whose cubs bark inside her, that is the generation of the end of time, when the young do not respect their elders, nor do they command good deeds and prohibit the forbidden. Their child curses his parents. As for the woman with the exaggerated makeup, that is al-Dunia [the world], crying with sorrow at her past life. The person playing at the well, pouring water in the punctured basin, is the man who steals and gives away alms (*sadaqa*), for it is Satan who takes them from him.' I wondered at him, 'O, Imam!', and I said, 'Yes. We take a meal every year on the roof of the Kaaba, and the drink that we take comes from the Zamzam Well.' I asked him, 'Where do you meet your brother?' 'On Mount ʿArafat,' he said. 'I take a hair from him and he takes a hair from me; I satisfy my longing for him and he satisfies his for me. God bless he who keeps close to his folks before his death.' Then he said, 'So you yearn to go back to your folks?' 'Yes,' I said. 'Do you know,' he asked, 'how many years there are between you and your folks?' 'Only God and His messenger know,' I answered. So he said, 'There are seventy-three years between you and your folks.' When I heard what he said, I cried. So he asked, 'What makes you cry?' I said, 'Who may live seventy-three years to be able to reach his folks?' 'Don't worry,' he said, 'I shall send someone who can take you to your folks, and, God willing, you will not sleep [tonight] except in your bed.' I became very happy. While he was talking to me a great cloud passed by and said, 'Peace be upon you, Prophet of God.' Al-Khidr answered. 'Peace be upon you, too, God's obedient servant. Where are you going to, blessed one?' 'To the cities, as you have commanded,' came the reply. Behind this cloud a small, airy, bright cloud appeared, with an inscription on it: "No God but One, and Muhammad is His messenger.' She said, 'Peace be upon you, Prophet of God.' And al-Khidr answered, 'Peace be upon you, too, God's obedient servant. Where are you going to, blessed one?' 'To the city of Muhammad, may God bless him, to water them with rain.' Al-Khidr said to her, 'Come close to me.' So the cloud approached until she faced him and spread herself on the ground. He then said to her, 'This is a man from the nation of Muhammad, may God bless him. He is lost, away from his folks.' 'Your wish is my command, sir,' she said. 'I shall take him back home, if God wills, and I promise that his heart shall not tremble and his body shall not be chained.' 'This is what I request and expect of you,' he said to her. As he put me on the cloud, I said to him, 'In God's name I beg you, give me something that may remind me of you.' 'You are most welcome,' he said. 'I shall teach you something with which God will make you win the source of life. Say: "My Lord, in your name with which you have defined the sea and the earth, summoned up food, spread protection, brought about heat, and chosen Muhammad, may God bless him, as your prophet and messenger, I beg you to help me on whatever you have granted me. Render me in no need of others, except your generous face, help me obey you as long as I am alive, grant me in my lifetime goodness and in my afterlife goodness, and protect me from fiery punishment."' Then I rode on the cloud, saying, 'You, Who are capable of doing everything, Who brings back home every stranger, bring me back home.' Suddenly the cloud threw me on top of my house. When I went down I saw a man there. That is what happened to me."

When the Ansari heard what Tamim had just narrated, he stood up and congratulated him for his safety and went away. At that moment, Imam [ʿAli] took Tamim, had his hair cut and his mustache shaved, and gave him one hundred dirhams from the Muslim treasury. At that time Hamza's *ghazwah*, in the company of Khalid ibn Al-Walid, where Hamza was killed, took place. May God pardon him and may He bless our master, Muhammad, and grant him peace, together with his entourage.

....

Translated by Bassam Abu-Ghazaleh; from *The Annual Journal of the Tunisian University*, no. 35, 1994.

VII

Tales of Love

75

A Love Story

Ishaq ibn Ibrahim al-Mawsili said:

When [Haroun] al-Rashid entered Basra [on his pilgrimage to Mecca] I was with him. One day Jaᶜfar ibn Yahya [al-Barmaki][1] told me:

"I've heard, Abu Muhammad, of a beautiful concubine and singer [for sale]. Her owner, though, refuses to have her shown anywhere but in his house. I've decided to go there in disguise to see her. Will you come with me?"

"If that's your wish," I said.

At noon, the slave vendor came and Jaᶜfar was told. He put on a turban, an outer shawl, and a pair of Arabic shoes, then he summoned me, and I put on the same. We rode on two donkeys equipped with saddles of the kind used by merchants, the slave vendor riding with us. On we went till we reached a house whose gate was a sign of old wealth and status.

The slave vendor knocked at the door, and a handsome young man, wearing a shirt, and with the marks of suffering on him, opened for us.

"Come through, sirs," he said.

As we entered, we saw a large corridor and a neglected courtyard. The young man brought a piece from a large old mat and laid it down for us, and we sat.

"Bring out the slave girl," the vendor told him. "The buyer's here."

He entered the house, and a girl came out, wearing the same rough shirt as that worn by the young man. For all its coarseness, she seemed as if in

---

1. Jaᶜfar ibn Yahya al-Barmaki was an important Persian chief and the greatest aide of Haroun al-Rashid. He was famous for his generosity, resourcefulness, honor, and eloquence. Accused by his enemies of conspiring to assume the caliphate, he was beheaded by al-Rashid in 187 / 803.

the finest attire, so great was her beauty. She was carrying a lute. Jaʿfar told her to sing, and she played well and sang beautifully; then she was overcome by weeping and couldn't go on. We could hear, at the same time, the weeping of the young man. The girl rose, then tripped and stumbled into the house, from which a [further] loud noise of weeping and sobbing was heard. Then they were heard no more, and we feared the two might have expired. We were making ready to leave, when the young man came out, still wearing the same shirt.

"Please forgive me," he said, "for what I'm about to do and say."

"Tell us," Jaʿfar said.

"God and you gentlemen are my witnesses," the young man went on, "that this girl is free herewith. And I ask you to marry me to her."

Jaʿfar gazed at the girl, perplexed, then addressed her.

"Do you wish me to marry you to your master?" he asked.

"Yes," she said.

Jaʿfar accordingly married her to him.[2] Then he turned to the young man.

"Whatever made you do this?" he asked.

"I'm such and such," the young man said, "the son of such and such. My father was one of the wealthy dignitaries of this city; this man here" (he indicated the slave vendor) "can vouch for it. My father put me to school. My mother had a young slave girl of my own age—this girl here—and she went with me to the school and learned all that I did. We'd go and return together. When she grew older, she learned singing, and I'd learn it from her.

"The greatest dignitaries of this city sought me for their daughters. My father, though, left the choice to me, and I made it clear I wasn't interested in marriage. I grew up well versed in *adab* and basking in my father's wealth, exposed to none of the things young people are usually exposed to. And that made people still more eager [to see me married to their daughters], since my chastity was seen as a mark of good character. But all this was solely on account of my love for this girl. My wishes never strayed from her to another. When, in her singing, she reached the level you've heard, my mother decided to sell her, knowing nothing of my attachment to her. Feeling ready to die, she was forced to speak of her feelings to my mother, and she in turn spoke to my father. They agreed together to give me this slave girl, providing her with all that was needed, and gave me a splendid ceremony. For a good while I enjoyed my life with her. Then my father died,

2. Jaʿfar is here playing the role of a guardian, who hears her consent and then gives her in marriage.

and I was careless with my legacy. I lived recklessly, throwing away great sums in eating and drinking and other luxuries, till at last all the wealth was gone, and we arrived at what you see. This has been so for some years now.

"Not long ago, I heard that the caliph and his minister, and many of his entourage, were to come [here to Basra], and I told her:

" 'Your youth's fading, your life passing. By God, I have no wish to sell you—I know I shall die if I'm parted from you. Yet it's better I should die, if you can find a comfortable, opulent life. Let me offer you for sale. Perhaps one of these wealthy people will give you the chance of living, with him, a life of prosperity and plenty. If I should die after you've gone, then that's according to my wish. Each of us would then be freed from wretchedness; and, if God should decree that I live on, I shall be patient and use the price I gained for you for my livelihood.'

"She wept when she heard that, her looks frantic. Then she rose, and said:

" 'Very well. Do it.'

"So, I went to this slave vendor and told him how things stood. He'd heard her singing in the days of my wealth and knew how matters were with us. I'd never, I told him, put her up for public sale, but only here in my house, for she's never once passed over this threshold. I wished the would-be buyer to see her alone, so she wouldn't be humiliated in a market or enter another's house. She had only this shirt of mine to wear, and we share it between us. I wear it when I leave to buy food, while she covers herself with her cloak. When I return to the house, I give her the shirt to wear and put on her cloak.

"When you arrived, and she came out and sang, I was plunged into bitter weeping and anxiety. She came up to me.

" 'How very strange!' she said. 'You've tired of me, would rather part with me. And yet you weep in this way.'

" 'By God,' I told her, 'I should find it easier to part from my soul than from you. I wished only to free you from your wretchedness.'

" 'No, master,' she answered. 'Were I to have authority over you, I'd never sell you. I'd die of hunger rather. Death would be the only thing that could part us.'

" 'Have no worry, then,' I answered. 'Do you wish to see the truth of what I've told you?'

" 'Yes,' she answered.

" 'Do you wish me,' I said, 'to go out to the buyer, free you before him, and marry you? And we'll then go on suffering as we do now, till God assigns relief or death?'

"'If,' she said, 'you're true in what you say, then do it. I wish for no one but you.'

"With that I came out to you, and the rest you know. Please forgive me."

"You are forgiven," Jaʿfar said.

He rose, and I rose with him, and so did the slave vendor. When the donkeys were brought for us to mount, I approached Jaʿfar and said to him:

"God is great! How can it be that a man as generous as you sees such poverty yet doesn't grasp the chance to do something? God knows my heart was torn for the young man."

"Woe to you!" Jaʿfar said. "My heart's torn for him, too. It was my pique at losing the slave girl, that held me back from giving him something from my bounty."

"And where," I said, "is the desire for heavenly reward?"

"You're right, by God," he said.

I turned to the slave vendor.

"How much," I asked him, "was the price given to you for the girl?"

"Three thousand dinars," he replied.

"And where are they?" I asked Jaʿfar.

"They're with my boy."

Jaʿfar spoke with me, then to the slave vendor.

"Take them," he said [to me], "and pay them over to the young man. Tell him to buy some clothes, then come to me so I can give him more and furnish him with employment."

I went back, weeping, to the young man.

"God has hastened your relief," I told him. "The man who's gone from your house is Prince Jaʿfar ibn Yahya al-Barmaki. He's ordered that you be given these and tells you such and such."

He was so astonished, I thought he might have fallen in a faint. Then he came to himself and thanked me. I mounted, followed on after Jaʿfar, and told him. He thanked God for His guidance, and we returned to his home.

When it was time for dinner, we went to al-Rashid. They began discussing matters of state for the day. Then Jaʿfar told him the story of the young man and the girl.

"And what did you do?" al-Rashid asked.

He told him, and the caliph found it fitting.

"Assign him some income from the treasury," he said (specifying a certain monthly sum). "Then do as you yourself think best."

Next day, the young man came to me wearing good clothes, his looks handsome, and I found him to be most eloquent and learned. I took him to Jaʿfar's assembly, where Jaʿfar instructed that things should be made smooth for him and appointed him one of his entourage, signing an order as the caliph had decreed, and another on his own account.

The matter became famous in Basra, and among the army, and all who could, presented the young man with something. By the time we left Basra, he'd become a wealthy man.

From Abu 'l-Muhassin al-Tanukhi, *Al-Faraj Baʿd al-Shidda* (*Reprieve After Hardship*), vol. 3; in *Qisas al-ʿArab* (*Stories of the Arabs*), vol. 1.

76

A Strange Vow

Abu Bakr Muhammad ibn Abdul al-Baqi al-Bazzaz relates how Abu ʾl-Qasim ʿAli ibn al-Muhassan al-Tanukhi quoted his father as saying: Abu ʾl-Faraj Ahmad ibn ʿUthman ibn Ibrahim, the jurist known as Ibn al-Nursi, told me as follows:

As a boy, when I was with my father in a company of people, my father was telling of people who'd found prosperity in various novel ways. Among those present was one of my father's friends, and I heard him tell my father the following:

I'd been invited by a friend, a merchant worth a hundred thousand dinars, and a man of many good qualities. The meal he offered us included some *dikabrika*;[1] but, seeing that he ate none of it himself, we held back, too.

"Take some," he said. "If I eat any of this, I shall suffer for it afterwards."

"Then," we said, "we'll help you by leaving it, too."

"In that case," he replied, "I'll eat some with you and bear the consequences."

He ate, then proceeded to wash his hands, but he was a long time about it. He washed them, I counted, forty times.

"What's this?" I asked. "Do you have an obsession of some kind?"

"By doing this," he replied, "I'm keeping myself away from harm."

"What do you mean?" I asked.

He declined to give any reason. Then, when I persisted, he said at last:

"My father died when I was twenty, leaving me considerable wealth, some capital and the furnishings in his shop. He'd been a cloth merchant in al-Karkh.

"On his deathbed, he told me as follows:

---

1. *Dikabrika* is a dish made from meat, chickpeas, vinegar, and fresh cow's or camel's milk, sometimes sweetened with sugar.

" 'You're my sole heir. I've no debts and I've committed no evil actions. If I die, be generous with provisions for my funeral, give away a certain sum on my behalf, and use another sum to provide for a pilgrimage. Then may God bless you with what remains. But remember the advice I'm about to bequeath you.'

" 'Tell me please,' I said, 'what that is.'

" 'Don't squander your money,' he said, 'so that, when you need it, it's vanished into the hands of others. Know that a little money coupled with honesty is a great deal, and a good amount coupled with corruption is small. Stay in the market. Be the first to enter and the last to leave—go in before dawn if need be. That way you'll prosper, in ways the future will unveil.'

"He died, and I took possession of his property. I did as he'd told me, going into the market before daybreak and coming out well into the night. I never missed a single person who might come looking to buy a shroud and could find no one else. And then I'd sell him other things he needed, too. For over a year I stayed in the market, in good standing with the people there, who recognized my honesty and were generous with me.

"As I was sitting there one day, while some of the market was still open, a woman came riding by on an Egyptian donkey,[2] its hindquarters covered with a shawl from Daibaq [in Egypt]. She wore the outfit of a housekeeper and was accompanied by a servant. She went right to the end of the marketplace, then, returning to my shop, dismounted from her donkey. I rose to meet her, greeted her with honor, then said: 'How may I serve you?' Viewing her more closely, I realized I'd never in my life seen a woman finer in every way, surpassing others in everything.

"She needed, she said, such and such material for clothing. I heard a melodious voice, and saw a form that captivated me. Straightaway I fell in love, with the most passionate love possible.

" 'Wait,' I said, 'till the other customers have gone out. Then I'll find you what you need. Here I've only a little that's suitable for you.'

"I brought out all I had. She sat talking with me, and knives were tearing my soul from love for her. She showed fingers I compared to the flowering of the palm tree, and a face like the full moon.

"I got up (before my feelings became too evident) and found what she needed in the marketplace, the whole, along with my own materials, coming to five hundred dinars. She took everything, mounted, but paid me no money.

2. Egyptian donkeys were known for their good appearance and were commonly ridden by caliphs.

"Such were my feelings of love for her, I did nothing to stop her taking the materials without payment. I didn't even ask the way to where she lived, or from which family's house she'd come.

"She was away a long time, and I began to fear she'd cheated me. The whole affair had left me short of money, but I dared not show my worries because of my debts to the other merchants. I sold everything I had in hand, and, with the little this brought, I was able to pay off all my debts and buy the bare necessities; then I contented myself with what I could collect on the property I'd inherited from my father. Sure now that I was finished, I carried on for one week more.

"Suddenly she reappeared; and, the moment I saw her, I forgot all that had happened and stood up to receive her.

" 'Young man,' she said, 'we're late in making our payment on account of a matter that arose. You must, we realize, have thought badly of us. No doubt, you thought we'd tricked you.'

" 'You've removed all such thoughts now,' I replied.

" 'Bring the scales,' she said.

"I brought them. She paid me all my money, then brought out a new list.

"I gave the merchants their money and placed new orders, gaining a healthy commission for myself. When the merchants brought the goods, I fixed a price for them, then sold them on to her at a good profit. And all this time I was gazing at her with passion, while she looked back, recognizing the signs. I was on the point of speaking to her, but finally didn't dare. All the merchandise was there, to the amount of a thousand dinars. She took it all, mounted once more, and again I didn't ask her for her address.

"Once more she vanished. So, I thought, that's the real trick. She gives five thousand dirhams and takes a thousand dinars' worth of goods. My only course now is to sell my property and embrace a pauper's life, picturing myself in poverty.

"This time she was away longer, for around a month, and the merchants were demanding their money. On the insistence of some of them, I put my property up for sale. As I was assessing all I had, in coins and in kind, she came to me once more. At the sight of her, I felt all my suffering melt away. She called for the scales, weighed out the money, then gave me another order—for more than two thousand dinars this time.

"I made a show of seeking out the merchants and handing them their money. This time we talked a good deal.

" 'Young man,' she said, 'do you have a wife?'

" 'No, by God,' I said. 'I've never known any woman.'

"I felt encouraged. Now, I thought, was the time to speak to her. If I didn't, she might never come back. I wanted to do it, but couldn't bring myself to speak. I rose, as if to go and ask the merchants to prepare the order. Then I took the servant by the hand, brought out some money, and asked him to take it in return for a service.

" 'I'll do it,' he said. 'I'll tell her of your love. But I won't take anything for it.'

"I told him how things stood and asked him to use his influence on my behalf.

"He laughed.

" 'What she feels for you,' he said, 'is stronger still. She doesn't really need these goods. She comes here out of love for you; she wants to sit and talk with you. Talk with her, use your charm, and leave the rest to me.'

"Plucking up courage, I talked with her, showed my love, and wept. She took all this well.

" 'The servant,' she said, laughing, 'will bring you a message from me.'

"She rose, but took nothing with her. I took everything back, having made a profit, from the first and the second sales, amounting to thousands of dirhams. That night I couldn't sleep, longing for her, fearful of losing her.

"A few days later, the servant came. I greeted him with honor and asked about her.

" 'She's sick from longing for you,' he said.

" 'Tell me about her,' I said.

" 'The lady who owns her,' he said, 'is the mother of Caliph al-Muqtadir.[3] She's one of her best slaves, and, longing to be able to come and go and meet people, she managed to be appointed her housekeeper. She's already told her lady about you, weeping in her presence, and she's asked her permission to marry you. "I'm not prepared to do this," the lady said, "till I've seen the man, to decide whether he's worthy of you. I won't leave the matter to your estimation of him."

" 'Now, that means you'll need to trick your way into the house. If you succeed, you may come to marry her; if you're discovered, you'll lose your head. That's the message she sent with me. If you're ready to take the risk, then try it. There's no other way to come to her, or she to you.

" 'If you're ready to try, then wait for night to fall, go through al-Mukharram,[4] into the mosque, and spend the night there.'

"I did as he'd said. Before daybreak, a riverboat came by with servants and empty chests, and the servants placed them in the mosque. As for my

3. An Abbasid caliph who reigned from 295 / 908 to 320 / 932.
4. A district of Baghdad, once the site of the ministry and later home to the Buwayhid and Seljuq rulers.

beloved slave, she left the boat and, coming into the mosque accompanied by the servant I knew, sat down, then sent the other servants out on various errands. She called to me, and kissed and hugged me for a long time; she'd never once kissed me before. Then she sat me down inside one of the chests and locked it.

"The sun rose, and the servants came back with clothing and provisions. She told them to put the goods in the other chests and carry them off to the boat. Then away we went down the river.

"Once inside the chest, I started regretting what I'd done. I'm killing myself, I thought, on account of my desires. Now I blamed myself, now I plucked up courage. I even made vows I'd fulfill if I could only come out safe. Then, at other times, I resigned myself to my fate.

"So I remained till we reached our destination. The servants carried off the chests, mine being carried by the servant who was in the plot. My beloved put mine in front of the rest, walking alongside it, and the rest followed. Whenever she came on a group of servants or doormen, they'd say: 'We have to search the chest.' Then she'd cry out: 'Who do you think I am, to treat me like this?' So they'd hold back, while I remained in mortal dread.

"At last she reached a servant she addressed as 'master'—the head servant, I supposed. 'I must search that chest you have with you,' the man said. She spoke to him softly, in a humble, submissive manner, but he didn't answer. She must, I thought, have run out of tricks now, and I felt ready to faint. Then, when he had the chest brought for inspection, I was sure I was finished. My bladder gave way, and the urine ran out through the cracks in the chest's boards. 'Master,' she called out, 'you've ruined five thousand dinars' worth of materials in this chest, along with dyed clothing. The rose water's been spilled onto the clothes. Now the dyes will run together. This will be the end of me with my mistress.' 'Take your chest off to hell, the two of you!' he said. 'Just move on.' She called out to the servants: 'Move it on!' And so I was carried in, relief flooding through me.

"Then, as we went on, I heard her cry out: 'Oh, mercy! It's the caliph, by God!' My fears came back worse than ever. I heard a lot of talking from servants and slaves, as the caliph said (addressing her by name):

" 'You, what's in your chest? Show me what's in there.'

" 'Master,' she said, 'it's clothes for my mistress. I'll open it straightaway, and you can see.'

"Calling to the servants to be quick about it, she had the chest taken into a room, let me out, told me to move to the room beyond, and had me sit down there. Then she quickly opened another chest, took out some of the stuff and put it into the one where I'd been before. Then she locked them both.

"Caliph al-Muqtadir came in. 'Open this one here,' he said. She opened it, and he, finding nothing of interest there, went off. Thereupon she came in to where I was and started caressing and kissing me. I was heady with joy, forgetting everything that had happened to me up to then.

"She left me, locked the door of the room, then came back at night with food and drink for me before leaving once more. Then, the next day, she came and said: 'My mistress will be here very soon. Prepare yourself how to address her.' In an hour she came back with her mistress, who told me to approach.

"The lady was seated in a chair, waited on by two attendants and my friend. I kissed the ground, then stood there before her.

"'Sit,' she said.

"I was her slave, I answered. It wasn't my place to be seated in her presence. She inspected me closely, then addressed my friend.

"'You've chosen well,' she said. 'Good looks and good manners.' With that she rose and left.

"An hour later my friend came back. 'It's all right,' she said. 'She's given me her permission to marry you. The only problem now is to get you out of here.' The next day came, and she packed me into the chest. I left as I'd come in, not without more adventures and more fear.

"I came out into the mosque, went back home, gave out money for charitable purposes, and thanked God for my safety. A few days later, the servant arrived with a bag containing three thousand dinars in gold.

"'My mistress,' he said, 'instructed me to give you this from her own money. You're to buy yourself clothes, a mount, and servants, smarten up your appearance, then, on the Day of the Procession,[5] come to the public gate and stand there till you're sent for. She's agreed with the caliph to have you marry in his presence.'

"I gave my answer on a note he was carrying. I took the money, used a small amount to buy what I'd been told to buy, and kept the larger part with me. Then, on the Day of the Procession, smartly dressed, I rode off to the public gate. People arrived and went in to see the caliph. I waited till I was sent for, then went in, into the presence of al-Muqtadir, along with the generals, judges, and Hashemites, struck with awe by my audience. I was instructed how to greet and stand and did as I'd been told.

"Approaching some of the judges present, al-Muqtadir spoke in support of my requested union. The marriage was performed, and I left his presence.

5. The day on which the caliph sat to receive the principal men of the realm and to consult on affairs of state.

"When I reached the alleys near the gate, I was conducted to a grand residence, elegantly furnished, filled with materials and servants, belongings and furnishings, such as I'd never seen before. There I was seated, and the one who'd conducted me went off, leaving me alone.

"I sat there all day, seeing no one I knew, not leaving my place except for prayers. Servants came and went, and splendid food was brought in. They were singing: 'Such and such' (calling her by her name) 'is marrying the cloth merchant.' I was so happy I couldn't believe it.

"Night fell, and I was beginning to feel hungry. The doors were locked, and, losing hope of my beloved slave's coming, I started walking around the mansion, till I found the kitchen, where the cooks were sitting. I asked them for food, and they, supposing me to be one of the upper servants, gave me an appropriate meal and two loaves of bread. This I ate, and, having washed my hands with some saltwort that was there in the kitchen, I decided they were clean enough and went back to my place.

"The night wore on. Then, suddenly, I heard drums and bugles and a general clamor. The doors were opened, and my lady was handed over to me. They brought her in, unveiled her, and paraded her in my presence. I was so happy I felt I must be dreaming. She was left with me there in the reception hall, and the people dispersed.

"When we were alone, she came up to me. I kissed her and she kissed me. Then, smelling my beard, she kicked me and brought me back down to earth. 'I might have known you wouldn't be up to it,' she cried. 'You base, common man!' And with that she rose to leave.

"I stood up, too, and clutched hold of her. I kissed the ground and then her feet. 'Just tell me what I've done wrong,' I said. 'Then, afterwards, you can do as you like.'

" 'Shame on you,' she said. 'You ate, and you didn't wash your hands!'

"I told her exactly what had happened. I swore to her, again and again, that, if I ever again ate *dikabrika* and failed to wash my hands forty times after the meal, that she'd be divorced from me, that I'd divorce any woman I married, I swore by my almsgiving and all I possessed, I swore to make the pilgrimage on foot, to become a disbeliever in God and Islam.

"She took pity on me, smiled, then called the slaves. Some ten slaves and attendants came, and she said: 'Bring us some food.'

"All kinds of delicious dishes were brought in, including some of the caliph's special delicacies. We ate, and washed our hands. Then the attendants left, and we went off to bed and consummated our marriage, spending a night fit for a caliph and not parting for a week thereafter. On the final day of the week, there was a huge feast, with many slaves present.

"The next day, she said:

" 'We can't stay here any longer, in the caliph's mansion. Without his special permission, which was hard enough to win, it wouldn't have been granted us at all. He's never done this for any other slave. It was all on account of my mistress's love for me.

" 'Everything you see here is a gift from her to me; and she's also given me fifty thousand dinars in gold and notes, in equity and jewels. There are treasures of every kind for me, outside the palace, and they're all yours. So, go home now, take your money, and buy a spacious house in an elegant district, with a broad courtyard and a garden full of trees. Then let me know, so I can have all these things here sent on to you. After that, I'll join you myself.' She handed me ten thousand dinars in gold, and the servant helped me carry it.

"I bought the house and sent a note to tell her, after which she brought all this wealth to me. And everything I own now is due to her. She lived with me for a great many years, and I with her, in princely style. Nonetheless, I didn't give up my trade. My fortune increased; on account of her I rose higher and grew wealthier still. She gave me all these sons" (he motioned to his children), "and then she passed away, may God rest her soul.

"The only harm that stayed with me, from the *dikabrika*, is what you've just seen."

From Abu ʿAli ʾl-Muhassin al-Tanukhi, *Nishwar al-Muhadara wa Akhbar al-Mudhakara* (*Snippets of Conversation and Memorable Tales*), vol. 4.

77

A Merchant and His Wife

Ahmad ibn Ayman, secretary to Ahmad ibn Tulun, told me as follows:

I went to Basra to visit a merchant, whose name I forget, and I saw with him two most smart-looking lads.

"If you will," he said, seeing how keenly I was gazing at them, "pray to God to protect them."

I did this, then said:

"You must have chosen their mother well, to have such splendid children."

"There's no woman in Basra," he answered, "finer than their mother, and none closer to my heart. My story with her makes a wondrous tale."

I asked him to tell it to me, and he narrated as follows:

"I used" (he said) "to go down to Ubulla[1] to trade. I brought some merchandise from there to Basra, and I made a profit. Then I took some merchandise from Basra to Ubulla, and again I made a profit. So I went on, taking goods between the two towns and constantly making a profit, till at last I became rich. People began to talk of my good fortune, and I finally decided to settle in Basra. I realized, though, that my stay here wouldn't be agreeable without a wife.

"Now, there was no one in Basra of greater dignity than the grandfather of these two boys; and he had a daughter he'd refused to marry off, so risking the enmity of all her suitors. I decided to approach him for her hand.

"I went to him when he was alone.

" 'Uncle,' I said, 'I'm the merchant——.'

" 'I know you well enough,' he said, " 'and your father's standing, too.'

" 'I've come,' I said,'to ask for your daughter's hand.'

" 'By God', he answered, ' I've nothing against you. But many people, from among Basra's dignitaries, have asked for her hand, and I've never

---

1. Ubulla was a town on the Tigris.

agreed, because I hate the thought of her leaving my care for someone who'd value her as slave girls are valued [i.e., for her physical attractions].'

" 'God,' I answered, "has raised her above such a status. And I ask you to let me become part of your family."

'Is that your firm wish?' he asked.

'It is,' I replied, 'and I should regard it as a favor and a privilege.'

'Then,'he said, 'come to see me with your men.'

"I spoke with a number of well-known substantial merchants and asked them to go with me the next day.

'You're taking us on a wild goose chase,'they said.

'Still,' I said, 'I ask you to come.'

"We all rode off to the merchant's home, sure he was going to refuse my colleagues' representations. He, though, gave them a positive answer, agreeing to marry me to his daughter. He honored them and spread a sumptuous feast for them; after which they left.

"When they'd gone, the merchant said to me:

'Do, if you'd like to, stay tonight with your wife. There's no reason to delay.'

"That, I answered, was very much my wish. We passed the rest of the day, till sunset, and we prayed the sunset prayer together. He praised God, and so did I; he asked for God's mercy, and so did I. When it grew dark, we prayed the evening prayer together. Then he took my hand and conducted me into a house that was well appointed, with the best furniture. It was spotlessly clean, and there were a number of men and women servants. When I had seated myself there, he rose.

'I'll take my leave of you,' he said. 'May God grant you from His bounty, and make your life an agreeable one.' And with that he left.

"I was now surrounded by older women from his family, who festively brought in my bride. When I looked at her, I saw there was no beauty there. When the curtains were drawn around us, she said:

'Sir, I am a secret of my father's, divulged to no one before—only to you now, since he saw you to be worthy of its trust. Don't, I entreat you, disappoint his faith in you. If what's required of a wife is mere good looks, without a wife's efficiency and chastity, then I shall be in a sad state indeed. But I have, I trust, enough of these two qualities to compensate for good looks.'

"With that she promptly rose and produced a bag full of money.

'Sir,' she said, 'God has permitted you to marry three more free women, in addition to me, together with any concubines you wish to have. You have my full agreement to marry those three, and to buy any of those slave women with the money in this bag, which I pass over to you to fulfill your desires. All I ask is that you will give me your protection."

" I assure you, when she said this, she took immediate possession of my heart, in a way no great beauty could ever have done.

'Here is your recompense,"'I answered, 'for what you have just said. By God, I will have no other woman but you. I will take my fortune in life along with you, possessing what a man most wishes for in a woman.'

"She was as tender and proper as anyone could be, and as efficient in running my household. I realized just how lucky I was. Then, as I grew older, I came in any case to have a greater need of levelheaded behavior. God has shown His approval of the way I received her initial address to me, and has given me these two splendid boys. We dedicate ourselves to His bounty to us, and to the charity He has shown us."

From Abu Jaʿfar Ahmad ibn Yusuf, *Al-Mukafaʿa* (*Recompense*), ed. Ahmad Amin and ʿAli al-Jarim (Cairo, 1941).

78

A Final Meeting

Bashir ibn al-Ashtar fell in love with a girl from his own tribe, called Jaida'. Quite enraptured by her, he finally became sick with love. Her family thereupon stopped him from seeing her, and a great enmity and quarrel sprang up between the two families.

As his longing for her showed no sign of abating and his state grew worse, he went to a friend of his, called Numair.

"Would you," he asked him, "do me a friendly service, so my soul may return to me?"

"Ask whatever you wish," Numair replied.

"Go to Jaida''s neighborhood," he said, "and, if you see her maidservant, tell her of my state. She may perhaps arrange for me to see Jaida'."

I went (Numair said), and I found the servant and told her; and she went to her mistress and received word he should go to see her after dinner, close to some trees there. When night fell, she went there, and Bashir came to meet her. I made to leave, but Bashir stopped me.

"By God," he said, "there is nothing more between us than what you see. Remain where you are."

We sat through a good part of the night. Finally I decided to leave. Bashir, though, almost fainted at this, asking Jaida' to stay the rest of the night with him.

"There is no way I can do that," she answered, "unless your friend here takes some compassion on us."

"Whatever you wish," I replied.

With that she flung some of her clothes toward me.

"Go to my chamber," she said, "as though you were me. My husband will come and ask for the drinking vessel. Withhold it from him till he becomes impatient (this is what I always do). When he returns with the milk, do not take it from him till he has stood there for a long time, or till he puts it down for you. After that he will not return to you for the rest of the night."

So I did (Numair continued). When he had stood there for a long time, with the milk, he decided to put it down. I went to take it, but we knocked against each other and the milk was spilled.

"This is unwifely forwardness!" he cried. With that he picked up a well-honed whip and began beating me till I felt close to death. I was about to stab him with my knife when people came to rescue me and covered me up. Then her mother came and rebuked me, warning me never to act against my husband's wishes.

"What is it you want with al-Ashtar?" she asked.

She left me then, saying she would send her other daughter to console me. When the sister came, she started weeping and calling down curses on those who beat me. Then she lay down by my side.

I put my hand over her mouth, then said:

"Your sister is with Bashir in such and such a place. What happened to me was for her sake, and you should be still more concerned than I am to hide the truth."

She trembled for a time, then became friendly, and we spent a wonderful night, gently and chastely, together. When morning came and Jaida᾽ arrived, she was shocked to see us together.

"She is your sister," I said. "She will tell you all that has happened."

I went to Bashir (Numair concluded) and told him what had happened. When he saw the marks of the whip on my body, and the bloody state I was in, he said:

"This is a wonderful service you have done me, and I owe you the deepest gratitude."

Bashir lived only one month more. Someone came to him as he was eating some grapes.

"You are eating fruit," this person said, "with Jaida᾽ newly dead?"

Bashir made a choking sound, and, when they came to move him, they found he was dead. When the news reached Jaida᾽, she tore her clothes and cut off her hair. Then she flung herself into a well, and she, too, died.

From Dawud al-Antaki, *Tazyin al-Aswaq bi Tafsil Ashwaq al-ʿUshshaq* (*Adorning the Markets with Tales of Lovers' Longing*), vol. 1, ed. Muhammad al-Tunji (Beirut: ʿAlam al-Kutub, 1993).

79

A Party Crasher's Reward

Ten men accused of heresy were sent off to al-Maʾmun. When they'd assembled to board their ship, a party crasher, thinking they were gathered ready for a banquet, added himself to their number. When he found they were all being put in chains, he regretted what he'd done, but he knew there was no turning back.

The others, all known to al-Maʾmun, were beheaded in his presence. Then al-Maʾmun asked who the further man was. No one knew, he was told.

"May my wife be divorced," the man said then, "if I knew these other people, or anything about them! When I saw them coming together, I thought it must be for a banquet."

"Has sponging," al-Maʾmun said, "come to this? Give him a good beating so he thinks twice about doing it again!"

"If, Prince of the Faithful," said Ibrahim ibn al-Mahdi, who was there in attendance, "you will hand him over to me, I will tell you an amazing story about party crashing."

"He is yours," al-Maʾmun said. "Let us hear your story."

"Prince of the Faithful (Ibrahim ibn al-Mahdi began), I was once riding through the city and passed by a house from which came the most appetizing smell of food and spices—I'd never smelled anything to compare with it. Then I saw, in a window, a wrist [of the woman preparing the food] that struck at my heart. I wanted to eat some of that food, but, since I didn't know anyone in the quarter, I realized I'd have to resort to trickery.

"I went to a tailor nearby and asked who owned the house. He gave me the name of the man—a merchant, he said, who loved the company of other merchants.

'Does he,' I asked, 'drink wine?'

'Yes,' he replied. 'And I think he's invited a group of his friends today.'

"I waited for a while, then saw them arrive.

" 'Here they come,' the tailor said.

"I spurred on my horse till I caught up with them. They were late, I told them, and the owner of the house (naming him) was waiting for them. In we went, they thinking I was one of the host's household and the host thinking I was with his guests. Each side honored me and offered me hospitality.

" 'I've satisfied my desire for the food' I said to myself when we'd all eaten, 'but there's still that wrist!'

"When the food had been taken away and drinks were brought in, a slave woman singer came with a lute in her hand. She sang a few short poems, which transported me along with everyone else. I envied her skill and perfect touch. 'But' I said to myself, 'we're not finished yet.'

"She flung aside the lute.

'Since when,' she asked, 'have you brought secret enemies into your midst?'

They all showed their hostility to me. I'll never, I thought, get what I was hoping for unless I win back their hearts.

'Do you,' I asked aloud, 'have a lute?'

"They said they did and brought one. I examined it, tuned it, then sang a short song. The singer came and kissed my hand, apologizing to me, and the people around me began to honor me more and more. I sang two further short songs.

'That's singing, by God,' the singer said. 'Not what we had before.'

"Apart from the host (who clearly had a strong head), the guests all drank till they were completely drunk, and the host gave instructions for them to be taken home. Me, though, he kept behind, asking who I was. I started hedging, but he insisted I should tell him the truth.

'My life's been pretty much wasted,' he said, 'not having met up with someone like you before.'

When I told him who I was, he gave a start.

'I'm going to spend the rest of the night,' he said, 'standing and serving you.'

"I insisted he should sit down, which he did. Then he started asking me why I'd come to his house, and I gave him an account. Nothing now remained, I concluded, but the "wrist."

'You shall have it," he replied, 'God willing.'

"He let me see all his slave women, but I couldn't find what I'd been looking for.

'There's no one left, sir,' he said at last, 'except for my mother and sister.'

'Let's begin with your sister,' I said.

"He brought her in, and she was indeed the one I'd been looking for.

'She's the one,' I said.

'You've made me very happy,' he replied.

"He called in witnesses and we signed the marriage contract. Then he took me to her chambers. The next morning he sent with her such possessions as are found only among us, Prince of the Faithful. And this boy here is my son by her."

From Dawud al-Antaki, *Tazyin al-Aswaq bi Tafsil Ashwaq al-ʿUshshaq* (*Adorning the Markets with Tales of Lovers' Longing*), vol. 1.

80

Parting and Reunion

A wealthy man from Baghdad, so it is told, fell in love with a slave girl singer of great beauty and accomplishment, highly skilled in singing and playing the lute. He lavished all his money on her, till at last he began to feel the pinch. Why, his friends asked him, didn't he have her sing at other people's gatherings (she was much sought after)? This would bring him in a good deal of money. The prospect, though, left him utterly downcast—death, he told them, would be easier for him.

She, for her part, told him to sell her. In this way he could recoup his money, or at least she herself would live amid affluence—for only a rich man would buy someone of her quality. He took her to the slave market, where a Hashemite from Basra bought her for fifteen hundred dinars. When the man had taken his money, and the two had parted, they both became cruelly wretched, plunged in weeping and misery. He tried to return the money and have her back, but to no avail.

I went off (he said) with no idea of where I was going. I couldn't go back to my house, which was empty of her now, quite desolate. I went into a mosque, put the bag of money under my head, and slept. After a while I woke to find a young man had stolen it. I tried to get up and run after him, but found my legs had been tied. By the time I'd freed myself, the young man was gone. In utter despair now, I covered my face and flung myself into the Tigris, wanting only to drown, but I was rescued by some people who supposed I'd simply fallen in.

When I told them what had happened, some of them criticized me while others expressed sympathy. An old man drew me close to him.

"You're not the first," he said, "to have fallen from wealth to poverty. Isn't it enough that you've lost your money? Do you really want to make away with yourself, too, and end up in Hell?"

I calmed down a little. Then I was seized with panic once more. I went to speak to a friend of mine, who gave me fifty dirhams and advised me to leave Baghdad. I might, he said, find someone to hire me to write for him, on account of my fine handwriting. I decided to go to Wasit, where a friend of mine worked as a scribe. I found a ship ready to leave and asked them to take me with them.

"We'll let you on for two dirhams," they said. "But the Hashemite captain doesn't like strangers on board. You'll have to dress like one of the crew."

Could this captain, I wondered, be the very same man who'd bought my girl? If so, I'd be able to enjoy her voice as far as Wasit. I bought a cloak, which I wore like any other member of the crew, and before too long I saw my girl approaching with her new master.

A screen was set up for her. After they'd set sail, and dinner had been brought, [the captain and some companions] began to eat and drink.

"How much longer," the captain asked my girl, "are you going to stay so sunk in grief and refuse to sing? Do you think you're the first who ever parted from her master?"

They went on pressing her, and finally she took the lute and sang two verses; then, though, she was overcome with weeping and fell into a faint. They sprinkled water on her and whispered the call to prayer in her ear, till finally she came to. They went on coaxing her, and eventually she sang two more verses—at which I began choking and almost fell into a faint myself.

"What's the matter with you," the others said, "bringing along a madman like this? Get him out of here."

I suffered grievously at their hands. Eventually the ship reached a port on the way, and they anchored and went on shore for a stroll, leaving the ship empty. I crept up to the lute and tuned its strings in a way only she and I knew. When the men returned, in the moonlight, they spoke kindly to her.

"You can see," they told her, "what a good time we're having. Won't you, by God, share it with us?"

She took the lute, then gave a loud gasp.

"This lute," she said, "is strung in a way my master loved. He used to play it with me. He's here with us!"

"If only he were!" they answered. "We'd get him to join us and cheer you up a bit."

"He *is* here with us," she insisted.

"Have you," they asked the sailors, "let anyone on board?"

Fearing the matter might be allowed to drop, I stepped forward.

"It's me, sir," I said.

He had me come nearer.

"By God," he told me, "I haven't made love to her. God's granted me plenty of wealth, and I bought her only to hear her singing. Come with us to our home, and I'll free her and marry you to her—but on one condition: that you'll bring her every night so we can hear her singing from behind the screen. After that you can go."

"How," I answered, "could I possibly refuse a man who's brought me back to life?"

"Are you in agreement?" he asked the girl.

She replied that she was, and thanked him, twice as happy as before. She started singing, and I helped her by suggesting tunes and songs. The man's joy grew, and so we went on, till, quite intoxicated, we reached the Maʿqil river. There I left the ship to relieve myself and fell asleep, and, not noticing my absence, they sailed on without me. When I woke, it was to find the sun fully risen and the others gone, and my ordeal began all over again. A ship of some kind passed, and I went on with them to Basra.

I entered the city, knowing not a soul or a place in it; and I hadn't thought to ask the man for his name and address. Then I saw a Baghdadi passing and decided at once to approach him and tell him of the wretched state I was in. I followed him to find out where he lived, then I went to a grocer's for a piece of paper so I could write to the Baghdadi about how things stood.

The grocer, liking my handwriting, started asking about me, but I didn't tell him much: only that I had no money left. At that he asked me if I'd work for him. He'd pay me half a dirham a day, he told me, and meet all my needs if I could provide a reliable record of his expenses. After a month he saw his accounts had been properly made and that all the thieving had stopped, and he accordingly raised my pay and gave me his daughter in marriage, then made me his partner. I, though, stayed constantly sad and brokenhearted.

One day I saw people hurrying about the streets with decorations and rejoicing, and, when I asked what it was all about, I was told it was Easter Sunday for the Christians and that people were going out to watch the spectacle. It struck me that, if I went out with them, I might come across my friends. I asked the grocer's permission, and, when he'd given me what I might need, out I went.

When I reached the place where the people were gathered, I saw the Hashemite captain there in the midst of the crowd and raced over to his group. They were overjoyed to see me.

"What happened to you?" they asked. "We thought you must have drowned! The girl tore her clothes, broke her lute, and cut off her hair.

When we got to Basra, we told her she could do as she wanted. She decided to dress in black, make a pretended grave, and sit down by it and weep."

They took me with them, and I found her in the state they'd described. When she saw me, she made a loud choking sound, and we were afraid she was dead. Finally she came to.

"I give her to you," her master said.

"No," I replied. "Do as you promised before. Free her and let us be married."

He did so, just as we'd arranged before. Then he gave me clothes and five hundred dinars.

"This," he said, "is what I was giving you daily before. We'll carry on in the same way."

I went to the grocer and told him the whole story, then divorced his daughter and lived in the greatest happiness with my girl.

From Dawud al-Antaki, *Tazyin al-Aswaq bi Tafsil Ashwaq al-ʿUshshaq* (*Adorning the Markets with Tales of Lovers' Longing*), vol. 1.

VIII

Excerpts from Seven Major Classical Works

81

From Ibn Tufail, *Hayy ibn Yaqzan*

1. The Death of the Doe

Wasting and weakness were taking their toll on the Doe, until at last she was overtaken by death, her movements at an end along with all her actions. When the boy saw her in this state, he was overwhelmed by grief, his soul almost spent with sorrow. He took to calling, using the voice she always answered when she heard it. He called at the top of his voice; but he could spy no movement or change. He gazed at her ears and eyes, but could see no evident defect. He gazed at all her limbs, but could see nothing amiss. His hope was to find the site of the ailment and to remedy matters, so she could be restored to her former state. But all his efforts were in vain. What had led him to the attempt was his own experience. He had found that, when he closed his eyes or covered them, he could no longer see till the obstacle was removed. When he placed his fingers in his ears, he could hear nothing until the blockage was taken away. When he pinched his nose between his fingers, he could smell nothing till his nose was free again. Perhaps, he concluded, all the various perceptions and actions of the doe might have been hampered by impediments of some kind and, when these were removed, the perceptions and actions would return to normal once more.

When the boy gazed at all the Doe's external organs and found no evident defect (even though the whole body had failed, with none of her organs spared), it occurred to him that the defect must have struck some organ invisible to the eye, hidden within the body, an organ whose function could not be replaced by any of these external ones. When that particular organ was struck, then the harm, the inability to act, became overmastering. If (he hoped) he could discover that organ, remove the defect that had overtaken it, then the organ would be restored to its normal state. The whole body would then benefit, and the functions would continue as before.

He had noted before this, in the dead bodies of beasts and other creatures, that all the organs were solid, with no cavity, except in the skull, the chest, and the abdomen. Therefore, he concluded, an organ with the quality he sought was to be found in one of those three places only, the middle one of these three being the natural one, since all the other organs must surely be in need of it? Its abode must be in the center. When, moreover, he turned to examine his own body, he sensed such an organ to be in his chest, since it was the key to all his other organs, like the hand, the foot, the ear, the nose, the eye, and the head. He was conscious that these last were separate entities; and this meant, he thought, that he was somehow independent of them. He was conscious of a similar quality in his head; of this, too, he was independent. But when he reflected on what he felt in his chest, he did not think he could do without it for a moment. He had felt the same when fighting the beasts, taking special care to avoid attacks by their claws on his chest—being aware of the organ within it.

Having decided the impaired organ must be in the Doe's chest, he resolved to search for it by exploring there, in the hope of finding the organ, spying the defect, and removing it. Might it not be, though, that his efforts would serve to make the impairment worse?

Then a further thought struck him. Had he ever seen other beasts restored to their former state, when brought to a condition like this? He could recall nothing of the kind. If he left her as she was, he reflected, there was no hope of her ever being so restored. If, though, he could find this organ and release it from its ailment, she might return to what she had been before. He thereupon decided to slit open her chest and explore what lay inside. He took some sharp pebbles, and some splinters of dry reed, which he used as knives, cutting through the ribs and the flesh till he came upon the diaphragm protecting the organs within. Something so strong, he felt, could only be serving to protect the organ he sought; if he could once pierce through it, then his goal would be reached. He strove to cut through, but his tools, mere pebbles and reeds, hampered his efforts. He sharpened the tools and went slowly through the diaphragm, which gave way at last, revealing a lung. For a while he thought this must be what he had been seeking, and he turned it around, looking for the place where the defect was.

Having first found one of the two lungs to one side, and seeing the lung so placed, when he had supposed the organ he sought to be squarely in the center of the body, he went on with his exploration, in the middle of the chest, till he found the heart, wrapped in the toughest of membranes, connected to the lung by tight ligaments on the side where he had begun his incision. "If," he said to himself, "this organ should have the same conditions on the other side, then it is truly in the center, and this must be my goal, especially being set, as it is, in such a noble place, with such a comely form, with a firm grip and strong flesh, protected by a screen of the kind I have seen with none of the other organs."

He explored the other side of the chest, seeking the diaphragm protecting the ribs, and he found a lung in a place similar to the one on the first side. Now, more than ever, he was certain this organ must be his goal. Bent on revealing it, he cut into its membrane, and with effort and perseverance, exhausting all his means, he contrived to win through.

Coming to the heart, he found it sealed on every side. He looked closely, searching for any visible defect, but found none. Then, pressing it, he felt a cavity. "It may be," he thought, "that my final goal lies inside this organ, where I have not yet come." So he cut through the heart to find two cavities, one on each side. The one on the right was filled with clots of congealed blood; the one on the left was quite empty. "My goal," he then said, "can only lie in one of these two chambers. As for the one on the right, I see it contains only this congealed blood. It could hardly have congealed before the whole body reached its present state." He had already observed how, when blood flows, it clots and congeals. "And this blood," he reflected, "is like any other blood, which I might find in any other organ; it is not particular to one or the other. Clearly my goal does not lie here. It is linked to this place I find myself unable to do without for a single moment since the time I began my search. As for the blood, it is like the blood I have lost many times when wounded by beasts or stones. I was not truly harmed then, or impeded in any of my functions. Therefore, this chamber does not contain my goal. As for the left chamber, this I find quite empty; yet surely it cannot be so without reason. Each of these organs, I have seen, exists for its own special purpose. How can a place of such dignity exist to no purpose? I can only think that what I sought lay there, before it departed and fled its abode. Then this body lost its powers, lacking all perception and motion."

When he found that the dweller in this abode had departed, before the place fell into ruin and was left to that state, it seemed to him unlikely that the dweller, after so much damage and destruction, would return. The whole body now became base and worthless in his eyes, compared to the thing he was sure must have dwelt there for a time before going on its way. Now he exerted himself to reflect on this thing: its identity and form; its connection with the body; its destination; the exits it had used when leaving the body; the cause of annoyance if it had left against its will; the reason why, if it had left willingly, it had found the body unpleasing and had resolved to depart.

All these things surged in his mind. He no longer had any care for the body before him. The mother who had nursed him so tenderly was, he now realized, not this disabled body but that departing thing, the source of all those actions. This whole body, therefore, was akin to a tool, or the club he used in fighting beasts. His interest moved from the body, for which he felt no more passion, to the possessor and mover of that body.

2. Hayy's Vision of the Divine Light

After deep trance, utter loss of self, and true spiritual attainment, he witnessed the highest sphere, which had no physical body. He saw an essence, free of matter, which is neither the essence of the One, the Truth, nor the essence of the highest sphere, nor different from either. It appeared like the image of the sun reflected in a polished mirror. It was neither the sun, nor the mirror, nor different from either. He saw the essence of that immaterial sphere graced with a reflection, a splendor, a beauty too great to be described in spoken words, too delicate to be clothed in letters or sound. With the highest pleasure and joy, happiness and delight, he viewed the essence of Truth, Glory be to His Majesty.

He viewed, too, the sphere next to it, the sphere of the fixed stars, whose essence was likewise free of matter. It was like the image of the sun reflected in a mirror that bore the reflection of another mirror facing the sun. This essence, too, was graced with splendor, beauty, and delight, very much like the one he had witnessed in the highest sphere.

Next to this, in the sphere of Saturn, he witnessed an immaterial essence that was neither like the ones he had seen before nor different from them. It was like the image of the sun reflected in a mirror that bore the reflection of another mirror facing the sun. In this essence, he saw what he had seen in the ones before: splendor and delight. In each succeeding sphere, he witnessed an essence free of matter, which was neither like the essences he had seen before nor different from them, not unlike the image of the sun reflected from one mirror to another, in a regular sequence following that of the spheres. In each of these spheres he witnessed a beauty and glory, delight and joy, the like of which no eye has seen, no ear heard, no heart known; until he came to the world of generation and corruption, which is all contained within the sphere of the moon. This he found to have an immaterial essence neither different from the essences he had seen before nor similar to them. This essence had seventy thousand faces, and each face had seventy thousand mouths, and each mouth had seventy thousand tongues, ceaselessly praising and glorifying the One, the Truth. In this essence, which he perceived to be multiple but was not, in fact, he saw the same perfection and delight as he had seen in those essences before. This essence appeared like the image of the sun reflected on the face of shimmering matter, a reflection from the last mirror to receive the reflection in the sequence before, beginning from that first mirror facing the sun itself. Then he saw a separate essence; were it possible for the essence of seventy thousand faces to break into parts, we would say this essence was a part. But this essence had come into being out of nonbeing. And, had it not been designated to his own body, when it came into being, we would have said it did not exist. Within this rank he saw essences like his own, belonging to bodies that had existed, then diminished, and to bodies that were still with him in existence. These were infinitely numerous (if it were possible to say so), or were all unified (if it were possible to say they were one). In his own essence, and in those essences of a rank akin to his own, he saw such beauty, splendor, and infinite delight as no eye has seen, no ear heard, no heart known; ineffable, unknowable for all but those who have attained true insight. He saw, too, many immaterial essences, which appeared like rusty mirrors, covered with dirt, turning their backs to the polished mirrors that reflected the image of the sun, looking away from them. In these essences he saw such ugliness and defect as he could never have imagined. They were, he saw, in never-ending pain, racked by unforgettable sighs, overwhelmed by a canopy of torture, burned by the fire of deprivation, and slit by jagged blades between allurement and vexation. Beside the tormented essences, he saw others that emerged then vanished, formed then dissolved. He looked closely and searchingly, and found a great calamity, a dreadful disaster, a constant creation, a supreme formation, a molding and inspiration, a creation and abrogation. When he had recovered a little, his senses returned to him, and he awoke from that trancelike state. He lost hold of his former state; the world of the senses loomed as the divine world receded. It was not possible for the two to meet. They were like two second wives: should you please the one, then you anger the other. You might observe: from your description of this vision, you appear to say that the immaterial essences are permanent where they belong to a permanent, nondecaying body, like the stars. If they belong to a decaying body, like that of a speaking animal, then they decay, shrink, and vanish. This may be understood from your analogy of the reflecting mirrors. Naturally, the image depends on the permanence of the mirror. If the mirror decays and vanishes, then the image vanishes with it. Then I would say to you: how quickly you have forgotten the agreement, breaking the terms we laid down. Did we not indicate that the scope of expression is limiting here, and that words, in every case, fall short of the truth? Your error was to place the real and the analogous on the same level, in every respect. This should not be done even in common speech; and how much less so in our case. Here, the sun and its light, its image and formation, the mirrors and the images reflected in them, are all matters dependent on bodies, without which they cannot exist. Therefore, their existence requires the existence of bodies; and, when the bodies are destroyed, those essences cease to be.

As for the divine essences and the lordly spirits, they are all free of bodies and the physical attributes of bodies, quite independent of them. These essences have no connection or relation to bodies, whose permanence or absence, being or not being, has no meaning for them, linked and connected as they are with the essence of the One, the Truth, the Being Whose existence is necessary. He is their First and their Initiator, their Cause and their Creator. He gives them permanence, provides them with eternity, with everlasting existence. They are in no need of bodies; rather, bodies are in need of them. Were it possible for these essences to perish, then bodies would perish, too; for these essences are the originator of bodies. Likewise, if it were possible for the One, the Truth, to perish—exalted and holy is He, and above such presumption, there is no God but He—then all essences would perish, too, and with all these essences bodies would perish; the whole world of the senses would perish, and not one being would remain, for everything is linked together. The world of sense, though depending on the divine world, is like its shadow. The divine world is dependent on nothing, free of the world of sense; yet it is impossible to presume the latter's nonexistence, since, inevitably, it follows the divine world. The decay of the sensory world is witnessed in change, not in total destruction. This is the meaning of the Holy Book when it speaks of the change in the mountains, of their turning to tufts of carded wool; of people being scattered like moths; of the collapse of the sun and moon; of the explosion of seas and oceans; of the day when skies and earth are to be replaced by other skies and earth.

So much I am now able to tell you of what Hayy ibn Yaqzan witnessed in that exalted state. So, do not ask for further elaboration in words. Such a thing is plainly impossible.

3. The Arrival of Absal on Hayy's Island

Absal had heard of the island where Hayy ibn Yaqzan was said to have been raised. He knew, too, of its fertility, natural benefits, and temperate climate; and that solitude was possible there for the one who sought it. He decided, accordingly, to travel to this island and live apart from others for the rest of his days. He gathered what money he had, used some to hire a boat to take him to the island, and then gave the rest to the poor. He bade farewell to his friend Salaman, and set sail. The sailors put him down on the shore of the island, then left him.

Absal remained on the island, worshipping the Almighty, glorifying Him, reflecting on His most beautiful Names and sublime attributes, enjoying peace of mind and a soul unperturbed. When he needed food, he found the means to satisfy his hunger from the island's fruit and game. And so he continued for a time with his prayers to his Lord, in utter happiness and great contentment. Each day he witnessed his Lord's grace and favors through the easing of his needs and provision of his sustenance, and this supported his faith and delighted his heart.

During all this time Hayy ibn Yaqzan remained in his rapturous state, leaving his cave just once each week to take any food found for him. And so Absal failed to come across him at first as he wandered through the various parts of the island, seeing no one, finding indeed no trace of any other person. At this his delight and peace of mind grew still further, for he was bent on utter seclusion and solitude. Then it happened, at a certain moment, that Hayy ibn Yaqzan came out in search of food when Absal was nearby, and each caught a glimpse of the other.

This person he had seen, Absal thought, was doubtless some religious devotee who had come to the island, as he himself had done, in search of solitude. And he feared that, if he approached this other, he would be unwelcome, as one coming between the worshipper and the goal to which he aspired. As for Hayy ibn Yaqzan, he had no notion of what this creature before him might be, a creature so unlike any of the beasts he had seen before. The black gown of hair and wool in which Absal was dressed was, Hayy supposed, some kind of natural coat. He stopped to marvel at Absal, who thereupon fled, fearful that Hayy might distract him from his concern. As for Hayy ibn Yaqzan, he pursued Absal, for it was in his nature to inquire about anything he might come across. When he saw Absal running ever faster, he hid himself for a time; whereupon Absal, supposing Hayy at a safe distance, and himself secure, resumed his prayer, weeping in devotion, till he lost all sense of things around him. Hayy now began, little by little, to draw closer, with Absal unaware of him, till he was close enough to hear Absal's recitation and praise of God and to see his supplication and tears. He heard a soft voice and a pleasant utterance, of a kind he had never known among the beasts. Then, looking more closely at Absal's form and features, he saw them to be much like his own. He realized, too, that Absal's gown was not after all a natural skin but clothing like his own. And, hearing Absal's heartfelt supplication and pious weeping, he was left in no doubt that Absal was one of those souls aware of the truth. He wished to know more of Absal and to find out the reason for his weeping and supplication.

Hayy now drew still closer to Absal until Absal, sensing his presence, began to flee. Hayy ibn Yaqzan followed and caught him, for God had blessed him with the strongest powers of body and mind. Hayy then held on to Absal and would not release him. For his part, Absal gazed at Hayy—this man clothed in the hairy skins of beasts, his own natural hair so long that it covered most of his body. And, finding Hayy endowed with such swiftness of foot and strength of limb, he was overcome with terror. He began to speak softly to Hayy, who could not understand him but sensed nonetheless that Absal's tone betrayed fear. And so he strove to calm Absal, using the sounds he had learned from certain beasts, stroking his head and arms, showing affection to Absal, making his friendly intentions clear. At that Absal grew calmer, convinced that Hayy meant him no harm. Having an interest in interpreting, Absal had learned several languages, becoming well versed in them. He began to address Hayy ibn Yaqzan in every language he knew, asking about his affairs, trying to make him understand, but all to no avail. As for Hayy, he stood there astonished at what he was hearing, having no notion of what it all meant, though he took care to make his own pleasure and approval clear. So it was that each marveled at the other.

Absal still had some food with him, which he had brought from the inhabited island, and some of this he offered to Hayy, who did not recognize it, having seen nothing like it before. Absal ate some of the food and invited Hayy to do the same. Hayy pondered his resolve about the food he might permit himself. Then, finally, not recognizing this thing he was offered, and so uncertain whether or not he could accept it, he refused the offer. Absal, though, persisted gently, and Hayy, who had grown fond of Absal by now, feared a continued refusal might give offense. And so Hayy approached and tasted the food, finding it delicious. He realized he had erred in this by breaking his own promise about the kind of food he might eat. Regretting what he had done, he thought he should perhaps part company with Absal and return to his own exalted state. But he was graced with no immediate revelation. And so he decided to remain with Absal in the world of the senses till he had found the truth about this world to his own satisfaction. Then, he thought, he could return to his own state without further distraction.

He stayed by Absal's side, and Absal, seeing Hayy silent, found his anxieties about his own faith diminishing. He might, he hoped, teach Hayy to speak, then instruct him in knowledge and religion, and so win favor with God. Absal began to teach Hayy language by pointing to different objects and pronouncing their names, doing this repeatedly and encouraging Hayy to pronounce the name while he himself pointed at it. Finally he had taught him all the names, and, quite quickly, Hayy began to speak. Absal then started to question Hayy about himself, asking how he had come to be on the island. Hayy explained that he had no notion about his birth or his father or mother, only about the Doe who had raised him. He told Absal everything about himself, how he had grown in knowledge till at last he had come to spiritual attainment. When Absal heard Hayy describe these divine truths and essences, which rest not on the world of the senses but on knowledge of the Almighty, and heard his description of the Almighty with His beautiful attributes, and heard him speak as best he could of the delights of spiritual attainment and of the pains of those who are veiled from Him, then he knew beyond all doubt that these things were linked to his own faith concerning the Almighty, His angels, and His scriptures, and messengers, and the Day of Judgment. God's Paradise and Hell were akin to all that Hayy ibn Yaqzan had witnessed. At that his heart was enlightened, his mind sharpened, and he saw a correspondence between Tradition and Reason. The means of interpretation became clearer to him. No problem of religious law was left without revelation, no ambiguity without explanation, and so he became endowed with understanding.

Now he began to gaze at Hayy ibn Yaqzan with veneration and wonder. This, he saw, was one of those favored by God who should have no fear, nor should grieve. He took to serving and following Hayy, heeding his advice on queries and doubts about the religious law he had learned among his own people. Hayy, in turn, began to ask Absal about his affairs. And Absal described his own native island, its inhabitants, their condition before they embraced the faith and thereafter. He explained the divine world as related in their religious law, Heaven and Hell, resurrection, judgment, balance, and the straight path. All this Hayy understood, finding nothing different from what he himself had experienced in his exalted state.

The man describing these things, Hayy ibn Yaqzan realized, was telling no falsehoods; he was speaking the truth, as a messenger from his Lord. And so he believed in him and bore witness to his message. He asked Absal, next, about the obligatory disciplines the Messenger had brought to his people, and about the forms of worship assigned to each discipline. Absal thereupon described the prayers, alms, fasting, pilgrimage, and other external practices. All this Hayy accepted and resolved to practice, on the injunction of the one he accepted as a truthful witness.

Yet there remained two aspects of religion that left him perplexed and unable to perceive the wisdom that lay behind them. The first was this. Why had the Messenger, when describing the divine world, spoken mostly in symbols, unwilling to give revelation directly? This, it seemed to Hayy, had led people to ascribe unfitting attributes to the essence of Truth, from which He was free. There was, in addition here, the question of crime and punishment. The second query was as follows. Why had the Messenger confined duty to the obligatory prayers and rites? Why had he permitted the amassing of wealth and overindulgence in food, so that people became fixed on vanities and were distracted from the Truth?

His own view was that a person should eat just enough to sustain him; and, as for money, this had no meaning for him. He studied the judgments of religious law in matters of money—the various types of alms, sales, interests, limitations, and punishments linked to each transaction—and found them strange, marked by fruitless detail. "If people," he said, "could only grasp the truth of such matters, they would shun all those follies. They would embrace the truth and be satisfied with that. No one would have a private fortune needing to be taxed, or risk the severing of a hand for stealing something, or risk losing his life for seizing it openly."

What had misled him here was his assumption that all men had inborn higher natures, acute minds, and lofty aspirations. He had no notion of how dull and inadequate they were, how poor in insight and weak in resolve—that they were like cattle, or worse still, that they had gone astray.

4. The Failure of Preaching on Absal's Island

The head of this island, whose name was Salaman, was a friend of Absal's, and he believed in life within the community, proscribing isolation. Now Hayy ibn Yaqzan set out to instruct these islanders and reveal to them the secrets of wisdom. After a time he was able to pass beyond the literal, to make clear what they had wrongly understood before. However, they began to feel uneasy at this, displeased and disturbed by what he was saying, harboring ill will toward him—even if they did appear pleased to his face, given that he was a guest among them, and out of respect for Absal as a leading figure.

Day and night, Hayy ibn Yaqzan remained patient and courteous to these people, setting out the truth openly or by implication. But all this only increased their hostility. They did indeed love the good and desire truth. But, deficient as they were by nature, they did not seek truth in the proper fashion, or follow the right path to realize it, or pass through the door that led to it. Nor did they wish to learn the truth from those endowed with it. And so, finally, he despaired of reforming them, losing all hope of teaching a way of life of which they were plainly incapable.

Reflecting on the various classes of people there, he realized each person was content with his present state. Passion was their god, desire their worship. Still they strove to amass worldly goods, till, sunk in this course, they went to their graves. No advice could win through to them, no good word found acceptance with them, no discussion led to anything but more obduracy still. Wisdom they had no way of attaining; they could not conceive even a part of it. They were plunged in ignorance, and their gains weighed heavy on their hearts. "Allah has set a seal on their hearts and on their hearing, and a veil on their eyes; great is the penalty they [incur]." He saw them canopied with torment and draped in darkness. Few only had thought of their religion beyond its worldly aspects. Good deeds, however light and easy, they disregarded and reckoned of small importance; they were turned aside from all thoughts of God by trade and sale, having no fear of the day when hearts and sights would be transformed. Hayy knew clearly now that he could find no direct way through to them and should not tax them beyond their limits. Most of them, he found, simply took from religion those things that aided them in their worldly lives and protected them against wrongdoing by others. Only a handful had the means to find the bliss of that other world—were among those "who desire the tilth of the hereafter and strive for it with genuine faith." As for those who transgressed, setting greater store by the life of this world, they would abide in Hell. What greater hardship could there be, and what misery more wretched, than the one suffered by those whose deeds, from the instant of waking to the moment of retirement to sleep, proclaimed only ways to some gain in base matters of the senses: wealth to amass, a pleasure to gain, a desire to fulfill, an act of spite to relish, a position to win, a religious deed to use for ornament or protection? All these were "layers of darkness on top of one another," on a perilous sea. "Not one of you but will pass over it: this is with your Lord a decree that must be accomplished." When he realized the state of these people, that most were like dumb animals, he became sure that all wisdom, all guidance, all fulfillment were to be found in the words of the messengers and the tenets of religion, which were perfect and complete. Deeds were attached to the person. Each was destined to that for which he was created. "[Such was] the practice [approved] of Allah among those who lived aforetime: no change will you find in the practice [approved] of Allah."

Hayy therefore went to Salaman and his companions, saying he now regretted the things he had explained to them. He was, he said, of their mind after all, guided in the same fashion; and he advised them to keep to the ways they were following, within the limits of religious law and common tradition, disregarding what did not concern them, shunning heresies and whims, following in the footsteps of their pious forefathers, avoiding anything that was new. Only, they should not imitate base people in setting aside religious law and coveting worldly gain; such behavior, he warned, they should shun utterly. He realized, as did his companion Absal, that this frail, unseasoned set of people could find no salvation outside the path he described. Removed from that path, they would lose their bearings, fall short of the progress of the blessed, stray this way and that, before falling back and meeting a woeful end at last. If, though, they held to their own ways until graced with faith, they would find safety and bliss in due time—even if those who reached the goal first were closer to salvation.

Accordingly, Hayy and Absal took leave of the islanders and prepared to return to their own island; and, in due course, the Almighty granted them the means to cross over. There Hayy ibn Yaqzan resumed the pious path he had embarked upon. Absal did the same, until his progress fell little short of Hayy's. And so they went on in their worship of the Almighty, on that island, until they met their destiny.

Translated by ʿAbd al-Wahid Luʾluʾa and Christopher Tingley

82

From Al-Jahiz, *Al-Bukhala'* (*Book of Misers*)

1. The Attenders at a Mosque in Basra

A group of men would meet regularly at a mosque in Basra. They were known for their frugality and for their eagerness to amass wealth while denying such wealth to others—a trait that made for a kind of bond of mutual affection, or covenant for mutual support. Whenever these men met in their circles, they would indulge the trait, relishing any appropriate news in a spirit of enjoyment and emulation.

1. One day an old man in the group addressed the others as follows:

"My dear old comrades, never underestimate little things. After all, everything that's big was small to start with. When the Almighty wills it, He can make a trifling object into a large one, He can turn scantiness into plenty. What is it that makes treasure, finally, but one dirham added to another one? And what's a dirham but one *qirat* added to another one? It's no different from the sands of Arabia or the water in the sea! How does the money build up in the treasury if it's not from a dirham here, a dirham there? I know a petty trader who came to own a thousand acres in Arabia. I'd seen him selling peppercorns and chickpeas, for the tiniest of profits. But still he went on, building up those small gains, till he was able to buy his thousand acres.

"Once, I remember, I was racked for several days with pains in my chest from a cough I had. One person suggested frosted sweets as a cure, another one recommended a bran porridge, with starch, and sugar, and almond oil, and so on. I wasn't going to pay out all that money! I just hoped it would clear up by itself. As I was soldiering on like that, this rich fellow said to me: 'Just try boiling bran and drinking the liquid hot.' So I did, and very tasty it was, too. What's more, I found I wasn't hungry afterwards. My appetite didn't come back before midday, and when I did finally finish my lunch and wash my hands, it was already late afternoon—so close to my suppertime I decided to do without supper altogether.

" 'Why,' I said to that wife of mine, 'don't you boil up bran every day for our children? The broth clears the chest, it's good, wholesome food, and it stops you feeling hungry. And when we've finished, you can dry out the bran itself to the way it was at the beginning. Then, when you've collected enough, you can sell it for the same price we paid to start with. That way we'll double our money.'

" 'May God,' she said, 'bless you a hundred times for that cough you had. The bran's done your body good and your pocket as well.'

"Now, wasn't that a lucky piece of advice?"

"You're right," his comrades agreed. "You can only get rich if you're thinking straight, and that's a gift from Heaven sure enough!"

2. Another old man came forward.

"I've never," he said, "known anyone do things properly, think everything through just right, like Maʿada al-Anbariyya."

"What about this Maʿada?" one of the group asked.

"Last year," the old man said, "a cousin of hers gave her a ewe for the sacrifice. But I found her gloomy, in a total quandary.

" 'What's the matter, Maʿada?' I asked.

" 'I'm a widow,' she said, 'all on my own. There's no one to guide me, no one to tell me how to manage sacrificial meat. The ones who did know are all gone. I'm afraid some of this mutton might be wasted because I don't know how to use the different parts. And yet I know God didn't create anything in this ewe, or in any other animal come to that, without its proper use. What am I to do? My fear is, if I waste the tiniest part, it might lead on to wasting a bigger part.

" 'Now the horn,' she went on, 'that's no problem. I can nail it to one of the beams on the ceiling, and it'll make a hook for hanging baskets and leather bags—for anything that needs to be kept clear from mice, ants, cats, cockroaches, snakes, things like that. The guts can be used as cords for a teasing bow—we need one badly. As for the head, the jaws, and all the other bones, they can be scraped, chopped up, and then boiled. Any grease that comes to the top I'll use for the lantern, spreading on bread, making broth, and so on. After that the bones can be used to light the fire. There's nothing like bones for making a good, blazing fire. It brings the pot to the boil quicker as well—bones make hardly any smoke when they burn. As for the hide, the skin makes a sack all by itself, and there are endless ways to use the wool. And you can make a wonderful fuel by drying the dung and the droppings.

" 'But now we come to the blood. The Almighty, I know, only forbade the eating or drinking of shed blood. There are ways we're actually allowed to use it. If I don't find some way of using the blood, it will be like a canker in my heart and eyes. I'll never be able to stop thinking and worrying about it.'

"Then, after a while" (the old man went on), "I saw her face light up in a beaming smile.

" 'So,' I said, 'you've hit on some way, have you, how you can use the blood?'

" 'Yes,' she said, 'I've just remembered, I have some new cooking ware from Damascus. There's nothing, so people say, that tans and strengthens them better than smearing them with hot greasy blood. I can relax now. Everything's fallen right, in its proper place.'

"Six months later, I came across her again.

" 'So,' I asked, 'how was your cured mutton?'

" 'Heaven bless you!' she exclaimed. 'It isn't time for the cured meat yet! We still have enough fat, and shanks, and scraped bones, and things like that. Everything has its proper time!' "

One of the other men there picked up a handful of pebbles and flung them down on the ground.

"You never realize how wasteful you've been," he yelled, "till you hear about the deeds of the righteous!"

3. Abu Yaʿqoub al-Daqnan used to say:

I never went without meat after I became rich. On the Friday I'd buy beef for a dirham, onions for a *daniq*, eggplants for another *daniq*, and a squash and a carrot for a *daniq* each when they were in season. Then I'd cook it all up together. That day my family and I would eat our bread with whatever was floating at the top of the pot: bits of onion, eggplant, carrot, squash, grease, or meat. On Saturday we'd crumble our bread and sop it in the broth. On Sunday we'd eat the onions, on Monday we'd eat the carrots, on Tuesday we'd eat the squash. As for Thursday, that was earmarked for the meat. And so, I never went without meat after I became rich.

4. Our companions related the following:

We made a visit to some people in the northern region and found their country rather cold. And yet they had a whole forest of tamarisk trees to use as firewood.

"There's no fuel more efficient than tamarisk," we told them.

"It certainly is efficient," they answered. "That's why we don't go near it."

"Why don't you go near it?" we asked.

"Tamarisk smoke," they told us, "sharpens the appetite. And we have large families."

5. Al-Jahiz and Mahfouz al-Naqqash

One night Mahfouz al-Naqqash and I came out of the Great Mosque together. We got close to his house, and, as it was nearer to the mosque than mine, he suggested I might stay the night with him.

"Where do you think you're going," he said, "in all this rain and cold? My house is yours. It's dark and you don't have any lantern with you. I've some buttermilk you couldn't beat anywhere, and some first-class dates, just right for you."

So, I went off with him. He left me waiting for a while, then back he came with a dish of buttermilk and a plate of dates.

"Abu ʿUthman," he said, as I stretched out my hand to the food, "buttermilk lies on the stomach, and there's no chance of getting any real exercise at night. It's a damp, rainy night, too, and you're not as young as you were, always complaining about your arthritis. And you're thirsty all the time, not used to proper dinners. Now, if you take a little of this buttermilk, but not too much, it will be as if you hadn't eaten and hadn't gone without either. You'll have taken the edge off your appetite but resisted the temptation to eat something you find really tasty. If you eat too much, though, we're going to have a wretched night trying to take care of you. We haven't any liquor or honey ready for that sort of crisis. I'm saying this now so you won't start going on about it tomorrow. I'm in a real quandary. If I hadn't brought you what I promised, you would have said I was a miser. But if I'd brought it without giving you any warning, without making clear what it might lead to, you would have said I was being uncharitable and hadn't given you the proper advice. Well, now I've cleared myself of both charges. The choice is yours: a mere meal that's going to kill you, or a bit of self-discipline, then a nice sound sleep afterwards."

I never laughed as much as I did that night! I ate up all the food, which I reckon must have been digested with the help of sheer laughter and jubilant delight. If there'd been anyone with me to appreciate the wonderful talk we had, I would have died laughing. But laughing on your own isn't like laughter shared by comrades.

6.

Once in a while Ibn al-ʿAqdi might invite his friends to his orchard, but I don't think his heart was in it. One day I questioned some of his visitors.

"Tell me something," I said, "about those visits."

"Will you keep this confidential?" one of them asked.

"Yes," I replied. "As long as I'm in Basra."

"He'd buy unhusked rice for us," the man said, "and bring it along. Nothing else under God's heaven, just that rice. When we got to his orchard, he'd tell his laborer to husk the rice in his own hand mill. He'd winnow the rice, and sift it, then he'd husk, all over again, any grains that had escaped the mill. When he'd finished with all the husking, winnowing, and sifting, then the extra rehusking, plus the extra winnowing and sifting, he'd tell his laborer to crush it, using his own ox-driven mill. Then, when the rice was crushed and milled, he'd tell his man to boil some water, gather firewood, then knead the ground rice, which would rise better with the warm water. Then he'd tell his man to bake it. He's been known to ask his visitors to set up fishhooks and block the exits for small fish so they wouldn't escape into the water channels. After that they'd run their hands among the rushes and roots, and any fish that was caught he'd cook under the baking plate of the fire so he wouldn't need extra firewood. And we'd be there like that from noon till nightfall, tired and hungry, and still waiting. All for a supper of black rice bread. And he wouldn't have given us that if he could have thought of anything worse."

7. Al-Makki told me the following anecdote:

I once spent the night at Ismaʿil ibn Ghazwan's house—he'd asked me because he knew I'd eaten supper with Muwais and I had a cask of wine with me. When it was past midnight, I couldn't keep my eyes open any longer, and I lay down on the rug, resting my head on my hand. There was no bedding in the house except his prayer rug, a mattress, and a pillow. He handed me the pillow, but I refused to take it and gave it back to him. He insisted, and I refused again.

"How can you lie there like that, with your head on your hand," he demanded, "when I've a pillow here for you?"

So I took the pillow and put it under my head. But I couldn't sleep in that strange place, on such a rough bed. When my host thought I'd fallen asleep, he crept softly up to me and pulled the pillow out from under my head. When I saw him going away with it, I started laughing.

"Did you have to do that?" I asked.

"I only came," he answered, "to put the pillow in a better position under your head."

"But," I told him, "I didn't say a word till you were going off with it."

"I did mean to do it," he replied. "Only, when I had the pillow in my hand, I forgot what I'd come for. I reckon drink makes you forget everything!"

8. Here's another anecdote I heard sometime ago:

A certain person was, it seems, an utter miser and somehow managed to become an imam in a mosque. Whenever he got hold of a dirham, he'd address it in a reverent, friendly way, holding it there in his hand.

"How many lands you must have passed through!" he'd say to the coin. "How many purses you must have left behind! How many humble people you must have raised up! How many prominent people you must have brought down! You'll never, I promise, be exposed or sacrificed."

With that he'd drop the coin into his bag, saying:

"Live there in God's peace. In a place where you won't be insulted, or despised, or disturbed."

Once he'd dropped a dirham in his bag, he never took it out again.

One day his family pressed him to spend a dirham on some food they desperately needed. He tried his best to head them off, but at last he went out, carrying a single dirham. Then, on his way to the market, he saw a snake charmer who was ready to put the snake on his body if anyone paid him a dirham.

"Am I," the imam said to himself, "going to squander something for which a life can be lost, just to eat and drink? Here, surely, is a divine lesson I need to learn."

With that he returned to his family and put the dirham back in his bag. His family was distraught at this. They wanted him just to die so they could be rid of him and live on without him.

When he did die, and the family thought they were rid of him at last, his son came to take possession of the money and the house.

"What," he asked, "did my father butter his bread with? Bad habits usually start with butter."

"He'd always," they said, "have a little cheese with his bread."

"Show me where it is," he said.

They did as he told them, and he found a hollow in the middle of the piece of cheese where the bread had been rubbed against it.

"Why is it hollowed out like this?" he asked.

"He never cut the cheese," they told him. "He'd just rub against the edge of it. That's where this hollow came from."

"This," he said, "is what reduced me to the state I'm in now. If I'd known about this, I would never have prayed behind his coffin."

"So what are you going to do now?" they asked him.

"I'm going," he replied, "to set the cheese up somewhere, a long way off, and point to it with a piece of bread!"

9. Abu ʾl-Hasan al-Madaʾini told the following story about a date merchant:

There was a date merchant in Madaʾin who grew worried when he saw his servant going into the shop and spending some time there. He was afraid the servant might be eating some of the dates.

One day he taxed the boy with this, and the boy denied it. So he called for a piece of white cotton and told the boy to chew it, which he did. When the boy took it out of his mouth, it looked yellow and sweet.

"So," he said to the boy, "this is what you've been up to, is it, day after day, and I knew nothing about it? Out of my house!"

10. Al-Masri told me this anecdote. He was a neighbor of al-Dardarishi's, who was extremely rich:

I was once at al-Dardarishi's house when a beggar came to the door asking for alms. Al-Dardarishi shouted at him. Then came another, and he shouted at him, too, in a furious rage this time. I went up to my host.

"Why," I asked him, "do you hate beggars so much?"

"The fact is," he answered, "most of these people are richer than I am."

"I had an idea that might be why you hated them," I said.

"If any of these people," he said, "had the chance to pull my house down, or take my life away from me, they'd do it. If I'd listened to them and given to them whenever they asked, I'd have ended up like them long ago. How do you expect me to feel about people who feel that way about me?"

11.

Abu ʾl-Hudail once took Muwais a chicken as a gift. It was cheaper than the gifts Muwais usually received, but he was so courteous and good-natured that he made a show of marveling at this plump chicken with its delicious meat. He was well aware, though, how miserly the other man was.

"How did you find that chicken, Abu ʿImran," Abu ʾl-Hudail would ask from time to time.

"It was absolutely wonderful," the good man would reply.

"But do you know," Abu ʾl-Hudail would continue, "the breed of chicken, and its age? A good chicken's known by its breed and its age. Do you know what we used to fatten it, and where we'd feed it?"

And so he'd go on, and his host couldn't stop laughing, for reasons that are clear enough to us, though Abu ʾl-Hudail suspected nothing. He was an innocent, quite artless and naive. Whenever a chicken was mentioned, he'd ask: "How does it compare with that other chicken, Abu ʿImran?" If a duck or a kid, a lamb or a cow, was mentioned, he'd ask (for example): "How does this lamb, if you put it alongside other lambs, compare with that chicken alongside other chickens?" If a particular fowl or cow turned out to be plump, he'd say: "But not as plump as that chicken!" If any fat thing was called tasty, he'd say: "There's taste in beef and duck, in fish and chicken, and especially in that breed of chicken." If the date of someone's birth was mentioned, or the date a particular person arrived in the place, he'd say: "That was just a year after I gave you that chicken." Or: "That was just the day before, or the day after, the day I gave you that chicken." The chicken served as a point of reference, and a date, for everything!

12. Ramadan told me this anecdote:

I was once on a boat with an elderly man from Ahwaz. I was at the back of the boat and he was at the front. When it was time for lunch, the old man took a chicken and a small chilled bird out of a basket and started eating and talking without offering me anything, even though there were just the two of us on the boat. He saw me looking, now at him, now at what he had in his hand, and realized I wanted a share of it.

"Why are you staring at me like that?" he said. Then he went on. "If somebody has something, he eats, like me. And if somebody doesn't have anything, he stares, like you."

Then he looked at me, just as I was looking at him, and said:

"Oh, how I'm enjoying this! I'm a man who eats well, only the best for me. But I don't like that jealous look in your eye. An eye like that's quick to strike. Stop looking at me, will you?"

I flung myself at him and grabbed his beard with my left hand and his chicken with my right. Then I went on hitting his head with the chicken till it fell to bits. He moved over to my side of the boat and wiped his face and beard.

"Didn't I say," he remarked, "you had a jealous look in your eye? Didn't I say you'd make trouble for me?"

"Where do eyes come into all this?" I asked.

"The evil eye's a misfortune," he answered. "And your eye's brought me a big misfortune!"

I laughed as I'd never laughed in my life, and we went on talking as if he'd never said anything amiss, and as if I'd never treated him so roughly.

13. Ibn Hassan related this anecdote:

We knew a man who was poor but had a rich brother, an utter miser and thoroughly pretentious. The poor brother said to the wealthy one:

"Shame on you! You know I'm poor with a family to support, and you're rich and don't have any dependents. And yet you never help me out with my livelihood, or use any of your wealth to support me, or give me a hand when I've a problem. I've never seen or heard of anyone more miserly than you are."

"I assure you," his brother said, "things aren't that way at all. I'm not as rich as you imagine, and I'm not the miser you seem to think. By God, if I had a million dirhams, I'd offer you five hundred thousand of them. Oh, you good people! How can a man offer five hundred thousand, all at one go, and still be called a miser?"

14.

"I've only ever enjoyed eating dates," Ibrahim ibn ʿAbd al-ʿAziz would say, "with blacks or Isfahanis. A black man never picks out dates when he eats them—not like me. And an Isfahani grabs a handful and doesn't look at what's in front of him, or eat anything there, till he's finished his handful. That's fair enough. But, as for choosing, that's all wrong. If someone picks and chooses the dates in front of him, just how are the ones that are left any use to the family?" He'd also say: "It's not polite to run your hands over the plate. You should only pick up the dates you want to eat."

15. Sari ibn Makram, a nephew of Moussa ibn Janah's, reported the following:

"Moussa used to tell us to stop eating when one of us was drinking water or asking for it. When he saw we weren't taking any notice, he called for water one evening, drew a line with his finger in a plate of rice we had in front of us, and said: "That bit's mine. Don't touch it till I've finished drinking my water!"

16. Ibn Abi Karima reported as follows:

Al-Kinani, the singer, was given an empty cask as a gift. When he was ready to leave, the cask was put down at the door for him to pick up. But he had no money to pay a porter to carry it, and, being haughty like most singers, wasn't prepared to carry it himself. So he started kicking the cask along—the harder he kicked it, the further it rolled. Each time he kicked it, he'd hide by the side of the road so no one could see him and watch to see how far the cask had rolled. Then he'd come out, give it another kick, and off the cask would go while he took refuge again. And so he went on till he got the cask home.

17. Thumama ibn al-Ashras related the following regarding the miserly ways of people in Marw:

All the roosters I've seen, in any town, spit out the seeds in their beaks for the hens to take—all except the roosters in Marw. In Marw the roosters won't let the hens have any of the seeds in their beaks. When I saw that, I realized what natural misers the people there were. There must be something in the water, because even their poultry was affected.

When I told this to Ahmad ibn Rashid, he added as follows:

"I was visiting an old man in Marw, and he had a child playing there in front of him.

"Give me some of your bread," I said to the child, as a joke, to try him out.

"You wouldn't like it," he said. "It's bitter."

"Give me some of your water then," I said.

"You wouldn't like it," he said. "It's salty."

So on I went, saying give me some of this, give me some of that. And he kept saying, you wouldn't like it, it's such and such. Then I asked for a lot of other different things, and he wouldn't give me any of them—there was always something wrong with them.

"It's not our fault," the child's father said, laughing. "Here's what taught him all those things!" He meant that miserly ways were rooted in them, in their very nature.

18.

Some of our friends reported how a group of Khorasanis shared a room in a house, and patiently did without a lantern at night. Finally they agreed to share the expense of a lantern—all except one man, who refused to pay his part. So, when it was dark enough to use the lantern, they used to tie a kerchief around his eyes so he couldn't see the light. They'd keep him like that till it was time to go to bed. Then they'd extinguish the light and uncover his eyes.

19. Abu Saᶜid Sajjada told a story about some people in Marw.

They only, he said, wore slippers for six months of the year; and when they did wear them, they walked on their toes for three months and on their heels for the other three. That way they really only wore their slippers for three months, and the soles didn't get worn or pierced.

20. A friend of mine told me the following:

I paid so-and-so a visit and found the dinner table hadn't been cleared, even though the guests had finished eating. I stretched out my hand to take some food.

"Finish off the wounded," our host said, "but don't go near the sound!"

What he meant was: "You can eat some of the chicken that's partly eaten already, or the small bird with just one leg left, but don't touch a whole chicken. And feel free to take any of a loaf smeared with broth and half-eaten."

21. This same friend added:

We once ate at the same person's house, and his father was there. A little boy was going in and out of the room, noticing that we were still eating.

"You're eating too much," he piped up at last. "May God not let you have enough!"

"By God," the grandfather exclaimed, "that man's my son all right!"

22.

I've never seen anyone to match Abi Jaᶜfar al-Tarsousi. He once visited some people who made him most welcome, perfuming his upper lip and mustache with rare scents. Then his upper lip started itching. So he stuck in his finger and scratched the inside of his lip, for fear his finger might scrape off some of the perfume if he scratched the outside.

Incidents like this are wonderfully funny when you see them with your own eyes. Written down in a book they lose much of the extra detail, and something of the essential flavor, too.

23. Our comrades reported the following anecdotes by Ibn al-Muqaffaᶜ [of which this is the first]:

Ibn Judham used to attend my classes and would sometimes go with me to my house. He'd have dinner with us and stay on for a while. I knew what an utter miser he was, for all his vast wealth. He insisted I ought to visit him, but I always said I couldn't.

"Bless you!" he said. "Do you think your visit's going to cost me a lot, so you're taking pity on me? I'm only talking about a few dry crumbs, some salt and some water from the pot."

He was trying, I thought, to cajole me into suggesting a visit that wouldn't cost him much. So I said:

"That's like saying: Young man, give us a crumb to eat, and give the beggar five dates. But the meaning goes far beyond the words. I don't think anyone would invite me all that way, to where you live, just for a few crumbs and some salt."

When I did finally make it to his home, a beggar came to the door.

"Feed us from what you're eating," the beggar said, "and may God feed you from the food of Paradise."

"May you be blessed," Ibn Judham replied.

The beggar repeated his plea, and the same answer came back to him. The beggar repeated his words for the third time.

"Get out of here, curse you!" my host shouted. "You've had your answer."

"May God be praised," the beggar said. "I've never seen anyone refuse to give a bit of food when it's there in front of him."

"Get out of here, curse you," my host yelled again, "or I'll come out and break your legs for you!"

"You'd better go while you're still in one piece," I told the beggar. "If you knew him as well as I do, you'd know he means every word of what he threatened. I wouldn't stay a moment longer."

24. Abu Ishaq Ibrahim ibn Sayyar al-Nazzam told the following about his neighbor in the town of Marw:

This neighbor wouldn't wear any shoes or slippers till the cherry season was over, because the streets and markets would be covered with dried cherry stones. And once this same neighbor saw me sucking a piece of sugarcane and collecting the juice in my mouth, ready to spit it out.

"If you don't," he told me reprovingly, "have a baking oven, or some children, then find someone who does and give them what you were going to spit out. Be careful, don't get into a habit like that while you're still free of responsibilities. You never know when a family might start springing up!"

25. Abu ʾl-Qamaqim said:

The first step in getting on is not to give you back what's come into my hands. If what's come into my hands has become mine, then it *is* mine. It wasn't mine before, but I've more claim to it now than the one who put it in my hands. If someone takes a thing out of his hand, without any compulsion, and puts it in someone else's hand, then he's made it available to the other person. Taking and putting a thing is like making it available to others.

"Abu ʾl-Qamaqim," a woman once said to him, "I've married a man who only comes to see me during the day. He's due now, and I'm not properly prepared. Please, take this *daniq* and go and buy me some basil for this loaf of bread, and some face cream. You'll have your reward from God, Who'll soften my husband's heart toward me. And because of the help you've given me, I'll make some headway in life at last. I'm quite worn out."

Abu ʾl-Qamaqim took the bread and the *daniq*, but he never came back. A few days later, the poor woman spotted him.

"God be praised!" she said. "Don't you have any pity on me?"

"Shame on you!" he replied. "The *daniq* fell out of my hand, and that upset me so much I had to eat the loaf of bread!"

Translated by ʿAbd al-Wahid Luʾluʾa and Christopher Tingley

83

From Ibn al-Muqaffaʿ, *Kalila and Dimna*

1. The Ringed Dove

The king said to the philosopher:

"I have understood the example of those whose affections for others are spoiled by the treachery of backbiters. Now tell me about those who are brothers in happiness. How does their friendship for one another begin? And how do they enjoy one another's comradeship?"

"The wise man," the philosopher replied, "doesn't recompense his supporters by showering them with favors and rewards. Those who are bound to one another in the brotherhood of goodness do good whenever called upon to do it, and they're always ready to bring comfort to others in trouble. Such was the case with the ringed dove, the deer, the crow, the rat, and the turtle."

"What of them? Tell me their story," the king commanded.

It's told (the philosopher began) how there was, near a city called Marwat, in the land of Dostad, a hunting ground where hunters came in search of game. A great tree stood there, thick with intertwining branches and lush foliage; and in this tree was the nest of a crow called Haʾir. One day, as the crow was perched on top of the tree, he saw a hunter, ugly and shabbily dressed, approaching the tree with a net around his neck and holding a stick and a trap in his two hands. The crow took fright at this, sensing villainy afoot.

"Something," he said to himself, "has driven this hunter here. What could it be, I wonder? Is it me he's after, or someone else? Whatever he's about, I'll stand firm here and see what he does."

The hunter laid out his net and scattered his seed over it. Then he hid himself nearby. Soon a ringed dove flew over with some other doves. She caught sight of the seed but not the net, and, with all the others, she swooped down to the bait. And so they were all trapped. The other doves fluttered frantically to try and get free, but the ringed dove called out to them to stop.

"No," said the dove, "not everyone for himself! Let's work together. Perhaps we can get the net away from here and help one another escape."

This they did, all fluttering upward together. Combining their efforts skillfully, they raised the net off the ground. Then, slowly but surely, they soared up, with the net still over them, high into the air.

The hunter watched them fly off, then rushed after them, still hoping to catch them.

"They can't fly far," he said to himself, "weighed down with the net like that."

The crow, meanwhile, had been following the whole thing.

"I'll follow on," he said to himself, "and see what happens to them, and to him."

The ringed dove saw the hunter in hot pursuit.

"There he is!" she told the others. "If we stay here in midair, we'll be exposed, out in the open, and he'll be able to follow us easily. If, though, we land and hide among some trees, we'll be hard to spot. In the end he'll get tired of looking and go away. Close by here there's the hole of a rat, a friend of mine. If we call to him for help, he'll gnaw at the net and free us."

The other doves agreed to this; and, since they were so well hidden, the hunter searched for them in vain and finally went off in despair. Meanwhile the crow, perched high up in the tree, was watching the doves carefully. They might, he thought, have some other tricks, which he could learn to his advantage should he ever be trapped himself. The ringed dove and the other doves flew down, with the net still over them, and landed by the rat's hole. In fact, as they saw, he'd prepared a hundred other holes to use in case of need. The ringed dove called out to the rat by name.

"Zayzak!" she cried.

"Who is it?" the rat called back.

"It's your friend, the ringed dove."

"Sister!" the rat exclaimed, hurrying out to her. "How did you come to fall into that snare—and you so wise, and careful, and wary?"

"Don't you know," she answered, "that no good or evil ever happens unless it's so ordained? There's no escape from what's written; what's destined to be is meted out exactly. It's fate that led me to the seed and hid the net till it closed on me and my friends. You can hardly wonder if I don't escape what fate decrees! Even those stronger than I am, by far, can't overcome their destiny. Fate eclipses sun and moon alike, didn't you know that?

Every fish caught in seas where no man bathes, every bird brought down from the sky and caught—all this happens by the dictates of almighty fate. If the weak fall short of their goal, then so, equally, do the strong."

The rat, true brother that he was, set swiftly to work, gnawing at the knots that kept the ringed dove snared.

"No!" she objected. "Work to free the others first. You can attend to me afterwards." Still she kept asking this, and still the rat took no notice of her plea.

"You keep on and on, saying the same thing," the rat objected reproachfully. "Don't you have any thought for yourself? Don't you have rights for yourself, too?"

"Don't blame me for asking you this," the ringed dove said. "I've been entrusted with the task of leading these others, and that's a heavy responsibility. They owe me obedience, and it's their duty to listen to my advice and accept it. They acted as they were supposed to do, and I did the same; and so we escaped from the hunter. My fear is that, if you cut my knots first, you'll exhaust yourself and grow tired of cutting theirs afterwards; and so they'll never be free. If, on the other hand, I'm left to be freed last, then you, as a true brother, will never leave me captive, no matter how tired you are from all that weary work of freeing the others."

"You're quite right," the rat said approvingly. "And what you've suggested will make your companions love you even more than they do now."

With that he began gnawing at the net, till, finally, he'd freed them all. And then the ringed dove and her companions flew safely homeward.

After the rat had freed the doves, the crow decided to go and make friends with the rat. "I'm not completely safe either," he said to himself. "I need the rat as a friend." He approached the rat's hole and called out to him by name.

"Zayzak!" he cried.

"Who is it?" the rat asked.

"It's the crow," came the reply. "When I saw how loyal you are to your friends, I decided I wanted you as a brother. I've come to ask you to take me as one."

"There's no reason why we should be friends," answered the rat. "The wise seek only what can be attained. What can't be attained they leave be. Anyone who acts otherwise is regarded as a fool—like those who try to move ships on land or drag wheels over water. I can't do any such thing. How could we be friends? I'm flesh and you're an eater of flesh. I'd be your prey."

"Just stop and think," the crow replied. "You might be food for me, agreed, but my devouring you wouldn't make me any richer. But if you're alive and my friend, I'll be enriched by your comradeship. Think back on all your experience of life. Have you ever once come across someone who sells what's useful, knowing what he's doing, to buy something harmful? I want your friendship for the benefits it would bring. Your being alive will be useful to me in times of difficulty, when the going gets hard. I want to be friends with you. Don't, please, reject my offer or harbor doubts and suspicions about me when I'm speaking to you frankly, opening my heart to you truthfully, in good faith. I've had clear enough sight of your own loyalty and good faith. Goodness can't be hidden, however hard someone may try to hide it. It's like musk: you can quickly hide the thing itself, but not its fragrance. Don't turn your friendly feelings away from me. Don't deny me your friendship."

"Enmity," the rat replied, "or the lack of enmity is a matter of the kind you belong to. The elephant and the lion are enemies. The lion can kill the elephant, or the elephant the lion. And there's enmity between your kind and mine, apart only from periods of quiet between hostilities. The trust of an enemy isn't to be trusted. The nature of things can't change. Water, even if brought to the boil over fire, will always put it out; heated by fire it may be, but it's still fire's enemy. The wise shouldn't be deceived, or lulled into a trusting comradeship. If they were, they'd be like the snake charmer who sees his snake half-frozen and puts it in his sleeve to give it some warmth. Brought to life by the warmth, the snake moves and strikes its master. 'And is this how you reward me,' the master asks the treacherous snake, 'for keeping you and caring for you?' 'It's my nature,' the snake replies. 'My instinct. My way. Only fools seek to part a creature from the instincts born in it.' The wise shouldn't be trusting when an enemy approaches with beguiling offers of friendship. Indeed, they should arm themselves with greater wariness still."

"I understand what you say," the crow replied. "You're right, indeed, to be aware of the natural instincts born into your kind. But I say again even so: don't make things hard for me by saying we can't be friends. The wise who are also magnanimous seek out every path to friendship and goodwill. Goodwill is quick to bring one another closer, and slow to fragment. A gold goblet is slow to break; even if dented or chipped, it can be easily repaired. Between the wicked, though, goodwill fragments swiftly and is repaired slowly; like an earthenware pot, easy to break and hard to mend. The gracious befriend the gracious, after a single meeting, after knowing one another just for a day. The mean and base befriend no one except for reasons of greed, or avarice, or fear. You are gracious, and I need your friendship. I shall stand here fast at your door, without food or drink, till you take me as your friend and brother."

"As a brother I accept you," the rat replied. "I've never turned away anyone in need. I take you at your word—but with reservation even so. Then, if you betray me, you won't be able to say: 'I found the rat to be weak-minded, easily deceived.'"

With that he came out from his hole and waited.

"What's keeping you from coming closer?" the crow asked. "Do you still have doubts?"

"Those who live in the world," the rat replied, "have dealings with one another through their hands or through their souls. Those whose souls are pure treat one another righteously and honestly. Those, though, whose thoughts are merely for what might come into their hands see the other, for the most part, in that light alone. The one who does good only because he expects material gain is like the hunter who scatters seed to lure birds. What honest souls gain from one another is worthier, by far, than what hands may dole out, or receive, in expectation. I've trusted the goodness of your soul, and I've offered you the goodness of mine. I've conquered any natural hostility and come out to meet you. I fear even so that other crows, your friends, who share your instincts but don't know me as you do might spot me, swoop, and make a meal of me."

"The sign of a good friend," the crow replied, "is that he's a friend to his friend's friend, and an enemy to his friend's enemy. Anyone not ready to befriend you is no friend of mine. I can forsake any, easily, who make an enemy of you. Gardeners tear up harmful weeds and toss them away."

At that the rat, his mind at rest, came safely from his hole to meet the crow. Greeting each other, they exchanged vows of loyalty, friendship, and goodwill, each quite sure in his mind of the other's total trust. Some days later the crow told the rat his hole was too near the highway. Both of them, he said, might come to harm when there was so much coming and going just nearby. "I know a secluded spot," the crow observed, "where the waters are filled with fish. I have a friend there, a turtle. I hope to live there, in peace and safety."

The rat agreed to be his comrade in the venture.

"I'll go with you," he said. "To tell you the truth, I dislike this place myself."

"What makes you dislike it?" the crow asked.

"When we reach our new home," the rat answered, "I'll tell you all about it."

The crow picked up the rat, held him in his beak by the tail, then flew off, landing, finally, by the turtle's spring. When he saw the rat along with the crow, the turtle took fright; not knowing the two were friends, he plunged into the water and swam off. The crow set the rat down safely. Then, perching on the top of a nearby tree, he called out to the turtle by name. The turtle recognized the voice and swam back to meet him, asking where he'd come from, and the crow told him all about the doves, and what had passed between him and the rat. The turtle, astonished at the rat's wisdom and loyalty, approached him and welcomed him warmly.

"What brought you to this place?" the turtle asked him.

"I've heard so many things about you," he replied, "from my friend the crow. He told me, too, how peaceful and secluded this place is. And so I've come to make my home here."

"And what," the crow asked him then, "of the stories you promised to tell us when we arrived? Let's both hear them. You can trust the turtle, now, as much as you trust me."

The rat accordingly began his account.

My first home (the rat said) was in a city called Marout, in the house of a man who lived alone. Each evening he'd bring home a basket of food, and some of this he'd eat, then put the rest to one side to keep. I'd watch him as he ate. Then, when he'd finished eating and gone out of the room, I'd spring onto his basket and devour the food, flinging some aside for the other rats there. The man knew rats or mice were pilfering his food, and he did his best to hide the basket, but all in vain. Wherever he hid it, I'd find a way to it.

One evening the man had a guest, and, after supper, the two sat down to talk.

"What country are you from?" the host asked the guest. "And where are you heading?"

The guest was a traveler who'd been to strange lands and seen wonders there. He recounted to his host what he'd seen in different lands. The host, though, noticed that I'd come close to the food basket, and, as he listened to his guest's stories, clapped his hands loudly to scare me away. This annoyed the guest.

"I'm talking to you," the guest exclaimed angrily. "And you're clapping your hands to make fun of me!"

The host at once explained:

"I'm not making fun of you at all," he said apologetically. "Quite the reverse. I find your adventures fascinating. I was just trying to scare off a rat that eats up every piece of food I keep in the house. I don't know how to stop it."

"Is it just one rat," the guest asked, "or are there several of them?"

"There are several," the host complained, "but one of them's a bigger nuisance than the others. I just can't stop it. I don't know what to do."

"That reminds me," said the guest, "of the story of the woman who sold sesame seeds."

"What about her?" the host asked, encouraging his guest to embark on a new account. "Tell me."

I was the guest of a man (the traveler began) in such and such a city. We had supper, then, after making up a bed for me, he and his wife retired for the night. There was a reed screen between me and them, and I heard him tell his wife:

"I'd like to invite some people here to dinner tomorrow."

"How can you," she objected, "when there's barely enough in the house to feed your children? You never save anything. Whatever you get, you spend."

"Don't worry about the food we offer to other people," he advised her. "Thrift and saving lead to what happened to the wolf."

"And what happened to the wolf?" she asked.

"A hunter," he said, "went out seeking game with bow and arrows. He shot a deer, and, as he was carrying it home slung over his shoulders, he was attacked by a boar. The boar was mortally wounded by the hunter, but the boar gored him so seriously that he died, too. Then a wolf came along and found a hunter, a deer, and a boar all lying dead.

" 'I ought to be thrifty,' the wolf said to himself 'and save what I can from this sumptuous feast. You don't get anywhere if you don't save.'

"Showing quite remarkable thrift, the wolf left the three bodies to one side and started chewing, of all things, on the hunter's bowstring. Once the string was cut, the bow snapped back violently against the wolf's head, killing him instantly."

"That sounds fair enough," the wife said approvingly. "I've enough rice and sesame to feed six or seven. I'll go off now and prepare the meal. Invite your guests for tomorrow."

The next day she spread the sesame out in the sun to dry. "Now, you scare away the birds and dogs," she told her husband. He, though, went off on an errand and left the sesame unguarded. A dog came into the yard and started eating some of it and the wife, seeing the dog eating the meal intended for their guests, decided the food was unclean now and not fit for humans to eat. Off she hurried to the marketplace, with the hulled sesame the dog had eaten from, and exchanged it for some much cheaper unhulled sesame.

So I watched (the traveler went on) and heard the market man say: "This woman's exchanging hulled for unhulled sesame. There must be some reason." Now, the same applies to this rat that gets into your food basket wherever you hide it. Fetch me a hatchet. I'll break a way into his hole and find the reason for you. And so the host brought him a hatchet.

All this time (our rat continued), I was in the hole of another rat, listening to their conversation. In my own hole there were a thousand dinars; I know the rat who placed them there. I used to spread the coins out and enjoy the sight of them, turning them over with delight. The guest put his arm through the hole, reached the hoard of coins, and took it.

"How did this rat," he said, "ever get to the food basket? You would have thought he'd be always here, guarding the treasure! At any rate, money increases power and reputation. Now, deprived of his treasure, be sure he won't be what he was before. He'll have no power or influence over the other rats."

I knew, as he spoke, that what he was saying was true. When I moved to another hole, I felt weak and powerless. I felt inferior. After a time, the other rats said: "We're starving. We don't have the food you used to provide us with. What are we to do now?"

So I scurried to the place where I used to leap into the food basket. I tried several times, but I couldn't jump in. I realized I'd changed. The other rats held me in contempt now. I heard some of them say to others:

"He's finished. Don't bother with him anymore. He can't do what he used to do. He's helpless, it seems."

So they all turned away from me and joined my enemies, talking ill of me to them.

"I only have friends," I said to myself, "when I'm prospering. People only ever show goodness, and generosity and chivalry, to the rich. The poor who strive to better themselves are left to stagnate, like the summer rains trapped in wadis, flowing neither to river nor to sea. Those without friends are without relatives; and the childless are soon forgotten. Those without strong, healthy minds lose both this world and the next. The penniless, stricken by hardship, are turned away by friends, shunned by kith and kin, forced, by dire necessity, to seek a livelihood by wayward ways that lead only to perdition. And so they lose both the here and the hereafter. There's nothing harder than poverty. The poor, in their desperate need of what lies in the hands of others, are like a bare, stark tree, standing leafless in a salt flat. Poverty is at the base of all affliction, earning nothing but contempt. Poverty steals away mind and manners alike, drains away learning, knowledge, wisdom. It draws unfounded accusation, invites hardship and affliction. The impoverished lose all sense of what's shameful. Those without shame are without virtue or chivalry, are loathed and shunned. Those who are loathed will be harmed. Those who are harmed will grieve, and grief does away with a sound, balanced mind. The impoverished will be accused by those they trusted, reviled by those they respected. The wealthy are always praised, the poor despised. Generosity, in the poor, is deemed foolishness. Mild manners are deemed weakness. In them gravity is seen as dullness, eloquence as chatter, calmness as stupidity. Death is easier, more welcome, more to be desired than poverty that obliges someone to ask alms of others and so be driven down into the abyss of humiliation and ignominy. Poverty lowers someone to cavernous depths, where before he soared in prosperity to the sublime. It banishes to a cold, harsh exile, after knowing a warm, snug closeness to loved ones. It is mere wretchedness after prosperity, contempt after honor. Most insufferable of all for the poor is to beg assistance from the miserly, the mean-spirited, and the closefisted. For someone fallen from prosperity to penury, it is easier to snatch poison from a dragon's mouth and swallow it than to ask the miserly and mean-spirited for aid.

"It's been said that for those afflicted with incurable disease; those languishing in alien lands without house or home, family and friends; for those afflicted with bitter, grinding poverty—for all such wretches, it has been said, life is a living death, and only death brings rest. A man may be so firm in refusing charity as to be forced, in spite of himself, to resort to theft. Muteness (it has been said) is better than eloquence thick with lying, impotence better than whoring, impoverishment better than growing rich by criminal means, fortitude in poverty better than ill-won gain wastefully spent."

Now, I saw the guest, having taken the hoard out from the hole, divide it with his solitary host, who placed his share in a bag. I coveted some of those coins—for I felt an urgent need to restore my strength and regain my former friends. I moved toward him as he slept. My movement, though, woke him. He struck at me with a stick, and I scurried back into my hole. My pain died down at last, and I was seized, once more, with a greedy desire for the coins. Again I approached him, while he watched me. He struck me on the head once more, making me bleed, and, writhing this way and that from injury and pain, I dragged myself, barely conscious, back to my hole. The fearful pain made me hate the money now; so much so that the very word made me quake with fear and horror. Reflecting on all this, I concluded that adversity and distress spring from greed. I saw the vast gulfs dividing generosity from miserly ways. It struck me that braving dangers, enduring the challenge of travel into the unknown in search of fortune, are lighter than putting out one's hand to ask or take. Contentment, I realized now, is the source of all wealth. "No mind," I heard the wise say, "is greater than a contented mind, no piety greater than abstinence, no illustrious lineage greater than cultivated manners, no wealth greater than contentment." Enduring what cannot be changed—this is the summit of all. The highest form of good, it has been said, is compassion; the highest form of amity lies in constant accord with others. The most useful mind is the one that knows what may and may not be, and so turns away, without rancor, from the unattainable.

So it was that, fully persuaded and fully contented, I moved out from the house of the solitary man, into the wilderness. A man of chivalry will always be honored, even if he lacks wealth—like a lion, always feared, even when quite at rest. The unchivalrous man, though, will be held in contempt for all his wealth. A dog is vilified, even if he has a collar and leash. Don't make too much of your loneliness or estrangement, for the wise are never truly lonely or estranged. Their goodness and wisdom will never fail to suffice, as with the lion, who lives through his strength alone. Make the most of what you have, using this to do the greatest possible good. Do that, and good will seek you out, as waterfowl seek out the water. Good fortune seeks the farsighted, the firm, and those diligent in making the most of what chance provides. The slothful, the hesitant, the weak, the dependent seldom find good fortune attending them. A handsome, comely, personable young woman does not seek out the company of feeble, broken-down old men.

The turtle now took up the moral theme.

"Don't distress yourself," he said, "by saying, I was rich once, and now I'm poor. Wealth, like worldly pleasures, is quick to come and quick to go, bouncing like a ball, now up, now down. The wise have marked out the transient, the mutable, the impermanent as being the following: the shade of clouds, evil company, love of women, false praise, and great wealth. The wise man never rejoices in his substantial wealth, or grieves when it grows meager. He rejoices in the largeness of his mind and in the good he's done. Never, he knows well, never will he be stripped of his good deeds. Always he fixes his thoughts on the hereafter, seeking to win a favored place there. Death is always sudden in coming, its advent never known. But you, my dear friend, hardly stand in need of my sermons, for you have your mind fixed, always, on what is good and right."

The crow listened intently to these words of the turtle to the rat and, convinced as he was of his friendliness, goodness, and wisdom, he was filled with delight.

"You've brought me," he told the turtle, "much pleasure and satisfaction, as you always do. You have every right to be pleased with those words of yours. People in the world aspire to live happily and well, to be well praised by brothers and friends, through mutual vows of faith and assistance. The good, when they fall, will rise up again if helped to their feet by the good. The elephant, if mired in the mud, is helped by other elephants. The wise do not refuse some good deed, holding it to be demanding or strenuous beyond bearing. There may be great risk in doing good, but such risk the wise will readily take; they do not regard such a course as foolhardy, or injudicious, or overventuresome. The wise man knows that, in acting thus, he is selling the transient to purchase the enduring—is buying the great for the price of the small."

The crow went on, still addressing the turtle:

"No one is to be considered wealthy if he fails to share his wealth. No one has truly lived if the favors he has done are few. No demands for recompense are considered grasping where generous favors have gone before, performed from sheer goodness of heart. And no favors are considered generous where grasping demands for recompense have gone before."

As the crow was speaking, a deer suddenly appeared and raced toward them. Startled, the rat scurried into a hole, while the crow flew off to a treetop, and the turtle plunged into the spring. The deer tripped lightly up to the water and drank a little. Then, suddenly, she turned rigid with fear. The crow flew across to see what could have frightened the deer. But, seeing nothing, he called out to the rat and the turtle:

"I see nothing you need fear."

With that they all approached together. The turtle, though, saw how the deer was looking at the water, without coming near.

"Drink if you're thirsty," the turtle told her. "There's nothing to be afraid of."

With that the deer approached and greeted the turtle.

"Where have you come from?" the turtle asked.

"From the wilderness," the deer explained, "where I was chased this way and that by hunters. Today I saw an apparition I took to be a hunter, and I ran here in fear."

"Don't be afraid," the turtle said. "We've seen no sign of any hunters. Stay here with us. We'll take care of you. The meadow isn't far off."

So the deer joined them and stayed there with them. Each day they'd meet all together by a bower to talk, exchange memories, and discuss. One day the crow, the turtle, and the rat were there at the bower, expecting the deer to arrive. When she failed to appear, though, they grew worried. Something, they felt, might have happened to her.

"Have a look," the turtle and the rat said to the crow. "See if she's anywhere close by." The crow flew over the area, and, seeing the deer caught in a hunter's net, wheeled straight back to tell the others. The crow and the turtle thereupon appealed to the rat.

"Only you," they said, "can help this sister of ours and yours."

The rat scurried up to the deer.

"How could it happen," he asked the trapped deer, "that you, so wary and sure-footed, fell into this?"

"Can wisdom," the deer replied sagaciously, "alter fate—fate that is unseen and so cannot be avoided?"

As they were speaking, the turtle appeared. The deer turned to him.

"You shouldn't have come here," she said. "If the hunter returns when the rat's cut the net, I can outpace the hunter and escape with ease. The rat has many holes to hide in. The crow flies wherever he wishes. You, though, are heavy and slow, and unable to run. I'm afraid for you."

"Life loses all point when loved ones are gone," the turtle replied. "When affliction strikes, it helps soothe sadness, and calm the soul, to meet a brother and unburden yourself to him. Separation from those to whom you're bound by friendship and affection steals away joy and veils insight with darkness."

As the turtle finished speaking, and just as the rat had freed the deer from the net, the hunter appeared. Amazed to see his net cut, he gazed around and saw only the turtle. The crow, the deer, and the rat watched with grief as the hunter bound the turtle up.

"We free ourselves from one snare," the rat said, "only to fall into another. It's truly said, indeed, that to be free is not to stumble. Those who stumble will stumble constantly, even on smooth, straight paths. Ill fortune isn't content with denying me my own family and friends, my wealth and well-being; it denies me even the company of the turtle, who showed more affection than a father to a son, an affection only death could take away. Woe to this body bedeviled by affliction, forever tumbling and turning, with no semblance of stability or calm. The grief I find myself mired in is like a healing wound that awakens a double pain when struck: the pain of the blow and the pain of a healing wound reopened."

The crow and the deer felt deeply for him.

"We share your sorrow," they said. "And yet, whatever any of us may say, however moving and eloquent, it will be no use to the turtle. Better, surely, to find some way out. It's said the strong are tested in the face of adverse events, the honest in giving and taking, while the family is tested during poverty, and friends during hard times."

"We need to show resource," the rat said. He turned to the deer. "Follow the hunter's trail," he went on. "Then lie down and pretend to be injured. The crow will pretend to be picking at you. Then I'll follow the hunter. If all goes well, he'll see you, lay down his bow and arrows, and leave the turtle to run toward you. When he approaches, get up quickly and run off, but pretend to be lame so he'll be encouraged to go after you for as long as possible. Let him come close. Play this game with him just as long as you can—make sure he doesn't lose interest in the chase. In the meantime, I'll have gnawed at the cords long enough to cut the turtle free."

The deer and the crow followed the plan through. The hunter went after the deer, the rat cut the turtle free, and they were all safe. The hunter was thunderstruck by what had happened.

"This is a land of jinn and sorcerers!" he cried.

With that he fled in fear. As for the crow, the deer, the rat, and the turtle, they returned safely to the bower together.

The philosopher then said to the king:

"If the smallest, weakest animals can work together to help one another, as we saw in this story, and save one of their number from certain destruction, then how pressing is the need for humans to follow their example."

2. The Ape and the Turtle

The king said to the philosopher:

"Tell me a fable of a man who strives for what he needs, then squanders and loses what he fought so hard to gain."

"To win," the philosopher replied, "is easier than to keep. What happens to a man who wins a thing yet is careless in keeping it is like what happened to the turtle when he lost the ape he'd caught."

"Tell me this story," the king commanded.

It's told (the philosopher began) how a colony of apes had a king named Vardin. He lived to a great age, becoming feeble and broken down at last. At that a young ape of his house sprang on him and turned to the others.

"He's grown old and weak-minded," the young ape cried, "incapable of ruling now. Let's depose him!"

The other apes supported him, banishing the old king Vardin and installing the rebel in his place. The old, banished ape, stricken with grief, fled, then wandered aimlessly till he came upon a fig tree by the seashore. He climbed the tree and began eating the figs; and one fig fell into the sea, to be gobbled up by a turtle. The sound of figs plopping down into the water pleased the ape. He went on throwing figs into the sea, all of them instantly eaten up by the turtle, who was convinced by now that the ape was feeding him deliberately, from the goodness of his heart. The turtle came out, approached the ape, and made friends with him. Amity and affection flourished between the two, and they stayed together for a long time, the turtle unwilling to leave his newfound friend to rejoin his own kind in the sea. Meanwhile the turtle's wife, grieved at her husband's absence, complained to a friend:

"I'm afraid," she said, "he's met with some mishap."

"Don't be too worried," the friend advised. "From what I hear, your husband's on shore with an ape he's made friends with. They eat, drink, and make merry. He's been away for a long time now. If he's forgotten you, then forget him. But if you can make away with the ape to get your husband back, then do it. If the ape should perish, your husband will come back to you."

The turtle's wife grew sick from grief and worry; she looked pallid, drained, and wasted. Luckily for her, though, the turtle said to himself one day: "I must go back home. I've been away long enough."

There at home he found his wife sick and exhausted. "How are you?" he asked her. No answer. He asked again. Still no reply. When he asked for the third time, a woman, a neighbor of his wife's, replied:

"Your wife's very sick, close to death."

"Can nothing cure her?" the husband asked.

"Yes," the neighbor replied. "The heart of an ape will cure her."

"That's a knotty problem," the husband observed. "Where am I to find an ape's heart, apart from my friend's. Shall I murder my friend, or let my wife die?"

He thought for a while. Then, at last, he said:

"A wife has her rights. What a wife offers her husband is beyond price. She's always close by her husband, in this world and the next. I'm bound by the vows of marriage, by honor and duty, to put her first and save her whatever the cost."

And so he went off to meet the ape, confused, hesitant about what he ought to do.

"To kill a loyal friend for a woman," he said to himself, "that's a deed to be feared, a deed God will never forgive."

He greeted the ape, who asked him, with concern:

"What kept you away so long, brother?"

"What held me back," the turtle replied, "greatly though I missed you, was a sense of shame. I haven't returned your favors. You don't, I know, expect your favors to be returned, and yet I feel I really must do you a good deed in return. By nature you're good-hearted, noble, and generous. You give to those who don't give, and you don't expect to be given in return."

"Don't shame me by talking like that," the ape replied. "I've been a burden to you. I was an outcast, chased out of my home. You've given me refuge, friendship, and affection. Through that, and through you, God's driven away my sorrow and gloom."

"And yet," answered the turtle, "three things make for a close friendship: dining, visiting, and socializing with each other's families. A friend should seek only amiability and affection from his friend. Those who seek material gain from friends would do better to stay away from them. A man shouldn't make too great demands on his friends, for that merely gives rise to irritation and rupture. A calf, sucking too much at the udders, greedily and insistently, is kicked away by the vexed mother cow.

"I mention all this" (the turtle went on) "because I'm so well aware of your virtues: of how good-hearted, hospitable, and honest you are. And now I'm inviting you to come and visit me at my home. It lies in a wooded island, thick with trees, heavy with fruit. Do accept my invitation. Climb on my shell, and let's go to my house."

The ape, longing for the fruit, climbed on the turtle's back. Once at sea, though, with the ape on his back, the turtle began to have qualms of conscience.

"This deed I'm planning," he said to himself, "is heinous treachery. Females aren't worth committing crimes for. They inspire no trust. Gold, it's said, is tested and revealed by fire, a man's honesty by what he gives and takes, and the quality of a beast of burden by the weight it can bear. But there are no standards by which women can be tested and known."

The ape, seeing how the turtle had stopped swimming, became suspicious.

"The turtle," he said to himself, "had something on his mind when he stopped. How can I be sure he hasn't turned against me? Nothing, as I've learned, is more fickle than the heart, nothing is quicker to change. It's said a wise man should always know what his wife and children, friends and acquaintances, are thinking—every day, through every word they utter, since that shows what they have in their hearts."

With that he turned to the turtle.

"Why have you stopped?" he asked. "Some anxiety, I can see, is weighing you down."

"I'm concerned," the turtle replied, "my house might not be suitable to receive such a good friend, and such a worthy guest, as you are. It doesn't, now I reflect, seem to be so. My wife's sick, and the house is gloomy and neglected."

"Have no worries about that," the ape said comfortingly, sitting there on the turtle's back. "Just find medicines and physicians for your wife. It's said: 'Let a man spend his money in three places: on charity, if he seeks the next world; on the ruler, if he wishes for honors in this world; and on the women of his household, if he seeks to hold his family together.' "

"The physicians," the turtle admitted guiltily, "say there's no cure for her but an ape's heart."

"Woe is me!" the ape said to himself. "Greed, in my old age, has dragged me down to this. That man spoke well who said once that the contented are safe and secure and extend their safety and security, their peace and comfort, to others. The covetous and greedy, though, live in fear of what they might not gain. I have to set my mind to work now, to find a way out of my plight."

"My friend!" the ape told the turtle. "One friend shouldn't withhold favors or advice from another. Had I known your wife needed an ape's heart to be cured, I would have brought my own heart along with me."

"And where is your heart?" the turtle asked, astonished.

"I left it behind."

"And what made you leave it behind?"

"It's a thing we apes do. When we visit a friend, we leave our hearts at home. If you like, I could return home and fetch it for you."

The turtle, pleased at the ape's goodness, swam back with him to the island. Once on shore, the ape climbed up his fig tree. The turtle waited for an hour, then called out to him:

"Come on, my friend! You've kept me waiting long enough. Fetch your heart and come down!"

"You seem to think," the ape replied, "that I'm like the ass. The one told by the fox that he had neither heart nor ears."

"How was that?" the turtle asked.

It's told (the ape replied) how once a lion was feeding on a carcass, and a fox was feeding there with him. The lion had become fearfully afflicted by mange, a malady so severe that it disabled him, and he could no longer hunt as he'd done before.

"What's happened to you, king of beasts?" the fox asked the ailing lion. "You've changed. You kill hardly anything. Why is that?"

"It's the mange, as you can see," said the sick lion. "There's no cure for me but an ass's ears and heart."

"I know a place nearby," the fox said, "where a washerman brings his ass to a meadow. He unloads the laundry, then he turns his ass free in the meadow to graze. I could, perhaps, bring the ass here to you. You could have its ears and heart."

"If you can do that," the lion replied gleefully, "then do it quickly. That's where my cure lies."

So the fox trotted up to the ass.

"How lean and wasted you look," the fox said. "And just look at those sores on your back!"

"It's that miserly washerman," the ass complained. "He gives me hardly anything to eat. He sets me to work for long, long hours. And the loads he gives me are too heavy."

"Why do you put up with such ill-treatment?" asked the fox.

"What can I do?" the ass replied. "Where can I go? How would I escape from people?"

"I could show you a secluded spot," the fox suggested, "lush with grazing, where no man has ever set foot. And there's a she-ass, more comely than any that's ever been seen. She needs a mate."

When the ass heard mention of a female, he replied joyfully:

"Why are we waiting?" he asked. "Lead on! Even if I didn't wish—as I do—to have you as a friend, I'd follow you to where she is."

And so they went to the lion. The fox hurried up to the lion first and told him about the ass. Then, stalking the ass, the lion leaped at him from the rear. But he missed him, and the ass escaped.

"What do you think you're doing?" the irate fox asked the fumbling lion. "If you couldn't even kill the ass, why did you put me to the trouble of bringing it? Woe to us all if our Lord Lion, the king of beasts, can't dispatch a mere ass."

The lion knew that, if he said, "I missed him deliberately," he'd merely seem foolish. Yet if he said, "I missed him because I'm sick," he'd seem like a weakling.

"If you could just bring me back the ass," he said, "I'll explain everything then."

"The ass has found out my sly ways," the fox said. "But I'll try, even so, to deceive him one more time."

The fox accordingly returned to the ass.

"What do you have planned for me now?" the ass asked warily.

"I really did mean the best for you," the fox reassured him. "Who do you think it was attacked you? It was the she-ass. She was crazed with desire for a mate. If you hadn't run away, but waited for a while instead, you could have had her."

When the ass heard all this about the female, he was inflamed with desire, and he cantered off toward her, with the fox trotting alongside. Lying in wait was the lion, who let the ass come close, then leaped on him, killing him at once.

The lion turned to the fox.

"The cure prescribed," he said, "was that I should first bathe, then devour the two ears and the heart, then, finally, offer the rest of the carcass as a sacrifice. Now, guard the dead ass till I've bathed and returned."

With the lion gone, the fox ate the ass's ears and heart, hoping the lion would see a bad omen in this and leave the rest of the carcass.

"Where are the ass's ears and heart?" the lion asked.

"Didn't you see?" the fox replied. "This ass has no ears or heart!"

"I've never," the lion said, "heard anything so strange!"

"If he'd had ears and a heart," the fox objected, "he wouldn't have come back to you after what you did to him the first time."

"I've told you this story" (the ape concluded, turning to the turtle) "to show you I'm not the simpleton you seem to think. You deceived me, and I've returned your deception. I realize now how naive I was."

"What you've said is true," the turtle admitted. "Those whose minds are sound and strong say little and do much. They admit their faults, take care before embarking on anything, and set their minds to work to repair any damage their faults have caused. Their minds are the ground upon which they rise after stumbling."

"This," the philosopher said to the king, in conclusion, "is a story of one who sought something and gained it, then afterward lost it."

3. The Man and the Ferret

The king said to the philosopher:

"Tell me a fable about a man who acts without first reflecting."

"The man who doesn't take care," the philosopher replied, "and fails to reflect before making a decision will regret it bitterly. An example of that is the story of the man and the ferret."

"Tell me this story," the king commanded.

It is told (the philosopher began) how there lived once, in the land of Jurjan, a man whose wife had long been barren, then was with child.

"This is joyful news!" the delighted man cried to his wife. "I hope for a son who will be our pride and joy. I shall look for a wet nurse and choose the best of names for him."

"Man!" the wife exclaimed. "Why are you talking like that? You don't know yet whether he'll be born or not, whether he'll live or die. Leave that kind of talk. Be content with what God gives us. A wise man doesn't speak about things he's ignorant of. He doesn't try to predict what destiny may or may not decree, what will or won't happen to him. A man can't make things happen as he wishes. He'll just end up like the man who poured oil and honey over his own head."

"Oil and honey?" the man said. "How was that? Tell me about it."

It is told (the wife began) how a man once received a gift from a wealthy merchant of flour and oil and honey. The man kept the oil and honey in a jug he hung from the beams of his house. One day the man was lying down, gazing at the jug hanging there above him and thinking how expensive oil and honey was.

"I shall sell what's in the jug for a dinar," he said to himself, "and with that I'll buy ten goats. And the goats will have kids." In five years, he calculated, he'd have more than four hundred goats. "Then," he went on, "I'll sell them all and buy a hundred head of cattle—an ox for every four goats. Next, I'll sow seeds and plow land with my oxen. Within five years I'll be rich. I'll build a fine mansion and furnish it with the best money can buy. Then I'll marry a beautiful woman, who'll bear me a fine son. He'll be raised to be well mannered, well behaved, well educated, and, most important, he'll be fully obedient to his father's commands. If he disobeys me, then, as God's my witness, I'll beat him with this stick, like so."

With that he lifted the stick alongside him and brandished it high above his head. The stick struck the earthenware jug and shattered it. And the oil and honey poured down all over his head and beard.

"I've told you this story," the wife explained, "to stop your talking of things you know nothing about."

The man admitted the sense of what she'd said. In time, the wife bore him a fine son. The father was delighted.

"Sit by the boy," the wife told her husband, "till I've bathed and come back."

As the father was sitting with the child, the king's messenger came and summoned him, and the child was left all by itself. Now, the man kept a ferret as a house pet, and, as he was being escorted away, he told the ferret to look after the child. A snake crawled out of its hole, inside the house, and wound its way to the child's cot; and the ferret, pouncing on the snake, tore it to pieces.

When he returned home, the man was met by the ferret, which was about to tell him how it had defended the child against the snake. But the father, seeing the ferret spattered with blood he took to be his child's, became crazed with fury. He brought his stick down hard on the ferret, killing it instantly. Then, seeing the child safe and well and the snake dead, he fell into an agony of remorse. "I wish," the anguished man cried out, "this child had never been born! Then I would have been spared this vile, treacherous act I've committed."

"What's the matter?" the wife asked, seeing him sobbing so bitterly. "Why is this snake dead, along with our ferret?"

He told her the whole story. "This," he cried out finally, "is the price to be paid for acting in too much haste."

4. The Wildcat and the Rat

The king said to the philosopher:

"Tell me a fable about a man besieged by enemies on every side, who is about to perish, then finds a way of appeasing his enemies and saves himself by conciliating them. Tell me about truce and conciliation."

The philosopher obediently began his account.

"Enmity and hatred," the philosopher said, "are, like affection, never permanent. Often affection turns to hatred, and hatred to affection. The wise will always keep a channel open to their enemies, so as to explore the enemy's means. What the enemy possesses, a wise man may well use to allay that enemy's hostility, leading to a truce and, if all goes well, to conciliation. Ways should always be sought to keep contact and exchange views. The one who judiciously seeks such ways and follows his notion firmly through will win his prize. An example of this is the story of the rat and the wildcat. The truce they agreed on saved them both from a great danger that might have proved mortal."

"Tell me this story," the king commanded.

It's told (the philosopher began) how there was once, in the land of Sernedib, a huge tree that soared to a great height. In the base of its massive trunk was the hole of a rat called Fraydoun and the lair of a wildcat called Rumi. There were hunters in the lands round about the tree, and, one day, a hunter laid his net near the tree, and he caught Rumi. The rat came out from his hole to forage for food, looking around him warily. He saw the wildcat entangled in the net. But then, looking back, he saw a ferret heading toward himself and, looking up, he saw an owl perched on a branch, watching him, ready to swoop. Surrounded as he was by danger, he said to himself:

"I'm trapped, with nothing to save me but my wits. I mustn't be taken by surprise but stay fully alert. The wise should always keep their presence of mind. The mind of wisdom is deep like the ocean. Adversity never conquers those who set their minds tirelessly to work. Prosperity should never intoxicate the wise nor should it veil their insight or dim the clarity of their vision.

"The wisest course" (the rat continued) "would be to make a truce with this snared wildcat. I could help him in his plight. If he hears me speak truthfully and honestly, without any deception or treachery, then it may be he'll trust me and trust the truce I offer him. And that, perhaps, could lead us both to a safe escape."

With this in mind, the rat approached the snared wildcat and greeted him, asking:

"How are things with you?"

"As you see," the wildcat replied sullenly, "I'm tightly bound."

"Indeed you are," the rat agreed. "In the normal way, it would have pleased me to see you trapped. But today I have a fellow feeling for you. We're both of us trapped. Why don't we work together to free ourselves? I'm not seeking any deliverance separate from yours. You'll see, in time, that I'm harboring no deception or treachery. You can see the ferret over there, waiting to pounce on me, and the owl up above, waiting to swoop down on me. Both are your prey, just as they're my enemies, and both fear you. If you'll let me approach you in safety, so I can escape safely from them, then I'll cut you loose. Trust what I'm saying. By nature, I trust no one, and you yourself are trusted by none. But we're both of us trapped. We must trust each other if we're to come out alive. Be quick to trust me. The wise never delay what must be done. Find relief in my survival as I do in yours. Each of us will be rescued by the other, as happens with a ship and its crew at sea. The crew are delivered safely by the ship, the ship by its crew."

The wildcat liked the words he heard, realizing the rat was quite sincere.

"What you say is the plainest truth," the wildcat answered. "I wish for this truce, which will bring both of us out safely. I shall thank you for it as long as I live and reward you most handsomely."

"As I approach you," the rat said, "let the ferret and the owl see we've come to an agreement. That will make them leave in despair. And then I'll have time to gnaw at the net and cut you free."

So it happened. But the wildcat saw the rat was taking his time gnawing at the net, as if not truly bent on his work.

"I see you're not serious about cutting me free," the wildcat said. "Now you have what you wanted, you seem to have changed—unwilling to lend your help. It isn't honorable to hesitate in relieving a friend after finding relief yourself. You saw what a good friend I was to you in saving you from certain death. It's only right you should do the same for me. You ought to forget the natural enmity that persists between your kind and mine. The good deed we've done, each for the other, should make you forget your natural instincts. The honorable are always thankful, never perfidious. One good deed makes the honorable forget countless bad ones. Treachery, bearing false witness, refusing heartfelt pleas for forgiveness—all these lead on, swiftly, to severe punishment."

"There are two kinds of friend," the rat replied. "Willing friends and those forced into friendship by necessity. Both seek their own interests, and guard themselves against harm. The willing friend is one the heart opens up to; he's always trusted, implicitly. The friend by necessity can be trusted in certain cases, but he's to be avoided in others. The wise man carefully weighs his need for such a friend. For the most part, relations between people are based on mutual interest and on any advantage sought. I'm loyal to you only in so far as I hold myself accountable—I'm on my guard against what you might do to me. There's a right time for every deed, and a deed out of its proper time is futile, even harmful. That's why I'm cutting you totally free only at the right time. For the moment I'm leaving a few knots uncut, till I know I'm completely safe from you."

They went on talking in this way till the hunter appeared in the distance. "Now it's time to cut you free completely," said the rat; and this he did. The wildcat scampered up the tree, the rat vanished into his hole, and the hunter, picking up what was left of his torn net, went off empty-handed.

After a while the rat came out from his hole, but, seeing the wildcat some way off, was wary of going too close to him.

"My brave friend," the wildcat called, "why don't you come closer? Come, we're friends! If someone makes friends, then loses the proper feelings of warmth and loyalty, he loses the fruits of friendship and despairs of friends' assistance. How could I forget the helping hand you stretched out to me.

You deserve a reward, from me and from my kind. Don't be afraid of me. Rest assured, what I have is yours."

"A friendship," the rat replied, "may well hide an enmity more dangerous than open enmity itself. To relax your guard is to be like those who ride on elephants' tusks, then fall asleep. A friend is a friend for the good he can provide. An enemy is an enemy for the harm he can inflict. If the wise seek benefits from their enemies, then they should make a show of friendship. And if they fear harm from a friend, then they feign enmity. Young beasts follow their mothers in search of milk, and when the milk no longer flows, then the young ones turn away. Clouds can gather now and release rain, then, later, disperse and withhold it. The wise will change their ways toward friends according to how their friendships change. You can open yourself up to friends, be frankly talkative, or draw back and be warily silent. Enemies may become friends by force of circumstances. When the circumstances are gone, the friendship goes, too, and the path's set for the old enmity to return.

"Friendships of this kind" (the rat went on) "are like water heated by fire. Take away the fire, and the water cools. By natural instinct, no enemy threatens me more than you do. But the two of us were forced into a friendship by pressing circumstances: you needed me, and I you. Now all that has passed, a sign that the old enmity, for ever prevailing between your kind and mine, may now return. It isn't good for the weak to be too close to a powerful foe; nor for the humble to be too near a proud and insolent enemy. You have no need of me now, except as your next meal. I see no reason to trust you. The weak are closer to escape from a powerful enemy when they're on their guard, when they're not beguiled by shows of feigned friendship. The wise conciliate, appease their enemies when obliged to do so, then swiftly turn away from them when the means appear. The wise are loyal, as best they can be, to those they befriend, and they're wary of their enemies, with all the wariness they can muster. You avoided the hunter, and I avoid you, which shows us both to have sound, sensible minds. I'm well disposed to you, but from a distance, and you should be the same. There's no way we could ever be too close. Now, peace be upon you!"

5. The Traveler and the Jeweler

The king said to the philosopher:

"I have heard of what goes on between kings and their confidants. Tell me about kings. On whom should they bestow favors, and who has the right to take a king into his confidence?"

"Kings," the philosopher replied, "are, like others, in duty bound to show favor to the deserving, to give hope to the grateful, and not solely to consider relatives and courtiers, the wealthy and those with influence. Kings should not hold back from doing good to the weak, to laborers, to the poor. They should have dealings with the lower orders as well as with the higher, should know how grateful and loyal, or how thankless and treacherous, they are; and should know how to deal with each kind accordingly. The physician doesn't cure his patients by observation alone. He analyzes their water, examines their veins, then dispenses his medication. The judicious man, knowing who the grateful and loyal are, strengthens his ties with them—he may, after all, need them in the future. The wise should be wary and cautious, not hasty in trusting others. It was said of old that the wise man should show no contempt either to small or great, among people or beasts. Rather he should test them out, then have dealings with them in the light of what he discovers. There is a fable on this theme, recounted by the wise."

"A fable?" the king said. "How does it go?"

It's told (the philosopher began) how some hunters once dug a pit to trap lions, and into this pit fell a man, a jeweler by profession. Later some beasts—a mountain cat, a snake, and an ape—fell into the pit, too. They didn't attack the man, but nor could they find a way out. The pit was too deep.

A traveler, passing by, looked down into the pit and saw them all together there.

"I can do no better deed," he said to himself, "to stand for me in the hereafter, than to save that poor man there from all those beasts."

He lowered a rope down into the pit. The nimble ape grasped it first and quickly scampered up to freedom. When the rope was lowered once more, the mountain cat clung on to it and was hauled up. Next the snake coiled itself around the rope and was pulled out. They all thanked the traveler but warned him, too, against helping the jeweler to come out.

"No creatures on earth are less grateful than man," they all warned him, "and above all that one down there."

The ape, introducing himself to his rescuer, said: "My home is at such and such a mountain, close to a city called Barajoun." "I, too, come from those parts," said the mountain cat. "And I live in that city's walls," the snake said, "should you ever pass through it." Then they all said together: "Visit us. We're in duty bound to repay you."

The traveler, though, ignoring the beasts' warnings, lowered his rope to the jeweler, now solitary down in the pit. Once hauled out, the jeweler bowed low to his rescuer, thanking him profusely.

"You've done me a very great kindness," he said, "for which I shall always be grateful. Should you ever come to Barajoun, do, please, visit me. That's where I live. Simply ask for me."

They all went their separate ways. Sometime later, the traveler found himself on his way to Barajoun. As he was passing by a mountain nearby, the ape came running toward him, welcoming him warmly, kissing his hands and feet in a gesture of utter affection and loyalty.

"Wait for me here," he said, "while I fetch you some refreshment."

Soon after, the ape returned with all kinds of luscious fruit. After enjoying this, the traveler moved on toward Barajoun, and, on some hilly ground outside the city walls, was met by the mountain cat.

"You did me a good turn," the mountain cat said, "and a very great one, too. I feel I must repay you generously. Wait here till I return."

Late that night, the mountain cat found his own way into the city, headed for the royal palace, then stole into the bedchamber of the king's daughter, who was sound asleep there. With swift, deadly movements, he killed the hapless girl and made off with her jewelry; and the traveler, awaiting his return, was presented with the booty.

"This small treasure," the mountain cat lied, "I discovered hidden here in these hills. Now it's yours. I must apologize for rewarding your priceless help so meanly."

"These poor beasts," the traveler said to himself, "have given me such excellent reward. How much more won't the jeweler—a man—repay me? Even if times are hard for him and he's nothing to spare, he'll at least be able to sell the jewels and share the proceeds with me."

The traveler arrived in the city and was welcomed by the jeweler.

"Make yourself at home," the jeweler said. "Excuse me for a moment. I have to go out and fetch you something to eat. What I have here in the house isn't fit to be set before such an honored guest as you are."

The jeweler, leaving the traveler waiting there at his house, then hurried off to the royal palace and presented himself before the king in the audience chamber.

"The man who murdered your daughter," he said, "and stole her jewelry is now detained at my house. I've caught him red-handed with the stolen jewels. He came to try to persuade me to sell the jewels for him."

The king at once sent a detachment of the royal guards, who arrested the traveler and brought him to the king. When the king saw the stolen jewels in the man's possession, he ordered that the traveler be first tortured, then paraded around the city as a thief and murderer, and finally crucified. Led through the city, reviled and spat on by an angry, outraged mob, the traveler sobbed loudly in his anguish.

"If only," he cried out bitterly, "I'd listened to the ape, and the mountain cat, and the snake, I would have been spared this. Oh, such a shameful, fearful plight!"

The snake, hearing the traveler's pitiful howls, came out from his hole in the city walls. Seeing the poor man in such a lamentable state, he couldn't bear simply to stand by and do nothing; and he thought of a clever ruse to save the wretched man from his misery. Crawling purposefully to the royal palace, he slithered swiftly into the apartment of the king's son and, finding the prince at his meal, bit him in the leg. There was uproar in the palace, everyone quivering with anxiety and fear. The distraught king summoned the royal astrologer and the court physicians to treat the stricken prince, who was now grievously sick and close to death. Giving him a potion that induced him to talk, the knot of anxious people around the prince's bed was dumbfounded by the words the young man uttered.

"I won't be cured," the prince said from his sickbed, weakly but fervently, "till the traveler's brought to me. When he lays his hand on me, I shall be cured. You, my father the king, have committed the fearful injustice, indeed the most heinous crime, in condemning a quite innocent man to torture, public ridicule, and death."

Now, how was it these strange words came from the lips of the dying prince? The truth is that the snake had told a jinn friend of his about the traveler, about the good deed he'd done and the heartrending misfortune he'd suffered. The jinn had then wafted itself, invisibly, to the sleeping prince and cast a spell on him, infusing in him a dream in which all the traveler had done, all that had happened to him, was revealed. The snake then sped off to the traveler and told him all about the jinn, the prince, and the dream.

"I warned you against helping that man," the snake said reproachfully to the hapless traveler languishing in his dungeon and awaiting death. "But you wouldn't listen."

Then the snake gave him a sprig of herbs that would dispel the effect of his poison.

"Should the king," he directed, "summon you, then give the sick prince this sprig. Tell him to have it boiled, then drink the infusion. It will cure him. Tell the truth to the king, and you'll be safe, God willing."

Meanwhile, the prince told his father the king from his sickbed:

"My cure lies with the traveler you arrested, tortured, and condemned to death."

The king relented at this, brought the traveler to his presence, and commanded him to cure his son.

"I cannot do as you command," the traveler replied. "But I pray, indeed, for the prince's health."

"What brings you to this city?" the king inquired. "What's your business here?"

The traveler thereupon told him the whole story: of the pit, the ape, the snake, the mountain cat, and the jeweler against whom the beasts had warned him. Then he prayed aloud:

"Almighty God! If You know I have spoken the truth, then hasten the prince's cure and restore him to health."

The young prince quickly recovered and was soon in the best of health. The king rewarded the traveler handsomely and ordered that the jeweler be executed.

The philosopher then said to the king:

"The jeweler's treachery, after what the traveler had done to save his life, the way the beasts supported the traveler and exerted themselves to save him from certain death—all this is a lesson to be learned, a lesson of loyalty and good faith."

6. The Host and the Guest

The king said to the philosopher:

"Tell me about those who turn away from their own quite suitable professions, which they carry on well enough, to follow other professions for which they're unsuited."

It's told (the philosopher replied) how there lived once, in a land called Karkh, a man who was pious and devout. One day the man had a guest and set before him a platter of choice dates.

"How sweet these dates are!" the guest exclaimed, after eating a few. "How delicious! In my own country, there are no palm trees and no dates. We do, though, have other kinds of fruit, especially figs. And dates, after all, aren't as good for the health as figs are."

In reply, the host embarked on a moral discourse.

"He isn't to be considered happy who needs what he can't find, or can't acquire. Such a man will grow greedy, covetous, and restless. Then gloom and despondency will follow, and his health will suffer. He'll overburden himself with worry and care. You, who have a firm will and a good appearance, should be content with what you have and hold back from seeking the unattainable."

"That's well said," the guest remarked approvingly. "But tell me one thing. I've heard you speak a foreign language I find intriguing and pleasing. Would you teach me that language? I'd like very much to learn it."

"What would happen to you," the wise host replied, "were you to turn away from your native language and take up a foreign one, would be like what happened to the crow."

"The crow?" the guest said. "Tell me, please. What did happen to the crow?"

"It's told," the host began, "how a crow once stood watching a partridge as it went about. Liking the way the partridge walked, he tried to imitate it. But no matter how hard he tried, the crow's steps looked awkward and clumsy compared to the quick, light, graceful steps of the partridge. At last, after repeated failures, the crow grew confused and disconsolate. I give you this fable," the host explained, "to show how, were you to abandon your native language (which might sound less attractive to you than a foreign one) and choose to attempt that foreign language instead, you wouldn't master it and would merely appear foolish trying to speak it. You'd lose what you already have but wouldn't gain the thing you covet. It was said of old: a person will be deemed ignorant if he attempts what is unapt, unfitting, and unbecoming; what his forefathers were never known to have attempted in their time."

The philosopher then explained to the king:

"Rulers who fail in their duty to keep those they govern in their present stations but rather encourage them to move beyond themselves will be making them act like the crow in this fable, who aspired to be something not his by destiny. A wise ruler should see to it that people know their places in society and don't covet positions above their own. For people, when driven by the urge to rise above themselves, to move out from their ordained places, find themselves embroiled in uncalled for hardships: hardships of displacement, uncertainty, and instability. This hectic movement, up the social scale, entails ever-mounting dangers, till, at the highest point, the exalted position so longed for and attained becomes a visible challenge to the ruler himself."

Translated by Ibrahim al-Mumayyaz and Christopher Tingley

84

From *Rasaʾil Ikhwan al-Safa* (*Epistles of the Brethren of Purity*)

The Epistles of the Brethren of Purity, *or* The Epistles of the Brethren of Purity and Loyal Friends (Rasaʾil ikhwan al-safa wa khillan al-wafa) *is a collection of works of an obscure and mysterious organization of Neoplatonic Arabic philosophers who lived in Basra, Iraq, sometime in the tenth century, during the Abbasid caliphate.*

Scholarly sources are unclear as to who they were, but it is generally accepted that this group authored at least the fifty-two rasaʾil (epistles) in the collection. The subject matter of these epistles is vast and ranges from mathematics, music, and logic through mineralogy, astronomy, ethics, botany, and embryology to philosophical and theological topics, concluding with a treatise on magic.

The work professes to contain a systematized and harmonious view of the universe and of life, its origin and destiny, forged from many discordant, competing notions. It also claims to offer "a complete account of all things"—to contain, in effect, all that was known at the time it was written.

Some scholars argue that the group's appellation is taken from the story of the ringed dove in Kalila and Dimna,[1] *in which it is related how a group of animals, by acting as "faithful friends" (ikhwan al-safa) to one another, managed to escape the snares of a hunter.*

Like all conventional Arabic Islamic works, the Epistles *contain numerous quotations from the Quran, but these works are noted especially for the didactic fables interspersed throughout the text. One in particular, "The Island of Animals" (or "The Dispute Between Animals and Man," embedded in the twenty-second epistle, "On How the Animals and Their Kind Are Formed"), is one of the most popular animal fables in Islam. It recounts the story of a group of seventy people, survivors of*

---

1. The original book of fables titled *Kalila and Dimna* is, as shown above, a collection of Eastern tales translated into Arabic by ʿAbdullah Ibn al-Muqaffaʿ (102/725–139/760).

a shipwreck, who discover an island where animals rule and decide to settle there. Soon the humans are trapping the animals for use as beasts of burden, or killing them for food, clothing, and even sport.

Unaccustomed to such harsh treatment, the animals complain to the king of the jinn (devout spirit beings). The king convenes four sessions of debate between the humans and various representatives of the animals, such as the nightingale, the bee, and the jackal. In these exchanges, the animals are highly critical of certain human attitudes, ideas, and practices, such as corruption, unfair rule, prejudice, greed, and brutal repression. The animals nearly defeat the humans, but a wise man ends the series of debates by pointing out that there is one way in which humans are superior to animals and thus worthy of making them their servants.

The following excerpts from the fable are highlights of the debate.

The Island of Animals

Once upon a time, a ship carrying seventy merchants, craftsmen, and scholars from different countries and cultures ran aground on Blasaghoun Island, near the equator. The island was fertile, teeming with springs and fountains, fruit trees and gardens lush in bloom. The castaways roamed throughout the island and were pleased by what they saw. They settled and built houses and began making use to their liking of all the creatures they found there.

DAY 1

At last the creatures could no longer bear the servitude and oppression and rose up in revolt against the humans. The leaders and the learned among the animals went to see the wise Byorasp, king of the good jinn on the island, who then summoned the humans as well. Byorasp was a fair, generous, and tolerant king, hospitable to strangers and merciful to the beleaguered. He stood against injustice and commanded the pursuit of good and avoidance of evil, so that he may earn the grace and blessings of the Almighty God.

"What is it that brought you to our island?" he asked the humans.

"It was a shipwreck that led us to your domain. But we already knew of your virtue and fairness in governing. We have come to your court today to put forward our arguments in this conflict with our runaway servants, these beasts who deny us the right to rule them and have now rebelled."

The jinn king replied, "What are your arguments, and what do you propose as evidence in support of your claims?"

"Your Majesty, we have both sharia and reason on our side."

One of the humans then rose and, after appealing to God Almighty to bestow His blessings upon the Prophet Muhammad (pbuh), said, "God created man from water, and from them wives, and carried them on both land and sea. God said:

> God is He Who raised the heavens without any pillars that ye can see; is firmly established on the throne [of authority]; He has subjected the sun and the moon [to his Law]! Each one runs [its course] for a term appointed. He doth regulate all affairs, explaining the signs in detail, that ye may believe with certainty in the meeting with your Lord. (13:2)[2]

"And said:

That has created pairs in all things, and has made for you ships and cattle on which ye ride,

In order that ye may sit firm and square on their backs, and when so seated, ye may celebrate the [kind] favor of your Lord, and say, "Glory to Him Who has subjected these to our [use], for we could never have accomplished this [by ourselves],

"And to our Lord, surely, must we turn back!" (43:12–14)

"There are many verses in the Quran, and in the Torah as well as in the Gospels, confirming that animals have been created for us. They are our slaves and we are their masters."

The jinn king turned then to the animals and said, "You have now heard what the humans argue, quoting the Quran to support their case. What do you offer in support of your own?"

The leader of the farm animals, the mule, rose and said, "Your Majesty, nothing in what this human has said supports his claim. God wished to show His mercy in the aid He has brought to humans. He also said:

And cattle He has created for you [men]: from them ye derive warmth, and numerous benefits, and of their [meat] ye eat.

And ye have a sense of pride and beauty in them as ye drive them home in the evening, and as ye lead them forth to pasture in the morning.

And they carry your heavy loads to lands that ye could not [otherwise] reach except with souls distressed: for your Lord is indeed Most Kind, Most Merciful,

---

2. Quranic verses cited here are taken from the authoritative interpretation by A. Yusuf ʿAli, endorsed by the Department of Scientific Research and Interpretation and Advocacy and Guidance in Riyadh, Saudi Arabia; Dar al-Qurʿan al-Karim, Beirut, A.H. 26/11/1403/1981 C.E.

And [He has created] horses, mules, and donkeys for you to ride and use for show; and He has created [other] things of which ye have no knowledge. (16:5–8)

The mule continued, "Do you, Sire, also believe that these are slaves for the humans? We lived upon this earth long before God Almighty created Adam, the forebear of all humanity. We led our lives happily, in meadows and mountains, busily raising our children and enjoying what God gave to us in food and drink. God then created Adam and made him His successor on earth. Humans multiplied and spread on land and sea in all parts of the world. They chased us and made prisoners of sheep, cows, horses, mules, and donkeys to burden them with hard labor."

The two parties went on exchanging their arguments before the jinn king. The animals, each in turn, presented their accounts of torture at the hands of humans. The donkey, the ox, the sheep, the camel, the elephant, the horse, the rabbit, the mule, and even the pig enumerated their virtues and valued services to the humans, but at the same time described the harsh and repressive treatment they received. They argued that humans buy and sell animals just as they do other commodities and goods. What is more, they said, the humans slaughter the animals for food and even use their hides and skins for clothing and adornments, all without appreciation of such benefits.

The leader of the humans then asked for permission to speak. "It is taken against us that we sell, buy, and slaughter these animals. But is this not what Persians do to Romans? And Romans to Persians where one party achieves victory over the other? Do they not all become either master or slave? Is this not the case between Abyssinians and Nubians? Arabs, Kurds, and Turks?

The jinn king then ordered one of his attendants to conclude the session and said, "Humans and creatures, the hour grows late. You will return to your quarters and come again tomorrow, God willing."

•••••

As the king summoned the vizier, Bidar, to his chambers, the humans convened among themselves to express their fears and apprehensions. They suspected that the vizier's counsel to the king might not reflect their interest. Some suggested sending him gifts to bribe him into their favor, but others said that he was an honest adviser and any attempt of that sort might antagonize him, prompting him to side with the beasts. A quarrel ensued, with some continuing to insist that a form of enticement was warranted, and indeed necessary, and again came the contention that such a move would surely backfire if the judges and jurists were found to be genuine and honest agents of justice.

One human spoke up, "What if the judge orders that all these animals be sold, and that the money be put into the king's coffers?"

Several others replied virtually in unison, "Should this come to pass, we would be left with no milk to drink, no meat to eat, no wool clothing to wear, no shoes for our feet. Death would then come to us more easily than life in starvation, cold, and want.

DAY 2

In the meantime, the beasts also gathered for consultation. "We must not each present our case one by one to the king and the judges," advised the donkey. "By this we will only complicate our approach and confuse the judges with contradictory statements."

One animal said, "The proper thing to do, in my view, now that the livestock have spoken, is to send emissaries to all the other families in the kingdom of animals—those who are eloquent and capable of presenting the case persuasively."

All those in attendance agreed. Six emissaries were sent to six families—farm animals, predators, birds, vermin, swarming insects, and creatures of the sea. There followed long and heated discussions within each family on which among them should serve as representative to the king's court.

The lion, as master of the predators, gathered his fellows and announced to them that the assembly of animals had asked him to send before the king and other jinn leaders a delegate who would speak on behalf of his own family in the ongoing conflict between humans and animals.

"You are our king," said the tiger, "and we are your subjects and soldiers. The king, the subjects, and the soldiers are the head, the body, and the limbs. And it is the king who assigns to each the role that befits him. If this consultation calls for someone who excels in leaping, crouching, darting, and striking, then I am the one."

"No," said the lion. "This will not do."

"Does the mission involve raids, clashes, and darting turns?" asked the wolf.

"No," replied the lion.

"If it calls for modesty, entreaties, and appeasement, then surely it is me!" exclaimed the wildcat.

The lion shook his head.

"If this assignment entails digging up graves and retrieving carcasses and goring bellies, then think of me, Your Majesty," offered the hyena.

The lion again declined, and then addressed the entire gathering: "All the characteristics and traits that you have put forth will be of no avail. They apply only to human kings, soldiers, sultans, princes, army commanders, and governors. Consider that this presentation shall be made before a council of philosophers, jurists, scholars, and thinkers. We should not think of brute strength and agility, but rather of shrewdness, prowess, and cunning. Whom can you recommend that possesses these?"

It was the tiger who answered then: "The only one endowed with these qualities, Your Majesty, is the jackal Kalila, brother of Dimna."

"What do you say to this, Kalila?" asked the lion.

"I hope that God will reward the tiger generously for his wise judgment," Kalila replied.

"Then you will proceed to the court of the jinn king to act on our behalf," replied the lion. "You will be rewarded when you return to us in victory."

•••••

At the same time, another messenger reached the bird family and met with their king, Simurgh, who immediately summoned all his subjects from land, sea, plains, and mountains. They all descended in countless flocks. Simurgh turned to his adviser, the peacock, and asked, "Who is the most articulate and eloquent speaker among the birds? We must send him to the debate between humans and animals."

"We have quite a few," replied the peacock. "The hoopoe spy, the cock muezzin, the pigeon guide, the pheasant herald, the lark crooner, the sparrow songster, the marten builder, the crow vicar, the crane guardian, the swallow squire, the heron weeper, the nightingale cantor, the ostrich nomad . . ."

The owl was also suggested by some members, but then it was recalled that the owl is regarded by humans as an ominous figure.

Then came forward the birds of prey with their ferocious beaks—vultures, eagles, falcons, and hawks. But their own chief, the phoenix, did not approve, as humans are often wary of these creatures. He and his fellows then nominated the parrot, noting that he is fancied, even beloved, by humans—kings, men, women, children, learned and illiterate alike—for its vivid colors and ability to imitate their speech. Humans talk to him and listen with intent delight as he repeats their words and phrases.

"They all have fine qualities," Simurgh replied. "And they are all beautiful and noble . . . eloquent as well, even in their murmurs and most private of whispers. But tell me, peacock, who is the best qualified to speak for us?"

"I would say that the nightingale is the master of oratory. His voice is musical and enchanting."

The nightingale accepted the mission, in the company of the parrot.

Simurgh turned to the them and said, "Godspeed. Now make your way to the king's court and deliver our argument."

•••••

Another messenger had reached the drone, the king of the swarming insects, and advised him of the mission awaiting one of his subjects. All the creatures that fly with wings and have no feathers on their bodies gathered to discuss the matter. The chief hornet recommended himself, as did the senior locust, saying that such a representative should be of hefty size and imposing manner. The drone king asked the group to think seriously of the matter and to pass on more prudent recommendations.

"Do not rush headlong into your nominations," he cautioned.

In turn, the wasp, the chinch, the mosquito, and the horsefly spoke highly of their own qualities and abilities, but they were each turned down by the other members of the gathering, as they are all in one way or another harmful. Then a wise bee stepped forward and said, "I can perform this duty, God willing."

This nomination received a warm welcome by the drone and the assembly. The bee set out immediately for the king's court.

And so it went in the other families. The vermin, including lizards, snakes, scorpions, and beetles, appointed the cockroach.

Their king, the snake, warned him, "When you arrive there, do not mention that it was I who sent you!"

"Why is that?" asked the cockroach.

"Because there is longstanding enmity between snakes and humans," he replied. "So much so that humans always ask God why He created us. When they think of us, they think of venom and of the murder of humans and animals alike."

With that the cockroach scurried away toward the court.

•••••

Elsewhere, an emissary met with the chief of the sea creatures, the dragon, at the shore. All were summoned, including the shark, the whale, the eel, the crab, the ray, the sea horse, the monkfish, the dolphin, the tortoise, and the frog. It was the whale that received the first nomination, in view of its enormous size, but was later dismissed for precisely that reason. The crab was also considered, but he himself acknowledged that he was a treacherous, angry sort. The crocodile then nominated the frog, saying, "He is a sober creature, and a pious one, praying day and night, accustomed to navigating both land and sea. He is also familiar to humans and can enter their houses freely."

The dragon asked for the frog's opinion.

"I will be proud to represent us," he replied. "Pray for me and wish me victory."

DAY 3

The following morning, representatives of the humans as well as the animals paid their respects to the jinn king, who was rather surprised by the various and distinct personalities of the humans. He observed them all, with their different colors, customs, and dress and, pointing to each in turn, asked his adviser who they were. He then understood that they included, among others, an Indian, an Assyrian, a Hebrew, a Greek, another from Khorasan, in Persia, and an Arab from the tribe of Quraysh—a thin brown man bowing and kneeling in prayer.

The jinn king asked, "Tell me, all of you, who is your king?"

"We have many kings," they replied.

"And may I ask why you have a multitude of kings, while I see that each family among the plaintiff animals has one king and one representative here?"

One of the humans stepped forward and said, "It is true, Your Majesty, that animals are more numerous by far than humans. But they choose kings by reason of craft and brute strength, whereas human kings are smaller in size but infinitely wiser and more concerned with the affairs of their subjects. We presume that our kings have greater political skills and abiding belief in the need for justice and equity in their rule. There are those who stand for fair treatment of their enemies as well as the rebels, the outlaws, and the corrupt in their land. Their subjects include ministers, supervisors, and tax collectors as well as farmers and craftsmen. There are judges and scholars who help apply justice and the tenets of law. There are servants and merchants and many other groups and classes. It is for all these considerations that God the Almighty has chosen kings to be His successors on earth, but only so long as they work in the service of righteousness and uphold a balance between the rights and duties of their subjects.

"You have spoken well," replied the jinn king.

As the representative of the humans concluded his opening statement, the king cocked his head to follow a humming sound that had begun moving through the air. It was the gentle music of a bee, made as if in praise to God.

"And who are you?" asked the king.

"I am the bee, Your Majesty. God Almighty has blessed me with many of His endowments."

"Please tell me what you mean," the king replied.

"Of course, Your Majesty. God has inspired us with all the engineering and architectural skills that humans use in building their houses and monuments. He also guides us to feed ourselves on flowers and fruits and to produce a sweet and healing syrup. This is testified by the word of God Almighty:

> And thy Lord taught the bee to build its cells in hills, on trees, and in [men's] habitations;
>
> Then to eat of all the produce [of the earth], and find with skill the spacious paths of its Lord: there issues from within their bodies a drink of varying colors, wherein is healing for men: verily in this is a sign for those who give thought. (16:68–69)

"We have also been blessed with a beautiful form—golden wings, a well-divided body, and a barb to defend ourselves against our enemies. Our kings and leaders care for us well and maintain an organized, cohesive community."

"You speak well. But what is your grievance against humans?" asked the jinn king.

The bee replied, "We live on mountaintops and hills, among trees and close to fields and gardens, as well as to humans. But as soon as they discover our honey, they begin destroying our homes and killing our offspring, even taking our honeycomb for their own purposes. And that is why we try to escape their savage advances."

The jinn king commanded all parties to retire from the court. He turned to wise Bidar and said, "You have witnessed the entire scene today and heard the arguments from both sides. What do you advise me to do?"

"May God guide your steps, Your Majesty," Bidar replied. "I suggest that you ask your judges and jurists for their views on this very grave matter. Joint counsel, Your Majesty, will be of greater use than one opinion."

•••••

All the judges and jurists were summoned to the king's court. The chief jurist spoke first: "I recommend, Your Majesty, that the animals put in writing the story of their servitude and ordeal under the humans. They will then submit it to wise interpreters of jurisprudence, who will pass judgment that they be sold, freed, or treated well. And if the humans do not heed the verdict, the beasts should flee, by all rights."

Another jurist said, "I believe that Your Majesty should advise these animals to escape together one night and move far away from where the humans live, as zebras and gazelles do. Humans would then be deprived of using the animals for riding and bearing loads."

A third counselor proposed, "Your Majesty ought to send the jinn tribes tonight to open the gates of all the barns and loosen the ties that bind these beasts. By this they earn the mercy and reward of God for delivering the animals from the cruelty of their rulers. God says in one of the revealed books: "You, tyrant kings, I have not given you sovereignty in order for you to collect money and enjoy all kinds of pleasures, but in order that you not oblige those who are wronged to deliver their pleas to me, as I will fulfill their demands even if they are infidels."

The king pondered for a while and said, "What you have counseled will not resolve the conflict between the parties. What I need from you is a course of action that will allow us to overcome this dilemma that grows ever more dangerous and threatens to unleash chaos on my island. Think well on what I should do."

The king then turned to his attendant. "Tell the parties that they are now dismissed. But advise them in no uncertain terms that I will grant them audience only once tomorrow morning before the judges deliver their verdict. And caution their chief delegates against repeating arguments already presented in the last three sessions."

DAY 4

Having discussed their tactics and coordinated their roles the night before for the final session, the defendants and plaintiffs entered the court once again and bowed in respect before the jinn king.

Once given permission to begin, the leader of the humans stood to speak: "Your Majesty, we have yet to name some other essential qualities that differentiate us and give us superiority over these beasts. Take, for instance, the way we look and behave. Unlike them, we are well mannered and respectable, kind and compassionate to one another. We humans dress properly, cover our private parts, and use silk, wool, and genuine leather for garments and shoes, and hides for our water and drinks, as well as mink coats and vests for our women. We decorate our furniture and adorn our utensils and implements with ivory. Our nomads pitch knit-wool tents for living, and we for celebrations and hunting expeditions.

"It also goes without saying that we eat well. Apart from meat, vegetables, and fruits, our meals abound in milk, butter, and other delicacies.

"We implore you, Sire, and the honorable judges to look upon these monsters and compare. See how wretched and unsightly they appear, and how ill-mannered they are. Such naked creatures have no shame, no civility, and no sympathy. Their saber-toothed predators and sharp-beaked vultures kill and devour their own kind, and even assault and murder humans with poisonous fangs, vicious claws and talons, and fierce incisors.

"With this," the chief representative concluded, "and on behalf of all humans, I rest my case."

The animals were well prepared for their rebuttal.

"We will not say much, Sire," said the parrot. "But have you ever seen anyone less ignorant, naive, or negligent than this man and other members of his species? They brag about their looks, their fashionable attire, elegant footwear, and leather flasks. But how indeed would they enjoy all these luxuries were it not for our hides, fur, and wool and for the tireless efforts of our little mate, the silkworm? They boast about their fine cuisine, overlooking that their gluttony thrives on our flesh and blood. They denounce our slaying of prey yet fail to say that this is precisely what they do to us so pitilessly—and even more cold-bloodedly to other humans. It is those creatures who are our mentors and coaches in savagery and indiscriminate brutality. What is more, we never assault humans, even when we are starving, but rather act in self-defense.

"In sum, I have this to say to the humans: stop blowing your own horns! And remember, even those horns come from us!"

The judges seemed amused and even swayed by the parrot's wit. However, a stern look from the jinn king prompted them to restrain their lighthearted reception of the plaintiff's statements and to maintain strict order. With a wave of his hand, the king instructed the judges to begin their deliberations.

An air of nervous anticipation prevailed as the judges entered a prolonged and querulous discussion. The humans looked especially anxious. There seemed to be no sign of reaching a unanimous decision among the judges.

"You are trying my patience with all this dithering," the king interrupted at last. "The parties have been presenting their arguments for four long, exhausting days. You cannot keep them on tenterhooks like this. More important, I have many other duties to tend to on this island."

The judges fell silent as the chief looked timidly at the king and held out his hands in resigned apology.

"We have among us," the chief justice began, "a judicious, prudent, and knowledgeable sage from the holy cities of Mecca and Medina. He holds the combined wisdom of Arabs, Muslims, Christians, Hebrews, Persians, and Greeks. I trust he can guide us to a resolution."

The noble, poised, yet modest man stood up. There was a long pause as he prepared to deliver the trump that all were awaiting. "Sire," he said at last, "the petitioners have put forward an array of divergent views, some valid and true, some excessive, narrow-minded, and unfair. The truth of the matter is this . . . the humans are the only ones upon whom God has bestowed reason, so that they might think and innovate, be creative and constructive. Furthermore, should they heed His tenets, the chance of eternal life is theirs. Men alone will have a Day of Judgment. The prophets, and Muhammad especially (pbuh), may plead for men to be spared Hell and rewarded with Paradise. Humans hold mastery over animals not by virtue of superiority but because they alone are answerable for their deeds at the time of death, with an afterlife that depends upon their conduct."

The jinn king reflected for a while on the sage's pronouncements. He then addressed all those present in his court with the final verdict.

"Humans are indeed superior, but animals are not merely inferior creatures to be subjected to wanton rules and gratuitous wishes. God has created them to assist humans, not to be their slaves.

Let us have peace and harmony on this island . . . and let it be known to all that men are accountable to Almighty God for all their deeds, among them their treatment of animals."

Translated by Fayez Suyyagh

85

From *Al-Maqamat* (*The Assemblies*)

From *The Maqamat of Badiʿ al-Zaman al-Hamadhani* (356 / 968–398 / 1008)

1. THE BALKHIYYA ASSEMBLY

ʿIsa ibn Hisham told us the following tale:[1]

The cotton trade took me to Balkh. So, in the prime of youth, without a care in the world and bedecked in wealth, I went there. My only concern was thought's restless filly that I tried to keep reined in and discourse's shy creature that I kept hunting. Throughout my travels nothing more eloquent than my own speech reached my ears. As we were on the point of leaving or almost so, a youth in eye-catching garb came up to me, fresh stubble visible on his cheeks and a gaze so clear that it had drunk of the waters of the Tigris and Euphrates. He greeted me with a display of generosity that I surpassed with plaudits. "Are you planning a journey?" he asked, to which I replied that I was. "Then may your scout find fertile pasture," he said, "and your leader not lose his way. When do you intend to leave?" "Early tomorrow," I replied, whereupon he recited:

Morning of God, not morning of departure;
Bird of arrival, not of separation.

"Where are you going?" he asked. "I am returning home," I replied. "Then may you be conveyed to your homeland," he said, "and may you complete your business there! When will you return?" "Next year," I replied. "Then may you fold up the robes and twist the thread tight! How do you feel

1. For literature on the *maqamat*, please consult the introduction.

regarding generosity?" "Just as you desire," I replied. "Then, should God bring you back safe and sound from this journey," he said, "bring me back that enemy in the guise of a friend, the gold-colored kind, the one that lures people into disbelief, that can dance on a nail just like the sun's own disk, that lightens the burden of debt, and shows the two faces of hypocrisy!"

ʿIsa ibn Hisham said: I realized he was asking for money. "Take this in cash now," I said, "and a similar sum as a promise." With that he recited:

Your own scheme exceeds what I asked for;
May you continue to perform worthy deeds!
May your wood still be sturdy, may you remain generous,
Your branches o'ertopped, your roots still strong.
I cannot bear the burden of receiving charity,
Nor tolerate the weight of begging.
My estimation fell short of the extent of your generosity,
While you have indeed outpaced my own expectations.
O buttress of fate and high aspirations,
May you never be bereft of fortune!

ʿIsa ibn Hisham said: I gave him the dinar. "From where does such eloquence come?" I asked. "My origins are with the Quraysh," he replied, "and my nobility stems from an upbringing in their valleys." However, some of the people standing around said: "Are not you Abu ʾl-Fath al-Iskandari? Didn't I see you in Iraq doing the rounds in the markets there and begging with bits of paper?" Whereupon Abu ʾl-Fath intoned:

God has many servants,
Who have adopted life in great variety.
In the evening they may be Arabs,
Yet next morning they are Nabataeans.

2. THE ASADIYYA ASSEMBLY

ʿIsa ibn Hisham told us the following tale:

I have come across some of the *maqamat* and epistles of the man from Alexandria, works that are enough to tempt the flighty beast to pay attention and the timid sparrow to tremble. He recites his poetry to us; its refinement blends with the very soul and its subtle diction is beyond the range of the very imagination of shamans. I beg God to keep him with us so that

I may be lucky enough to meet him and to marvel at the way his ambition remains unsatisfied in spite of his exquisite craft. Fate has imposed its barriers between him and its successes, and so on and so on, till some business happened to take me to Homs. Toward it therefore I set my aspirations, traveling in the company of a group like stars in the night, as close-knit as saddle blankets on horses' backs. We set out to cover the terrain and eradicate the distance. We kept edging along the humps of plateaus mounted on our steeds till our line was as straight as any stick and then as curved as a bow. Now a valley loomed ahead along the base of a mountain range that was covered in fruit trees and tamarisk looking like young maidens who have let their hair down and combed out their tresses. In the mid-day heat we headed toward the trees in order to both find shade and take a nap. Having tied up the horses, we nodded off.

All of a sudden our horses started neighing loudly. Glancing at my own horse, I saw that he had pricked his ears and was staring wildly. He kept gnawing at the rope with his lips and kicking the ground with his hooves. Now all the horses started panicking and pissing. They managed to sever the ropes and headed for the hills. We all rushed to our weapons, and there confronting us was a fearsome lion in its deathly garb, having emerged from its lair strutting along arrogantly and baring its teeth; its eye had a malignant glare, its nose was stuffed full of disdain, and its chest contained a stalwart heart that knew no fear. We told ourselves that this was a pressing danger and a significant event. From among our troupe a young man rushed toward the beast

Olive complexioned from among the Arabs,
One who fills the bucket to the very brim,

with a heart impelled by fate and an efficacious sword. However the lion's strength overwhelmed him; first he slipped on the ground, then fell flat on his face. The lion now moved from his first victim to a young man who was with him. Fate now summoned him just as it had his companion. He moved forward, but terror paralyzed his hand. He, too, fell to the ground, and the lion pounced on his chest. However, I threw my turban at it and managed to keep its mouth away, thus sparing the young man's life. With that the young man got up and stabbed the lion in the chest. While it collapsed of sheer fright, the lion actually died from the wound to its chest. We now went to look for the horses; we brought back the ones that had stopped and left the others that had run away. Now it was time for us to prepare our comrade for burial

As we poured the soil on our comrade's grave
We were grief-stricken; what a desolate hour it was!

We set out for the desert once more and penetrated its terrain. We kept moving until our supplies ran low and our food was almost completely used up. We were at the point of no return and feared those two killers, hunger and thirst. Just then a horseman appeared in the distance. We moved toward him. When we reached him, he dismounted from his splendid horse, placed his hands on the ground, and kissed it with his lips. From among the group he selected me; he came over, kissed my stirrup, and sought refuge by my side. I looked down at him and was astonished to see a face as radiant as a rain cloud and a physique such that "when the eye beholds him, it relaxes." His cheek had sprouted its first growth along with a mustache; his arm was muscular, and his penis was supple. While he looked Turkish, his garments were regal.

"Well, you rogue," we all said, "what is your story?" "I am a king's servant," he replied, "but he was on the point of slaying me. I therefore made my escape and have been wandering around just as you now see me." His general appearance supported his story and suggested he was telling the truth. "Today," he went on, "I am your servant and my property is yours." "That is good news for you," I replied, "and through you, for me, too. Your travels have brought you to a welcoming space and a fruitful livelihood."

Everyone in the group started congratulating me. He looked at everyone, and his glances slew them all; when he spoke, everyone was entranced. "Gentlemen," he said, "there is a spring by the base of this mountain. You have been riding in the open desert for a while, so why not pause to take some water over there?" With that we reined our animals in the direction he indicated. When we reached the spot, the noonday heat had melted our bodies and even cicadas had climbed up into the trees. "Why don't you all take a nap," he suggested, "in the welcoming shade by the side of this sweet water?"

"We will do so," we replied.

With that he dismounted from his horse, undid his belt, and took off his shirt. Now his body was concealed from us only by the thinnest of undergarments. None of us had the slightest doubt but that he had had an argument with the heavenly angels, so he had managed to flee and escape the clutches of Rudwan. He now went over to our riding animals and took off the saddles, then he fed the horses and laid out some straw for us to sleep on. All the while the eyes of our entire group were riveted on him, as we stared at his beauty in disbelief. "Young man," I said, "your service is excellent and your total appearance is exquisite. Unlucky is the man who loses your company, and blessed the one whose companion you are! How can I thank God for giving me such bounty as you?"

"I still have yet more to offer you," he replied. "If my services so far and my comely appearance have pleased you, then how will it be if you see me in a situation where I can show you all another aspect of my skill? Then you will be even more delighted." "Go ahead!" we said.

With that he went over and took a bow, strung it, took an arrow, and shot it high into the air, then followed it with another. "Now," he said, "I'll show you something else." He came over and took my quiver, then mounted my horse. He now fired an arrow at one of our number and pierced him through the chest, and followed it with another that emerged from a second traveler's back. "Curse you!" I said, "what are you doing?" "Shut up, you dolt!" he replied. "Now everyone tie his companion's hands, or else I'll make him swallow his own spittle."

We had no idea what do to next; our horses were tethered, the saddles were on the ground, and our weapons were out of range. What is more, he was mounted on horseback, while we were on foot, and he was using the bow to pierce people in the back and chest. Once we saw the serious situation we were in, we took the ropes and tied one another up. I was the last one, and there was no one left to tie my hands. "Take your clothes off," he said, and so I did so. He dismounted and went around slapping everyone one after another. He, too, took off his clothes and then came over to me. I happened to be wearing a new pair of boots. "Take them off, you bastard!" he said. "These boots were still fresh when I put them on," I replied, "so I can't get them off." "I'll do it," he said and came right up to me. At that moment I grabbed a knife that I had kept hidden in my boot; while he was busy trying to get the boot off, I plunged it so hard into his chest that it came out of his back. One gasp was the only sound he made before he fell to the ground dead.

I now went over to my friends, untied their hands, and then distributed the property of the two dead men among us all. We went over to our friend but found that he, too, had died. Thus he went to his grave and we set off once again. We reached Homs five days later. When we arrived at its market square, we spotted a man with a bag and walking stick accompanied by a son and daughter. He kept saying,

God bless the man who fills my bag with his generous gifts,
God bless anyone who takes pity on Saʿid and Fatimah.
He will be a servant for you, as will she—no doubt.

ʿIsa ibn Hisham said: "This is that man from Alexandria," I said, "the one I've heard and asked about. It's the very man in person." I went over and spoke to him: "Say what you want!" "A dirham," he replied.

A dirham you will have multiplied by its like,
So long as my life breath supports me.
Make then your calculation and request
So I can hand over what is demanded.

"Here is one dirham," I told him, "multiplied by two, by three, by four, and by five," till I reached twenty. "Now how much do you have?" I asked. "Twenty loaves," was his reply, so I ordered that he be given that amount. "There can be no success if God's help is withheld," I said, "and no strategy can work in the face of deprivation."

3. THE BAGHDADIYYA ASSEMBLY

ʿIsa ibn Hisham told us the following tale:

While in Baghdad, I had a craving for some dates but had no money in hand. I went out looking for somewhere to buy some, till I reached Karkh. There I encountered a country yokel doggedly pulling his donkey behind him, with his money belt strapped to his waist. Aha, I told myself, we have found a victim! "God preserve you, Abu Zayd!" I yelled. "Where have you come from, where are you staying, and when did you get here? Let's go to my house." "My name is not Abu Zayd," the yokel replied, "it's Abu ʿUbayd."

"Oh, that's right," I said. "God curse the devil and banish forgetfulness! Being apart for so long has made me forget your name. How's your father, still young as I remember him, or now grown old?" "The spring grasses have long since grown on his grave," the man replied, "and I hope that God will conduct him to His paradise."

"Indeed we belong to God," I said, "and to Him do we return. To God the Almighty, the Great, belongs all power and authority!" With an impetuous gesture I now grabbed hold of my shirt, fully intending to rend it apart. The yokel grasped me by the waist. "Don't tear your shirt, I beg you," he said. "Well then," I said, "come to my home and we'll have some food. Or rather, let's go to the market and buy some meat; it's closer, and the food is better."

The mention of delicious mouthfuls of food aroused his appetite and diverted his attention. He was keen to go, not realizing that he had fallen into the trap. We reached the stall of a meat seller whose meat oozed with juice and pastry dripped with gravy.

"Give Abu Zayd a portion of this meat," I said, "then weigh out a piece of halvah and a selection of these other dishes. Make a side order of bread and sprinkle some summaq water over it. Then Abu Zayd will be able to eat with relish."

With that the meat seller took his cleaver, chose the very best cut from his oven, and proceeded to pound and tenderize it. Abu Zayd took a seat, and so did I; his hopes were high, and so were mine. Eventually we finished.

"Now," I said to the halvah seller, "weigh out a couple of pounds of that walnut cake for Abu Zayd; it slips down the gullet and flows through the veins. Make sure it was made last night and is fresh today; thin-crusted, well filled, covered in pearly oil, and gleaming bright. It should melt like unchewed gum. Then Abu Zayd will be able to eat with relish."

The halvah seller cut up some cake. Abu Zayd sat down, and so did I; he bared his arms, and I did likewise. Eventually we had eaten our fill.

"Now, Abu Zayd," I said, "we really need some ice-cooled water to quench the burning from such a hot meal. Sit here, Abu Zayd, while I bring us a water seller."

With that I left and took a seat where I could watch him without his knowing. I wanted to see what he would do. When I took a long time coming back, he got up and went over to his donkey. The meat seller grabbed him by the belt. "So where's the cost of that meal?" he asked.

"But I was a guest!" Abu Zayd replied.

The meat seller cuffed him, then gave him a slap. "Come on, you rogue" he said, "pay up fifteen dirhams!"

The yokel started weeping and untied his purse with his teeth. "How many times did I tell that stupid idiot that my name was Abu ʿUbayd? But he kept saying Abu Zayd."

Whereupon I recited the following lines:

To earn a living use all kinds of tricks
And do not be satisfied with any situation.
Undertake any enormity,
For mankind is weak, and that's the way it is!

4. THE MAWSILIYYA ASSEMBLY

ʿIsa ibn Hisham told us the following tale:

On our way home from Mawsil, our caravan was attacked; riding beasts and baggage were all taken. My very last breath took me to some villages in the region, accompanied by that Alexandrian named Abu ʾl-Fath. "What tricks do we have up our sleeves?" I asked, to which he replied, "God is sufficient."

We found ourselves drawn to a house whose owner had just died; the mourning women had just started their keening. It was full of people whose hearts had just been rent by shock and their pockets torn by grief; women were loosing their hair, beating their breasts, slashing their necklaces, and slapping their cheeks. "Ha!" said Abu ʾl-Fath, "we'll find a palm tree in this terrain, a delicious lamb within this flock." He went inside the house to look at the dead man. By this time, the man's chin had been bound for carrying, and water was on the boil to wash him. The bier was ready to take him away, the shroud had been stitched to wrap his body, and the grave dug to bury him. When Abu ʾl-Fath set eyes on him, he grabbed his neck and felt his pulse. "You people!" he said, "don't bury him, by God. He's still alive. He's had a seizure and is unconscious. I'll return him to you with eyes open in two days."

"How can you say that?" they asked him. "When a man dies," he replied, "his anus[2] goes cold. I've felt this man and discovered that he's still living." They put their hands in his anus. "Things are exactly as he has described," they said, "so do whatever he demands."

Abu ʾl-Fath went over to the dead man and took off his clothes. He wrapped his head in a turban, hung amulets on him, and smeared him with oil. Then he had the house cleared. "Let him be," he told them. "Don't restrain him in any way. If you hear him groan, don't respond."

With that he left. By now news had spread far and wide that the dead man had been resurrected. We were inundated with charity from every household; every neighbor gave us gifts, so much so that our saddle packs were bulging with silver and gold and our bags with cheese and dates. We kept looking for an opportunity to get away, but none arose. The appointed time arrived when the false promise had to be fulfilled.

"Have you heard any sound from the sick man," Abu ʾl-Fath asked, "or noticed any sign of life?" "No," they replied. "If he hasn't made any sounds since I left," he went on, "then it's not the right time yet. Leave him be till tomorrow. If you hear any sound out of him, you'll know for sure that he's not dead. In that case, inform me at once so that I can decide on the best treatment and put his sickly constitution to rights." "Don't delay things beyond tomorrow," they said. "No, I won't," Abu ʾl-Fath replied.

As morning's visage smiled and daylight's wings spread across the horizon, men arrived in crowds and women, too, in droves. "We want you to

2. The original text indeed gives the Arabic, "ist," here.

cure the dead man now," they said, "and cut out the small talk." "Let's go to him," said Abu ʾl-Fath. He removed the amulets from the man's hand and unwrapped the turban from his head. "Lay him on his face," he told them, and they did so. "Now stand him up on his feet," and that was done, too. "Now let go of his hands," he ordered, whereupon the body collapsed in a heap. "He's dead," said Abu ʾl-Fath with a sigh, "so how am I supposed to make him alive?" With that he was set upon, slapped and punched, to such an extent that, whenever one hand was lifted, another immediately took its place. They occupied themselves preparing the dead man for burial, while we made good our escape.

We eventually reached a village on the edge of a valley that was being inundated by a flood of water. The inhabitants were in a panic, unable to sleep at night for fear of the flood. "You people," said Abu ʾl-Fath, "I'll solve this water problem for you and rid the village of the entire matter. Just do what I say, and do nothing without consulting me first." "What is your command?" they asked. "If you sacrifice a yellow heifer in the stream, bring me a virgin girl, and pray two *rukʿa* behind me, God will divert this flood into the desert. If He does not do so, then my very blood may be lawfully shed." "We will do all you suggest," they replied.

So they sacrificed the heifer, married him to the virgin girl, and prepared to pray the two *rukʿa*. "You people," said Abu ʾl-Fath, "be very careful that there are no mistakes in the way you stand, any slips during the kneeling, any lapses in the prostration, or any errors during the sitting. If that happens, our hopes will be dashed and the whole initiative will have been in vain. Gird yourselves for these two *rukʿa*, for they will be long.

With that he started the first *rukʿa*. He stood there as rigid as a palm tree till their backs started aching, then he did the prostration, which lasted so long that they thought he had fallen asleep. However, no one dared raise their head until he had pronounced the "God is great" as a sign to sit up again. He now bent over again for the second prostration and gave me the nod. With that, we headed for the valley and left them all there bent over in prostration. We have no idea what fate did with them.

And with that Abu ʾl-Fath recited the following poem:

May God never put the likes of me far from you;
Where, O where are the likes of me?
How stupid people are, by God!
I have fleeced them with such ease.
From them I have received charity,
But all I have given in exchange is deceit and fraud.

5. THE HULWANIYYA ASSEMBLY

ʿIsa ibn Hisham told us the following tale:

Returning with other pilgrims from Mecca, I stopped in the town of Hulwan. "My hair has grown long," I told my servant, "and my body is somewhat dirty. Find us a bathhouse and a barber we can employ. Make sure the bathhouse is spacious and in a decent neighborhood; the air should smell sweet and the water should be just warm enough. I want a barber who is deft with his hands and wields a sharp razor; he should have clean clothes and not prattle a lot."

With that my servant went out and only came back after a good while. "I've chosen a barber in accordance with your demands," he said. With that we made our way to the bathhouse. Once we arrived, I noticed it was not particularly grand. Even so, I went in and was trailed by a man who proceeded to grab a handful of mud, rub it on my forehead, and spread it over my head. With that he left. Another man now entered. He started giving me a rubbing that rattled my very bones, kneading the mud into my body enough to crush my joints, and all the while whistling a hail of spittle. He then set about washing my head and went over to pour some water. At this point, the first man came back and gave the second such a punch that it rattled his teeth. "You blackguard!" he yelled, "what are you doing with that head. It's mine." With that the second man delivered a blow that shattered the first's dignity. "To the contrary," he said, "this head is my property and my right, and what's more I have it in my control."

The two of them kept slugging it out till they were exhausted. With their remaining energy, they took each other to arbitration. Both of them went to talk to the owner of the bathhouse. "I am the owner of this head," said the first, "because I was the first to put mud on his forehead and rub his head with it." "That's not right," said the second. "I'm the rightful owner because I am the one who gave him a rubbing and kneaded his joints." The owner now spoke. "Bring me the head's owner," he said, "so I can ask him for myself to whom his head belongs." So they both came back to where I was. "We are in need of your testimony," they both said, "so fulfill your obligation." With that I had to get up and follow them willy-nilly. "My good man," said the bathhouse owner, "speak nothing but the truth and testify only to what is right. Tell me, to which of these men does this head of yours belong?" "God forgive you, sir," I replied, "this is my head, and it's been with me throughout my journey. It has done the circumambulation of the Kaʿbah with me, and I have no doubt at all that it belongs to me."

"Shut up, you babbler!" the man replied. He then turned to one of the two contestants. "Look," he asked, "how much longer is this stupid row going to continue over this head? Just forget about it and let it go to Hell. Just imagine that it had never even existed and that we never encountered this ass."

ʿIsa ibn Hisham said: So I left that place feeling slighted, donned my clothes in a hurry, and quickly made good my escape. I cursed my servant roundly and pummeled him like a lump of putty. To another servant I said: "Go and find me a barber who can relieve me of this load of hair." He returned with a man of pleasing build and decent garb, almost like a doll in appearance. His demeanor was enough to make me relax. Once inside he said: "Greetings to you! Where are you from?" "From Qum," I replied. "May God grant you long life!" he replied. "So you hail from the land of blessings and ease, the haven of the Sunnis and other Muslim sects. In the month of Ramadan I attended the mosque there, when the lamps were lit and the special Ramadan prayers performed. But all of a sudden the Nile overflowed its banks and snuffed out the lights. But God made me a shoe that I had put on when it was moist, but the embroidery on it did not reach as far as the sleeve. Then the boy returned to his mother after I had prayed the evening prayer when the sun's shadow was equal. But tell me, how was your pilgrimage? Did you manage to complete all its rituals as required? And they yelled: 'How amazing, amazing!' I glanced at the minaret. How trivial a matter is war—to the spectators! I found the soup just as it was and realized that the entire matter was in accordance with God's decree. How long will this aggravation last, today and tomorrow, Saturday and Sunday. I will not prolong things any further. What is all this verbiage about? But I would like you to know that al-Mubarrad is as sharp as a razor on matters of grammar. Don't bother yourself with the language of the plebs. Were potential to precede action, I would have shaved your head by now. Do you think we should get started?"

ʿIsa ibn Hisham said: His would-be eloquence had me baffled with so much nonsense. I began to worry that he might keep this session going. "Let's wait till tomorrow, God willing" I said. I asked the people around about this man. "He's from Alexandria," they replied. "The water here doesn't agree with him so he has gone crazy. He spends the whole day babbling as you can see for yourself. Even so there is a good deal of virtue in him." "I have heard about him," I replied, "and I am sorry to hear of his madness." With that I recited as follows:

I hereby give God a solemn binding pledge
I shall not shave my head ever again even though I suffer hardship.

Abu Muhammad al-Qasim al-Hariri (446 / 1054–515 / 1122)

THE DAMASCENE ASSEMBLY

Al-Harith ibn Hammam narrated to us as follows:

I was traveling from Iraq to Al-Ghuta, being the possessor of princely stallions and envied resources. I found myself tempted by inactivity and cosseted by plenty. Once I arrived after much hardship with my travel-weary camel, I found it to be just as it had been described, containing things to refresh the heart and delight the eye. I therefore offered thanks to the hand of distance and entered headlong into the realm of pleasure, unlocking the seals of desire and plucking the ripe fruits of delight. Then came the time when a caravan made preparations to depart for Iraq; meanwhile I had recovered from my exploits. I felt a strong nostalgia for my homeland, a pull toward my own fold. With that I packed up my tents for departure and saddled my beast for the return journey. However, when my companions were ready to leave and everyone was agreed, we were still wary of setting out without a guard to accompany us. So we searched for someone among every tribe and used every device possible to trace such a person, but we failed to find anyone among the clans, so much so that we came to doubt whether such a person even existed. Our failure to find anybody diminished the caravan's eagerness to leave, and everyone gathered by the Jayran Gate to discuss the situation. There, people kept wavering between leaving and staying, tying themselves up in knots and then untying them again, till they ran out of things to say and fell into despair.

In their midst was a person who appeared to be still young; he was dressed in monk's garb, was carrying a woman's rosary, and had about him the demeanor of someone inebriated. He had fixed the company with his gaze and pricked his ears to pick up their conversation. Thus their innermost fears were abundantly obvious to him. Just when they were all on the point of dispersing, he addressed them: "You people," he said, "let your distress be resolved and your minds be comforted. I will serve as your guard in a way that will banish your fears and show you my devoted service."

The narrator continued: "We now asked him for more details about his offer and raised the sum involved higher than that of an ambassador. In reply he claimed that his protection consisted of some words that he had learned in a dream as a means of protecting oneself against the wiles of mankind." Some of us started gesturing to others and expressing our misgivings through nods and winks. He realized that we found his story implausibly weak. "Why do you treat my serious proposal so flippantly," he asked, "and regard my pure gold as mere dross? By God, how many times have I crossed fearsome wastes and undertaken serious risks! In every single case I have felt no need of guards to accompany me or quivers of arrows to protect me. Even so, I have a way of removing your doubts and dispensing with the caution that has beset you all. I shall accompany you into the desert wastes and be your companion through the plateaus. If my pledge to you is fulfilled, then replenish my good fortune and give me wealth. If, however, I am telling you lies, then tear up my flesh and shed my blood."

Al-Harith ibn Hammam said: We felt inspired to accept the truth of his vision and believed what he had told us. We stopped arguing with him and cast lots as to who would balance him on his camel. His words had made us sever the bonds of hesitation and cancel all fear of things harmful and injurious. Once the saddlebags had been secured and the time came to depart, we asked him to teach us his magic phrases so that we could use them as a continuing source of protection. "Whenever daylight or nighttime approach," he said, "each one of you should recite the Fatiha of the Quran. After that, he should recite the following prayer in a humble, soft voice:

> O God, Who can revive the bones of the dead and ward off disaster, protector against terror and bounteous giver of rewards, resort of the penitent and guardian of forgiveness and restitution, let Your prayers be upon Muhammad, seal of Your prophets and conveyor of Your message, and also upon his illustrious family and keys to his victory. Protect me against the snares of the devil, the whims of rulers, the assaults of tyrants, and the trials of despots. Shield me from the attacks of enemies and the enmity of opposers, from the conquest of victors and the deprivations of despoilers, from the tricks of the crafty and the wiles of the deceitful. O God, rescue me from the outrages of neighbors and the proximity of the outrageous; keep far removed from me the hands of wrongdoers and extract me from the gloomy clutches of transgressors and by Your mercy include me in the company of Your righteous servants. O God, keep me, in both my own land and abroad, in my absence and my return, in my foraging and my coming home, in my transactions and my sphere of activity, in my travels and resorts. Preserve me in my own person and my valuable property, in my honor and reputation, in my money and household, in my family and home, in my strength and circumstance, and in my wealth and death. Do not cause me any change nor give authority to any of my foes. O God, provide me from Your bounty a bolstering power; with Your eye and Your aid

> keep watch over me and grant me the special favor of Your protection and bounty. Give me the security of Your selection and care, and do not hand me over to the charge of others. Grant me a welfare without risk, provide me with a continuing serenity, rescue me from the horrors of disaster, and wrap me in the warm coverings of favor. Let not the talons of enemies overwhelm me, for You are the One Who hears supplications.

With that he stared fixedly at the ground without moving his eyes or uttering another word. We all told ourselves that a fit of terror had struck him or that a fainting fit had prevented him from talking. But he raised his head once again, took a deep breath, and continued: "I swear by the heavens with their constellations," he said, "and the earth with its broad expanses, by rushing waters, by brilliant sunlight, by foaming sea, by winds and sandstorms, this prayer I have recited is the most trusted of talismans, offering more protection than wearing armor plating. Whoever studies it at the first smile of dawn's rays will have no peril to fear till twilight; whoever repeats it to himself as darkness falls will suffer no theft during the night."

The narrator said: So we kept repeating the words until we had it memorized and taught it to one another in case we forgot it. With that we began to urge our camels forward, using prayers rather than drivers and shielding our wares with words rather than warriors. The man stayed with us, offering his protection day and night, but never asked us to keep our promises. But, as soon as we spotted the outline of Al-ᶜAnah, he spoke: "Now for your assistance!" he said. With that we showed him goods of every kind, both what had been visible and hidden away, materials that had been tied up and stamped as precious metals. "Choose whatever you wish," we said, "for no one will disagree." The only things he craved were light jewelry and glossy clothes; all he seemed to want were silver and gold coins. Of each category he gathered a load and made off with plenty to keep poverty at bay. With that he slunk away like a pickpocket and sped off.

We felt deserted and were amazed at the way he left us. We kept inquiring about him in every gathering, requesting information from every guide, trustworthy or not. Eventually we were told that, ever since he had entered Al-ᶜAnah, he had been frequenting the tavern. So malicious was this story that I was tempted to test its validity by going somewhere I would never visit. I put on a disguise and entered the saloon. Lo and behold, there was our leader all decked out in bright-red garb standing close by the wine barrel and the press. All around him were handsome stewards and gleaming candles, myrtle and jasmine, panpipe and flute. At one moment he would be asking for a glass from the vat, at another he would ask for flute music;

sometimes he would sniff the perfumes, at others he would flirt with his lovely companions. No sooner had I uncovered his deceit, the enormous difference between his behavior today as opposed to yesterday, than I upbraided him. "Woe to you, accursed man!" I said. "Have you forgotten what you said by the Jayran Gate?" He gave an incredulous laugh and then recited the following poem in merry tones:

I have traveled continually, traversed deserts, and shunned separation, all so I can reap pleasure's delights.
I have waded through floods and tamed horses in order to drag my skirts through youthful ribaldry.
I have abandoned all dignity and sold estates, and all to sip wine and quaff a draft.
But for my passion for wine, my mouth would never utter amusing tales,
Nor would my skill have brought the caravan to Iraq, protected by the rosaries we carried.
So do not be angry with me nor upbraid my conduct, for my excuse is obvious,
And do not be surprised at an old man who can still resort to a place full of ripe pickings and overflowing vats.
Wine strengthens the bones, cures illness, and banishes sorrows.
The purest of delights comes when the respectable person rips off the coverings of his bashfulness and gives himself over to pleasure;
The sweetest of passions when the lover no longer suppresses his desires and flaunts them in public.
Reveal your desires and thus cool your heart, or else the flint of your sorrow will ignite.
So heal your wounds and calm your anxieties with the vintages you crave;
Demand the evening glass from a wine server who, whenever he glances, can drive away the lover's agony,
Or a singer who chants in such tones that, whenever he sings, mountains of iron are moved.
Disobey any counselor who will not permit you to have intercourse with a beauty who has consented.
Resort to trickery, though it be in the realm of the impossible; ignore what is said and take what is beneficial.
Abandon your father if he refuses you; set up your nets and catch whatever is trapped.

Be loyal to friends and shun misers; give generously and donate gifts.
Seek refuge in repentance before you die; for whoever knocks on the door of a generous person will see it opened.

"Your recitation is all well and good," I told him, "but your sinful behavior has been appalling. The contradictions you pose have worn me out, so tell me, by God, from which parts do you originate?" "I do not wish to be explicit," he replied, "but I will do it by allusion":

I am the gift of the age, the wonder among peoples,
Among Arabs and Persians I count as the master trickster.
Yet I am someone in need, crushed and humiliated by fate.
I am a father; my children's bones stick out in hunger,
In charge of a needy family, and thus not to be blamed if I use my wits.

The narrator continued: "With that I realized that he was Abu Zayd, notorious for his suspicious deeds, one who blackens the repute of old age. His defiance and disgraceful conduct, both, infuriated me." I responded to his excuses with the utmost disdain, making it clear that I knew full well who he was: "My good sheikh," I said, "isn't it time you put an end to all this debauchery?" That sent him into a rage, and he started ranting and denying things. After some thought, he replied: "This is a night for jollity, not abuse; we should be drinking wine, not arguing with each other. Ignore the way things look now, and let us meet on the morrow!"

So I left him as he was, not because I believed his promises but rather because I was worried his fierce temper might get the better of him. I spent the night wearing the mourning garb of utter regret because I had directed my steps toward the evils of wine rather than the pursuit of noble deeds. I made a solemn oath to God—may He be praised and exalted!—that I would never again enter a tavern, even if I were offered possession of Baghdad itself; no more would I consort with bibulous company, even if I were offered a return to my youth.

With the early dawn we prepared our riding beasts and put a distance between ourselves and those two sheikhs, Abu Zayd and the devil.

Translated by Roger Allen

86

From Abu ʾl-ʿAlaʾ al-Maʿarri, *Risalat al-Ghufran*

Abu ʾl-ʿAlaʾal-Maʿarri (363–449 A.H.) was one of the greatest classical Arab poets and thinkers, and one of the few major blind poets in Arabic and world literature. He was born in Maʿarrat al-Nuʿman in what is now called Syria, and after trying the ways of other poets, moving around and experiencing Arab life in the fourth century A.H. (tenth century C.E.), he went back to his birthplace and lived in relative seclusion until his death at a ripe age. Aside from his poetry, in which he, in his mature years, abstained from following other poets in eulogizing princes and living on their bounty, he wrote creative prose epistles and other intellectual, literary, and linguistic works, many of which were destroyed by the major invasions of the Crusades and the Mongols from which the Arab Middle East suffered greatly in medieval times.

Risalat al-Ghufran *is definitely his most famous epistle, which he wrote in answer to an epistle sent to him by a well-known man of letters at the time, Sheikh Ahmad ibn Mansour al-Halabi, known as Ibn al-Qarih, in which Ibn al-Qarih tried to show off his linguistic and literary knowledge, his experience and travels. Al-Maʿarri, irritated by these pedantic demonstrations, wrote his* Epistle of Forgiveness *in response. Here in the* Epistle of Forgiveness, *Ibn al-Qarih is made to go on an imaginary trip visiting both Hell and Paradise, where he meets many well-known poets, linguists, mystics, critics, musicians, and other prominent virtuosos from both the pre-Islamic and Islamic eras and has conversations relating to various philosophical, religious, linguistic, and literary questions. In these imaginary exchanges where the vast knowledge of al-Maʿarri in all these disciplines is displayed, something even more unusual and probably unprecedented in world literature is presented: the visit to Hell and Paradise. The visit to Heaven had already been made in the Miʿraj story about the Prophet's ascension to stand in the presence of God, and it must have been in al-Maʿarri's mind when he wrote his epistle. There have been quite a few strong arguments among literary historians about these works as the primary influences that inspired Dante's* Divine Comedy.[1]

•••••

Al-Maᶜarri is speaking here of Ibn al-Qarih, now roaming the stretches of Paradise:

And it occurred to him [our sheikh, Ibn al-Qarih], may God perpetuate his strength, this was something that used to be called a promenade in life on earth. Carrying with him a bottle of wine, he rode a strong and fast-running horse of Heaven, which had been created out of corundum and pearls in a place that is neither hot nor cold. And he went on with no particular destination in mind, carrying some of the food of eternity. . . . And then he raised his voice, chanting al-Bakri's poetry:

I wonder when a fast-running camel will carry me
Toward al-ᶜAdhib and al-Saybun
With me a skin of wine, thin bread,
Basil, and a piece of fish!

---

1. Editor's note: In my book, *The Classical Arabic Story: Genres, History and Influences*, ᶜAbd al-Wahid Luʾluʾa wrote at length about the close similarity of the Miᶜraj story and Dante's *Divina Comedia*. Other literary historians think that Dante was influenced by al-Maᶜarri's *Epistle of Forgiveness*, an observation also alluded to by the Catholic priest and Spanish scholar of Arabic Miguel Asin Palacios. In his book *La Escatología musulmana en la Divina Comedia* (*Islamic Eschatology in the* Divine Comedy), published in 1919, he drew parallels between the *Divine Comedy* and several Islamic sources he thinks greatly influenced Dante, including *Kitab al-Miᶜraj* and al-Maᶜarri's *Risalat al-Ghufran*. Facing a tirade of criticism from various groups such as Italian nationalists and religious Christians, he retorted by giving quite a few Islamic sources he believed influenced Dante's famous poem, insisting that the widely popular Islamic story of al-Miᶜraj was a basic influence on the *Divine Comedy*. The argument continues (see Philip Kennedy, "The Muslim Sources of Dante?" in *The Arab Influence in Medieval Europe*, ed. Dionisius A. Agius and Richard Hitchcock [London: Ithaca Press, 1996]) and may go on until people abandon national and religious fanaticism and realize that intercultural connections and borrowings have existed throughout literary history and will continue.

In Heaven with al-Aʿsha

(Al-Aʿsha was a great, half blind, pre-Islamic poet.)

And then a voice called, "Do you know, O forgiven slave of God, whose poetry this is?"

"Oh, yes," the sheikh answered, "our knowledgeable people had related . . . that this poetry belonged to Maymun ibn Qays ibn Jandal of Bani Rabiʿah."

And the man raised his voice, "But that's me, I'm that man! God had been merciful with me after I was at the brink of Hell, desperate of being forgiven."

And our sheikh looked happily and satisfied when he saw a fair, relaxed young man, whose weak eyes had turned attractive and his hunchback straight, and he said to him, "Do tell me, how was your escape from Hell, and your rescue from your shameful deeds?"

"The angels of punishment," he said, "were pulling me toward Hell, when I saw a man standing in the yards of doomsday, with a face that glittered like a moon, while people were calling him from all directions, 'O, Muhammad, O, Muhammad, your mediation, please, your mediation!' And I shouted while still in the clutches of the punishing angels, 'O, Muhammad, O, Muhammad, save me, for I have an immunity with you!' And Muhammad said, 'O, ʿAli, see what immunity he has!' And ʿAli ibn Abi Taleb, may God bless him, came to me while I was being pulled into the abyss of Hell, and he stopped the angels of punishment and said to me, 'What's your immunity?' And I said, 'I'm the poet who said:

O, you who ask me, 'Where's your camel heading to?'
She has a date in Yathrib,[2]
I've decided not to pity her exhaustion
Nor the blisters of her feet
until we meet with Muhammad.
When you halt at the door of Ibn Hashim,[3]
You'll have rest and you'll gain his blessings.
. . .
If you depart [this life] without a store of piety
While seeing after death those who have done,
You'll regret you are not like them
And not safeguarding what they safeguarded.

---

2. Yathrib, now called Medina, where the Prophet was at the time of al-Aʿsha's intended visit.
3. The Prophet's tribe.

. . .

A prophet who sees what you cannot see
His fame has spread in all directions.'"

Then al-Aʿsha said, "I told ʿAli, may God complement the pleasure of gatherings with his presence, knowing what has been said in this poem . . . that I used to believe in God and Judgment Day and in resurrection even when I lived in pre-Islamic times."

•••••

And ʿAli went to the Prophet and told him, 'Messenger of God, Aʿsha Qais had eulogized you and attested that you were a prophet sent by God.'

And the Prophet asked, 'Couldn't he have come to me in the previous world?'

And ʿAli said, 'He did, but his love of wine and [your tribe of] Quraish stopped him.'

"So, on ʿAli's intercession, I was allowed to enter Paradise on the condition that I would not drink any wine there. And I was happy and content, and found an alternative in honey and milk. All those who did not abstain from wine in the mocking world, cannot drink it in the eternal world."

With Zuhayr ibn Abi Sulma

(Zuhair was a great pre-Islamic poet famous for his wisdom. He lived a long life and wrote memorable verses on the ennui of long living and on pre-Islamic ethics.)

And the sheikh looked around in the orchards of Heaven and saw two high palaces, and thought, "Let me go to these two palaces and ask whom they belong to." As he approached, he saw written on one of them: "This palace belongs to Zuhayr ibn Abu Sulma al-Muzni," and on the other, "This palace belongs to ʿUbayd ibn al-Abras al-Asadi." And he wondered and said to himself, "Those two men died during al-Jahiliyya [pre-Islamic time], but the mercy of our Lord must have included them. I must try to see these two men and ask them how God has forgiven them." And as he started with Zuhayr, and found before him a young man like a flower who had been granted a palace built of pearls, as if he had never grown very old and fed up with his long life, as if it was not he who had said:

I'm fed up with the exigencies of life
For he who lives eighty years will surely be bored.

And as if it was not he who had said:

Don't you see I'm already ninety years plus ten plus seven?

And [our sheikh] asked him, "Are you Abu-Kaᶜb?" And when he answered yes, [our sheikh], may God perpetuate his dignity, asked, "How were you forgiven, in spite of the fact that you lived during the time of disobedience when people had no guardian and were unguided to do good deeds?"

And [Zuhayr] answered, "I had an aversion to bad behavior, and I met a forgiving Lord. I had faith in God Almighty, and I saw in a dream a rope dangling from Heaven. Those inhabitants of earth who got hold of it were safe. And I knew it was the command of God. So I told my sons at my deathbed, 'Should someone call you to worship God, you must obey him.' Had I been alive at the time of Muhammad, I would have been the first believer. In my poem, at the time of al-Jahilyya and atheism, I said:

Do not hide what lurks inside your souls
For God will verily know it.
It may be postponed for a time, but is recorded
For reckoning on doomsday, and punishment may come fast and hard."

Al-Khansaᵓ and Her Brother Sakhr

(Al-Khansaᵓ was the most famous woman poet in classical Arabic literature, who lived part of her life before the advent of Islam and the other part after Islam. She was famous for her elegies on her brother, Sakhr, who was killed in battle before Islam. One of the most famous was her description of him as a mountain whose top is afire. This last image has lived in Arab memory up until now and is used even in conversation.)

At the far end of heaven, [our sheikh] found a woman standing near the exit to Hell. And he said to her, "Who are you?"

"I'm al-Khansaᵓ al-Salamiyya," she answered. "I wanted to have a look at Sakhr, and I saw him tall like a mountain with fire burning around his head. He said to me, 'What you said about me was right!' referring to my description of him:

Sakhr is one whom guides ask for guidance
Like a mountain with fire on its peak."

With al-Hutaiʾa

(Al-Hutaiʾa was a well-known Umayyad poet who was famous for satirical poetry even against himself, as the two lines below show.)

Our sheikh, may God make him happy on all of his paths, went on until, at the very far end of Heaven, he reached what looked like a tiny house of a female slave shepherdess. Inside was a man who did not have the bright appearance of the people of Heaven. . . . And he said to him, "O, slave of God, are you satisfied with the least of property?"

"By God," the man answered, "I couldn't obtain it except after great tumult, sweating, and distress, until Quraish mediated for me. I am al-Hutaiʾa ʾl-ʿAbsi."

And then our sheikh asked him, "What made them mediate for you?"

"It was because I spoke the truth," the man answered.

"In what?" our sheikh asked.

"In the following lines of verse:

My lips today insisted on uttering ridicule
But I did not know whom I should satirize.
I see my face that God has created ugly
Fie, how ugly it is, and how ugly is its bearer."

And our sheikh said, "Were you not granted forgiveness for your following verse?"

He who makes good won't miss its good consequences
Benefaction won't be lost between God and men.

And al-Hutaiʾa answered, "Other good people have preceded me with something similar. Moreover, I said this, but did not follow it; therefore, I was not given credit for it."

Iblis and Bashar ibn Burd

(Bashar ibn Burd was a famous poet of Persian origins who lived in both the Umayyad and the Abbasid eras. He was blind and impudently sharp-tongued.)

Our sheikh looked and saw Iblis, may God damn him, chained with fetters and pulled by the angels of punishment. And our sheikh said, "Thank God who has taken you, O enemy of God and His holy men! Of the sons of Adam, you have ruined such a great number that only God might know."

And Iblis asked, "Who's this man?"

And our sheikh said, "My name is so and so. I come from Aleppo, and I was a man of letters, with good connections to kings."

"What a bad profession!" Iblis said. "It only produces a tiny income that is not enough for a family. So many people, like you, have been ruined by it. Congratulations on being safe. . . . Do tell me, though, how come you were forbidden to drink wine in your worldly life, but are allowed to here, in the afterworld? And do the people of Paradise do with the everlasting boys like the people of Lot?"

Angrily, the sheikh answered, "May God curse you! Aren't you busy with your suffering now? Haven't you heard God say [in the Quran]:

They have in it [Paradise]
Immaculate mates, and in it they are everlasting.

"Well, Bashar ibn Burd, unlike other humans, was good to me; I owe him a favor that I owe nobody else among Adam's children, for he said,

Iblis is better than your father, Adam
Be aware of that, you gang of evildoers.
Fire is his element, while Adam is of clay
And clay cannot be superior to fire!

"He said the truth," commented our sheikh, "yet the man is still hated."

No sooner did our sheikh say that, than a man among the punished lot appeared. He would close his eyes so as not to see the revenge that was applied to him, but the punishing angels would force open his eyes with a pair of tongs made of fire. It was Bashar ibn Burd, given two eyes after his blindness, so that he would be able to see his own punishment. And our sheikh, may God keep him in high status, said to him, "O, Abu-Muʿadh, you were good in that you wrote well, but bad in belief. I used to remember some of your poetry and ask God's mercy for you, hoping that you'd repent. Your following verses are one example:

> Go back to where you'll find peace and harmony
> Time has gone by and you are lonely still,
> You hope for tomorrow, but tomorrow is like
> An expectant woman,
> No one can predict what child she'll beget.

Translated by Bassam Abou-Ghazalah

87

From *The Adventures of Sayf Ben Dhi Yazan*

AN ARAB FOLK EPIC

The folk epic of Sayf Ben Dhi Yazan, composed sometime between the thirteenth and sixteenth centuries, during the Mamluk period, is based on the story of the sixth-century Yemeni king who fought against the Ethiopian forces occupying the country. He is portrayed in the tale as a Muslim warrior of the time before the advent of Islam who fights successfully against pagan forces, establishes the dominion of Islam, and is one of the first genuine Arab heroes. We encounter him when he has already established himself as the one destined to lead, successfully undertaken a quest to win the hand of his first love, Shama, daughter of the Ethiopian king Afrah, and foiled numerous attempts by his enemies against him. Here he has just been rescued by his half sister, ʿAqisa, a princess of the jinn, and is being flown home by her to his wife and child over a forbidden island with an enchanted royal garden. This chapter tells of his encounter on the island with his greatest love, the beautiful princess Munyat al-Nufus, and his marriage to her, before he loses her later in the tale and has to undertake a perilous journey to reclaim her:

"ʿAqisa," King Sayf then said, "the days have passed, and patience is exhausted. I can stay no longer. Take me back now to my land, and to my wife and mother and children."

"And how can I take you back," she replied, "to her who every hour seeks to harm you?"

"Sister," he said, "do me this service, for I can no longer endure to be parted from them."

"I hear and obey," said ʿAqisa. Then she rose and, lifting him onto her shoulders, soared up with him into the lofty heavens; and as they flew, all of a sudden there was a sweet and lovely fragrance. "ʿAqisa," he said.

"Here I am at your service." she replied.

"What is this fragrance?" he asked.

"Brother," she said, "do not question me on these matters, but let me rather deliver you to your home and abode." Then, when still he insisted, she said:

"This is the fragrance of the valley set aside for the enchanted Garden of Delights, fashioned, through their wisdom and secret sciences, by the masters of sorcery and magic. It is called now the Garden of the Wizards, and none may enter it; for the wizards have made it for the use of their daughters, as a place for their recreation, where others may not wander. Should any but the offspring of great kings enter it, the servants bear him off into the wilds and hills and destroy him, causing him to drink the cup of death."

Now ʿAqisa uttered these words to strike fear into King Sayf Ben Dhi Yazan, so that he would enquire no further and would not ask her to descend into that garden and tarry there. But King Sayf said: "ʿAqisa, my sister, I desire to view this garden, to see what plants and trees it has, and what are their flowers and fruits and colors."

"Brother," she replied, "hear my words and do not, in your obstinacy, disregard my advice. You have no need of this. Follow my counsel and cease to insist, and let me rather deliver you to your land. I seek only your good, and I fear harm and evil will befall you."

Then folly tightened its grip on the king, and he said: "I will not listen to advice in this matter, nor will I heed your counsel. I must see this garden and gaze on the beauty of the people of this time. I enjoin you by the inscription on Solomon's ring, and by the great temple presiding over all the jinn; for should I return to my family and people and tell them I passed over the Garden of Delights, they will say: 'Tell us what it is you saw there,' and if I do not describe it, they will mock me. Nor would it be right to invent an account, for falsehood dishonors a man."

"Is it for this," she asked, "that you wish to view it?"

"Indeed, Sister," he replied. "And so it must be."

"I hear and obey," she said then; and with that she bore him down to the ground, he being ready to faint from the sweet fragrance.

"Brother," ʿAqisa said then, "permit me, in God's name, to counsel you; for, by God, though caution has no power against destiny, I do not hold you lightly, now that God's pledge stands between the two of us."

"ʿAqisa," said King Sayf Ben Dhi Yazan, "of what do you wish to warn me?"

"I must warn you," she replied, "on two accounts. First, there is in this garden a building fashioned and made firm by the secret sciences. Should you encounter it, do not draw near or view it, for so you will find more ample fortune. And second, do not remain more than two or three hours, for should you stay longer, you will drink the cup of death. Such is my counsel to you. And do not, either, approach the trees, or seek to pick any of the fruits whose fragrance is sweet like allspice, for all this was made by sorcery and enchantment. Be doubly cautious, Brother, and do not go against my counsel, lest you destroy yourself. I myself have no power to come to your aid, for the servants would destroy me."

"I hear and obey," said King Sayf.

"Go then with the blessing of Almighty God," she said, "and since neither I nor others can enter, I shall sit here awaiting you, Brother, till you have viewed the place and returned in safety. Now I have told you. Do not cause me anxiety on your account."

Then King Sayf Ben Dhi Yazan, placing his trust in Almighty God, walked up to the gate of the garden, and he saw that it was open, and fragrances like ambergris issued from it; and when, filled with wonder, he entered, he saw channels and wheels, plants and trellises, the wheels turning of their own accord with none to attend them. The plants of the garden were two of each kind, some identical and some not, such plants as plums, and pomegranates, and apricots, and almonds, and walnuts, and hazelnuts, and peanuts, all of good variety, together with succulent apples, and figs, and firm grapes, and golden quinces, and lemons on the branch, apricots from Hama and Khorasan, narcissi and jasmines, roses and lilies, myrtle and sweet basil and anemones. He saw, too, birds on the branches praising the Sovereign Lord in all languages with their different tongues and words. The turtle dove would give praise to God, and the sparrow would answer and the lapwing lilt, and then the thrush would warble back in rhyme; all the birds giving praise to God, the All-Forgiving Sovereign, and invoking the name of He Who is One and Almighty, to Whom alone all things return. Such a garden it was as has been said:

O man of resolute will, do not be hesitant,
Arise and gaze upon the garden's beauty.
Enter the gate and see the ripening fruits
And take enjoyment of their lovely hues,
While the soft breeze is sporting with the waters
And the linnet repeating his melodious tunes,
And branches are proud of the fruits which they bear
And the lovely forms of maidens are swaying.
Come, gaze upon the roses and the flowers,
On the jasmine and on the chrysanthemums.
Praised be my God, the Painter of all creatures;
May the Founder of the universe be exalted.

Then King Sayf Ben Dhi Yazan began to walk around that garden, looking right and left, forward and back, to see the wheels turning, and the fountains spurting, and the birds flying among the branches; and so he continued till he came to the building ʿAqisa had warned him not to approach. As he drew near to it he saw that it was a feast for the eye and a joy for he who sought delight, a thing to bewilder the minds of the knowledgeable, mounted on forty columns of silver, and between each column and its neighbor, a window of yellow brass with frames of red gold. Round about it, within the single platform of brass, half a fathom high and four cubits wide, circling it from door to door, were many cabinets for storing necessities, all in marble and upholstered with silk furnishings fashioned by magic so that no dust could settle on them, and they could be neither folded nor lifted from the floor; and there were chairs, too, inlaid with red gold and studded with gems. Forty chairs there were, each facing a cabinet beneath the platform and having behind it a sign in gold to show that each who had a chair had one of the cabinets also. The sight filled King Sayf with longing and wonder, and when he opened the door of a cabinet, lo, inside it was upholstered, and its walls lined with silk, the whole made from gold and brass. Within was a set of clothing woven from gold and silver thread, its buttons made from gemstones, such a thing as only a king and lord of castles and villages and cities might possess; and the clothing was stored within in a bundle of silk. Then King Sayf opened all the cabinets, finding each to be like the first, and he knew that ʿAqisa had spoken truly, that these garments belonged to the daughters of kings who came to this place borne on the shoulders of the jinn. Wishing to know whether each set of garments had its separate owner or whether all belonged to the one owning the building for the use of whoever might come there, he examined them and found that every set of seven outfits was of the same exact colors.

"To what end is this search?" the king said then. "And who can tell what such people are minded to do? The garments I have seen, but what is the aspect of those that wear them? Surely those possessing such garments are unmatched in this world. I shall not leave this place till they have come, so that I may see them with my own eyes, to know whether they are human or jinn. Yet if ʿAqisa warned me not to approach this building, it was because something here would do me injury." With that he drew back from the building, till he reached a spot with tall and dense foliage, and there he sat watching the building.

Now as he was seated there, some birds came flying from the open country, winging their way toward that garden, and they hovered, then descended, till they alighted before him on the roof of the building, then slid down it, flocking together and using small ledges specially contrived for their descent and ascent.

"What a size these birds are," thought King Sayf as he viewed all this. And as he still marveled at the sight, one of the birds descended to the ground and began to look right and left, forward and back. Then, raising its head, it said to its companions: "Come down now, for we are safe here. There is none from outside." When the birds heard this, they all flew down alongside the first, as doves fly down beside doves, following it into the building. Then each bird stood before one of the chairs, undoing the buttons that were beneath their arms; the holes for these buttons were rimmed with gold thread and the buttons were of gold, spread from beneath their arms to the very tips of their wings. Then, when they had finished undoing their buttons, they took off the feather robes and set them down on the chairs, and maidens like radiant stars were revealed, like the full moon when it rises. They all acted in this fashion, save for one who flew up over the dome and alighted on the ledge, refusing to descend with the other maidens and disport herself with them. The others then took the feather robes off their bodies and each, opening one of the cabinets in the building, took a silk wrap and enveloped herself within it.

Now, set in the midst of the building was a marble fountain, filled with water like bars of silver, over which wheels turned. All the maidens now seated themselves on the edge of this fountain and began to move their hands and dangle their legs in the water; and all the while King Sayf Ben Dhi Yazan remained concealed in the foliage, watching them and seeing what they did. Then they all went out to the middle of the fountain, their hair spread on the face of the water, and began swimming together, diving and frolicking and laughing, swaying around one another; and so things continued for an hour.

All this time the one maiden had remained on the ledge of the building, disinclined to come down with the others and take off her robes. At last one of the girls raised her head, saying: "Queen Munyat al-Nufus, why have you not come down with us and taken off your garments, as we have? If the queen does not seek to cheer her spirits, what is to become of the attendants in her service? The wise course, O Queen, would be to descend with us and take off all your garments, responding to your companions and rejoicing in your youth."

"As for me," the queen replied, "my spirit has been cast down and my breast filled with foreboding since I descended into this garden, for my heart tells me there is a man here."

"What is this you say, O Queen?" said the maiden. "How is a man to come to this place? Had one come, the sentry of the place would have destroyed him, for it is set aside for maidens alone, with no place for a man to alight."

And still she spoke such words, till at last the queen descended from her ledge and came to stand before her chair, which was the greatest of them all, encrusted with gems and inlaid with red gold. Then she undid her buttons as her companions had done, and like them stripped off all her garments and enveloped herself in a wrap of silk, yellow and red and green. Then she approached the fountain, minded to enter it like her companions; and she was as the poet described it when he said:

A beautiful girl stood there with loosened garments
And I asked her, "Wherefore have you painted your fingers?"
She said, "I wiped with them my lips of honey."
I said, "That's true enough, but why are your lips so honeyed?"
She said, "A bee visited them, mistaking them for its hive."
I said, "That's true enough, but why does your hair hang loose?"
She said, "My nurse is coming presently to comb it."
I said, "That's true enough, but why are your eyes darkened with kohl?"
She said, "Some black eyes have been gazing upon us."
I said, "That's true enough, but why are your roses withered?"
She said, "The morning breeze withered them for jealousy."
I said, "That's true enough, but why is your neck so slender?"
She said, "From the weight of the necklaces I wear."
I said, "That's true enough, but why are your breasts showing?"
She said, "From the tightness of the buttons which I use."
I said, "That's true enough, but why is your waist so slim and small?"
She said, "From the weight of my belts and tunics."
I said, "That's true enough, but why are your pantaloons so loose?"
She said, "I tripped over the girdle and it broke."
I said, "That's true enough, but why are your genitals wet?
She said, "I have my monthlies just like your women do."
I said, "You're a fibber, I won't take that excuse!"
She said, "You've asked about something that's not your property,
To me you are a brainless nincompoop.
How can your sort ever gain one like me
Without the risk of death and of spilling blood?"
Alas for me, how can I have any hope
Of ever gaining possession of such a girl?
I ask God's pardon for all I say and do,
From every misdeed of which I am guilty!
And may God's blessings rest on the purest of men,
Muhammad, who delivered the eloquence of the Quran.

Now, as King Sayf gazed on her, he was seized with imaginings, becoming ever more possessed, transported from one state to another. As for Queen Munyat al-Nufus, she went down into the fountain with the maidens and began to disport herself with them, and they with her, all making merry together, with none to keep watch over them. They began to embrace as a lover embraces his beloved, their perfumes wafting out from them, so that the garden was filled with musk and scent. At that King Sayf sensed fire and flame kindling in his loins and was seized with torment; unable to endure, he was ready almost to lose his mind, afflicted by love's ailment over which no physician has power. "This is a plight indeed into which I am fallen," he thought, "a thing from which I find no refuge or escape. Here I am now, trapped like a bird in the cage; for if I should come out and these maidens see me, it may be they will join together against me and destroy me, and I without power to lay so much as a hand on them. Were they to strive against me, I should lack all strength to withstand them in war and combat, so comely and lovely are they, above all this Munyat al-Nufus, to whom all dreams and hopes return. Were she to seize me, with her right hand or her left, my limbs would lose their vigor. She would consume me, striking me with the cutting swords of her glances, casting arrows into my soul from the bows of her eyes. Such a thing, by God, I never expected to find. In such affliction and tribulation none can aid me save God, the Exalted and Generous One. I shall return to ʿAqisa and recount to her what has passed."

All this while the maidens remained together in the water, mingling in joy and delight, and performing the strangest of deeds; each would spread her two palms for another, to aid her in floating on the face of the water, and they would tumble and turn across one another's hands, and so it continued for a long time, until the sun began to set. Then King Sayf left them, contriving to make a way out of that garden and hasting between hills and mounts to where ʿAqisa stood awaiting him.

When she saw the distress he was in, that he had departed from her sound of body and had returned sick and ailing, she said: "What has passed with you? Tell me what has occurred to afflict you in this fashion." But he had no power to speak, for sorrow had overwhelmed him, and he fell into a fit of anguish, sobbing and sighing and moaning, in such a daze he could utter not a word, his soul ailing and his heart heavy with love.

It was hardship for ʿAqisa to be parted even for an hour from King Sayf, so tenderly did she love him; and seeing him now in this condition, weeping and lamenting and stammering in his speech, she said once more: "What has passed with you?" And when he told her of the things he had seen, she beat her face, saying: "Did I not warn you, Brother, on no account to enter the building? Yet you paid no heed. This is a distant hope, hard indeed to attain. To this garden it is that the daughters of kings come to disport themselves, borne there by the jinn, and some have garments fashioned by sorcery, through which they have power to fly. Did you discover the name of her you saw?"

"Her name," he replied, "is Munyat al-Nufus."

When ʿAqisa heard this, she once more beat her face, weeping so that the tears streamed down.

"I weep from love and passion," King Sayf said then. "But for what reason do you weep, daughter of noble lineage?"

"Brother," she said, "it is for the passion that has afflicted you. This is an ailment that has no remedy, for this Munyat al-Nufus you have named has a father called Qasim al-ʿAbous, who is the ruler of the Diamond Isle, an enchanted island lying at the end of the world, at a distance of thirty-four years from us. He is an obdurate and mighty king, full of malice, with troops more numerous than the pebbles or grains of sand. Over forty realms he rules on that island, each with its cities and fortresses and villages and regions and lesser provinces, not one of them lacking a king of its own, with troops and men and warriors and elephants and wizards and sorcerers. As for his own city, where he himself holds sway, it has a full four million troops, set one and all in readiness for war and combat. They have no wives, nor do they possess crafts or houses of merchandise, nor do they have any kind of work to do; rather, they await war and combat, prepared to enter the tumult and tribulation of battle. He has, too, three hundred and sixty wizards, one for each of the days of the year, and each day one of them appears before him. All the kingdoms stand in utmost awe of his might; China and all its followers send him tribute and fear his unrelenting wrath. Sagacious in such weighty matters, he has made for his daughter and her companions enchanted feather robes, as though they were birds, and when a maiden puts one on, she takes on the very likeness of a bird, able to fly whenever she wishes and go anywhere as she desires; for in a single hour of daylight she will traverse the span of a full year's journey. All the world is theirs; the lands with their cities and valleys and plains and seas are like a mere quarter in which they move swiftly from house to house, and the road does not stretch out long before them as it does for the traveler. If such, Brother, is the condition of your beloved, how are you to meet with her unless Almighty God, the All-Generous and Exalted One, should will it?"

"For what reason," King Sayf asked then, "did they come and alight in that garden?"

"Brother," she replied, "it is their custom to come every year to that place for recreation and repose. There they dwell for seven days, in prosperity and joy and laughter, eating and drinking wine; and then, when the seven days have passed, they depart in safety. Such is their custom, son of noble lineage. Deliver yourself therefore from the burdens of love and passion, for they will bring you only misery and sickness. I counseled you against the course you took, and you paid no heed, and now this is the affliction and punishment into which you have fallen. The wise course is to let me bear you back safe to your land, where you may comfort yourself with your wives and children, and all your troops may have sight of you."

"Sister," said King Sayf, "I will not, by God, hear such talk from you or any other. I will not listen to the chider's reproof, nor will I turn back from this queen till I have attained my hope with her and lain in union with her; or else I shall perish beneath the hooves of high-stepping horses, my breath choked from me by the blades of well-tempered swords and the spikes of tapering lances."

"Will you dwell in a land that is not your own," asked ʿAqisa, "and forsake all your family and children and troops?"

"Sister," said Sayf, "I have neither children, nor family, nor kinsfolk, nor friends, nor loved ones. I will heed nothing and brook no question. My beloved I must have, by craft or through war and combat."

"And how will you come to meet her?" asked ʿAqisa.

At that the king wept, the turmoil within him growing ever fiercer. "Sister," he said, "my patience and endurance are at an end and the fire of passion burns in my body. If you have power to help me, then help me; and if you lack such power, Sister, then you stand excused and may go about your business. As for me, I shall not move from this place till I have possession of this queen, Munyat al-Nufus, though I were to drink the cup of bitterest death."

When ʿAqisa saw how King Sayf Ben Dhi Yazan was fallen into the net of love and passion, and that wise counsel would be all to no avail, she wept for him, the tears of compassion streaming down her cheeks. "Brother," she said, "I have, by God, no power to come to her country, nor am I able to enter the building where she is."

"ʿAqisa, my sister," he replied, "I do not ask you to bear me to her country. There she is in the garden. How could I bear to wait till she flies on her way, leaving me to dwell here after her, ablaze in the scorching fire?" Then he sang out the following words:

O ʿAqisa, cease to blame me. My heart is ground down with love,
My ears complain of the din of words
And they are intolerable to me.
I have seen in this place the sister of celestial nymphs.
She had my heart drink deep of love
O ʿAqisa, what shall I do? I have seen Munyat al-Nufus,
Her beauty's greater than the sun's, and I want her to be my bride.
My heart burns in the fire of longing. My body and my patience are spent.
There's no escape from the spilling of blood
Until I reach the fulfillment of my hope,
For now I have nothing left but tears.

King Sayf Ben Dhi Yazan it was who recited these verses, the tears streaming down his cheeks, while ʿAqisa listened, her heart ready to break with sorrow on his account. And when she knew that he had fallen into the trap from which there was no escape, she said: "By God, Brother, if such is your condition, I will come to your aid, striving for you to have possession of this maiden, though my soul should perish and I be torn from all my family and kin. But so that I may know rest and reassurance, recount to me everything that passed. When you entered the garden, did you view them there, or did they come to it after you reached it?"

"Sister," he said, "when first I entered, I viewed the whole garden, and then I went into the building, where I saw the chairs and cushions and furnishings but no living being, human or jinn. Then, seeing the foliage, I sat on the ground in the midst of it, finding its scent sweet. So it was that things began, and before I knew it these birds were descending and all that happened, happened. Then, when my heart grew heavy, I came to you and told you of what had passed. Such is my tale, Sister, and peace be upon you."

With that King Sayf wept, the tears streaming down, he being rent by love and passion as the mighty had been before him. Then ʿAqisa said: "The day is at an end. Rise now, so that I may bring you food, then rest your heart with sleep; and after that return to them under cover of darkness, and strive to steal the feather robe. If you are able to take it, place it beneath your clothes, then conceal yourself beneath the waterwheel. They will search all through the garden for you, everywhere except that place, for they have acquired the nature of birds, and birds will not venture to approach a thing that spins round. When they have searched for it and do not find you, she will tell them to go and bring her another robe like the first. Then, when they leave her and she remains there alone, reveal yourself to her and show her the robe, saying: 'This is yours.' At that she will rise and hurl herself upon you, and you must turn and run full tilt not stopping till you are forty feet beyond the garden. Return then and seize her. I will be with you when you do so and keep hold of her for you."

"And what, sister," said King Sayf Ben Dhi Yazan, "if she should send some of the birds only, keeping the rest in her company?"

"Brother," said ʿAqisa, "that would be your evil fortune. But things will not pass so, because the country is a distant one and only the whole group may journey to it. When you have taken the robe, conceal yourself, as I said, beneath the waterwheel. She will not come out before the end of the day, and when she sees that the robe is not on the chair, she will think one of the maidens is playing a prank on her. 'Maidens,' she will say then, 'which of you has taken my enchanted feather robe?' Then they will say: 'By God, O Queen, we have no knowledge of it.' Then she will be filled with anger, crying out at them furiously, saying: 'Woe to you! Search the garden and see who has come here to this place.' They will conduct their search with fear and foreboding but will not venture near the waterwheel. Then, when they have searched the whole garden and failed to find it, they will say to her: 'O Queen, we have not found it and do not know who has dared take it.' And she will say: 'It may be that its servant has taken it and fled, but I will stay here in this place, which is enchanted, as you know, and you I command to go to my country and bring me another robe. But hasten back to me, lest harm befall me from some enemy.' When they see her vexed, they will all rush off, putting on their clothes and departing straightaway for their country, leaving her there. And know, Brother, that, even traveling with all dispatch, through daylight and darkness, it will take them a full three days to reach their country, and three days more to return in full haste. Know, too, that she rules over the Island of Maidens and everyone on it, and that her soldiers number a hundred thousand; bold and resolute she is, one of the great and mighty. When you see, Brother, that the maidens have departed for their land and she remains alone in the garden, come out as I told you and reveal yourself to her. And if she says, 'Who brought you to this place?' tell her: 'The power of God, the Sovereign Lord, brought me here.' Then she will say: 'Leave this place.' 'And you,' you shall say then, 'why do you remain here without your people?' She will say: 'On account of something that has been lost.' Say to her: 'No doubt it is this feather robe.' Then, keeping your distance from her, take a single feather from the collar. When she sees this in your possession, she will spring at you, and you must take care to keep yourself from her, running always ahead of her. She will pursue you with the swiftness of the ostrich, and you must take heed she does not catch you while you are there in the garden, for there she will destroy you were you the most accomplished knight on earth, and give you the cup of destruction to drink. Run still ahead of her till you are forty feet beyond the garden, then return to her, as I said. There she will be humbled at your hands, for when you take hold of her braid, she will submit, saying: 'Take pity on your captive.' But pay no heed to her words, drawing her on to me by the ends of her hair, and then I will tell you what you should do. All this is if you succeed in taking hold of her. If you do not, then be patient for a further year."

When Sayf heard these words, he rose and walked on to the gate of the garden, placing his trust in God the Almighty Sovereign. Then he entered beneath the cover of the trees, treading lighter than the dust of the air, till he reached the building where the maidens were. There he found them still as they had been before, within the fountain, tumbling and turning in the water like glittering stars; and there was Munyat al-Nufus among them, like the moon amid the stars.

"Praise be to Him," King Sayf said then, "Who created you and gave you form, the One True God, the Eternal and Everlasting." Still the girls were lost in their sport and song, looking like the flowers of the field. Then King Sayf said: "O Compassionate, All-Concealing One, Who are Yourself shrouded in mystery, conceal me from all eyes and turn all glances from me, Almighty and All-Forgiving One." And God answered his prayer, hiding him from all eyes by virtue of that which had lain within the knowledge of Almighty God since ancient times, which had been writ by destiny on the brow; and the thing that had been concealed became manifest.

Then King Sayf Ben Dhi Yazan reached out and took the feather robe, placing it within his garments, while the All-Compassionate and All-Concealing One kept him hidden; and he made his way back from the shelter of the trees till he reached the place beneath the wheel, his tongue never ceasing or forgetting all the while to invoke the Lord of Lords Who had aided him in seizing that robe. It seemed to him then that he possessed the world and all that was in it. So things passed with King Sayf.

As for Queen Munyat al-Nufus, she left the water, together with all the maidens, and each maiden, going to her chair, began to take her clothes and put them on. Then, when they had done so, they put on their feather robes, all except Munyat al-Nufus. When she did not find her feather robe, she felt the world closing in on her; she no longer knew what was before her, her eyes rolling upward and mind and reason gone. "Woe to you!" she said to the maidens then.

"Who, wishing to jest with me, has taken my feather robe? Come, bring it here to me."

"Mistress," they replied, "of what robe do you speak? None of us, by God, left the water before you."

"It is my feather robe I mean," she said. "The one who has done this surely wishes my death. Come, bring it here and put aside this dissembling; for since I came to this place, I have felt my heart hold back and my mind fail me. Some enemy, I think, lies in wait for us in the heart of this garden. If you have not taken the robe, then search this place."

"Mistress," they replied, "this garden is enchanted and none may enter it." But they began to search through the garden, till they had combed every spot and place of concealment, except beneath the wheel, for it creaked as it turned, and the maidens could not endure to draw near it. When she had lost all hope of recovering her robe, she turned to her companions in sport, saying: "I cannot leave this garden except by flight, for the way is too long to pass on foot; and now flight is lost to me. I shall remain here in this place while you strive to traverse the valleys and bring me my other robe from my palace. Make all haste with this, or enemies will overcome me."

"We hear and obey," the maidens replied. And with that they flew off toward their country, leaving Queen Munyat al-Nufus in the garden. Entering the building, she sat there deep in thought; while the king, viewing her solitary state from the shelter of the trees, knew that he had attained all he could ever desire or hope for. Then his face sparkled with light, and he approached the door of the building, full of joy at the course things had taken.

"Why do you remain here in this building?" he asked. "Why have your friends flown off, yet you have not flown with them?"

"Who are you," she replied, "and how have you come into this place? Are you man or jinn? You I believe it was who stole my robe and took away my joy, leaving me in the condition I am in."

"It was indeed I," he replied, "who took the robe, to attain my goal and desire from you. Here it is now, comfort of my heart." With that he took a feather from within his garments as a sign that this was indeed the robe; and when she knew he had taken it, the light before her eyes turned to darkness.

"What has drawn you to such a deed," she said, "by which you have cast yourself into the way of destruction and the worst of snares? By God Who is great, you have now come to an evil pass." With that Queen Munyat al-Nufus sprang toward Sayf like a lion, pouncing on him like punishment itself, and he ran from before her, making for the gate without once looking back, summoning all his resolve as she threatened to catch him. Once he stumbled over the roots of some tree, almost falling onto his face; but then he steadied himself, and still he raced on, while Munyat al-Nufus, knowing now that her robe was with him, pursued him in her turn till he had gone out of the garden. Still she followed wherever he went, till two miles or so separated King Sayf from the garden, and he had left the whole enchanted land around forty feet behind him. Then, as she bore down on him, he turned back toward her like a lion and pulled her by the ends of her hair, hardly able to believe his good fortune.

Then Munyat al-Nufus felt sure of drinking from the cup of destruction, knowing there was no longer any release or escape from his hands. Then, her distress growing ever stronger, her heart ready to break, she said: "Sir, now that you have attained your goal, take pity on your captive." But he gave her no answer or any speech at all, still holding her by the hair till he had brought her to ʿAqisa, who was there awaiting his arrival.

ʿAqisa approached Queen Munyat al-Nufus and greeted her, saying: "Queen of all time, mistress of maidens and women, know that you have attained what none attained before you; for this is the king of the kings of all time, the most accomplished of all knights."

"ʿAqisa," Munyat al-Nufus said then, "is it come to this, that you bring humans to our land, permitting them to enter our garden and view our dress and appearance, and that you spur this scoundrel on to take hold of the daughters of kings? Who now, when my father learns of this, will deliver the two of you from his hands? He will surely give you both the cup of destruction to drink and will lay waste the lands of Qarnar and the source of the Nile, destroying all that live there and sparing none."

"Mistress," said ʿAqisa, "this is no scoundrel, but indeed the highest of kings, who has soldiers and helpers among man and jinn alike, whose hand commands wizards and sorcerers and sages and masters of the secret sciences, commanders and supporters. You alone have no knowledge of him, acting according to the common saying that he who knows not the falcon roasts him. But I shall tell you now, O Queen, who he is. This is the king of the kings of Yemen, the vanquisher of infidels and evildoers; this is King Sayf, son of King Dhi Yazan, son of King Tubbaʿ the Yemeni, who is matchless among kings, with none to approach his measure. My brother he is by suckling, a valiant hero and indomitable foe. But do not suppose he has taken you captive; rather, you have made a captive of him, taking him hostage with your beauty."

"And why," asked Munyat al-Nufus, "has he come to this place, entering the garden never approached by man or jinn. This place is protected by charms and spells, the skilled work of the wizards of other days."

"Know, O Queen," said ʿAqisa, "that, after staying some days at my palace, he asked to be borne to Hamraʾ al-Habash; and then, as we chanced to pass over this place, he asked me to set him down so that he could relieve himself. I descended with him accordingly, and he, leaving me, went on to look into the building. Then love that humbles the mighty cast him toward you; able to endure no longer, he ventured to steal your robe, and all that happened, happened. This is a thing foreknown by God, the Mighty and All-Powerful, Lord of this world and the hereafter. Do not fret at this, O Queen, for he that possesses you well knows your worth and status, and with him you will be honored above all your followers and dependents."

Still ʿAqisa spoke such honeyed words to her, beguiling her with pleasant smiles, till at last Munyat al-Nufus relented and smiled in her turn, knowing no escape was left to her, that she remained solitary and powerless whatever she might say. "ʿAqisa," she said then, "why do we not enter the garden, where we can sit and eat and drink and make merry?"

"I have no power to enter, O Queen," said ʿAqisa. "Rather, I shall seat you in a palace better than the garden." With that she set the two of them on her shoulders and sought the lofty heavens, continuing thus till she bore them down over the palace of the One-Armed Snatcher, whom King Sayf Ben Dhi Yazan had slain before, when ʿAqisa sought his aid earlier in this tale. This palace had furnishings of the finest jeweled satin and beds of wood, inlaid with sheets of red gold; and there she seated Queen Munyat al-Nufus on a bed, and King Sayf on another like it, saying: "Converse together while I make arrangements for you to be served."

With that she called out to the servants and attendants of the palace, commanding them to prepare food to bring health to the body. Then they labored to produce pigeons and *hudari* and quail, slaying the birds and setting them in the pots. Then ʿAqisa asked for drink, too, and sweetmeats, and served King Sayf and Queen Munyat al-Nufus with fare to smooth away all frowns. And ʿAqisa began to mollify Queen Munyat al-Nufus, saying: "O Queen, you are mistress of this place, my brother Sayf Ben Dhi Yazan and myself your mere servants and attendants. Cast off all care now and be happy. Know that all that happens to a person is ordained from ancient times, and gotten goals are attained only through hazard and endeavor. Had King Sayf Ben Dhi Yazan not been decreed fortune and success by God, he could never have viewed you, never seen your shadow. You, O Queen, have taken possession of his heart and overwhelmed his innermost soul. You are meant only for him and he only for you; for you are endowed with loveliness and worth, splendor and perfection, and he, too, takes pride in his valor and prowess over heroes, his steadfastness in war and combat, his kingdom and sovereignty over cities, regions, and districts, villages, castles, and domains."

Still ʿAqisa spoke such words to Queen Munyat al-Nufus, till she ate with the gallant King Sayf Ben Dhi Yazan, and they ranged wide in their converse, the queen laughing and smiling. Then ʿAqisa was happy and, placing their hands one in the other's, she said: "Join hands now and make your marriage contract according to the creed of Our Master Abraham, the Friend of God." And lawful contract was accordingly made between them.

King Sayf Ben Dhi Yazan, knowing then what he should do, did it to the utmost of his strength, according to the law of those days. ʿAqisa departed from them for a time, then returned with a garment in which she clothed Queen Munyat al-Nufus, so as to make her a bride for King Sayf, and set on her crown and necklace, little as she needed such things; and she became resplendent beyond the sun and the moon.

From *The Adventures of Sayf Ben Dhi Yazan* (Bloomington: Indiana University Press, 1996). Translation and retelling by Lena Jayyusi.

Notes on the Translators

The pieces from the initial sections distinguished by general subject category were variously translated as follows. First translators: Lena Jayyusi, May Jayyusi, Faisal al-Khadra, Leila al-Khalidi al-Husseini, Fayez Suyyagh, Matthew Sorenson, and Bassam Abu-Ghazaleh; second translator: Christopher Tingley. The two short surrealistic stories were translated by Hilary Waardenburg-Kilpatrick.

The long texts were translated as follows:

Anecdotes from Al-Jahiz, *The Misers*, ʿAbdul-Wahid Lulua and Christopher Tingley
Excerpt from *The Adventures of Sayf Ben Dhi Yazan*, Lena Jayyusi
Excerpts from Ibn al-Muqaffaʿ, *Kalila and Dimna*, Ibrahim Mumayiz and Christopher Tingley
Excerpts from Ibn Tufail, *Hayy ibn Yaqzan*, ʿAbdul-Wahid Lulua and Christopher Tingley
Selections from *Al-Maqamat* (*The Assemblies*), Roger Allen
Selections from *The Epistles of the Brethren of Purity*, Fayez Suyyagh
"The Story of Tamim al-Dari," Bassam Abu-Ghazaleh and May Jayyusi
"Tales of Juha," Matthew Sorenson, Faisal Khadra, and Christopher Tingley
"A Vision of the Next World," from *The Wahrani Dreams*, Fayez Suyyagh

Name Index

TO FACILITATE RESEARCH, NAMES OF AUTHORS ARE LISTED ACCORDING TO THE WAY THEY ARE KNOWN IN ARABIC HISTORY OR LITERATURE.

Subject Index